BELLES & BEAUX

A BLUESTOCKING BELLES COLLECTION

THE BLUESTOCKING BELLES   SHERRY EWING

SUSANA ELLIS   ALINA K. FIELD   RUE ALLYN

CAROLINE WARFIELD   JUDE KNIGHT

ELIZABETH ELLEN CARTER   CERISE DELAND

Cover Design by Jude Knight

ePub: ISBN: 979-8-9855874-2-5

❀ Created with Vellum

Print ISBN: 979-8-9855874-3-2

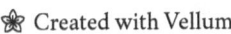 Created with Vellum

BELLES & BEAUX

Just in time for Christmas 2022 comes this boxed set of eight charming stories of love, family, and miracles. Each Belle has contributed a tale set in the festive season—one just long enough to fit in between tasks at this busy time of the year. The tales are unrelated, except by the festive season.

Some have been written for this collection, some are made-to-order stories never before published, some have been used as fan giveaways. All are delightful.

So, pour the drink of your choice, find a favorite chair, and step into one of our worlds.

A Mistletoe Kiss: Sherry Ewing

As Christmas approaches, Sophie Templeton's one wish is a kiss beneath the mistletoe from the man who holds her heart. Spencer, Earl of Wilmott has been quietly waiting for Sophie to grow up. Has he left it too late to make his offer?

The Magic Christmas Stew: Susana Ellis

The life of an idle spare is no life at all for retired Captain, Daniel Winthrop. He is capable of doing many things, but they all required a wealthy bride. Governess Emily Bainbridge fears being pursued for her fortune, so she keeps hers a secret. Will this pair find the courage to conquer their pride and risk all for love?

Flowers for His Lady: Alina K Field

After her fall from grace years ago, Eleanor Gurnwood has made a family of the villagers in her vicar-brother's parish. His rising career means she must choose between continuing as his minion or staying with the village. Then her past rides in on a white horse in the form of Major Sir Bramwell Huxley.

An Angel's Promise: Rue Allyn

Artis MacKai might be only a little girl, but she is not going to let a blizzard, wolves, or a deadly enemy stop her from rescuing the stolen mare and foal who are the hope of her family. It will take the spirits of her parents, a determined boy, and her desperate brother to save her.

Room at the Inn: Caroline Warfield

A fatherless child requires a village with room in their hearts. A hard-hearted baroness makes it impossible. The Honorable Declan Alworth steps up to make room in his heart and his home for the little treasure. How can the vicar's niece, Maera Willis, resist either one of them?

Zara's Locket: Jude Knight

After Zara MacLaren is dismissed from her post on Christmas Eve, things go from bad to worse. When a goldsmith recognizes the locket he once made in the hands of a would-be seller, he sets out to find her. What seems bad fortune might just turn into a Christmas miracle.

Three Ships: Elizabeth Ellen Carter

Laura Winter lives on a tidal island that is home to a lighthouse. On a late November day, a violent storm brings not only the handsome Lieutenant Michael Renten but also a clutch of pirates bent on wreaking mischief.

The Beau of Christmas Past: Cerise DeLand

Years ago, Alyssa and Gabriel were caught enjoying a Christmas kiss, which broke Alyssa's betrothal to another man, and caused the pair to be exiled, far from their families and one another. Home for

Christmas, will they find the past something to be overcome? Or fulfilled?

A MISTLETOE KISS

BY SHERRY EWING

All she wants for Christmas is a mistletoe kiss...

Miss Sophie Templeton has been waiting a lifetime for the one man who owns her heart, but he seems to court a different woman every Season. As Christmas approaches, Sophie's one wish is a kiss from him beneath the mistletoe.

Spencer, Earl of Wilmott has quietly watched Sophie through the years, holding her in his heart, and biding his time until he can offer for her. He appeases his parents by being seen with a variety of eligible women. But Sophie is grown up now, and he must put aside his worries that she'll find him too old and make his offer.

One chance encounter, one dance in which he all but claims her; can Spencer convince Sophie to make this a Christmas romance that will last a lifetime?

CHAPTER 1

The Village Rectory
Edington, England
December 1817

Miss Sophie Templeton reached for a red ribbon and began to tie the fabric into an intricate bow. Her sister Margaret, who was happily married, went around their father's small house decorating as though she owned the place. She was on a mission to see the rooms properly decorated and Sophie had been roped into helping despite preferring to stay in London for the holiday season. She had friends to call upon and possible connections to be made to find a man suitable to become her husband, after all. She had no time to while away the hours in the country! At ten and nine she was practically on the shelf.

Sophie handed the newly-made bow to Margaret who attached fabric to a bunch of mistletoe. Her husband Frederick had begun a ritual when they had married to hang mistletoe from every available doorway in their house. It was his way to capture his wife at every opportunity to give her a kiss. Sophie sighed at the thought of such a romantic gesture. She only wished she had her own beau to steal a kiss or two herself.

"Sophie," Margaret called from the foyer. "Bring that bunch of garland for the mantel in the front parlor. We can decorate that room next."

"Coming, Margaret," Sophie answered, relieved that she could take a break from making bows. She took up the garland and walked to the front room where her father, Joseph, sat in his favorite chair reading the newspaper. Tall and lean with his dark brown hair becoming greyer as the years passed, he had been a doting father as best as he knew how after Sophie's mother had passed away. Her father missed his wife to this very day, but back then, he concentrated more on his parishioners than he did Sophie while she was growing up. It was the reason Margaret took Sophie to live with her when she married. Sophie didn't have any ill feelings toward her father for his lack of attention and Margaret, being older, had been more of a mother to her than a sister.

"Is your sister keeping you busy, poppet?" he asked lovingly.

Sophie could never ask him to stop using his favorite endearment for her, since apparently her mother had also used the term before her passing. "Yes, papa. Your house will look just lovely when we're all done and ready for visitors."

She came over to kiss his cheek and he patted hers. "Such a good girl," he murmured softly as though she was still a small child. "I don't know why you both bother every year. It's not likely I'll have too many people dropping by to pay their respects to an old man."

"You're not old," she scolded, smothering a laugh. "Besides, you know that's not true, Papa. Before you know it, the whole village will have come by to ensure you have enough food on your table and a sweet treat or two to see you through the entire winter."

Her father chuckled. "I suppose you're right. I'll probably gain ten pounds just from the desserts alone." He stood, set down the newsprint, and picked up his bible from the table. "If you need me, I'll be in my study working on this Sunday's sermon."

She watched him leave, all the while pondering if their father ever got lonely when they weren't here visiting. She would mention it to Margaret when they could have a private word together.

Sophie took the garland to the mantel and was putting it in place when Frederick and Margaret entered the room. Enter being a figurative word since Frederick stopped her sister to do what? Give her another kiss beneath the hanging mistletoe, of course. Sophie held back a groan of despair. She wasn't sure she could stand many more of their public displays without her emotions getting the best of her. Was it right to be jealous of her beloved sister's happiness? Perhaps not, but Sophie couldn't help being pea green with envy.

Sophie cleared her throat hoping this was enough of a hint to break the two love birds apart. Honestly, you would think they were still newlyweds instead of being married for the past five years with a three-year-old son!

"Margaret, my darling, we are embarrassing your sister," Frederick stated, holding his wife at arm's length.

"Nonsense, Freddy. Sophie has been living with us all these years. She's used to us by now," Margaret replied, strolling into the room. She began fussing over the garland that Sophie had just placed on the mantel. Sophia glared at Margaret whose brow rose haughtily. "What? It needed to be perfect."

"It was perfect, Margaret. I don't know why you even brought me along, if all you're going to do is nit-pick over everything I've done." Sophie plopped herself down into her father's vacant chair and crossed her arms. Her foot beat a rapid staccato on the floorboards.

Frederick came over to give Sophie a kiss upon her cheek. "She's a bit bothersome when it comes to these things, Sophie. Please forgive her," he said softly. His charcoal grey eyes twinkled mischievously as if his words would take some of the sting out of whatever Margaret might say next.

Margaret huffed and sat down in a chair opposite her sister. "You two are in cahoots against me! I knew I should have traveled here alone, Freddy. You could have easily stayed in London with Colin and his nursemaid. But no… you insisted that you and Colin come along. *Family being together is important during the holiday,* you said."

"Now, Margaret—"

Margaret waved her finger at her husband. "Not. Another. Word! Otherwise, I swear you'll be sleeping in the barn tonight."

Sophie giggled, knowing her sister would never force her viscount to sleep in a cold barn. "Best listen to her warning, Freddy, elsewise you'll never get back into her good graces," Sophie declared with a laugh.

Margaret looked at the two of them before they all burst into laughter. "Enough! You two will have me at my wits end before the Christmas holiday is over. I am glad you came, Freddy. I do so love to take advantage of all the hanging mistletoe." Margaret smiled before she continued. "I forgot to mention; Jennette Morledge will be coming over for supper tonight along with her two boys. I've asked Cook to prepare something extra special."

Sophie folded her hands in her lap, trying to remember when she last saw Joseph and Michael Morledge. Had she seen them since the last Christmas season? A memory of the two brothers when they weren't much younger than her flashed across her mind. They had both grown up to resemble their deceased father probably more than Sophie would have liked. She held back a shudder thinking of Sander Morledge and their brief association when Margaret was possibly going to wed the man. Thank goodness Freddy had come to their rescue... and Jennette's as well.

"Joseph is now eighteen, sister, with Michael only four years his junior. It might be best if you at the very least stop calling the elder a boy," Sophie stated, rising from her seat.

"They turned out to be well-behaved young men," Frederick announced before giving a wink in Sophie's direction. "If I remember correctly, Joseph has a small crush on you, my dear, despite him being a year younger than you."

Sophie blushed, remembering how Joseph followed her around her father's house, hanging onto every word she spoke. The memory of another flitted across her mind. Once there, it was difficult not to blurt out that her heart cried out for another. Sophie had resigned herself to the fact that Spencer, the Earl of Wilmott, was far beyond her reach. Whenever she had encountered him in the past, it had always been at a distance. Her heart would race just seeing him, but he never seemed to notice her. Perhaps it had been her age, since she was much younger. And then there were his visits with his parents to the rectory during the holidays...

"Sophie?" Margaret's concerned tone brought Sophie back to the present and the conversation about Joseph.

There was no sense in her dreaming about a life with Spencer or even Joseph for that matter. "He's more like a step-brother than husband material," Sophie said, with a slight grimace. Joseph was nice but she could never think of him in a romantic fashion. And yet, if she couldn't have Spencer, then who would make her a proper husband? She had no answer for herself.

Margaret's eyes lit up. "He would be perfect for you, Sophie!"

Sophie's eyes narrowed. "No. He would not and don't even think about playing matchmaker, Margaret, or I'll disown you as a sister," she fumed.

Margaret began humming a little tune and Sophie could tell her sister was already scheming away inside her head to make a match.

Sophie gave a heavy sigh, knowing her sister would do as she pleased. "I'll see if Cook could use an extra set of hands since we are having visitors this evening. Freddy... I leave Margaret in your tender loving care."

Frederick bowed. "You are too kind, my dear."

Sophie patted his arm. "I'll expect the rest of the decorations to be put into place when I return, or I'll know what you both did instead with your free time."

Margaret blushed, but a slight smile crept up at the corners of her mouth. Sophie had the idea there wasn't going to be much decorating going on once the couple were alone. Her sister was one lucky woman!

CHAPTER 2

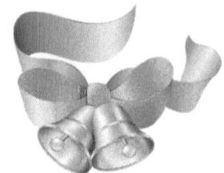

Spencer, Earl of Wilmott, tightened the cinches on the saddle for his horse. An afternoon ride was just what he needed to clear his head from a morning spent with his parents. He was tired of the young, titled women they put in his path. Their intentions were good if not honorable, and he certainly understood their desire to see him wed. But he was only three and twenty. He still had plenty of years ahead of him before he settled down. Hence his need to leave their manor home for a ride in the country with the freshly fallen snow.

He took the leather reins into his hands and led his steed over to the mounting block but turned when he heard another horse approaching the manor. Spencer waved his hand and his friend, Lord Evan Charville, returned the gesture. They had grown up together, even attending the same school, and were more like brothers than just good friends.

Spencer handed the reins to a stable boy and clasped Evan's hand once he dismounted from his horse.

"It's good to see you. Here for the holiday, Evan?" Spencer inquired with a smile.

"You know my mother would never forgive me if I didn't come

home," Evan said with a chuckle before lowering his voice. "I'd rather be spending Christmas with my mistress in London, but she'll just have to do without me until the new year."

"I'm certain she'll understand," Spencer murmured.

Evan ran his hand through his hair. "I'm not so sure, but that's not why I'm here."

"I thought we were going to meet this evening at the local pub for a drink or two. What's so important that you raced over here to see me?" Spencer asked.

Evan's devilish grin had Spencer cringing at whatever news his friend had to impart. "The Vicar's house is full of his relatives who are busy decorating, inside and out," Evan began, then placed his hand on Spencer's shoulder. "I saw Miss Sophie myself with her dog in the front yard. She's become a beauty!"

Sophie... the last time he had seen her was when she had been skating in a park near London. That had been the year of the Frost Fair, which made it nearly three years ago. She had been only sixteen at the time. Spencer remembered how her face had turned up toward the sky as the snow fell onto her dark blonde hair. Green eyes to rival a springtime forest were filled with wonder and excitement as she enjoyed her time on the ice. Although she had not noticed him, he could not take his eyes from her. If he had not been otherwise engaged with a young woman whose name he didn't even remember, he would have asked Sophie if he could join her. Alas, their timing always seemed to be off, and Spencer let the years pass despite his attraction to her.

He had known Sophie since the time her family had taken up residence in the village rectory. She had been a teenager with a puppy with an odd name following her around. Tulip, if he remembered correctly. Tall and gangly with freckles caressing her cheeks and nose, she had been awkward and unsure of herself as only someone that young could be. But as she had grown, Spencer's feelings for her had also changed even though he was four years older. She would be nine and ten by now and of marriageable age. Would she think him too old for her?

"Spencer?"

He shook his head as memories of Sophie's yearly return for Christmas teemed through his mind: Her laughter filling her father's house warmed his heart when he and his parents called upon the vicar and his family; her enchanting smile when they passed out small gifts to the children in the village; and those mesmerizing green eyes whenever she chanced a glance at him from across a room. Yes... there had been something there, he would swear it, and he was a fool for never acting upon his attraction in the past. He would not wait any longer. If he did, he might not get the opportunity to see if they could make a match. Unless she was already spoken for... God forbid!

"A beauty, you say?" Spencer asked already knowing Sophie's physical beauty but more importantly her heart as well. There wasn't a mean bone in that young woman's body, and any man would be lucky to take her as his wife.

"Thought I lost you there for a minute," Evan chuckled again.

"You did," he replied, with a knowing smirk.

"Should we ride over to the rectory and see her for ourselves?"

Spencer thought of the possibilities of what could be. "Yes, but give me a moment to run into the manor. I borrowed a book from the vicar that I should return. It's as good excuse as any for coming over unannounced."

He made his way inside and up the stairs to his room. Finding the leather-bound book on his dresser, he picked it up and headed back outside. Lucky for him he didn't run into his parents and have to explain where he was going. He shook his head, wondering when they would ever think of him as a grown man. If he was old enough to marry, then he certainly did not need to give them an update on his whereabouts minute by minute.

He tucked the book away inside the leather satchel attached to his saddle, and Spencer and Evan mounted their horses and took off across the countryside. The rectory wasn't far and before too long, they arrived at the small house with a low stone fence around the dwelling. The church stood off to the right with a tall steeple but was vacant now. They dismounted, slipping their reins into the hitching posts. Taking off his leather gloves, Spencer placed them inside his jacket.

Spencer almost forgot the book in his eagerness to see Sophie. He ran back for it and had just walked through the front gate when a dog came barking to see who was intruding.

"Tulip, you come back here," a woman's voice called out from the back yard.

The dog continued to loudly bark. Spencer's eyes looked at the hound. "Tulip, sit!" he commanded. The dog promptly sat on its rear haunches, wagged its tail, and began panting with her tongue plopping out to one side.

"You, bad little dog," the woman called out before coming to a skidding halt. "Oh! Forgive me. I didn't know we had visitors," Sophie said, while a becoming blush streaked across her cheeks.

Spencer could only stare at the woman across the space between them. Clearly, she had been in the kitchen if the wooden spoon she held was any indication of her whereabouts before her dog decided to run away from her. Flour dusted her hair and face, her apron had what appeared to be jam across the front, causing Spencer to wonder what she had been attempting to bake.

"Hello, Sophie," Spencer said liking the sound of her given name as it passed his lips.

"Spencer... it's so good to see you," she said affectionately until she remembered herself. "I mean, Lord Wilmott."

He came over and took her hand without the spoon and bowed over it. "There is no need to stand on formalities, is there?" he asked.

"B-but y-you're an earl..."

"I am just a man..."

"Well... of course you are!" A gasp escaped her, and she wrench her hand from his. "M-my f-father would n-never a-approve," she stammered shyly.

Spencer straightened. What a pity Society's rules must be applied. "If we are to stand on formalities, may I present my friend, Lord Charville," he stated, waving a hand for Evan to come forward.

Sophie gave a brief curtsey, hiding the spoon behind her back.

"I would ask you to call me Evan, but I suppose that would be too forward of me," Evan said with a wink.

Sophie didn't say anything but only continued to stare at Spencer, not that he would complain. "Are you here to see my father?" she inquired, making her way to the front door.

"Yes, to return a book I borrowed," Spencer said, taking off his hat once he entered the foyer.

"I'm certain he'll be glad to see you, Lord Wilmott," she stated with a smile. She appeared as if she would say something further, but they were interrupted by her father coming out of his study.

"Lord Wilmott! What a pleasure. Come in, come in. No sense standing there in the entryway getting cold. Sophie, you daft girl, close the front door," Joseph Templeton ordered.

Embarrassment flooded her face before she did what she was told. She took their coats and hats and mumbled an apology with a bowed head.

Spencer frowned then introduced Evan. Remembering the book, he held it out for the vicar to take. "I thought it was about time I returned this, sir. Thank you for lending it to me."

Joseph took the book and tucked it under his arm. "No need to thank me. You're welcome to anything in my library. You must stay for dinner... Lord Charville, too. I won't take no for an answer. Sophie, please let Cook know we'll have two more for dinner. Now, come with me to my study. We can talk there without interruption from all the decorating my girls are doing."

"Miss Sophie... A pleasure to see you again," Spencer said with a bow.

Her hands full, she bobbed an awkward curtsey, reminding him of that shy little girl from years ago. "And you as well, Lord Wilmott. Lord Charville... If you'll excuse me, I'll see to your things and then inform Cook you'll be joining us for the evening meal."

Spencer watched her leave and wished he could have said something more to her. If he was lucky, he'd get his opportunity before the night was over.

CHAPTER 3

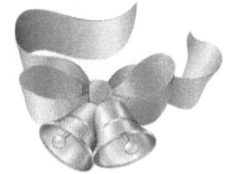

*S*ophie pushed her food around on her plate. Her appetite waned as the evening progressed. Conversations flowed around her, including the gentleman seated to her left. Her short answers had left Joseph Morledge struggling to keep up some form of interaction, but Sophie didn't care. She wasn't trying to be rude to Joseph or her father might have taken her to task in front of the entire table… Heaven, forbid! It was just that all she could concentrate on was the man seated across from her who kept up a lively conversation with not only her father, but everyone seated around him.

Spencer, Earl of Wilmott… He was the one man of her acquaintance who had been like the forbidden fruit offered to Eve in the Garden of Eden. His tawny-colored hair and amber eyes would be any woman's downfall and Sophie was no exception. In truth, she had hidden a secret attraction to the man since he first came to the rectory all those years ago with his parents. He had been on the brink of manhood, a rake in the making, if she were to guess, and always with a different woman whenever she saw him in London. Not that she was keeping tabs on the man but it was hard not to notice that his attention appeared to waver between the various blondes, brunettes and redheads of each Season.

Then to see him today of all days when she looked her worse! She had resembled a kitchen maid with flour in her hair and a dirty apron. Those jam tarts had better be the most delicious dessert item on the table this evening or she'd toss the whole batch into the rubbish!

His hand when it grasped hers this afternoon had been warm, sending shivers of delight racing through her entire body. If she could have been folded into his arms, she would have died and gone to heaven! How many nights had she dreamed of this man over the years? Too many to count and, as she had grown to womanhood, those fantasies only grew as each night rolled into the next. To have him so close had only fueled her thoughts of what his kiss would taste like. How would those broad shoulders feel beneath her fingertips? His hair as she brushed it from his forehead... would it be silky to the touch? How rapid would her heart beat if he turned those amber eyes to her with a fair amount of affection? She was dying inside to know...

"Sophie..." Margaret's voice from her right shook her right out of her daydreaming.

"Hmmm?" she muttered quietly.

"Joseph was speaking to you, dear heart," Margaret said politely, although the look she gave Sophie told her she had better start paying attention to the conversations going on around her.

She turned to look at the man to her left. Joseph had also grown up over the years and seemed to have a maturity far beyond his eight and ten years. Perhaps this came from the responsibility he felt for his mother and younger brother. And who could blame him! His father, what Sophie could remember of him, had been the very devil. He had hidden away his injured wife as though she were dead and had been looking to marry again. That man had charm and plenty of it but there had been something sinister hiding beneath his wicked smile.

Jennette Morledge had borne the brunt of his displeasure so, when he had died, she had sold the country house and moved her family near the rectory. It wasn't unusual for the two families to get together often, which was why Sophia thought of Joseph and Michael like the brothers she never had.

"My apologies, Joseph," she murmured politely, hoping he would excuse her poor manners. "What were you saying?"

"No need to apologize, Sophie. I was just wondering if you would allow me a dance at the village social next Friday evening? That is, if you're attending," Joseph asked flashing a confident smile.

Before she could answer, Margaret spoke up. "Of course, she would love to dance with you. Isn't it lovely of him to ask, Sophie?"

Sophie gritted her teeth until her jaw hurt. She caught her father's glare and plastered a smile upon her face. "Thank you for asking, Joseph. I'd be delighted."

Joseph appeared relieved when he sat back in his chair raking his hand through his black hair. He began speaking with his brother who was on the other side of him, and Sophie was happy she didn't have to further respond to another strained conversation.

Her eyes moved to the man seated across from her. Her breath hitched to find him staring at her, and her body became flushed. Spencer was the only person who could make her flustered, so she raised her chin as though to prove, if only to herself, that she could keep a handle on her racing emotions. A slight grin began to etch its way across his handsome face, and for a moment Sophie thought he might be staring at another woman behind her. After all, Spencer had never looked at her in *that* way. But clearly there wasn't anyone. He was looking at Sophie and his roguish smile only continued to widen, causing her heart to beat rapidly in her chest. She would never survive through dessert if he continued staring at her like this!

"I would be honored if you would also allow me a dance, Miss Sophie," he said, and the husky baritone of his voice almost made her melt into her chair. She could hardly believe her good fortune. He was actually asking *her* to dance with *him*.

She heard Margaret take a breath as if to answer for Sophie again, and she quickly reached over to take her sister's hand and give it a squeeze beneath the table. She would answer for herself this time. "Of course, Lord Wilmott. I'd be honored to dance with you."

He gave her a brief nod, took up his glass of wine and sipped, all while holding her gaze. If she was ever jealous of an object, it was that crystal goblet that had briefly touched his lips. She gave him a small smile, not trusting herself to speak because she knew she'd be tripping over her tongue like she did earlier this afternoon.

The dinner dishes were cleared. Her freshly baked tarts were a success, thankfully, and her father led the gentlemen back to his study so they could partake of an after-dinner brandy. This left Sophie with Margaret in the parlor. Sophie went to the pianoforte and began to play, hoping that Spencer would hear how accomplished she was and rejoin her.

"You shouldn't ignore Joseph, Sophie. Can't you see he cares for you?" Margaret asked, crossing the room and sitting in a chair by the hearth.

Sophie continued playing. "And you should mind your own business, Margaret. I know you meant no harm, but I can answer for myself. I am a grown woman, after all." She took her eyes momentarily off the keys before continuing. "Joseph Morledge is like a brother to me. Nothing more"

"But Sophie—"

"*A brother to me,*" she said interrupting. "He'll never be anything more."

"It's such a shame, dear heart. He really does care for you," Margaret declared trying again.

Sophie stopped playing to look at her sister who clearly was only attempting to see to Sophie's best interest. "You found your happily ever after with the man of your dreams. Don't you wish me to find mine?"

Margaret sat back in her chair. "Well, of course, I do. Everyone deserves to find love."

"Then let me worry about my own love life, please. You know how much I love you for all your efforts on my behalf over the years, but trust me when I tell you, everything will eventually fall into place… *in time.*"

"Very well. I'll try my best not to meddle," Margaret said with a frown of displeasure.

"If only it was that simple," Sophie muttered beneath her breath.

She began playing again. One tune after another until she grew bored with the keyboard. What difference did it make how well she played if Spencer wasn't in the room to hear her? As if she conjured the man with her thoughts, the men returned to the parlor, causing Sophie to lose her breath when Spencer came to stand by her chair.

"I am sorry to cut our evening short, but I must return home. In my eagerness to visit with your family, I completely forgot that I had agreed to dinner with my parents," Spencer stated, looking a bit embarrassed. "I'll have some explaining to do."

"Let me get your coat and hat. I'll inform a lad to bring your horses out to the front."

She left the room, delivered her message to one of the staff, and then went to a closet to retrieve Spencer's and Lord Charville's things. Taking hold of Spencer's jacket, she held the fabric up to her nose and inhaled while the heavenly smell of spice filled her senses. She heard footsteps coming closer to the foyer and didn't want to be found out, so she quickly retrieved the other coat and their hats.

Spencer came into view, took Evan's things and handed them to the man who returned to the parlor to say his farewells.

His hand brushed hers when he reached for his coat. "Will you walk me out, Sophie?"

Her heart would never be able to stand being this close to him, but she would take the chance she might survive their brief moment of privacy. She took her own redingote from the closet but before she could slip her hands in the sleeves, Spencer took the garment from her.

"Allow me..."

He went behind her to assist her with putting on the garment. His hands briefly resting on her shoulders caused her to tremble. He then went to open the door, giving her the opportunity to bow out if she felt so inclined. Nothing could be farther from her thoughts.

The night was cold, and Sophie could see her breath in the air as she exhaled. The clip clop of horses was getting closer. He would be leaving her soon. Plus, Lord Charville would be exiting the house at any moment. She didn't have much time!

"Spencer... I—"

He took her hand this time bringing it to his lips. "Ah... there it is..."

"What?" she asked in confusion.

"The sound of my given name passing your lips as though you are happy to be alone with me," he answered tucking her hand in the crook of his elbow. He began walking toward the road. "I have waited years to hear such a sound, if I am being perfectly honest."

"You have?" she gasped out.

"Yes, I have. It's been torture waiting for you to grow up," he said caressing her hand.

She halted their progress to the road, not believing he was speaking the truth. "You've been waiting for me?"

"Yes." A simple answer with so many possibilities.

"Why me?" Her eyes widened when she realized she had spoken the words aloud.

He took his hands to caress her cheeks. Leaning down, he stared into her eyes. "Because you were worth waiting for, my dear."

She closed her eyes, hoping for her first kiss. But she was to be disappointed when the front door opened, and they broke apart.

"I will look forward to our dance together next week, Miss Sophie," he said as he put on his gloves. His fingers then went to the brim of his hat giving it a slight tip as he took his leave.

There was no further time for any whispered words. Lord Charville bid her goodnight and the two men mounted their horses. She would spend the rest of the week with her head in the clouds waiting until she could be held in Spencer's arms while they danced.

CHAPTER 4

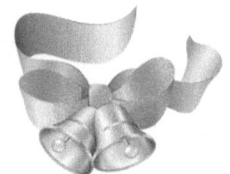

The assembly was much as Spencer expected. The room filled with all the local villagers and landed gentry who had come to the country for the holiday. Bright decorations hung from the walls and hearths and even a bit of mistletoe had managed to find its way to hang near the entrance. Spencer smiled with thoughts of kissing Sophie beneath it. Now, if only he could claim his dance as she had promised.

One wouldn't think such a feat would be that difficult but, to his annoyance, Sophie was in much demand as one gentleman after another claimed her to the sound of a merry tune. She would no sooner leave the dance floor to recover from the fast patterns of a dance before another would come to whisk her away. Spencer was tired of standing on the sidelines waiting for his opportunity.

"She's lovely, isn't she?" a voice said next to him.

Spencer turned to see none other than Joseph Morledge. "Yes, she is." Spencer was uncertain as to the younger man's feelings, but if his expression was any indication of how he felt about Sophie, then he was in love with her.

"I saw the way she looked at you at dinner last week," Joseph said before sighing. "She's never looked at me that way before, more's the pity."

"You wish to marry her," Spencer assumed. A muscle in his cheek ticked in annoyance.

"I wish for her happiness. There's a difference."

Spencer's brow rose. "How so?"

"I could marry her, of course. Her father would approve as would her sister, but I would never make her happy," Joseph informed him.

The man certainly had Spencer's attention. "And why couldn't you make her happy?"

Joseph placed his hand on Spencer's shoulder. "Because of the way she looked at you last week at dinner," he repeated, patting Spencer. "You should make your intentions known, and soon, or you'll miss your opportunity with the fair lady."

Spencer watched the younger man leave. The band stopped playing, and he saw Sophie leave the dance floor. She made her way across the room and picked up a glass of punch. It was now or never!

Several acquaintances tried to stop him to have a word or two, but he only nodded and continued to make his way to the lady while she was still alone. He bowed before her. "Miss Sophie. I hope I can now claim my dance?"

The smile she gave him was radiant. "I was beginning to wonder if you had forgotten, Lord Wilmott."

"Never," he vowed placing his hand over his heart. "I only gave you the opportunity to dance with whomever you wished because once I claimed you, I plan on never letting you go."

Her brow lifted, and she appeared as though she was hard pressed to keep her laughter inside. "Is that so?" she smirked.

"Yes, it is," he replied while his gaze swept over her. She never looked more beautiful. If she were his wife, he'd adorn that graceful neck with diamonds and emeralds to bring out the color of her eyes.

"More than two dances, and we'll cause such a scandal we may never recover. Whatever would we do?" She waved her fan in front of her flushed cheek before snapping it shut and tracing it across her cheek.

A smile lit his face. If he correctly remembered the language of the fan, Sophie just said she loved him. "I guess we'll just have to wait and see. Shall we, my dear?" he asked offering his arm. He swore he felt her fingers tremble, and he covered her hand briefly with his own. Smiling down at her, he led her to the dance floor. The beginnings of a waltz filled the room. He held out his hand, and she placed hers in his palm, the other upon his shoulder while he took her waist. My God, she was so tiny she barely reached his chest. Rose perfume filled his nostrils, and he prayed she wouldn't become such a heady distraction that he stumbled over his feet.

"Did you pay the musicians to play a waltz for us?" she teased again, her eyes sparkling mischievously.

"Sheer luck!" he murmured looking down into her lovely face as he twirled her around the floor. "You look lovely this evening. Blue becomes you."

She fingered the edges of his jacket. "And you look very handsome, Spencer," she whispered softly. "You kept me waiting long enough to claim me."

He chuckled. "Surely you only waited an hour or two."

"More like years…"

He was so startled by her reply that he did indeed stumble but quickly recovered. Her soft laughter caused his heart to lurch. He pulled her a step closer into his embrace, and her green eyes widened. She looked around in a panic. "Don't worry, Sophie. I would never do something inappropriate on the dance floor that might damage your reputation. Your father and sister might never forgive me," he remarked to acknowledge the sudden fear that sparked in her face.

She relaxed, squeezing his hand, then looked up into his face. "You'd best behave, if you want to stay in my good graces, too," she murmured.

His laughter rumbled inside his chest. "My only desire is to remain forever in your good graces, dearest Sophie."

Her brow rose. "Are you about to inform me of your intentions, my lord?"

He twirled her around. The faces of the other dancing couples became a blur. He had every intention of asking her to become his wife, but not here… not in a crowded room full of curious people just waiting for a bit of gossip about why he had hurried his marriage proposal. He had always dreamed of asking Sophie to wed him in a setting far more intimate and private. A moment to be shared with just the two of them together.

"Spencer?" His name crossing her lips brought him back to the present, and he smiled down at her.

"Not here," he remarked and watched her disappointment so he quickly continued, "but soon." Her eyes lit up, and he couldn't be happier that he was the cause.

The music chose that moment to end, leaving Spencer no choice but to bow before his lady while she curtsied in return. He took her hand, tucking it into the crook of his elbow while he escorted her from the floor. They stopped to talk to several acquaintances, including his parents, although Spencer couldn't tell if they were happy that Sophie was on his arm… not that he cared. They would have to learn to love her just as he did. *Love*… yes… love her he did and he vowed that Sophie would know it, too, before the Christmas season was over.

CHAPTER 5

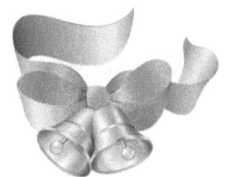

hristmas Eve

Sophie, full of excitement, twirled around in her bedroom in front of a full-length mirror. Margaret had informed her of the earl's arrival a short time ago, but he had asked for a private word with her father. Memories of the past two weeks spent in Spencer's company filled her head. Sleigh rides in the freshly falling snow, skating on the nearby frozen lake, dinner at his parents' manor that also included her sister and husband, and even sitting in her father's parlor having lovely conversations after dinner. She almost cherished those moments together more than all the others because it gave her, and her family, the opportunity to get to know Spencer further.

A knock on her door gave Sophie a second of panic. What if he wasn't asking her father for her hand? What if he had changed his mind? She went to the door to find Margaret holding Colin who squirmed in her arms. Her nephew started crying, and Margaret heaved a heavy sigh.

"He's late for his nap," she said as though she had to make an excuse for the child. "But come downstairs. You have a visitor."

Sophie leaned over to kiss Colin's cheek and made her way down the stairs. She stopped short on the next to last step. The person waiting with his hat in his hands wasn't exactly who she was expecting.

"Joseph! What brings you here?" Sophie said coming forward. She noticed her father's study door was still closed, then took Joseph's arm to lead him into the parlor. Not giving him the opportunity to answer her question, she continued. "I'm actually glad you've come over."

"You are?" he said taking off his coat and laying it over a vacant chair. He followed Sophie over to a worn sofa and sat next to her.

She took his hands not knowing how to begin this difficult conversation that must be said because she wanted no hard feelings between them. She cared for Joseph but not in the way that would make a good marriage.

"Joseph... I wanted to tell you"

"I already know, Sophie," he said, and yet his tone was somber as if he regretted the fact she did not love him.

"You do?"

He brought her hand up to his lips and kissed the air between them. "You want to inform me, very nicely by the way, that your affections lie with another. It hasn't been very easy to see for myself the attraction you feel for Lord Wilmott but as long as you're happy, then that is really all that matters," he said. It was probably the most she ever heard Joseph speak all at one time.

A sigh of relief escaped her. "Then you're not mad at me?"

"How could I be mad at you? We're family. We may disagree on things from time to time, but in the end, we all just want what is best for one another, don't we?" Joseph replied before he stood.

She gave him a brief hug that she'd done a hundred times or more in their past. "I want your happiness, too, Joseph, and hope you'll find the lady of your dreams one day."

He nodded and took up his coat and walked toward the front door.

Sophie's brow furrowed. "You never mentioned why you came over."

Joseph looked embarrassed. "I almost forgot! Mother wanted to invite your family over to celebrate the New Year together. Just let us know if you can attend," he said, opening the door.

"Please thank her for the invitation," Sophie answered with a smile. Jennette was always so considerate, another mother figure toward Sophie that she appreciated.

He bent forward and kissed her cheek. "Goodbye, Sophie," he said staring into her eyes before taking his leave.

She touched her cheek where his lips had been just moments before. Somehow Joseph's farewell was solemn, as if she had lost something that could have been if only her heart hadn't gone in another direction.

She had no further time to ponder her reaction to Joseph's departure because suddenly Tulip came bounding into the house barking and tracking mud onto the clean floor.

"Tulip! You bad dog. Don't you dare... Ack!"

Tulip's muddy paws as she placed them on the front of Sophie's dress left dark brown prints on her otherwise pretty green gown. The misbehaving dog continued its antics, running circles around Sophie until the hem became just as dirty. Tulip then did the unthinkable by trying to weave her way in and out of Sophie's legs. Sophie screeched when the dog and the fabric of the dress wrapped around her legs. Sophie began to trip and fall over her obnoxious pet. She was going to land in a heap on the floor!

Falling backwards, Sophie was unprepared to be enfolded in strong arms while she breathed in the heavenly scent of Spencer's cologne. Brought up against his chest, she took hold of his arm to steady herself.

"I've got you," Spencer whispered in her ear.

"Thank goodness," she whispered, her voice faint from the proximity of being held in his embrace.

"Tulip, sit!" he commanded the barking dog until she finally obeyed. Spencer then assisted Sophie to stand, and she swayed once she gained her feet. His hand stayed upon her waist, pulling her close.

She tried to step back, but the man continued to keep her near his side. "I'll make a mess of your clothes," she said quietly, knowing how muddy her gown had become.

"It hardly matters, Sophie," he replied with a grin spread across his handsome face. "Can we go outside for a walk? The day is lovely, and we should take advantage of the sunshine."

"I would love to but only after I've changed. Just give me a few minutes," she said. Rushing up the stairs, she ran into her room and began to quickly change her soiled gown. Looking in the mirror, she patted her hair back into place and returned downstairs. Spencer already had his coat, and hers, in hand. Once they were dressed to brave the cool weather, he took her hand, tucking it into the crook of his elbow, and escorted her outside.

The snow crunched beneath their shoes and Sophie became conscious of the stupidity of not changing into boots. But it was too late to worry about shoes that would certainly be ruined. She was with Spencer... alone... and she waited patiently for the words she had longed to hear.

He finally halted their progress beneath a tree, causing Sophie to gaze upward. A smile lit her face from what she saw above before returning her attention to the man who held her heart in the palm of his hands.

"You must be wondering why I asked you to take a stroll outside," he began looking somewhat apprehensive of what he would say next.

"To share a bit of witty conversation?" she teasingly asked.

"Perhaps afterward." Laughter rumbled in his chest while the sweetest grin slipped across his mouth.

"After what?" she said, and her breath caught in her throat when he took her hand, bringing it up to his warm lips.

"After I ask you to become my wife," he said in that husky voice that caused her heart to flip end over end.

"You wish to marry me." Her answer was more of a statement than a question.

"You may not have known it, but I have watched you from afar for many years now. I've seen you grow up from a little young miss getting into mischief with her puppy to the beautiful woman you are today. Is it any wonder I want to marry you?" He kissed the inside of her wrist and Sophie practically melted right there on the spot.

"I can't believe you've thought of me for all these years. I've noticed you, too, but always saw you with other women on your arm. I figured my chances of catching your eye were beyond hope." A burst of jealousy at the women who came before her rushed through her but, as Spencer brought her closer, she realized they meant nothing to him.

"My apologies, dearest Sophie, but that was the doing of my parents. If I had had my way, there would have been only one woman on my arm, and she would have been you. I just needed to have a fair amount of patience while I waited for you to grow up."

She stared up into his amber eyes with golden flecks sparkling in the sunshine. She would never tire of being held in his arms. "Ask me..." she whispered reaching up to play with the edges of his tawny hair.

"I adore and love you, Miss Sophie Templeton. Will you do me the greatest honor by becoming my wife?"

"I love you, too, Spencer," she happily said, "and yes! Yes, I'll marry you."

Spencer breathed a sigh of relief before leaning down to seal their fate with a kiss. It was a gentle claiming, and Sophie matched his movements as he taught her what she had dreamed about all her life. To have the man she loved giving her her own mistletoe kiss. She opened her eyes and looked upward toward the bunch of mistletoe hanging above their heads before she closed her eyes once more. Spencer had fulfilled her Christmas wish, and a lifetime in his arms would never be enough.

EPILOGUE

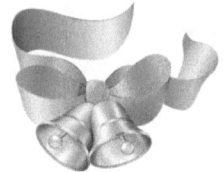

One Year Later...
Spencer's gaze swept around at his decorating efforts and nodded his approval. It was a passable job if he did say so himself. Their country home was now ready for the holidays and all the visitors who would soon descend upon them. Now, to get his lovely wife's approval. He left the front parlor and made his way to the library which had become Sophie's favorite room in the house... except for their bedroom.

With thoughts of how they had spent the previous evening, he opened the door to find his wife curled up in his favorite chair with Tulip at her feet. The moment he entered, the hound bounded up and ran the distance to Spencer, barking and wagging her tail. Spencer bent over to scratch the dog behind her ears while her tail beat furiously in approval upon the floor.

"Good dog, Tulip," Spencer said going to his wife. He held out his hand, and she put down her book. Tugging her to her feet, he placed his hand over her stomach, the developing mound proof that the baby within was growing stronger each day.

Sophie placed her hand over his. "You won't be doing this in front of our parents, now will you? It would be quite embarrassing," she said with a laugh.

Spencer kissed her cheek. "I don't see why. It's not like they haven't all had children. Besides, I'm thrilled we are expecting a baby soon."

"You'll be a very devoted father, my love," Sophie said reaching up to caress his cheek.

"And you every bit the devoted mother. Now, come with me before our guests arrive. I have something to show you," he said, leading her from the library.

A gasp of surprise left his wife when she saw what he had accomplished in her absence. Mistletoe hung from every doorway and Spencer wasted no time bringing her to the closest bunch to give her a kiss beneath the greenery.

"I hope you don't mind that I stole Frederick and Margaret's idea. She mentioned how it had become a family tradition when I asked her if I could do the same for you," he murmured as his wife gave him a fierce hug.

"Never let it be said we turned our noses up at tradition," she beamed in approval pulling on his hand until they were beneath the next doorway. "Kiss me…"

"Today and every day for the rest of our lives," he answered, before his lips met hers in a kiss that enflamed the love they shared between them.

Sophie's arms wound their way around his neck, and he swore he would never let this woman go. She was the love of his life and had been worth the wait.

He broke off their kiss to stare at the woman in wonder. He was the luckiest of men. He had the love of a lady who had held his heart for years, a baby on the way, and a lifetime of happiness to look forward to. He thanked the good Lord above for all his blessings, especially at Christmas. He gave a slight chuckle thinking how their journey together all began last year with a mistletoe kiss…

THE END

ABOUT SHERRY EWING

Sherry Ewing picked up her first historical romance when she was a teenager and has been hooked ever since. An award-winning and bestselling author, she writes historical and time travel romances to awaken the soul one heart at a time. When not writing, she can be found in the San Francisco area at her day job as an Information Technology Specialist.

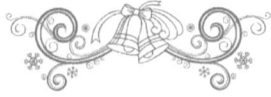

Sophie Templeton made her first appearance as a secondary character in my Regency novellas, *Under the Mistletoe* and briefly in *A Second Chance at Love*. Now that she was all grown up, she was looking for her happily-ever-after and found it with Spencer, Earl of Wilmott. I hope you enjoyed their journey to having a first kiss under the mistletoe! You can learn more about my other Regency, medieval, and time travel stories on my website at https://www.sherryewing.com/books.

SOCIAL MEDIA FOR SHERRY EWING

You can learn more about Sherry Ewing at these social media links:

Bookbub: www.bookbub.com/authors/sherry-ewing
Facebook: www.Facebook.com/SherryEwingAuthor
Goodreads: www.Goodreads.com/author/show/8382315.
Sherry_Ewing
Instagram: https://instagram.com/sherry.ewing
Pinterest: www.Pinterest.com/SherryLEwing
TikTok: https://www.tiktok.com/@sherryewingauthor
Twitter: www.Twitter.com/Sherry_Ewing
YouTube: http://www.youtube.com/SherryEwingauthor
Newsletter Sign Up: http://bit.ly/2vGrqQM
Facebook Street Team:
www.facebook.com/groups/799623313455472/
Facebook Official Fan page: https://www.facebook.com/groups/
356905935241836/

THE MAGIC CHRISTMAS STEW

BY SUSANA ELLIS

The life of an idle spare is no life at all for retired Captain, Daniel Winthrop. He is capable of doing many things, but they all required a wealthy bride. Governess Emily Bainbridge fears being pursued for her fortune, so she keeps hers a secret. Will this pair find the courage to conquer their pride and risk all for love?

This story is dedicated to some very special people who never stopped believing in me.

The Bluestocking Belles: Jude Knight, Caroline Warfield, Sherry Ewing, Rue Allyn, Cerise DeLand, Elizabeth Ellen Carter, and Alina K. Field. I can't even imagine writing without you at my side. You all deserve medals for patience, that's for sure!

The Maumee Valley Romance Writers, particularly Shay Lacy, Denise Frazier, Lesley Blanton, and Marilynn Rice, for the candid and heartfelt pep talk at our Brainstorming Weekend at Middle Bass Island (Put-in-Bay). Additional thanks to my traveling companion, Marilynn, who helped me brainstorm this story in London. You are all the BEST!

CHAPTER 1

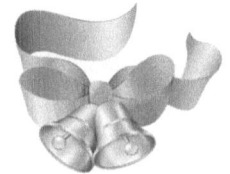

December 1815
Edenthorpe, Yorkshire

"Miss Bainbridge! Miss Bainbridge! I found a *perfect* branch over by the brook, but it's too high for me to reach!"

Emily looked up from her efforts in fastening a length of holly into a crown for
Nora's head.

Kitty's cheeks were red from excitement as she traipsed over the snow-covered ground.

"It will be perfect for the mantel! And there are lots more as well, if only we could reach them!"

Emily smiled at her oldest charge. "Excellent work, my dear. Nora and I will be there directly." She finished tying the stem and placed the crown on the younger girl's head. "There! I think it will look better when you can remove the cap, but it becomes you well enough now, sweet child."

Nora beamed at her governess, and they strolled hand-in-hand toward the brook where Kitty had made her holly tree find.

"It's that one," she pointed. "Don't you think it is beautiful, Miss Bainbridge?"

Emily assessed the height of the branch. "It is indeed, Kitty dear. But it is too high for me, as well. Another few inches and I could possibly—"

"Perhaps I may be of service, madam?"

A tall, dark man in a worn overcoat appeared behind them. Emily whirled around, her heart in her throat. They hadn't strayed far from Winthrop Hall, but now she regretted not having brought a groom along.

"Sir, this is private property..." she began, making an effort to draw the children nearer.

Kitty broke free and ran to the stranger. "Uncle Daniel! You're back! Papa said you were returning soon. It has been so long since we saw you last!"

He lifted her in his arms and twirled her around. "A few months only, poppet!" He took a long look at her. "But my, how you've grown! Another few months and I should not be able to lift you!"

Nora could wait no longer for her share of attention, tugging determinedly on the hem of his coat. "I've grown too, Uncle Daniel. I'm six now, you know."

Setting Kitty on her feet, 'Uncle Daniel' bent down and surveyed his other niece. "Why, so you are, poppet. I missed your birthday, did I not? I shall have to find a way to make up for my gross negligence, your highness."

Nora looked puzzled until he pointed to the crown of holly on her head. Then she giggled.

"Isn't it pretty? Miss Bainbridge made it for me. We've been out looking for greenery to decorate the house."

He gave her a quick hug and rose to his feet, bowing to Emily. "Ah, Miss Bainbridge, I presume? Forgive me for not introducing myself previously. I'm Daniel Winthrop, uncle to these incorrigible little monkeys."

His blue eyes twinkled at her, and Emily felt slightly giddy. How ridiculous, she chided herself. She had conversed with attractive gentlemen before, most of whom had been far better dressed. No doubt it was the suddenness of his appearance. She straightened her back.

"No need to apologize, sir," she said stiffly. "I am Emily Bainbridge, the children's governess. I am pleased to meet you, Captain Winthrop." She gave a quick bow. "As Nora has mentioned, we are searching the wood for holiday decorations." She swallowed. "But I'm sure you are eager to continue on to the Hall to reunite with your family. You mustn't let us keep you."

Captain Winthrop cocked his head. "They won't miss me for another few minutes or so, Miss Bainbridge. As I recall, when I interrupted you, you were bemoaning the fact that the branch you sought was too high."

He strolled to the tree. "Is it this one? I think I might be able to retrieve it for you." He took out a pocket knife and sawed the branch from the tree.

"Oh yes! That's it!" Kitty seized it from his hands. "There is another one over here I think you can reach, Uncle Dan. And some mistletoe too!" She placed the branch on the pile they had been building, and clapped her hands excitedly. "Oh, we shall have lots of them for the house. What good luck that you came along when you did, Uncle Daniel! Don't you agree, Miss Bainbridge?"

He smiled at her. In spite of the stubble on his face and the unkempt strands of hair beneath his cap, Emily felt herself flushing and hoped it could be attributed to the chill in the air. "Indeed it was, children. Nora, I see some mistletoe over there I believe you can reach. Let us investigate, shall we?"

"Mistletoe?" Emily took a quick glance at Captain Winthrop's wide grin and knew immediately what he was thinking. Oh, what nonsense! There was no reason in the world that he should be thinking of *that!* But she could feel her cheeks heating up and turned away quickly, hoping he didn't guess the direction of her thoughts.

"DEAR DANIEL, if I'd known you were coming, I'd have put on a proper dinner rather than the simple fare we are accustomed to," fussed his sister-in-law as the white soup was served. "A nice roast beef, perhaps, or braised lamb. Cook does a fine lamb in savory jelly."

"Louisa, my dear, I'm sure my brother will find our simple dinners to be far superior to fare on the battlefield," chided her husband. "I can't imagine beans and hardtack were all that appetizing."

Touching a napkin to his lips, Daniel shook his head. "My stomach is still not accustomed to proper meals, even after four months in London." He grinned. "There was a chap in my regiment who used to make what he called 'Magic Stew.' We all contributed whatever we had from our food allotment and such things as we could forage, and no matter what was in it, we thought it the best stew we had ever tasted."

"What was in it?" inquired Louisa. "Perhaps I could get Cook to replicate it."

Daniel laughed. "I shouldn't even attempt it. The 'magic' came from being on the march and having long lost the expectation of having tasty meals. I am convinced, Louisa, that you would not find a pot of assorted army rations with the odd vegetable tossed in at all tasty."

"Perhaps not," she conceded. "But I warn you that I have every intention of tempting your appetite now that you are home. You are far too thin. I don't believe you have gained an ounce since you returned from Waterloo thin as a rail. Did the Home Office have you on starvation rations while you were working with them?"

Seeing his brother's expression, Theo jumped in. "Now Louisa, you mustn't try to mother him. He's a grown man and a former soldier, and two years older than you are." At Louisa's grimace, he continued, "But I heartily agree with your plan to organize a party for him. To become reacquainted with the neighbors after all the years he was away in the wars."

His wife's eyes lit up. "Of course! We have been talking, Daniel. A party is just the thing. Wait until you see Cecilia Throckmorton from the Grange. She has grown up to be a beauty. She is to come out next year in York, and will no doubt have a dozen suitors hanging out for her, but you might get in ahead of them..."

"Louisa, please!" Daniel said sharply. Then his face relaxed. "I'm sorry, my dear, but I am not in the market for a wife at present." Although they all knew that was not strictly true. He had to find either a wife or a post of some sort. Sooner rather than later.

Two footmen entered the room, and the table was silent while the soup bowls were removed and the plates for the next course were placed in front of them.

Louisa stared pointedly at her husband, who cleared his throat.

"I understand how you must feel," he began.

A vein pulsed on Daniel's neck. "But you don't, do you, Theo? Know what it's like to have to find your own way in the world? All your life you've always known you would be the next viscount and spend your life as lord of the manor. I never wanted to be a soldier, but when Father offered to buy me a commission in the infantry even though he really could not spare the cost, I couldn't refuse, since I had no alternative." He speared a piece of ham. "Perhaps I should have remained in France in the army of occupation, after all." He brought the ham to his mouth and chewed noisily.

Louisa whimpered, bringing her napkin to her eyes. Theo glanced at her uneasily, and then turned to his brother.

"You're not being fair, Daniel," he said quietly.

Daniel swallowed hard, mentally berating himself for his outburst. "You're right; none of this is your fault. Please forgive me, Louisa, Theo. My manners have gone wanting over the past ten years." He gave a wry smile. "Perhaps that governess of yours could tutor me in social niceties. Pretty girl, isn't she?"

Louisa's face perked up. "She's a marvel, really. The children love her. We are so fortunate to have found her. Theo and I didn't want a stuffy old bat like I had myself as a child, and when my friend wrote me about Miss Bainbridge in September, we asked her to come for an interview right away, and hired her on the spot."

"She came all the way out here for an interview. Is she a local girl?"

He couldn't recall ever seeing her before, although she would have been very young when he'd left to join the army.

"No, I think she's from Norfolk. Or perhaps Cambridgeshire? In any case, she comes highly recommended by the vicar's wife in my friend's parish in Norwich. Lucy Hall, now Lady Grimsby. Theo knows her, don't you, darling?"

Theo nodded, and continued on with his dinner.

"I see." But his curiosity about the new governess remained unsatisfied. Who was she, really? How did she happen to come to their attention at that particular time, not to mention her willingness to travel so far for a mere interview? He was determined to find out, one way or another.

In any case, he couldn't fault his sister-in-law for her assumption he would be looking to marry. Besides the fact that at twenty-eight he was of an age to marry, he still had to deal with the problem of finding a means of support. The modest income Theo and his family lived on could by no means be stretched to include an allowance for his brother, if Daniel had been inclined to accept one. He'd decided against continuing in the army, and he had no calling for the Church, so marriage to an heiress seemed, however distasteful he found it, the best option open to him.

He drained his glass and held it up for the footman to refill it. After all he'd endured on the Peninsula and—oh God, Waterloo!—he had no reason to complain about his lot in life. Perhaps he could find an heiress who was not too objectionable, possibly even one he liked.

The image of Miss Bainbridge came to mind, but he pushed it out of his mind. Marriage to a governess was out of the question. Unless she had a fortune hidden away somewhere, and that wasn't likely. He'd do better with the Throckmorton chit, who presumably had some sort of dowry, at least.

A fortune hunter. He'd become a damned fortune hunter. What the hell?

EMILY DISCOVERED at breakfast the next day that there was to be a house party a fortnight off, and that, due to the spontaneity of it, her assistance would be required.

"Daniel has been away all of his adult life," explained Lady Winthrop. "A party is the perfect way to reintroduce him into the neighborhood. But Theo and I agreed that a single evening event is not sufficient. A few friends I have in mind to invite live too far away to come for an evening, and besides, I wish for them to have the time to become a bit better acquainted with him."

"But it seems likely that most people would have made their plans by now," Emily pointed out. "Do you really think you will receive many acceptances?"

Her employer smirked. "I think the families I have in mind will make the effort to come. Those with daughters to marry off will find it impossible to turn down the opportunity to meet an unmarried gentleman with a connection to a viscountcy, not to mention his good looks."

"Do you find him attractive, Miss Bainbridge? Or is it simply his relationship to my darling Theo that influences my opinion?"

Emily felt caught off guard. "Well…"

Lady Winthrop laughed. "How ridiculous to ask you such a question! You could hardly say otherwise, could you? In any case, my dear, I shall need your help to put this together. I shall write to invite my friends immediately, of course. I wish for you to put together a list of the locals to invite to the ball on Christmas Eve. The vicar's wife can help with that, I believe. And we will need additional servants. There will be meals and games to organize—I told Theo the holiday season would provide many more amusements for our guests than anything we might do in the dreary winter months—and isn't it fortunate that you and the children are decorating the house. Of course, we shall need a great deal more decorations for the assembly room, I believe. Oh dear, I do hope it is not taken, as we have no ballroom here…"

Emily sagged into the nearest chair. "But the children— Their lessons! Surely, they are my first responsibility?"

Their mother waved away the objection. "The baby's nurse can keep an eye on them when you are unavailable. As far as lessons go—a fortnight's holiday will scarcely matter. I daresay they will enjoy taking part in some of the activities." She planted her hands on her cheeks. "Goodness, there is so much to do, I hardly know where to start." Biting her lips: "Guests! The invitations must go out immediately. Today, if possible!"

And that is how Emily was sent to the vicarage—after hastily giving her charges a few lessons to work on for the morning—to obtain a list of local gentry to invite to the ball.

Mrs. Dean had her hands buried in bread dough, but nevertheless welcomed Emily to her kitchen. "A house party? And a Christmas Eve ball? How fabulous! I daresay it will be the event of the year."

She directed Emily to the vicar's study to obtain paper and pen, and then focused her gaze on her guest. "It's for Master Daniel, I reckon. I heard he'd returned."

At Emily's nod, she continued. "I see her ladyship isn't wasting any time, and why should she? It's past time he settled down. He's done his lot for king and country."

Emily gave a pinched smile, unwilling to participate in any of Mrs. Dean's gossipmongering. But the older woman had turned her attention to the dough, parting it into two mounds and then placing them each in loaf pans waiting nearby.

"'Twill take a special woman for Master Daniel," she mused. "Not a silly young girl out of the schoolroom. Someone more mature, warm-hearted, capable..." She sighed deeply as she wiped her hands on a towel. "Preferably an heiress." She pulled up a chair and sat down next to Emily. "I don't suppose you have an inheritance tucked away somewhere, do you?" Not waiting for Emily to respond, she shook her head. "Not likely, you being a governess. A real shame, that. You might have done well for him otherwise."

Emily cleared her throat. "Perhaps we should begin our task now, Mrs. Dean. I must return to the children, you know."

"Of course, Miss Bainbridge. Let me think—the Pevensys and the Denhams must be invited, of course, and the Throckmortons too, although their daughter gives herself airs, I think. And then there is..."

She went on, and Emily dutifully wrote the names all down until the page was filled and she was able to take her leave of the vicar's wife.

Nevertheless, the two-mile walk back to the Hall gave her more than sufficient time to ponder over the suddenness of the ball and its intended purpose—to find the returned soldier brother a wealthy bride. He didn't seem the fortune hunter type, at least not the sort with whom she'd been acquainted. Not like Simon, in any case.

Her cousin's sophisticated charm and honeyed words never reached his eyes, and soon turned to resentment at her persistent rejections. While she could banish him from her home, somehow, he managed to be present whenever she left it, to the point where she could not feel safe walking on her own property, even in the presence of a maid or a groom.

There was in his eyes a determination to get his hands on the family property, which would belong to her on her twenty-fifth birthday, only weeks from now. After that, she would have full control over her inheritance and no amount of persuasion would induce her to marry Simon, or indeed, anyone at all. She'd sign it all away to a widows and orphans fund before she'd let a fortune hunter get his hands on it.

CHAPTER 2

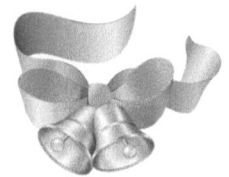

"Captain Winthrop, do tell us all about your adventures on the continent. And Waterloo too! How many Frenchmen did you kill? Did you catch a glimpse of Boney?"

On his morning calls, Daniel had become accustomed to such curiosity, though only the children were as frank in their questions.

"Ella!" the girl's mother admonished. "Did we not discuss this earlier? It is not polite to interrogate a guest, particularly not about such things as war. Apologize and then go upstairs and read *Letters on the Improvement of the Mind, addressed to a young lady* for the next hour."

Ella's face fell. "I beg your pardon, Captain Winthrop. I just wanted to know..." "Ella!"

One look at Mrs. Pevensy's face induced her to give a slight bow and leave the room.

The older woman turned toward Daniel and grimaced. "My apologies, Captain Winthrop. Waterloo has been a topic of conversation for months now, and the children seem to think it was all a great lark and not the dreadful tragedy it turned out to be." She bit her lip. "A dozen young men from near here lost their lives, and many more from York. So many families impacted, and those of us with marriageable daughters feel it as well."

Daniel cleared his throat.

She laughed. "You needn't feel I'm tossing my eldest daughter your way. Amelia is only sixteen and far too young to consider marriage. As her mother, however, I am excessively conscious that the pool of eligible gentlemen is smaller than it might have been."

Daniel shook his head. "I do understand, Mrs. Pevensy. The consequences of the war are far-reaching, despite its end proving victorious for Britain."

She reached over and patted his hand, even as a young woman with tousled hair hastened into the room. "Ah, here is Amelia at last. Darling, this is Captain Winthrop, the viscount's brother, recently returned from the Continent. Captain Winthrop, this is my eldest daughter, Amelia, returned from her morning ride."

He rose and bowed over the younger girl's hand. "I am pleased to meet you, Miss
Pevensy."

She blushed and gave a small bow. "I am honored, sir."

"Ah, the tea trolley has arrived," announced his hostess, rising from her chair to pour the tea.

When everyone had been served, she brought up the subject of horses. "My daughter is horse-mad, Captain Winthrop. I believe she prefers horses to people. Although she *has* learned to change out of her riding habit before greeting callers, I am pleased to say."

She cast an indulgent look toward her daughter.

"Oh, Mama! How could you say such a thing? I like people well enough—"

"But not as much as horses," her mother insisted.

Amelia shrugged and looked sheepishly at Daniel. "Perhaps she's right. I do prefer horses to *some* people, at least. Do you like horses, Captain Winthrop? Did you ride one in the war? Do you have a horse now?"

He set his teacup on the table nearby and leaned forward as he related a few of his more notable experiences with the 95th Regiment of Foot. Not too much about the battles, but his reminiscences of daily life and sketches of his companions seemed to enthrall his audience, including his hostess, who seemed to have forgotten her objection to pressing him for details on his military career.

By the time he made his exit, he was surprised to comprehend that he had rather enjoyed his time with the Pevensys and would relish meeting them again. In fact, it was the first morning call he had made that hadn't made him feel uncomfortably aware of his marriageable state. God bless sensible women like Mrs. Pevensy!

He had thought it was best for him to leave his sister-in-law at home, as she had a tendency to make it seem as though he had come to interview potential wives. It was implied rather than stated, but it made him feel like a prize horse being led around the paddock at Tattersall's. And goodness knows, he was no matrimonial prize, possessing no home or fortune, only years of battlefield living and the ghastly memories that came along with it. How could he saddle himself on some well-to-do young lady? On any woman? Even a governess.

Daniel bit his lip. Why had the image of the pretty Miss Bainbridge come to his mind at that moment? He wouldn't be averse to becoming better acquainted with her, but he could not afford to make a penniless marriage.

Without realizing it, he pounded a fist on the seat beside him, so hard the coach came to a stop.

"Everything all right, sir?" The coachman called down to him.

"Yes, Hayes. You may continue."

As the wheels rolled on, he remonstrated with himself. This was no way for a grown man to go on. He'd seen so many soldiers die in battle. Many more who returned to England to face poverty and misery in return for their service. So many widows and orphans with no means of support. He had family. The money from the sale of his commission, which Theo had refused to take back. It wasn't much, but he and his mates had managed to survive on considerably less while on the march on the Peninsula.

He sat up straight as a thought came to him. He'd use the "Magic Stew" idea to initiate a project to help soldiers less fortunate than himself.

"You may carry our parcels to the kitchen," Emily instructed as she stepped down from the coach and assisted first Nora, and then Kitty to alight.

"Did we buy everything on the list? Do you think we have enough for all?" Kitty continually worried that there wouldn't be enough in the Boxing Day baskets.

Emily chuckled. "My dear, by the time the hams are delivered, the baskets will be full to overflowing."

"Hats, mittens, and scarves will keep them warm," Nora added, eyes sparkling. "We have jams, apples, and sweets too. Don't forget we are to make biscuits as well, Miss Bainbridge!"

"I'm certain you will not allow me to forget, dear child. But we'll have to wait for Cook to find available time in the kitchen, as it's in a bit of disarray at the moment."

The housekeeper opened the door to admit them, and she helped Emily remove her own outer apparel and then that of the children.

"Miss Bainbridge, a letter arrived for you in this morning's post. I put it on the hall table for you."

"A letter?" Emily's brow wrinkled. Who could have known she was here? Only a handful of close friends had been entrusted with her whereabouts, and she was certain none would betray it. If Simon had somehow ferreted it out, she was no longer safe. And then what would she do?

Swallowing hard, she instructed the children to run upstairs to the schoolroom and resume their project to write notes for all the basket recipients. "I'll be along shortly."

"Are you well, Miss Bainbridge? You seem rather pale. Can I get you something? Tea, perhaps?"

"I suppose I'm a bit tired, Mrs. Cotton. A cup of tea would be much appreciated, thank you. I'll be in the drawing room reading my letter."

When she broke the seal and unfolded it, she was relieved to see that it was from her father's (and now her) solicitor, who had agreed to keep her location a secret between the two of them. He wrote that the documents necessary to formalize the ownership of the estate had been prepared and were ready for her signature on the day of her birth, the twenty-fifth of December, and that he planned to bring them to her himself, having secured lodging at a nearby inn for both Christmas Eve and the following day.

Emily paused at that point, as she comprehended that the time to expose her true identity to her employers was rapidly approaching. The Winthrops had been so kind to her; she had become fond of them all, especially Kitty and Nora. The entire household had welcomed her wholeheartedly to the point where she had come to think of them as the family she had never had herself.

This was something she hadn't considered when formulating her escape plan. After all, she'd had a good reason for her deception; she would fulfill the role of governess for them until it was safe for her to return home. It hadn't seemed like living a lie when she thought of it that way. But now, she found herself feeling both remorseful for her deception and sorrowful at the prospect of leaving them to return to her old life.

A solitary tear dropped onto the letter, and she drew a breath as she returned her attention to the final paragraph.

As your late father's friend as well as his legal advisor and now yours, I must caution you that you would be well advised to find a suitable husband at the earliest opportunity. As a wealthy woman, you are likely to remain the target for desperate men. And, I hope I may be forgiven for adding a personal note—that a marriage between two like-minded individuals can be a great comfort as the years pass by, along with the children and grandchildren. It is my sincere prayer that you will find this joy in your own life.

The letter blurred in front of her. Mr. Hill was right; she hadn't seen that in her own family—her mother had died too young. She'd never known the true value of having a relationship such as the one shared by Lord Winthrop and his wife. And the children. Suddenly the life she had anticipated as an independent woman seemed empty and lonely, as her father's had been, she concluded. They had never been much of a family, more just two people living in the same house. Melancholy fell over her.

"Is something wrong, Miss Bainbridge? Might I get something for you?"

Emily startled, shaking herself out of her thoughts. She hadn't noticed Captain

Winthrop's entrance into the room.

"N-No, Captain Winthrop. A letter from home, that is all."

He bent over her, concern in his gaze. "Not bad news, I hope?"

She hurriedly folded the letter and put it in her pocket. "Not at all, sir. I hope you will excuse me. I must get back to the children."

He moved back. "Of course, Miss Bainbridge."

She felt his eyes on her as she scurried out of the room and swallowed. For some reason, she found herself excessively distressed at the thought of what he would think of her once the truth had been revealed. What was that about? A man she scarcely knew?

"YOU'VE DONE WELL with it, Theo. The land is productive, the tenants well cared for, and all on your own too. I'm happy for you."

Daniel and Theo, both mounted, surveyed the snow-covered fields in the terrain below them.

Theo nodded, a satisfied smile on his face as his gaze roamed over the estate.

"I appreciate that, Daniel. It hasn't been easy over the years, eking out an income sufficient to support the family. I've read up on the latest farming techniques, joined a local farming collective, and have managed to build up a bit of a nest egg for the future." He grinned at his brother. "Dowries for the girls, you know. And we've added a servant or two, although I'm damned lucky to have a thrifty wife."

Daniel winced. "As to that, I wish I could have dissuaded Louisa from persisting with her plans for this house party and a ball, of all things! In all honesty, I am not seeking a wife at the moment, despite the prevailing opinion that I am in dire need of a fortune."

Theo burst out laughing. "Once she gets an idea in her head, my wife is as stubborn as a mule. Neither you nor I could have put her off the idea. Besides, we discussed it before your return, Dan, and we both agreed that it's the least we owe you, under the circumstances."

"You owe me nothing, Theo! I confess I have been a bit envious of you at times, especially now, seeing you and your family settled and happy."

"You're a member of that family, Daniel. We owe you—the country owes you—a great debt for the sacrifices you have made in the defense of England and Europe. We expect to support you in all things now that you are returned." He reached out and took Daniel's hand. "You could not do anything to make us prouder of you than we are now." He chuckled. "And if you choose to remain a bachelor, we will happily call upon you to escort Kitty and Nora to balls and protect them from unsuitable fortune hunters—"

"—Like me, you mean?" Daniel snorted.

"Exactly!"

The brothers contemplated each other in perfect understanding for a moment, until Daniel cleared his throat.

"As it happens, Theo, I have an idea for a scheme that I wanted to discuss with you. Not one to benefit me, but an endeavor to help those who returned from the Continent to find little but poverty and hardship for their sacrifices."

"Go on."

"Remember what I told you the other night about the 'Magic Stew' we would make when our food allotment was low?"

"On the Peninsula, when you and the other men combined what you had into a pot and it

provided food for all of you?"

"Exactly! The resulting stew wasn't suitable for Prinny's dinner, but it tasted all the better to us because we shared in the making of it and we all had something to eat."

When Theo looked puzzled, Daniel shook his head and grinned. "Sorry, I'm not making myself clear, am I? The horses have been standing long enough. Let's turn back and I'll explain my idea more clearly."

As they walked their horses slowly back to the house, Daniel recounted what he had seen of the misery faced by returned soldiers, unable to find work to feed themselves or their families, some of whom had lost limbs and other body parts in the bloody conflicts they had fought.

"At Waterloo, particularly," he said with a catch in his throat. "So many dead and oftentimes, not a surgeon in sight. Trapped under horses, speared by the enemy or the thieving peasants looting everywhere. A terrible number of my soldier brothers fell right in front of me, the casualties in the 5th Brigade were massive, and yet there was nothing to do but to fight on until the end."

"My God," said his brother, slack-jawed.

Daniel shook his head. "I beg your pardon. I didn't mean to go there. It's not something I like to think about. It was what it was, and nothing can change the tragic loss of human lives it cost us. But Theo," he turned to face his brother, "we must do something to help the rest. Those who returned alive, whole or maimed, and the families of those who did not. It's the very least we can do, do you not see?"

His voice cracked at the end and Theo's eyebrows drew together.

"Of course I do, Daniel. I can see you feel very strongly about this, as should we all. What can I do to help? You know my financial situation won't stand a large contribution, but we'll do what we can."

Daniel snorted. "And *you* know that I have only the money from the sale of my commission—which has not yet been finalized—and am a half-pay officer in the meantime. But I've been thinking: there aren't enough wealthy people to make a great difference, and even fewer who care enough to actually do anything. No, it's about all of us doing whatever we can to contribute to the effort. Not only money, but a spare shirt or blanket, a pig or a goat. Or taking on a widow as a servant and providing a cottage for her family to live in."

Daniel's voice shook with excitement. "Don't you see, Theo? When we all contribute what we can, we all get something in return. Nobody goes hungry."

Theo nodded. "The 'Magic Stew.' Of course. Now tell me what you have in mind, brother. I can see you've seriously studied on this matter. How can we make it happen?"

"I've received three acceptances today in the post," boasted an animated Louisa that evening at dinner. "The Norwoods, the Rochesters, and the Blackthornes, I am pleased to say. A bit of a journey for them, but Priscilla has been out for several years now, and I'm sure her parents must be desperate to find a husband for her."

"Louisa, please," her husband demurred, with an apologetic glance at Daniel, who shrugged nonchalantly.

"Priscilla Blackthorne?" The name sounded familiar to Emily, who had of late been required to dine with the family so she and Louisa could discuss ideas for the upcoming festivities. "Is that the Blackthorne family from Cambridgeshire, do you think?"

"Indeed. From some village near Ely, I believe." She took a bite of a buttered roll and gave Emily a curious look. "Are you acquainted with them, Miss Bainbridge? I believe you come from around there, do you not?"

Emily forced herself to finish chewing the bite of pigeon pie in her mouth without choking, although it took a heroic effort to do so. She had already decided to confess the truth to them, but she hadn't expected to have to do it so soon, at the dinner table. But she wasn't willing to tell them any more lies than she already had.

"Er—yes, I believe we have met in the past, but only in passing," she managed.

While neither Louisa nor her husband seemed to notice her agitation, she was acutely aware that the captain across from her was scrutinizing her intently. She took a quick sip of her wine and licked her lips, forcing herself to avoid his gaze.

"What a happy coincidence! You shall have the opportunity to become much better acquainted, will you not?" Louisa picked up one of the letters from the table. "They are arriving on Saturday. I'm thinking of the Peacock Room for the parents. Miss Blackthorne will have to share with one of the other young ladies."

While she prattled on about the other guests, Captain Winthrop leaned forward and whispered, "Are you well, Miss Bainbridge? You seem a bit... flustered."

"I'm simply a bit tired, sir. It's been a long day," she said to his cravat. She felt his eyes on her, but couldn't meet them. Such a coward she was!

By the time dessert arrived, Louisa seemed to realize she had been dominating the

conversation and inquired as to what the gentlemen had been doing that afternoon.

"I'm glad you asked, my dear. My dear brother has come up with a brilliant plan to lend assistance to needy soldiers and their families." Theo grinned at Daniel. "It's called 'Magic Stew.'"

CHAPTER 3

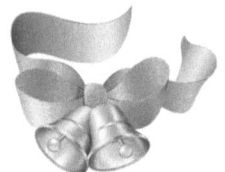

*a*s the days passed, Emily learned more about the captain's "Magic Stew" proposal to gather the neighborhood together to help needy men returning from war. She was intrigued with the enthusiasm he displayed for the project, and frankly, so was everyone else. He had an air of command even in his simple civilian clothing, and his dark good looks didn't hurt either. His was the face of a mature man, with a chiseled jawline, well-defined cheekbones and a nose that was ever-so-slightly bent, identical to his brother's, which they jokingly referred to as the "Winthrop snout."

But what stood out in his appearance was the sincerity in his clear brown eyes when he set his gaze on a person. For Emily, at least, it seemed as though he knew she wasn't being completely truthful, and his eyes were seeking to ferret out her secret.

Which had the effect of making her nervous around him and desirous of avoiding him. Which turned out to be impossible because he made a determined effort to accompany her and her charges wherever they went. And everywhere they went, he greeted people and inevitably brought up the "Magic Stew" project.

Mr. Hake at the stationer's store, when he heard about it, was inspired to provide paper supplies to be used by the children to make flyers with "Magic Stew" pots on them to hand out to the villagers. The greengrocer promised to provide produce for families who could take soldiers into their homes for a time, and the same went for the butcher and the miller. People donated clothing, blankets, bags of onions, potatoes or apples from the cellar, and just about anything they could spare to the large bins at the church. Nora carefully wrapped one of her dolls and placed it in the bin, declaring, through brave tears, that Penelope would cheer up some other little girl's life. Emily helped Kitty do a creditable job knitting a pair of socks. Emily herself knitted a cap and scarf in the evenings during her spare time, vowing to herself that she would do more after receiving her inheritance.

As to that, Emily was well aware that she would have to speak to the Winthrops soon. The Blackthornes would likely recognize her, and she couldn't allow the Winthrops to find out from them. But the house was topsy-turvy with preparations for the house party and the "Magic Stew" project, and poor Louisa was torn in all directions, with new servants needing supervision and keeping track of orders and deliveries and other such errands. Hosting a house party was no easy feat, and making all arrangements in less than a fortnight was wearing them all down.

"WITH ANY LUCK AT ALL, there will be at least one good day for the gentlemen to hunt," Daniel remarked. "It's best in the early hours when the pheasants are up and foraging for food."

"Or in the afternoon as well," Emily offered. "They are often out and about seeking a second meal in the hours prior to sunset."

Daniel studied her with interest. "A governess who is knowledgeable about hunting. Have you an interest in shooting, Miss Bainbridge?"

She grinned. "I do, actually. My father used to take me with him when he hunted. I was the son he never had, and I had no mother to object." She straightened her back. "I've brought home a brace or two of pheasants more than once." Then she shrugged. "Though I've become sadly out of practice in recent years."

The two of them were in the library, his sister-in-law having set them to fine-tuning the activities for the house party, as the first of the guests were due to arrive the following day. Nora and Kitty had come down with coughs, resulting in both girls being confined to the nursery with a prescription of bed rest and Cook's best herbal infusion. There was a possibility they could recover in time to meet the guests, but their mother did not wish to take the chance that her guests might fall ill and turn her house party into a hospital ward.

For a moment, Daniel felt dazzled by Emily's animated face, her blue eyes sparkling as she spoke. He had the feeling that she was finally speaking from her heart, and not as a governess, and he wanted to know more.

"Tell me about your family," he urged. "You were reared in the country, I take it?"

She wrinkled her nose for a moment (and perky little nose it was, he thought), and then put her pencil down and sat back in her chair, seemingly having come to a decision.

"Yes, Cambridgeshire. My father owned a farm outside of Littleport. My mother died when I was a small child, and I was brought up by servants until I was ten, when my aunt and her son moved in, ostensibly to temper my incorrigible behavior." She rolled her eyes.

He tried unsuccessfully to swallow his laughter. "Incorrigible! I cannot imagine you, Miss Bainbridge, the exceedingly proper governess, tearing about as a hoyden. I must know more!"

The more he heard about her youth, the more complete a picture of her formed in his mind. She could hunt and fish, had her own horse, and had an extensive knowledge of farming and animal husbandry. How extraordinary!

"And your aunt, did she put a stop to all of those things when she arrived?"

Emily's shoulders slumped and the amusement left her face. "She did. I had lessons from a governess all day, and when I was allowed out of doors, I had to be accompanied by my hateful cousin Simon, who imagined himself lord of the manor. He was a boy, you know, and three years older."

A bully, Daniel thought. He knew the type. It made him sad to think about the poor child's spirits being flattened in such a way.

"Where was your father in all this?"

Emily blew out a puff of air as she shook her head. "My aunt had convinced him he had sadly neglected my upbringing and that I'd never find a husband unless she was allowed to take over my education. I soon learned there was no point in going to him with my troubles, because he always responded that I must mind my aunt and governess and not to bother him."

Seeing his face, Emily burst out. "Oh, you mustn't think he was unfeeling. It was his guilt, you see, for feeling neglectful of me, and also for my aunt and cousin. She was the widow of his younger brother, and had been left very little to live on. As the head of the family, he felt he had a responsibility toward them."

Ah yes, the inevitable lot of the younger son, thought Daniel. He knew what that was like. But he was determined that he would never leave his family destitute; he would be certain he could adequately secure their future before he started one.

For some reason, the wife he envisaged making that family with had the face of Emily Bainbridge who came to mind, but he forced the image away. He could never wed a governess, not unless his circumstances changed. Even if she could be persuaded to wed him. The whole idea was absurd.

He looked at his watch.

"Dear me, how the time as flown. We'd best get on with business, Miss Bainbridge. Have we everything in place for the scavenger hunt? Are we agreed on the prizes?"

Emily looked down at the papers in front of her. "The children made crowns of holly for the winners to wear for the remainder of the day. For charades as well. Is that sufficient, do you think?"

Daniel pursed his lips. "And forfeits, as well, I think. The losing couples must perform forfeits for the amusement of the rest of us."

"Forfeits? What do you have in mind, Captain? Not blindfolded kissing games, surely!"

He grinned at the wary expression on her face. "Nothing too indelicate, my dear instructress. Such diversions are *de rigueur* for house parties, or so I've been told."

She shook her head disapprovingly, but made no further comment, as they moved on to the skating party and then broke up for tea.

For some reason, he could not get out of his head the image of kissing the lovely governess, blindfolded or not. Would she be offended... or might she actually enjoy it?

STILL CONFINED TO THE NURSERY, the children were nevertheless allowed to make garlands decorated with tissue paper flowers to string about the house before the arrival of the guests. With Nurse's help, they had also made kissing boughs to hang about the house, pretty spheres of holly, ivy, and mistletoe, with red bows on the top. Emily was charged with supervising the servants in putting up these decorations. By the time they were finished, every room in the house was brilliantly decked out for the holiday season, wreaths on every door and a massive Yule log ready to burn upon the guests' arrival, some of whom were due at any moment.

In spite of the general chaotic state of the house and her knowledge of the many tasks waiting to be accomplished, Emily smoothed her apron and gave the dining room one last glance. The table centerpieces, created with the assistance of the local florist, were splendid; once the candles were lit, the entire room would be resplendent with the spirit of the Yuletide season.

"Ah, there you are, Miss Bainbridge." Captain Winthrop's voice was low and inviting. "I must congratulate you on the magnificent work you've done with the house."

He moved nearer the fireplace where she stood, so close she could smell his scent, bergamot, with mint and a hint of citrus, she thought, along with others could not identify. She should have moved away, but her body seemed frozen in place. The intent expression on his face had a mesmerizing effect on her. She wondered how it would feel to kiss him, instinctively knowing it wouldn't be anything like the sloppy kisses forced on her by her loathsome cousin.

"Have you ever been kissed, Miss Bainbridge? Properly, I mean."

No, she thought as his mouth came closer to hers. *But I believe I'm about to.*

His lips touched hers gently at first, as though he were waiting for her to protest, and when she did not, he put his arms around her and deepened the kiss, pulling her closer until she could hear the beat of his heart, as well as hers. When he finally put her away from him, she felt disappointed, as well as disconcerted at the intensity of her response. What was happening to her?

"Before you box my ears," he said in a low voice, "I must protest that my actions were clearly provoked by the spirit of the season."

Her gaze followed his finger to the kissing ball above them. She managed a weak laugh as they moved away from each other.

"Oh, there you are, Daniel, Miss Bainbridge. A carriage is pulling up. It may be the Salisburys, or perhaps the Carringtons. Do come to greet them." In her excitement, Louisa almost failed to notice the beautifully decorated dining room. "Oh my, it's turned out quite splendidly, Miss Bainbridge." At the sound of the door opening: "They are here. Oh, do make haste." She checked her hair in the mirror over the fireplace before scurrying out the door.

Emily and Daniel exchanged knowing looks. "And so it begins," he said. "After you, Miss

Bainbridge."

63

CHAPTER 4

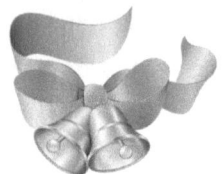

*a*s the guests began to arrive, Emily became increasingly anxious that she had been unable to find the opportunity to confess the truth about her identity to her employers… and to Daniel, of course. Curiously, she found herself thinking of him as Daniel in her mind, particularly since the kiss they had shared. What would he think of her once he discovered the truth about her deception and the reason for it? Oh, why hadn't she been honest with them from the start? Well, they might have decided it too much of a risk to hire her in the first place, and she would never have met them at all, including Daniel. She forced herself to shake it off. There was no point in agonizing over past decisions. The Blackthornes would arrive and surely reveal her secret, and even if they did not, the solicitor's arrival would have the same effect.

Emily tried to keep herself out of sight the next day, which was not hard to do, since the more guests arrived, the more effort was required to keep the household from dissolving into total chaos. She saw Daniel only in passing, although they shared warm glances from time to time. She knew he had escorted the gentlemen to the village to introduce them to some of the retired soldiers being temporarily housed there with the hope of offers of employment to be made. She overheard them discussing the "Magic Stew" project, often requesting advice as to what they could do to help.

But it was a house party after all, and the festive mood pervaded over all. Daniel's interactions with their guests proved him to be most charming and well-liked, especially by the young ladies in the party. Louisa had him placed near the Carringtons' daughter Isobel, who was rumored to be possessed of a handsome dowry, at dinner the first night, and the next day it was Serena Harding, whose father owned a cotton mill. At Friday's skating party, he partnered all the young ladies in turn, but she saw no sign of particular interest in any of them. It doesn't mean a thing, she told herself. He couldn't be interested in her, a mere governess. The Winthrops intended him to marry an heiress.

Well, she thought. I'm an heiress. And he's going to know soon. I wonder if…

At that point, the gentleman himself skated up to her. "Skate with me?"

Her heart skipped a beat at the heat in his eyes. "Of course, sir," and proceeded to demonstrate the skills she had learned from her childhood in the country.

"Is there anything you can't do?" he whispered as they left the ice to warm up at the bonfire.

"Well," she said looking up at him with sparkling eyes, "I am hopeless at needlework, sir.

And drawing as well, I'm afraid."

He chuckled. "Indeed? So, at the heart of things, you excel at all things besides governessing."

Well, she thought, he must know sooner than later. She had dragged her feet long enough.

"As to that," she began, her heart beating rapidly in her chest. "I'm not really a governess. Daniel, I wonder if I might prevail upon you to help me gain an audience with your brother and sister-in-law?"

"Not a governess, eh?"

Oddly enough, he didn't seem to be surprised at her statement.

"I take it your employers haven't been apprised of that fact?" He touched her cheek. "I don't think you have anything to worry about, darling Emily. "I feel certain they will understand why you omitted to inform them that you are the owner of Bainbridge Farm."

She gasped and swayed on her feet.

"Here, sit down," he said, leading her to a bench, where he carefully removed her skates.

"I did wonder, after our conversation the other day. Your father left it all to you, did he not? There was no entail?"

Tears of relief welled up behind her eyelids. "None at all. There never has been. Technically, the farm could be left to anyone, although it usually went to the oldest offspring. At one point it was called Hathaway Farm, after my great grandfather. Then my grandmother inherited it, changed the name back to Bainbridge, and it's been Bainbridge Farm ever since."

She looked up at him. "I know my aunt hoped I would be disinherited in favor of my cousin, but Father didn't trust Simon."

"The truth is," she added as they made their way to the house. "I don't inherit until my twenty-fifth birthday, unless I marry before that. That's the reason I came here. Simon has been following me everywhere in an effort to force me into marriage before my birthday. Although," she sighed, "my solicitor tells me he could still do it even then, by causing some sort of scandal."

"And once you are wed, your husband owns it all," Daniel concluded grimly. "When is your birthday, Miss Bainbridge?"

So, it was Miss Bainbridge again. His voice sounded distant, and she felt confused when he moved further away from her. Something was wrong. Was it something she'd said?

"The twenty-fifth of December. I was born on Christmas Day."

"DANIEL," began Theo, drawing him aside as the other gentlemen left the dining room to join the ladies in the drawing room. "Come with me to my study. There's something I'd like to discuss with you."

Daniel nodded and the two of them strolled across the hall to the study, otherwise known as the library, where Emily had opened up to him about her childhood. He could still see the animation of her face, the absolute trust in her manner as they conversed as equals, as friends. He'd been attracted to her from that first meeting in the park, but it wasn't until then that he'd begun to fall in love with her. The kiss had closed the deal for him, and he thought she might return his feelings, but he hadn't really thought through to the eventual conclusion of it all. A governess might not quibble over attaching herself for life to a second son, but a woman of means could certainly look higher.

"Miss Bainbridge has confided her true circumstances to Louisa and me, and she tells us you are aware of it as well."

Theo poured out two glasses of brandy and handed one to Daniel as he took a long drink and set the glass down on the desk.

"I know the truth, yes," said Daniel. "I regret that she felt she had to conceal her

background, but I understand the necessity for it." He studied his brother's demeanor. "I hope you don't intend to dismiss her."

Theo snorted. "You know me better than that, brother dear. But the point is moot, since it appears that Miss Bainbridge will be leaving on her own accord following her birthday."

"Leaving? But why?" Daniel sat down, feeling a sudden weakness in his legs. "The girls love her, and I know she's been happy here. And besides..." He broke off at the thought of the nefarious cousin's relentless pursuit of his darling girl.

Theo shrugged. "She didn't elaborate on that point. I suppose it has something to do with the farm." He took another swig of brandy. "It's a lot of responsibility, running a farm, as I have reason to know. Of course, she may well have an estate manager, but it would still be a heavy responsibility for a woman alone."

Emily was one who could manage it, thought Daniel with pride.

She was one strong, capable and independent woman. He'd not met many like her.

If it weren't for that nasty scoundrel Simon… Daniel's fists clenched unconsciously.

Theo took a deep breath. "Might as well come out with it, Dan. Louisa and I have it mind that you and our lovely governess have been smelling of April and May of late, and we think it's a perfect match."

Daniel's eyes widened and his mouth moved to speak, but his brother clapped a hand on his shoulder. "Now, don't deny it. Listen for a moment."

He dragged an armchair to a spot in front of Daniel, and leaned forward. "Look, Daniel, I know we've made a mistake in pushing you toward all the heiresses. Louisa and I—we've come to understand that you don't need our help in putting together the next phase in your life." He sighed. "You are a good man, and a strong one. You managed to survive in all sorts of appalling situations. You do not need to wed an heiress. Not ever, if it doesn't appeal to you."

"But… Emily is an heiress."

"She is," agreed his brother.

"I'm not a fortune hunter!" Daniel's body tensed.

"Of course not. We know that."

"Others might think so. *She* might think so," he muttered.

Theo snorted. "I'm willing to bet she doesn't. Hers is the only opinion that matters, and you'll never know if you don't speak to her."

Daniel fidgeted in his chair. "I don't know." Her cousin sought her fortune. Daniel wasn't at all like that wretched fellow.

Theo rose and headed for the door.

"I don't mean to press you on this, brother." He chuckled and Daniel smiled involuntarily. "Well, perhaps I do at that. The prerogative of older brothers, you know."

"It just seems to me that you fell in love with her before you knew she was an heiress. And if she loves you, what sense does it make to deny your feelings for each other simply because she has more money than you do?"

He opened the door. "I've never taken you for a fool, Daniel."

When he was gone, Daniel poured another glass of brandy. His brother was right. If he let Emily go out of his life, he would indeed be a very foolish man.

"MISS BAINBRIDGE? I must admit I never expected to find you here!"

The Blackthornes, the final guests to arrive, had joined the group for tea after settling into their rooms. Their daughter Priscilla, having already complained about having to share a room with two other young ladies, was quick to recognize Emily as the Bainbridge heiress and made sure to find a seat on the settee beside her.

"Your disappearance has been the talk of the county, my dear. When we learned of it, we could not begin to understand why you would not leave word of your plans with anyone. Such shocking rumors have come to our ears! Why, Mr. Bainbridge, your cousin, has been outside of himself with concern for your safety."

Of course he was, thought Emily grimly. He must be getting desperate now, with my birthday two days off.

She took a sip of tea and managed a forced smile.

"It all happened so quickly, I hardly had time to pack. I heard the Winthrops needed a governess and I— well, I had a notion to be a part of a family for a time. I really should have left notice of my plans."

Priscilla narrowed her eyes. "I don't suppose it had anything at all to do with the handsome captain. Mama has her hopes pinned on a match between us, but I'm beginning to think the mysterious governess has already captured his attentions."

Emily choked on her tea. "Of course not! I mean, I only met Captain Winthrop a few weeks ago!"

Priscilla appeared unconvinced. "He looks at you a good deal. I suppose he has his eye on the farm; why else would he set his cap for a governess when there are so many other young ladies to choose?"

Emily set her cup down with a clatter and jumped from her seat.

"You are wrong to believe Daniel to be a fortune hunter! He is far too noble! And if you persist in besmirching his name, I'll—I'll—well, I don't know what I'll do, but I vow you will regret it, Priscilla Blackthorne!"

The room had gone quiet, and Emily was aghast to see all eyes on her, including Daniel's. Oh, how dreadful! She could feel the heat in her face, and despite the weakness in her legs, she could think of nothing to do but flee the room. And the house too. She kept running, tears falling down her face so that she could barely see where she was going, without any sensation of the cold air around her.

"My dear cousin, have you forgotten your cloak? Do come with me, I believe I have a blanket in the carriage."

Simon! She came to an abrupt stop, looked up and with horrified eyes saw her cousin in front of her, arms reaching out toward her.

"No!" Backing away, she started to turn and run in the other direction, but he rushed forward and caught her.

"Now, now, you mustn't struggle. We've a fair amount of travel if we are to reach Gretna

Green before your birthday."

"I'm not going anywhere with you! Go away and leave me alone!"

He grabbed her arm and tried to drag her toward a carriage in the distance. Unable to free herself, she dropped to the cold ground, a dead weight.

Baring his teeth, he kicked hard at her rib cage. "Get up, you troublesome woman, or you'll suffer far worse on the journey."

Helpless and in pain, she watched as his boot was poised to kick her again, but just prior to impact, she saw him falling to the ground next to her.

"What the—" Simon managed to get out before the toe of Daniel's boot slammed into his ribs.

Daniel glared at him, his eyes cold and flinty. "She's going nowhere with you, you scoundrel. And you are going no further than the magistrate's." He rolled the other man over and sat on him, restraining his arms behind his back with an iron grip.

"Grimsby!" he roared in the direction of the stable. "Bring rope! Now!"

He turned to Emily with concerned eyes. "Emily darling, are you hurt? I'm sorry I couldn't reach you before this brute could abuse you."

Shivering on the snow-covered ground, Emily felt an ache in her throat. Darling? Had she imagined it? "Daniel, I–I..." she tried to answer him, teeth chattering.

"Don't try to speak, darling. You're freezing. We must get you into the house without delay." The look in his eyes left no doubt of his feelings for her.

"You said it... again," she murmured. "Darling."

"Oh, for God's sake," said Simon, struggling to get his hands free.

Daniel's nostrils flared. "Hold your tongue, you miscreant. You'll get a good trouncing from me as soon as my hands are free."

"I'll help you," Theo added as he and the groom joined them.

"Thanks, brother." They bound his hands and forced him to his feet. "Can you and Grimsby get him to the magistrate? I must get Emily back to the house."

"By all means," Theo replied. "We'll take care of the offal. You see to your sweetheart."

Sweetheart? Am I dreaming? Emily groaned slightly as Daniel gently lifted her enough to wrap his jacket around her shoulders.

"This might hurt a bit," he warned, as he made to lift her in his arms. "But it's crucial that we get you warmed up as quickly as possible. I can't bear to lose you now that I've found you."

Was that a break in his voice? Feeling utterly safe and content in his arms, a drowsy

Emily concluded that it must be true; Daniel cared for her.

CHAPTER 5

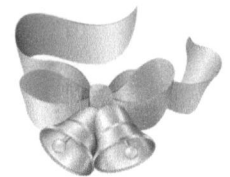

*D*aniel paced back and forth outside the nursery door, as Emily rested in her bed, where he had laid her only an hour ago. When he saw that a fire was lit, he had reluctantly left her to the tender care of Louisa, the housekeeper, and several servants, armed with towels, warm blankets and hot tea.

"Once she is out of her wet things, Daniel, we'll dry her off and get some of Cook's infusion down her before a chill can set in. The doctor has been sent for, and there's really nothing else to be done." She had placed a hand on his arm. "I promise you you'll be able to see her as soon as the doctor approves."

She smiled. "All will be well, dear brother. Why don't you go down to the library and have a brandy while you wait for Theo to come back with the magistrate."

As much as Daniel wanted to know that Emily's evil cousin was safely locked away, he found it impossible to put so much distance between them. He couldn't get the image of that cad Simon striking his darling Emily with his boot. If only he'd run faster. He should have been there to protect her. His fists clenched. If only he had given that rogue the walloping he deserved.

When he'd seen Emily shivering on the cold wet ground, groaning from the pain and white-faced with fear, he'd found himself wondering what he would do if he lost her, if he had to live the rest of his life without her. Nothing else mattered but that she be by his side as they built a life together, a family.

He gave a start as the nursery door opened.

"Uncle Daniel!" Nora raced over to him and hugged his legs. "We're all better now, but Miss Bainbridge isn't, and Mama says we can go downstairs to meet the guests!"

Daniel blinked as the real world intruded on his ruminations.

"Come, Nora," Kitty commanded. "Uncle Dan is waiting for Miss Bainbridge to feel better. Are you going to marry her? I would like that ever so much!"

Louisa appeared in the doorway. "Are you two still here? Stop plaguing your uncle and come with me to the drawing room."

To Daniel, he added: "She's doing much better. You may see her briefly. Until the doctor gets here, at least." She winked.

He took a deep breath and tried to keep from running to Emily's side. She was sitting up, in a buttoned-up flannel nightdress, her dark hair flowing against the pillows. She smiled when she saw him, and he was relieved to see she'd regained the color in her face.

"Daniel."

The housekeeper harrumphed, and left them alone, well, as alone as you can be with a maid sitting in a chair at the foot of the bed.

Emily flushed. "Captain Winthrop, I mean. I–I wanted to thank you for rescuing me this afternoon. I am forever in your debt."

He moved to her side. "It's Daniel. Call me Daniel. And you, well, I hope I may call you Emily? And believe me, there's no debt. I had a very good reason, perhaps a more selfish reason, for liberating you from that ruthless cousin of yours." He took her hand to his lips as if to kiss it, when the nursery door opened and a stocky white-haired gentleman padded into the room. Ah, the doctor.

Laying her hand back on the counterpane, he gave her a sheepish smile. "We shall finish this conversation later, my dear Emily."

"Of course," she said. "I'll be waiting."

The doctor looked from one to the other. "Harrumph!" he said as he escorted Daniel to the door.

"YOU'RE DAMNED lucky the doctor interrupted," exclaimed Theo, appalled. "Proposing marriage to an injured woman in a sickbed? Never thought you were such a nitwit, brother!"

Daniel rubbed the side of his head. "I don't know what I was thinking. I suppose I wasn't thinking at all. All I knew was that she was alive and it was my responsibility to make sure she stayed that way." He took a swig of brandy from the glass.

Theo chuckled. "You've got it bad, Danny boy. I never thought I'd see the day you'd be so eager to get yourself leg-shackled. You know," he said, tilting his head to the side, "we could have avoided the bother and expense of the house party and ball if we'd known it would be you and the governess."

Daniel shook his head. "I told you it was not at all necessary," he began, but then

stopped. He and Emily had been thrown together a great deal in the days leading up to the house party; if they had not had the opportunity to become better acquainted, she might have been sequestered in the nursery while he was out working on his "Magic Stew" project, and by the end of the month she would have been on her way back to Cambridgeshire.

He sat down abruptly. "What if she says no?" he whispered. "In two days' time she'll be twenty-five and on her way to Cambridgeshire, and I'll never see her again."

Theo clapped his hand on his brother's shoulder in sympathy. "What you're feeling is the agony every man in love feels before he declares himself. Makes for a damned unpleasant few hours… or days, as the case may be."

"And you, Theo, did it happen to you?"

"It did indeed. I thought it was possible Louisa loved me, but that filthy rich earl was sniffing around her, and…" he relaxed in his chair. "Well, I should have had more faith in her. Wasn't at all fazed to take on this penniless viscount, after all."

Daniel chuckled. "Hardly penniless, dear Theo. That's me. But you give me some hope, at least. There are more important things than money, at least for some. Emily, I think."

"And the heiress part? Have you resolved that in your own mind, Daniel?"

"I love Emily, and I want her by my side, heiress or not." He suddenly felt lightheaded. "Marrying someone just to gain wealth seems too– dishonest. I couldn't do that without feeling a scoundrel the rest of my life, not even if it would enable me to rescue a thousand former soldiers from poverty."

He rose and approached the fireplace, staring into the warm flames. "It's different when you love someone. I don't care that she has property; I'll sign it all over to her when we marry, that is, *if* we marry."

His shoulders slumped at the thought that it might not happen.

Theo sighed as he rose and headed for the door. "Sorry, brother, I'll leave you to your misery. The musical evening, you know. Leave me some of the brandy, will you? I'm sure I'll need it afterward."

EMILY'S RIBS were not broken, but the doctor prescribed bedrest and frequent applications of compresses of chamomile or lavender tea. Her dinner was sent up on a tray, and before bedtime, she read to the children to calm them down from the excitement of the party. After that, she tried to sleep, but could not be at ease. Daniel's face as he rushed into the room and took her hand kept popping up in her mind. What had he been about to say to her? He said his reason for rescuing her from Simon was a selfish one;

what could he mean? Her mind had leapt to the conclusion that he'd been about to propose to her, but that didn't seem likely. Did it?

Sleep finally found her, after the third compress change that night, and she didn't awaken until the maid came to open the drapes to allow the mid-day sun into the room.

She was drinking her tea when Louisa arrived to inspect her bruised side. "It looks dreadful, but then, bruises always look dreadful the second day, I believe. How do you feel, my dear?"

"Well, it hurts a bit when I move, but I can talk and breathe, thank goodness."

Louisa's brow furrowed. "Do you feel like coming downstairs this afternoon? The doctor said that, since your ribs aren't actually broken, we could wrap a bandage around your middle to minimize the movement. That would allow you a chance to come downstairs and enjoy the party."

"I don't think I'm up for charades," Emily responded after recalling the Christmas Eve day schedule.

Louisa fussed with the bed coverings. "Well, I wasn't thinking of charades, actually."

Emily wrinkled her nose. "Then what *were* you thinking?"

Louisa threw up her hands. "Listen, Emily, if you feel well enough, you really should dress and come downstairs." She opened the wardrobe and pulled out Emily's Sunday best. "This will have to do. I'll send Mary to do your hair, and when you're ready, Theo will help you downstairs."

Emily blinked. "What? Why?" she stuttered.

Louisa sighed deeply. "There is a certain gentleman downstairs who's been waiting to talk to you since yesterday afternoon, and if you don't come down and put him out of his misery, I'm afraid he will lose his mind."

Emily's heart leapt to her throat. "Daniel? You mean Daniel?"

Louisa rolled her eyes. "Who else could it be? Theo is right; the two of you have gone daffy!" She turned to the maid in the corner: "Hattie, get Mrs. Cotton to help you wrap Miss Bainbridge's middle.

I'll have some hot water sent up, and Mary will help you get her dressed."

"I can dress myself," Emily protested.

Louisa shrugged and left the room.

WHEN EMILY and Theo entered the library, Daniel's heart jumped in his chest. She was beautiful in a modest dark blue gown with white gloves up to her elbows, her wavy hair swept back into a knot at the crown of her head.

He suddenly had an urge to flee.

No. He would not bungle his proposal. She deserved better. He took a deep breath and walked over to greet them.

"You look lovely, my dear," he said, taking her hand to kiss it.

"Thank you," she said with a smile. "You are very distinguished in your uniform. Are you wearing it to the ball tonight?"

Theo cleared his throat. "I believe I hear Louisa calling for me. I'll just leave you two here alone—for a bit. If that's agreeable to you, Miss Bainbridge?"

At her assent, he left them.

"Miss Bainbridge," he began.

"You may call me Emily, Captain."

"Daniel."

They laughed, and it seemed as though some of the tension had gone out of the conversation.

He took her hand and led her to a chair.

"Dear Emily..."

"Oh, do sit down," she said. "I'm getting a crick in my neck from looking up at you." But she was smiling.

He grinned. "I'll do better than that," and he went down on one knee in front of her.

She went completely still.

"Miss Emily Bainbridge, I have fallen deeply in love with you and I would like nothing more than to take you as my bride. Will you marry me?"

Her face filled with tears, but she was smiling. "Yes, of course I will marry you, Daniel."

He closed his eyes for a moment and then looked up at her earnestly. "I vow that I will spend the remainder of my days making you happy, Emily. About your fortune—"

She put two fingers over his lips. "Not now," she said. "We can discuss that later. For now, I just want to relish in the knowledge that we love each other. Nothing else matters, really. Does it?"

He kissed her fingers and leaned in to take her in his arms, pulling her to her feet until both were standing, bodies pressed together, his hands around her waist. When she winced, he pulled away.

"Did I hurt you? Are you well, my love? I forgot for a moment…"

She pulled him back to her. "It's nothing, Daniel darling. Let's see… were you about to kiss me? Because I am actually quite eager to be kissed," she said, with a silly grin on her face.

Grinning back, he put his hands on her shoulders and moved his mouth to hers.

"Far be it for me to disappoint you," he murmured when they finally broke apart.

"Did I say I was disappointed?" She turned her mouth up toward his and moistened her

lips.

I'm the luckiest man on earth, Daniel told himself as he responded to her invitation.

"My dear child, it never occurred to me that that villainous cousin of yours would follow me to discover your location. I am so sorry that my negligence is responsible for the unpleasantness that occurred."

Emily leaned forward and clasped his hands in hers. "Dear Mr. Hill, please do not blame yourself. No doubt he ascertained that you and I would need to meet around the time of my birthday, and decided to use you to find me."

The solicitor wiped his brow. "In any case, I am relieved to learn that Mr. Bainbridge will be in no position to trouble you further."

"Absolutely not," said Daniel forcefully, clapping a hand on Emily's shoulder. "I will see to it myself that he never comes near her again."

Mr. Hill's gaze darted from one to the other. "Am I correct in assuming...?"

"Yes, it is true," said Emily with a blush, "Captain Winthrop and I are indeed affianced."

"It was all settled this morning," Daniel announced, taking her hand in his. "Once I ascertained that she suffered no lasting effects from yesterday's events, I lost no time in claiming her for myself."

Emily wrinkled her brow. "I do recall that my consent was required for that to happen, Daniel dear." But there was a smile on her face. "Will you be an imposing husband, I wonder? Run the household with military precision?"

"I shan't need to," said Daniel smoothly. "That's the advantage of taking a governess to wife. I expect the household will be run as efficiently as a schoolroom."

Mr. Hill chuckled. "You are a lucky man indeed, Captain Bainbridge."

He turned to some papers on the desk in front of him. "I'm afraid I wasn't aware that you were contemplating marriage, so I did not bring a marriage contract with me, but I do have with me all the documents that will be needed for you to sign for your inheritance."

"Tomorrow, of course," Emily added.

"Yes. And providing you aren't planning to elope to Scotland," he said with a chuckle, "I can have your marriage documents drawn up as soon as I return to Littleport."

Emily's hands flew to her face. "We haven't even discussed—"

Daniel drew her closer to him and winked at the solicitor. "We may not be going to

Scotland, but we will be marrying soon."

"But Daniel—"

"Another thing," Daniel added, "I want it put in writing that Emily's inheritance is hers alone after our marriage. I don't wish her ever to wonder if I married her for her fortune."

"But Daniel, I don't think that," she protested.

He gave her a quick kiss on the lips. "I know."

Mr. Hill nodded. "Whatever you wish, sir."

He packed up his papers. "I'll be on my way. You may expect me around two in the afternoon tomorrow. Happy Christmas!"

After his departure, Emily squirmed in his arms. "I thought you didn't mean to be imposing, Daniel dear. You just made two decisions without discussing them with me at all."

"What? Do you wish to go to Scotland after all?" he teased.

She punched his arm lightly. "Of course not. But as for the wedding date—"

"Well then, tell me your thoughts on the matter. Is late January too soon for you? The banns will need to be called."

She thought it over. "Earlier would be better."

Louisa and Theo sailed into the room. "You are discussing the wedding!" she exclaimed. "I love weddings! Shall you be married here or in Cambridgeshire?"

Emily and Daniel exchanged glances. "In my parish church?" He nodded.

"We can all discuss this later," Theo interrupted. "Daniel and I are expected at the assembly rooms, and there are guests to see to..."

"Yes indeed!" Louisa looked at the clock on the mantelpiece. "It's nearly time for supper to be served. Emily, are you well enough to join us, do you think?"

Emily had never felt better in her life. She smiled at Daniel.

"Of course. Please let me know if I can do anything to help, Louisa dear."

THE STREET outside the assembly rooms was crowded with carriages when the Winthrop party arrived with their house guests. Fires were blazing on both ends of the room, and the ballroom was dressed with wreaths over the mantels, greenery and garlands on the walls, and candelabras everywhere. Tables and chairs were set up along the far wall, most already taken by early arriving guests. Musicians were tuning up in the alcove, and Emily could see the refreshment table being set up in a corner.

Louisa, as hostess, was in her element, looking particularly lovely in a taffeta ball gown of celestial blue that matched her eyes, chatting easily with everyone and introducing Emily as her "friend from Cambridgeshire who came to help with the children." A few eyebrows were raised at that, but Emily knew it was a ploy to get people to think of her as more than just the children's governess. But where was Daniel?

The dancing began with the traditional minuet, followed by a series of country dances, and a Scotch reel. Following that, the music ceased, and Theo, standing in the center of the dance floor with Louisa at his side, indicated that he was about to speak.

"Lady Winthrop and I would like to welcome all of our friends and neighbors on this special night, the eve before Christmas. We are particularly thankful for those of our friends who traveled a distance from their homes in order to spend the season with us. It has made our holiday celebrations especially meaningful."

At that moment, Daniel appeared from the entryway, looking smart in his dark green uniform.

"Another reason for our gratitude is the safe return of my brother, Captain Daniel Winthrop, from years of service with His Majesty's armed forces." The crowd applauded enthusiastically, and Theo continued, "My brother would like to say a few words."

Daniel cleared his throat. "Any soldier will tell you that fighting a war is a group endeavor, one that requires a close camaraderie, a deep trust among its members. I've served with many courageous men who would, and did, lay down their lives to save others. I saw many fall in battle. I saw even more seriously wounded and maimed. In all cases, there are families left without a means of support."

His voice cracked. 'We have all seen these loyal, courageous men on the streets, unable to find jobs, begging for crusts of bread for their children. Thanks to them, the war is over, and our shores are once again safe from invaders."

The crowd cheered, and Daniel took a deep breath. "Most of you will have heard me or others involve talk of a project we have started in this village, where each gives a little: clothing, food, a chance of a job, whatever they can spare. We call it the Magic Stew project. No one of us can do what needs to done for those who fought so bravely and their families. But when we combine what we have, we can make a difference."

He paused while the locals in the crowd murmured their agreement, then continued. "The Yule season is a happy time, a time of celebration, and a time to help others. The act of giving itself causes joy in the giver. That, my friends, is the spirit of Christmas, the 'Magic Stew' that miraculously feeds us all."

He looked over at his brother, and searched the crowd until he found Emily and drew her out onto the floor. Emily felt her heart in her throat when she saw the heat in his eyes as he presented her to the audience.

"You look beautiful," he whispered.

"As do you," she whispered back.

The room was silent as Theo took a gloved hand from each of them and turned to the audience.

"And for the best news of the evening, Her Ladyship and I are delighted to announce the engagement of my brother, Captain Winthrop, to Miss Emily Bainbridge, of Bainbridge Farm in Littleport, Cambridgeshire."

There was a smattering of applause before the orchestra began playing a waltz, and Theo and Louisa left the happy couple alone on the floor.

Daniel bowed, she curtsied, and suddenly she was whirling across the floor in his arms. Her steps matched perfectly with his, and she felt as light as a butterfly in flight.

"How did you know I could dance?"

"Don't all governesses know how to dance?"

"Not all. They send for dance teachers. I had one myself."

He laughed. "That's good. I suppose I should have asked."

"It's all happened so quickly," she said with a grimace. "Do you think we might be rushing things a bit?"

The music stopped and a *Roger de Coverly* was announced. Daniel led her off the dance floor into a shadowy hallway.

"Not a chance," he said, and proceeded to convince her so thoroughly that her doubts fled, leaving nothing but pure joy in her heart.

The End

ABOUT SUSANA ELLIS

Susana Ellis is a retired teacher, part-time care-giver, sewist, cook, and fashion print collector. Lifelong reading and a fascination with history led her to writing historical romance.

SOCIAL MEDIA FOR SUSANA ELLIS

You can contact Susana Ellis at these social media links:
- susanaellisauthor@gmail.com
- www.facebook.com/susana.ellis.5
- https://www.pinterest.com/susanaauthor/
- https://twitter.com/susanaauthor
- https://susanaellisauthor.blog

FLOWERS FOR HIS LADY

BY ALINA K. FIELD

Shamed into spinsterhood by a fall from grace years earlier, Eleanor Gurnwood has found a home for herself in the tiny village of Upper Upton, and a quirky, sometimes annoying family in the villagers she's been serving as her vicar-brother's minion. Now, with his rising career, she's faced with a choice: succumb to his pressure to keep house for him elsewhere or stay on in genteel poverty with her new "family".

For now, she has only one goal in sight: to make this year's Christmas service beautiful for the parishioners of St. Tancred's. Until the Christmas eve when a man from her past rides in on a white horse.

Major Sir Bramwell Huxley, late of his Majesty's 95th Foot, has ventured on one last mission, a quest for a Christmas miracle: finding the lady he abandoned before leaving for Waterloo.

CHAPTER 1

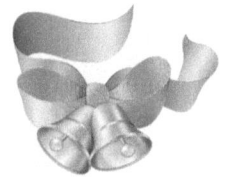

2 *3 December, 1820*

The helpers had departed St. Tancred's hours ago when the wet snow falling showed a determination to stick, as the last few December snowfalls had not done. Besides, some of the members of the Ladies' Society for the Improvement of Village Life had meals to prepare. Those with servants had children to tend to and husbands who would worry about their safe arrival.

Even the new curate, Mr. Godwin, had left, polite and pleased, after a cursory visit in the late afternoon. *He and his wife—a lovely woman due to give birth soon—would serve the people of Upper Upton far better than...*

With a steadying breath, Miss Eleanor Gurnwood shook off what would be an uncharitable thought.

She had stayed on in the peaceful solitude to finish arranging great urns of winter greens and holly, despairing of their broken organ, and the promised flowers from the Brockton Manor greenhouse.

Never mind. This would be a lovely Christmas at St. Tancred's, or at least better than last year's celebration when her brother's cheeseparing meddling had decimated the ranks of her helpful ladies.

He'd left weeks ago, and the ladies had come back.

No one waited at home for her but Millie, her landlord, Galt Wyman's housekeeper. Millie would be ready with her usual meat pie and cabbage mash keeping warm near the hearth. And despite that it was the Sabbath, old Galt would be at the Royal George, himself pie-eyed, and cabbage-mashed after too many pints.

The stained glass of the windows, depicting the medieval martyrdom of St. Tancred and his siblings, obscured the view, but outside, the winter night glowed with the sort of soft light that comes with a snowfall. She hoped the weather wouldn't spoil the plans for tomorrow night's Christmas Eve Carol service, or the Christmas morning liturgy, or the children's party Christmas afternoon at the Longview Children's Home.

She bent close to the lantern and reached for her watch, remembered she'd sold it to get through the quarter, and sighed. Next year her small trust would be her own to manage and draw from.

The remaining lit candle told her it was likely past seven. Well then, she'd best go rescue Galt before he stumbled his way to the church to fetch *her*. But first...

Three layers of skirts cushioned her knees against the cold marble as she bent her head and gripped her gloved hands together. *Lord, give me wisdom, guide my path; for pity's sake, send an angel, send someone, to show me the way.*

Tears sprang and she blinked them back. *And cleanse me of this nauseating self-pity.*

It was, after all, her own fault. She'd loved impetuously, with the natural consequence of losing emphatically.

And she wouldn't trade that one experience of love—of loving—for all the rubies in India. Pity herself, she might, and battle the hurt that had followed, but it seemed St. Paul was right—for the love had never quite gone away.

Besides, she wasn't entirely alone. There were good people here in the village of Upper Upton. Her landlord, for one, and his house-keeper. And the innkeeper and his wife. And the matrons and teachers and the young residents of the nearby Longview Children's Home.

She had friends, though those ties were still tenuous. She had hopes of a position at Longview. She also had her brother, who loved her in his own overbearing way.

If only he could display more *charity*.

What really was so terrible about what she'd done? It had been reckless, and foolish, and so wonderful that she pulled out the memory sometimes and savored it. She, destined to spinsterhood, had been loved.

In the end, she'd suffered no more than a wound to her heart and endless hours of tiresome lectures. She felt certain that God had forgiven her. So why did his servant, Reverend Matthew Gurnwood, keep reminding her of that one lapse from propriety?

A man's rumbling voice and the creaking of door hinges accompanied a blast of cold air that blew out the candle's flame.

Blasted Galt. "Please close the door and spare me a moment," she called over her shoulder, "and I'll add a prayer that God in his goodness may spare you the consequences of tonight's imbibing."

"I fear more than a prayer is needed for this fellow, madam."

A frisson of awareness shivered up her spine. The deep, gruff voice caressing her wasn't Galt's. Or Matthew's. Or Mr. Godwin's. And it was no angel's voice.

Memories flooded her with yearning—hopeless yearning for something her pride would balk at receiving. It wasn't him. It couldn't be him.

"Courage," she muttered.

Another blast of cold air swirled around her. She scrambled to her feet, snatched up her heavy mantle and the lantern, and hurried down the aisle.

WELL AT LEAST THE old man he'd unearthed from the snow was, apparently, no vagrant.

Major Sir Bramwell Huxley steadied the wispy-haired fellow, a hand clamped to each wiry shoulder while the only light approached like a bobbing specter.

It was dark as the Paris catacombs and just as cold in the church. He'd found the drunken sot sprawled in the lane and half carried him here, the nearest place of refuge.

"I thankee, sir," the fellow croaked in his thick local accent. "Slipped I did, is all. Ellie, you ought to be home. What fool notion is't to hang about here until the snow's as high as a pig's udder."

The shrouded figure arrived, and a feminine scoff came from under the drooping hood. "The same point might be made, Galt, about hanging about too long at the Royal George."

Bram's senses alerted, and he ticked through the incoming facts, sorting them.

That had been no country accent. The fellow was no gentleman, yet he'd called the woman by a first name. He sensed a youngish woman under that heavy wrap, tall and slim. Could she be the fellow's more refined daughter? Or a much younger wife? Surely not a saucy maid, nor one of the resident vicar's misses. And…

"Would this be the Royal George run by Alexander Grant?" Bram asked.

The woman visibly stiffened.

"The very one," the man said. "And a fine ale he serves too. 'S'not but a few paces from here. Let me buy you a pint fer yer troubles."

"Be off with you both then and make sure the church door is shut." The woman slid around them, her skirts brushing his leg, and a faint scent of lilacs raised the hair on the back of his neck.

Ellie. Could she be Eleanor? *His* Eleanor?

"I'll let Millie know you'll sleep at the inn, Galt," she called over her shoulder.

"Can't do that," the old man said. "Lest I make a bench me bed. Full up, he is. Folks heading to a house party at Lord Cathmore's stopped for the snow."

Lord Cathmore's party had been Bram's excuse for dodging a gathering of distant relatives and traveling to Sussex at Christmas. His excuse, but not his true reason.

"Why, we'll bring him home with us," the old man said. "Why not? Took you in, didn't I, Ellie? Got an extra bed. Room for the horse out back too." He straightened, the charitable impulse seeming to sober him, and turned for the door.

With a sigh, the woman dipped her chin, the heavy hood shielding her face. If he could just get a peek. He followed them out, his fingers itching to yank back the wool and have a glimpse.

Tied to an iron fence rail, his horse shuddered and sent him a baleful look.

"Fine feller he be," the old man said, and Bram chuckled, wondering if he meant the horse or himself.

"On my honor, I'll do you no harm," Bram said, "and since the inn's full, I'll take you up on the offer of hospitality. Allow me." He set his hand over the lady's where she was holding the door pull.

A current shot through him and she snatched her hand away as if she'd been burned as well. She glanced up, mouth agape and quickly turned away.

That moment's shadowed glance made him certain—almost—and he barely managed a breath to ask, "Shall we lock it?"

She shook her head. "The curate will see to it later."

He pulled the heavy door shut and followed her. Quick stepping was his Eleanor, despite the wet snow swirling around her plenteous skirts. She'd not been dressed so abundantly the last time they met.

Memories of that night stirred him, and in a few long strides he outpaced her and reached the horse. The old man was already there, stroking the white nose.

"Let me put you up on my horse, Miss, er..."

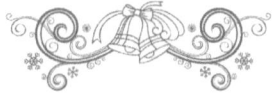

He wanted an introduction, did he?

"Take my arm, Galt," she said. "You, sir, may mount and follow us."

"I most certainly will not ride while a lady walks." He cupped his hands. "And if you won't ride, well, up you go, Mr. Galt."

Tugging her wrap tighter, she trudged on, eyes on the treacherous path ahead. That one glimpse, dark though it was, had revealed an iron jaw formed by generations of breeding, the hook of a powerful nose, and lips that could soften in the sweetest of kisses.

Swallowing a rising heat, she sensed him joining her, the reins swallowed up in one of his gloved hands. The heat of his big body swept through her, and his scent washed over her, a mixture of horse, his particular shaving soap, and the indefinable and not unpleasant musk that was his alone.

He was flesh and blood and all male. What was she to *do*?

She straightened her spine. The past was the past. He with his white horse was no knight come to seek her out. The promises he'd made—the promises they'd both made—had gone awry. Matthew had interfered, no doubt, but so had the Crown, and she couldn't begrudge a man who'd sworn his service there. It wasn't that he hadn't cared for her, but that duty had called more strongly.

He'd gone away, and now he was passing through the village. He hadn't come seeking *her*… yet, here they were, and the air around them all but vibrated with his curiosity.

She would face this squarely, head-on, with her dignity intact. "Yes," she said quietly, "It is I."

His free hand sought hers and, flummoxed again, she allowed it to be captured, holding her breath for an apology or explanation or— God help her—a sweet word. Or something.

And he said nothing.

Millie greeted them at the back door of the cottage, her dark eyes flashing fire. "Mind my clean floor. And who've you brought home this time, Galt Wyman. Who is this fellow, Ellie?"

A bounder of gigantic proportions, she wanted to say, but Galt spoke first.

"Picked me up out of the snow, he did, old woman, and a woman with eyes in her head can see he's quality. Lay the table for one more. And the bed in the spare room. Clean sheets. Come through, sir, come through," he said, beckoning.

Eleanor stepped into the room and pushed back her hood. She

fixed her gaze on the visitor and felt the heat of his hazel eyes. His light brown hair needed a trim, and the sight of his bristly whiskers, a shade darker, sent a shiver through her, remembering…

Swallowing a surge of lust, she steadied herself. "Perhaps introductions first, Galt?"

DARK HAIR SPILLED out over Eleanor's forehead and cheeks, making her look like the fresh young lass barely out of the schoolroom he'd met almost six years ago. Though, he supposed she hadn't been so young then. She'd only looked it. She must be six-and-twenty now, or perhaps seven-and-twenty. She was thinner, and something had happened besides his desertion, something to leave the dent of too many frowns between her beautiful dark winged eyebrows.

She cleared her throat, and he realized he was gaping back at her, tongue-tied.

"I am indeed a boarder here," she said. "Our host is Mr. Galt Wyman, and this is his housekeeper, Mrs. Millie Chatworth."

"Pleased to meet you," he said, finding his voice. "I am Bramwell Huxley."

Eleanor cocked her head. "*Major* Bramwell Huxley?"

He nodded. "On half-pay for now." And how the devil did she know about his promotion?

She raised an eyebrow. "Major *Sir* Bramwell Huxley?"

Blasted Alexander Grant must have been talking. He dipped his head.

"Why, you two know each other?" the housekeeper said. "Yer acquainted with our Miss Gurnwood?"

"And not to let on to me, Ellie," Galt said. "For shame, girl."

Anger flashed across her face, and he remembered her brother. The good reverend had called out her innocent friendliness more than once at that long ago house party. He could only imagine how he'd addressed the less than innocent behavior. If he'd learned of it.

He must have. Gurnwood had made sure there'd be no further connection between his sister and a lowly captain.

"The merest acquaintance," Eleanor said, "years ago."

It wasn't a mere acquaintance, dammit. It had been a heart-swelling affair with a soul-rattling ending, followed by war.

"Five years and nine months to be precise," he said. "And there is nothing for Miss Gurnwood to be ashamed of."

The shame was all his.

Eleanor shed her cloak, a heavy shawl, her gloves, and a bonnet, and he couldn't look away.

"Sir Bramwell is more a friend of my brother," she said.

He bristled with a flash of anger. Matthew Gurnwood, the pompous hypocrite of a clergyman, had never been his friend. He'd known him, briefly, at Oxford, before leaving to go into the army.

Why hadn't Gurnwood taken her in? Why was she forced to take a room with good-hearted yokels? "And where is your brother now?"

"In Chichester," she said.

"Aye," Galt said. "Promoted to sub-dean."

The housekeeper bustled about, setting a kettle to the fire. "He'll be back Christmas day, Ellie says."

"And there'd best be room at the inn for him," Galt said, "because he's not staying here."

The housekeeper clucked. "I suppose he'll go to the vicarage and push Mr. Godwin and his wife out of their bed, and her with a babe coming so soon."

Well, well; Reverend Matthew Gurnwood wasn't well liked by the locals either.

"What of the flowers?" the housekeeper asked. "Did her ladyship send them?"

"Flowers?" he asked. "In winter?"

"For the altar," the housekeeper said. "To add to the greenery. Our Ellie is always scrounging about to see the altar properly dressed, isn't that so? And her ladyship has a greenhouse with blooms all year round, isn't that right, Ellie? St. Tancred's had a small greenhouse until last year's storms and Mr. Gurnwood wouldn't make repairs."

"Your brother was vicar here?" he asked, more by way of confirming something he'd already heard. "For how long?"

"Too long," Galt muttered, and Eleanor sent the old man a quelling look.

She went to a cabinet and came back with a bottle and two glasses. "We came to St. Tancred's a little more than a year ago. And Millie, you well know the money was needed for repairs to the church roof. Come along, Galt. Why are you standing around here in your kitchen when you have a perfectly fine dining room?"

IT WAS Eleanor herself who led him to the small bedchamber under the eaves after his host had passed out midsentence in his small parlor.

Over dinner, Bram had done his best to answer Galt's many questions providing as little information as possible without outright lying.

Why was he here? To attend the party at Brockton Hall.

How did he know Lord Cathmore? They'd served together at Waterloo.

And the subject of Waterloo had pulled a shade down over the old man's face. Eleanor declared she knew Galt had questions and would leave them to talk.

Galt had lost a grandson at Waterloo and begged to know what had happened there.

By necessity, they'd polished off one bottle of surprisingly good brandy and opened another, helping Bram wade through those blood-soaked memories, helping him parse his words. Galt didn't need to know the full horror of what the lad might have endured.

He was clutching an empty glass and his host was snoring when Eleanor entered, threw a shawl over Galt, and beckoned him. He went readily. Following her was what he'd wanted to do the entire evening.

His shelter for the night might have once been a servant's room, sparsely furnished with a narrow bed, a plain deal bureau, and a washstand. It smelled of soap, clean linen, and wood smoke. He turned the bedside oil lamp higher. The bedding looked fresh, and a fire burned brightly in the small unadorned hearth.

While he and Galt drowned bad memories, Eleanor had prepared this room for him.

His heart lifted. The coldness she'd displayed this night was a false front. She was still the kindest girl he'd ever met, though she was no longer a girl. She was a woman, the woman for him.

When he turned back to thank her, she had already departed.

He hurried down the corridor after her and knocked at the door she'd just closed.

CHAPTER 2

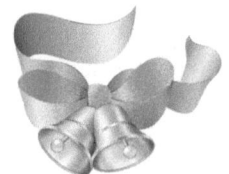

"*D*o you need something?" she called through the closed door. Not *Go away.*

His confidence soared and he tried the knob—it was unlocked—and stepped in.

Eleanor's room was only a tad larger than his own, with the same amenities, except that the fireplace was larger and the fire in it smaller. Was color flooding her cheeks? It was hard to see in the dim light, but he hoped it was so. He hoped she felt something.

He wanted her more than he ever had before, but he reminded himself to go slowly.

"What is it, Major? Do you need something?"

He'd caught her in the act of feeding the fire. She'd cast off her heavy shawl, and the coil of hair on the back of her head had loosened, dark tendrils touching her cheeks and shoulder.

The fireplace poker in her hand wobbled.

"Yes, I do need something," he said, and his feet carried him closer of their own accord. "I need you, Eleanor."

"That is the brandy speaking," she said with a brittleness she'd not shown all those years earlier. "Go to bed."

Gutted. His battlefield experience, his medals, his exploits, meant naught now. He'd given her his heart. They'd made promises, but she hadn't wanted to wait.

She blinked and pressed her lips together on an unmistakable tremor that passed through him as well, and he knew.

He'd hurt her terribly.

ELEANOR HELD HER BREATH, waiting to see what he would do next.

What she would do, if he decided to step even nearer.

A shiver passed through him. The room was chilly, but big men like Bram only shivered when they were ill or…

She set aside the poker. "You and Galt spoke of Waterloo."

When the subject came up, she'd seen pain in Galt's face and reluctance in Bram's and had left them to hash it out.

Oh, she'd been curious. She'd wanted to stay. She wanted to know where Bram had been, what he'd experienced. Whether he'd suffered.

But if she did, she'd be tempted to open her heart and be hurt all over again.

He stepped close and lifted her clenched hands, untangling them. "We did." He studied her face, clear-eyed. "I suppose I *am* foxed. And I won't… I won't trouble you tonight. Except to tell you, I've never forgotten you, and we must talk."

He lifted her hands and bestowed a kiss on the back of each one, sending her heart tumbling.

She shook her head. "What is there to say?"

"When I heard Matthew Gurnwood was the vicar here, I had to know what became of you. You're not married. Why didn't you marry? Your brother said—"

"*My brother?*" What exactly had Matthew done?

"You were betrothed to some clergyman fellow."

"I most certainly was *not*." Oh, Matthew had hoped to bring about a match between her and a widowed clergyman with powerful connections in the church hierarchy. Matthew had blamed the failure of the match on her fall from grace at the house party where she'd met Bram, but in truth, if she had to marry an old coot, she'd sooner marry Galt.

"What about you, Bram? Did Lady Felicity finally snare you when you returned to London?" Lady Felicity Spanning, newly widowed, had attended the house party. It was clear to all she'd set her sights on the handsome young military officer who was heir to a baronet.

"Who? No. Of course not. And I only passed through London on my way to Deal."

"But after you left, Lady Felicity told me—"

"No," he said, his mouth firming, his eyes burning into her. "She was nothing to me. I've only ever thought of you."

Some strong emotion—anguish perhaps—sparked in his eyes, quickly extinguished. His hands firmed around hers, warm and strong. The brash young man she'd fallen for had suffered. He was battle-hardened.

That young man hadn't forced himself on her before; she was certain the man he'd become wouldn't either.

But she'd hardened too, hadn't she? She wouldn't succumb to a man who'd left her with nary a goodbye.

One big hand pulled away and cradled her jaw. "Ah, Eleanor." He swallowed, and his eyes glistened. "Thank you for preparing a comfortable room for me." His lips brushed hers in a featherlight kiss, sending a tingle all the way to her frigid toes.

Hades. She was well on her way to losing her heart again.

He stepped back and bowed. "We'll talk tomorrow," he said, and then slipped out the door.

BRAM AWOKE with a start and looked around, seeking a memory of where he was and how...

Eleanor was here.

And she'd promised to talk. Although, as he threw back the covers and shivered in the chill morning, he recollected that she hadn't made any such promise. He'd been too foxed to try to extort one from her.

So foxed that he'd slept naked, a sure sign that this house had felt safe. He stirred the embers, fed the fire, and set the bucket of water someone had left to heat.

Someone had also brought up his kit—or maybe it had been here in the dark corner the night before. He quickly shaved, dressed, and made himself as presentable as a man could in wrinkled clothes and without a valet.

The housekeeper greeted him in the kitchen. "S'pose you'll be wanting breakfast after sleeping half the day away."

He glanced out the small window. The overcast sky revealed nothing about the hour.

"It's nigh onto ten of the morn. Go on then into the dining room and I'll fetch you a plate."

He pulled out a chair. "I'll eat here, and I'm grateful for whatever is on offer. Is Miss Gurnwood still about?"

"Went out earlier." She bustled about, the delectable odor of bacon and toast sending him back to his mostly happy childhood. The Huxley cottage had always been filled to the brim with friends and his female cousins from the nearby manor house that was now his. The toast appeared in front of him, along with a tub of butter, a pot of jam, and tea.

"Do you expect her back soon?" he asked.

"Who can tell? Ellie comes and goes as she pleases now that she's out from under..." She chewed her lip. "Now that her brother has left." She set down a plate laden with bacon, sausage, eggs, and beans. "Christopher Godwin called this morning, and Ellie fetched him home to his mama, along with my fresh biscuits."

The enticing smells made his mouth water. "Christopher Godwin?"

"The curate's boy."

"Ah. Did Miss Gurnwood move in here when her brother left?"

"Aye. She couldn't very well stay in the vicarage with Mr. Godwin before his wife and babes arrived. She thought to go and stay at

Longview, but the vicar squashed that notion. Didn't hold with Maria and Alex Grant taking her in neither. Wasn't happy about Galt, to be honest, him being a widower, never mind I'm here allus and old Galt has fifty years on her. Now, leave the dishes when you're done and I'm off to tidy up after Galt."

The vicarage, Longview, and the inn had been Eleanor's other choices.

"Miss, Millie," he said. "Whose home is Longview?"

"Belongs to Lord Cathmore, and I suppose Lord Hackwell too, since both their ladies are patrons. It's a children's home. Filled to the brim with 'em."

"A school?"

The housekeeper snorted. "Orphans, the lot, or as like to be orphans. The vicar didn't hold with his sister mingling with, beg yer pardon for plain-speaking, sir, bastards." She turned back at the door. "She'll most likely look in at the church after the vicarage. Make sure all is ready for tonight."

"Tonight?"

"It's Christmas Eve. There'll be a carol service."

Ah. She'd been in the church decorating. He remembered something about flowers.

"Too much brandy for me last night."

"And too much for Galt. I reckon he's off to the Royal George for some hair of the dog." She nodded. "Straight down the high street. You can't miss it. And it mayn't be my place to ask, but will you be staying on here for Christmas or traveling on?"

He looked down at his almost empty plate. He was expected at Brockton Manor for Christmas. But Eleanor was here until he could pry her away from the village and convince her to....

To what? He now had a manor house, filled as it was with an aunt and cousins. He didn't have the heart to throw them out.

He'd have to ford that river when he came to it and hope his cannon didn't sink and his horse drown. "I'll beg another night of your hospitality, Miss Millie, if I may." She harrumphed and departed.

He took one last bite and carried his empty plate to the sideboard.

Some hair of the dog was in order for him as well. One drink, a short chat with Alex Grant, and then he'd seek out Eleanor at the church.

"Do you think Auntie Liv has made scones for Wills?' Christopher Godwin turned up his freckled face and in doing so almost dropped the bundle of biscuits he was bringing his friend.

"Careful, young Chris," Eleanor said, "else you'll be bringing your friend mud pies instead of ginger biscuits."

A wicked gleam passed through his face, and she laughed. "Give them to me. Millie didn't spend hours baking these for you to drop them. I'll carry them and claim one for my troubles."

He straightened and clutched them closer to his thin breast. His clothes were warm, but ill-fitting. The poor lad was growing fast. When the opportunity for a promotion in Chichester came up, her brother had brought in Mr. Godwin to serve St. Tancred's. Matthew felt magnanimous about allowing the curate and his wife the use of the vicarage, but he really ought to be giving Mr. Godwin a greater share of the tithes.

The Royal George Inn looked busy today with more horses moving in and out of the stables. She waved to Barty, the Longview lad Mr. Grant hired as a groom when he wooed Maria away from her job at Longview and married her.

Grant, Cathmore, and Hackwell had all served together in the army. With Longview nearby, Lords Cathmore and Hackwell wanted a respectable inn for wealthy visitors and potential donors. They'd inveigled Grant, outcast son of a Scots laird, to take up the management of the inn. With his affable hospitality and their patronage, the inn had prospered.

She opened the inn door and felt a rush of warmth from the well-tended fire. It was Christmas Eve, and yet the taproom was busy. Most likely the men were getting out from underfoot of their busy wives. She waved a greeting to Galt, ensconced by the fire with some of his cronies.

Alexander Grant beamed his usual friendly smile. "Happy Christmas, Miss Gurnwood. And Christopher, what have you there?"

"Biscuits," the lad said.

"For me?"

Christopher's face fell. Grant laughed and tousled his hair. "Wills is back in the kitchen bedeviling Aunt Liv. Run ahead. Miss Gurnwood, before you go back to visit with Maria, will you greet my esteemed visitors?"

"Esteemed visitors? Would one of those be Lord Cathmore with my flowers?"

"Miss Gurnwood." Maxwell Hamish, Viscount Cathmore, rose from his chair, and the three other men at his table stood as well.

She recognized Lord Hackwell, who she'd met at the parish's spring assembly. The second man she didn't know, but he was, like the other two lords, tall, handsome, dark-haired, and aristocratic looking.

The third man was Bram.

She felt heat rising into her cheeks. Of course, he knew their lordships. His promotion and news of his baronetcy she'd culled from the newssheets. She might have puzzled out that they'd been in the army together.

She was naught but the vicar's spinster sister, no one of consequence, and grateful for Hackwell and Cathmore's courtesy. Not so grateful for the curious gaze and twitching lips of the man introduced as Lord Ottershaw.

And Bram... best not be grateful for his courtesy.

"We shall expect you at Brockton Manor," Lord Cathmore was saying. "Let me send a carriage for you this afternoon. Last night's snow has melted, and the roads are quite passable."

The invitation had already been extended by Lady Cathmore, and she'd turned it down.

"I thank you for the kindness," she said, "But I fear I have duties at St. Tancred's."

"Surely not," he cried. "Not now that your brother has hired a curate and gone off to Chichester."

"I am helping Mr. and Mrs. Godwin settle in. And speaking of that…" She took in a breath. In for a penny, in for a pound. "Did you perchance bring along the promised flowers from Brockton Manor's hothouse?"

Alex Grant chuckled at Lord Cathmore's puzzlement. Lord Hackwell smiled. Lord Ottershaw's lip curled up in a sneer.

Color was rising in Bram's cheeks, sending a flurry of heat into her own.

He was embarrassed. She swallowed a rising fury.

"Ach, Cathmore," Grant said, "flowers for the church, of course. Maria spoke with your lady about them."

"I am sorry, Miss Gurnwood," Lord Cathmore said. "I didn't know."

"Flowers?" a lady's voice said. "I adore flowers."

Lady Felicity Spanning sailed up to the group, parting the warm congenial air like a roving iceberg. Stiff blond curls peeked from under her bonnet, the red plumes of the elaborate piece dyed to match the fur-lined mantel draping her willowy figure.

Dressed for travel—thank heavens, she would be leaving soon.

"My dear sister, it seems our host, Cathmore, is also a florist," Lord Ottershaw said.

Lady Felicity tittered, and then caught sight of the sandy-haired man, the tallest one of the group. "Bram," she cried. "My dear brother, you didn't tell me Bram would be attending the party. You are, aren't you?" She sidled over, linked arms with Bram, and mimed a surprised face at Eleanor. "Why, if it isn't Miss Gormhall." She batted her eyes. "Or… surely, you're a Mrs. now?"

Bram's mouth firmed, his color still high. He glanced down at the arm linked with his but didn't try to pull away.

Eleanor dipped her chin a fraction, all that she would offer this haughty…

She took in a breath. "How do you do, Lady Felicity. Merry Christmas, my lords." She spotted Maria entering the taproom holding her daughter and managed a smile for Grant. "And now, I fear I must be off. Good day to you all."

Maria hurried to greet her and pass over baby Elspeth who'd crowed a greeting and put out her arms to the newcomer.

Maria leaned close. "Is aught wrong? I wondered what could be holding you up—oh." She set an arm about Eleanor's shoulder. "That woman," she muttered. "So unpleasant. So unlike Lady Cathmore and Lady Hackwell. I should like to attend the house party just to watch *our* grand ladies deal with her."

Eleanor smiled, and then laughed. "I'm sure they'll deal kindly with her."

"Says the vicar's sister."

She shuddered, feeling herself a fraud. If only Maria knew.

"Has she set her cap for the major?" Maria asked as they entered the kitchen.

Eleanor's heart sank. Felicity had set her cap for the major five years and nine months ago. Perhaps she was another reason he'd stayed away so long.

A cold knife pierced her heart remembering the words whispered in the night, the kisses, the feel of his big body over hers. The promises. Had Bram done with Felicity what he'd done with Eleanor? Had he made promises there as well?

They entered the kitchen, and she brought her attention away from a sudden surge of anger and grief to greet the chattering boys.

BRAM WATCHED Eleanor's proud back stiffen as she turned away and walked toward Grant's wife and infant. The babe reached for Eleanor who accepted it with delight, and then the ladies put their heads together like bosom friends.

"*She's* not aged well," Lady Felicity said softly. "Poor thing."

Bram scanned the painted face and looked down at the gloved talons wrapping his arm. "We've all aged, Lady Felicity."

She gasped dramatically, pulling her arm away, as he'd hope she would. "*Bram*. That is not a gallant thing to say to a lady."

Cathmore's lips twitched. "You're as lovely as the day we met, Lady Felicity."

"Which was last month in London," she said with a stiff smile. "The carriage is waiting outside, brother. I'm anxious to meet your ladies, my lords. We can all cram in if you like."

"Thank you, but Hackwell and I rode here. We have a call to pay and then we'll be along shortly."

"Certainly, Bram must ride with us," Lady Felicity said. "Oh, say that you will, Bram. Why, I'm sure my brother would be happy to ride outside while I grant you a chance to redeem yourself."

"How generous of you," Bram said. "Cathmore, a word, if you don't mind, before you depart."

Cathmore raised an eyebrow.

"Come along, Felicity," Ottershaw said. "Their lordships will catch up with us apace."

The four men watched them leave.

"One more round, innkeeper," Hackwell said.

Grant laughed, and led them to the bar, pouring a brandy for each of them. "Well, Huxley," he said, "mayhap you'll soon join the ranks of happily married men."

Bram shuddered. "*Happily*, indeed."

"She's certainly made her intentions known," Hackwell said.

Cathmore smiled. "And I'd say Huxley here has made his intentions known as well." He laughed. "Going to beg off from my house party, are you, and stay here with Grant?"

"Actually," Bram said, "as the inn was full, one of the generous locals took me in last night. I thought I might stay another night and attend tonight's carol service."

"Who took you in?" Grant blinked and then a sly smile spread. "Galt Wyman, was it?" He glanced at the other two men. "Since her brother left, Miss Gurnwood lodges there with old Galt and his housekeeper."

"Well then," Hackwell said, "you may as well attend the Christmas party at Longbourne tomorrow afternoon."

"The children's home?"

"Yes. Our ladies are patronesses of the establishment. In fact, we are running an errand there right now for our wives."

"Miss Gurnwood is quite involved there as well, now that her stiff-necked brother has departed," Grant said. "His support of Longbourne was lukewarm at best."

"He kept Eleanor away?" Bram asked, and then he remembered what Millie had said earlier.

Grant grinned. "Eleanor, is it?"

Three pairs of eyes studied him, and blast it, his cheeks began to burn. "I met her and her brother several years ago. In fact, Lady Felicity attended the same house party."

Grant nodded. "Miss Gurnwood—Eleanor—is cut from the same cloth as my Maria and I'd daresay Cathmore's and Hackwell's ladies. Her kindness isn't just put on for Sunday mornings. She's a lady who likes children, no matter how they were birthed."

Bram tossed back his drink and set down the glass, thinking.

A home for orphans, or ones who are like orphans, Millie had said. Why did Eleanor have such a particular interest in the place?

Cold slithered down his back. Had he got her with child all those year ago?

"I'll ride along with you today," he said.

CHAPTER 3

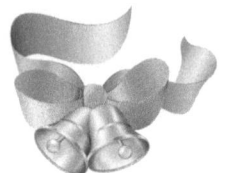

*E*leanor conveyed Christopher and his bundle of warm scones to the vicarage, then popped into the church to see the previous day's labor in the full light of day.

It was magnificent. Red, white, and gold banners streamed from the foiled star hanging over the large crèche. The manger stood empty, ready to be filled when the children brought in the baby Jesus at the end of the service. Lush boughs of pine, box, and juniper filled urns; holly and mistletoe berries added color. The promised Christmas roses and amaryllis would have topped off the adornments.

Perhaps next year, if she were still here.

Battling a heavy heart, she retraced her steps back to Galt's. Milly stood in the warm kitchen, laboring over more baking. It smelled divine.

"There you be," she said, retrieving the kettle from the grate. "Water's hot. Sit you down and try some of my current cake. Oh, and Galt brought back a letter for you."

She shed her outerwear and let Millie serve her, grimacing at the handwriting on the letter before opening it.

My dear sister,

You will be pleased to know that I've taken a goodly house with well-kept furnishings near the cathedral. You should be able to manage it quite well with a maid or two.

I know that you will be anxious to join me here, and so, I've advanced my plans and will arrive at the Royal George in time for the evening carol service. I've written separately to Grant, and you will remove yourself forthwith from your current abode to the inn, where a room will be waiting.

By another stroke of good fortune, I'm to be accompanied by the Archdeacon, the Venerable Felix Millington. He is recently widowed, and quite eligible, and dare I say, eager to meet you. It would not do for you to be discovered residing unchaperoned in the home of a single man.

Be sure to have your trunk conveyed to the inn as well, as we shall all depart for Chichester after the morning services.

You will, I trust, conduct yourself with the decorum fitting my new assignment.

She put the letter aside and stared into her teacup.

"Bad news?" Millie asked.

She straightened and inwardly shook herself. "It's from my brother. He's arriving tonight instead of tomorrow."

"Hmm," Millie said. "And when does he leave?"

"Tomorrow after the morning services."

Millie took a seat across the table. "He's not staying here."

"He's written to Mr. Grant to take rooms."

"Rooms? As in more than one?"

"Three, actually. He's bringing along the Archdeacon. And he instructs me to remove to the inn for the night so that I can be ready to leave with them in the morning."

Millie made a noise low in her throat. "We're not good enough I suppose."

Eleanor shook her head. "The Archdeacon is recently widowed and quite eligible. And Matthew doesn't want me to be found residing unchaperoned in the home of a single man."

The ridiculousness of it overcame her, and a laugh bubbled up and spilled over.

Millie reached across the table and took her hand. "Don't go," she said. "Stay here the night with us, and longer. Galt won't mind. Although." She grimaced. "I s'pose when your brother discovers the major here under the same roof, he might have an apoplexy."

"The major? No, he's off to Brockton Manor for the Cathmores' Yuletide party."

Millie shook her head. "Nay. He told me hisself before he left this morning, he'll be here tonight."

"Well then, he must have changed his mind. I saw him leave the Royal George with Lord Cathmore and some others attending the party."

"He'd best send someone for his kit, then."

"I'm sure he will."

And that would be that as far as Bram Huxley was concerned.

"You look peaked," Millie said. "Best go and have a lie down before dinner. I've a beef joint a-roasting."

"Should I not stay and help—"

"Shoo." Millie matched her hands to her words. "With only three mouths and my own to feed, I can manage with one arm tied behind me back."

Three mouths. She shoved down the foolish hope that Millie had the right of it, and Bram would return from Brockton Manor in time for their dinner.

But Galt and Millie kept country hours. Bram would never make it to Brockton Manor and back by dinner.

"You're still here?" Millie asked.

Eleanor managed a laugh and obeyed, climbing the narrow stairs to her room.

"WHAT ARE you so blue-deviled about, Huxley?" Hackwell asked.

"I'm not."

"Oh ho. Cathmore, has the major not been frowning since we left Longview?"

"Indeed, he has. Do you not approve of our wives' charity? Or does the long face have something to do with you seeking out children around the age of five?"

Blast it. Cathmore had overheard his conversation with the matron, the nosy bugger. He spurred his horse into a canter, but Hackwell kept pace with him and called, "Is there aught you wish to tell us about? I've told you my family's scandal, so you know there'll be no judging."

Hackwell had discovered both his own father's and brother's by blows living under the care of the future Lady Hackwell.

He reined up and rubbed his jaw, and the other two men stopped as well.

Perhaps Hackwell's history had unconsciously prodded his worries. But he'd found no children at Longview that fit his suspicions.

"I mentioned that just before Waterloo, I attended a house party in Leicestershire. It was at the home of a school friend. Friends of his from Oxford were in attendance, clerical types, along with others."

"Reverend Gurnwood?" Cathmore asked.

"Just so. Plus, some stuffy cleric he was trying to impress."

"And Miss Gurnwood?"

"Yes."

"Ah."

"I thought you were looking at her rather warmly," Hackwell said. "What happened... no, never mind, if you're looking around Longview for a child of a certain age, I can guess what happened. Did she cast you off?"

Had she? He'd gone off overnight to visit a friend recovering from wounds and returned to find that she and her brother had left. And then the summons had come to report for duty.

He'd sent her a letter, and she'd never replied. He'd sent an emissary in the person of his host and was told his attentions weren't welcome.

That information arrived after the battle, and he'd gone his way to other duties, shipped off to Canada and then the West Indies. The guilt and, dammit, the hurt had flamed back to life when he'd learned that Matthew Gurnwood was vicar in this small village only a few miles from Brockton Manor.

"Well, if you ask me," Cathmore said, "the problem lies with that pompous brother of hers. Never did think much of the fellow, but the living wasn't mine to manage."

"You and Miss Gurnwood." Hackwell laughed, and then sent him a sheepish look. "Sorry, old fellow. Miss Gurnwood seems a good sort of girl. Don't know what she sees in you."

"I rather think she despises me."

"Ah, no, not from what I saw," Cathmore said. "What are you going to do?"

Perhaps it wasn't too late. "I'm going to win her back."

"Hah," Cathmore said. "A woman once spurned," he grimaced, "or a woman who thinks she was spurned, requires a special kind of wooing."

"Cathmore learned this wooing his lady," Hackwell said. "Having also put the cart before the horse."

He recalled Cathmore's story of his temperamental bride.

Miss Gurnwood wasn't temperamental. She was a proud and sensible woman.

He hadn't spurned her, but she was still holding him at arm's length. Did she care for him? Did he have a chance with her?

"What does she want most in the world?" Cathmore asked.

He reined up and looked around the winter landscape, bleak and barren like the last few years of his life. Had Eleanor experienced the same sort of loneliness?

"You must make a grand gesture," Cathmore said. "It's Christmas after all."

"You must bring her the perfect gift," Hackwell said. "What does she want, man?"

He spotted a holly bush with its red berries. Galt's fireplace mantel had been adorned with them, a bit of color in the drab. But Eleanor wanted more.

"Lead the way to Brockton Manor, Cathmore," he said. "I know just what to bring her."

Heart heavy, Eleanor left right after dinner for the church. Bram had not appeared, as she'd known he wouldn't. Galt had arrived home well into his cups but had rallied over the excellent roast beef.

Millie had spared Galt her brother's news and commands, and Eleanor had kept mum about them as well. She wouldn't move to the Royal George tonight. All the same, she gave both her host and his housekeeper their Christmas gifts, embroidered handkerchiefs for Galt, and a summer shawl she'd knitted on the sly for Millie.

One never knew what lengths Matthew might go to. He'd whisked her away from the house party all those years ago, not even giving her a chance to wait for Bram's return.

The old hurt chilled her. Matthew had pulled her away, and Bram had not followed her.

Lifting her skirts, she picked her way down the High Street. She'd donned her best winter gown, a red wool with a beaded neckline and flounces, but in view of the muddy streets, she'd donned practical half boots with it. The dress had been a gift from the lady patroness of Matthew's last parish before coming to St. Tancred's. A hand-me-down, but not one that had been worn much. Matthew had frowned at the color and the scooped neckline, but she'd been thrilled both to receive it and to know that he couldn't object without insulting the giver.

She pushed open the church door and was surprised to find two people there already, going about lighting candles.

Mr. Godwin cast her a bright smile. "Ah, here is our savior, my love."

His wife—indeed it was her—waddled down the altar stairs and came to grasp Eleanor's hands. "Dear Miss Gurnwood," she said. "The church looks divine. What would we have done without you?"

"You have an excellent group of parishioners who—"

"Who don't know me at all." She smiled. "Not to mention, the children to see to, including this one." She rubbed her belly. "My dear aunt has arrived just this evening and is taking the little ones in hand and tucking them in. I'll go and fetch Christopher betimes so he can be with his choirmates and friends. By Christmas next year, I'll know all the ladies and even before then, I'm sure I'll be able to follow in your excellent footsteps when you leave for Chichester."

Her heart fell even further. She wasn't needed here, at least not in her old role at St. Tancred's. But there was still the chance for a position at Longview to pursue.

She forced a smile. "I'm afraid you won't see the last of me soon. I have no plans to go to Chichester."

Mr. Godwin had joined them, and a troubled look formed on his face. "I received a letter from your brother just this afternoon saying he was taking you away tomorrow."

"Yes. I received a letter with the same message. But I'm determined to attend the party at Longview Manor tomorrow. Lady Cathmore and Lady Hackwell will be there, and I intend to speak to them about a position at Longview."

"You don't wish to leave us?" Mrs. Godwin squeezed the hand she was still holding and smiled. "I confess, I'm glad, but..." She bit her lip.

"My brother's quarrel will be with me, not you. Now, what else needs doing before the service starts?"

THE EARLY ARRIVALS filtered into the church, greeting Eleanor and taking their seats. And just when she thought she might have a reprieve, Matthew walked in with an older gentleman who proved to be Felix Millington.

Where her brother made a show of his austere spirituality, the archdeacon fairly glowed with a kindness she didn't believe was feigned. Shorter than her own tall self, he was portly and jolly and sported a wreathe of white hair like a monk's tonsure. He beamed her a smile and a feeling of peace settled over her.

Or that circle of hair might be an angel's halo.

Mr. Godwin came to join them, and when introductions were made, the archdeacon's large gray eyes twinkled. Even Matthew softened a bit under the man's influence.

And that only lasted until the archdeacon drew Mr. Godwin away to meet Mrs. Godwin.

"You were not at the inn, nor have you moved your things there," Matthew said without preamble.

"No," she said. "I have not."

"What are you about, Eleanor, my dear?" he asked, infusing his tone with a patronizing patience. "I thought that you had abandoned this stubbornness. I've made a place for you in Chichester and even found the possibility of a match for you."

She gasped and laughed. "With that lovely old man? Are you mad?"

His skin mottled a dark shade of red. "Mind your tongue."

"You're being ridiculous, Matthew. I won't marry him. Nor will I be leaving with you in the morning."

Like a big fish seeking to suck in a smaller one, his lips pursed and then opened again, but before he could speak, the door rattled and the cold air carried in their choir, the children from Longview, with Mrs. McClintock and two of her staff.

"You *will* come with me to the inn tonight," Matthew muttered. "This stubbornness is unbecoming. We will talk after the service."

Despite her determination to go her own way, her confidence was shaken.

"Is anything wrong, my dear?" Mrs. McClintock had taken in the scene, perhaps even heard Matthew's words.

Eleanor forced a smile, shook her head, and turned to the fidgety children. "Now, everyone knows the program?"

The chorus of yeses led to a general hushing, and Eleanor led them to their seats while the rest of the congregation streamed in. With

119

much more fidgeting and arranging and rearranging, the children were finally seated. Christopher Godwin hurried in to join them, and Mr. Godwin appeared from the vestry, garbed and ready. Eleanor ignored her brother beckoning her and squeezed in next to Mrs. McClintock.

As the curate began his welcome, the church door slammed open again with a blast of cold and a late arrival. Mr. Godwin's mouth gaped, and then everyone turned to the shuffling at the door.

Bram was moving up the aisle, a huge bucket of flowers clutched in each arm. Galt followed with more, and behind him came servants.

Glorious white hellebores, Christmas roses, red and white striped carnations, and sprinkled among them vibrant, almost red blooms.

He stopped by her seat. "Sorry I'm late," he said in a stage whisper. "Where do you want these, Eleanor?"

Her breath froze even as heat flooded her cheeks. She tried to speak but her throat had thickened.

"How marvelous, sir." Mrs. Godwin appeared, clapping her hands. She led the men up to the altar.

"We shall have a short delay," Mr. Godwin said, "while we make room among the greenery for this Christmas gift—dare I say Christmas miracle? *The flowers appear on the earth; the time of the singing of birds has come.* In our case it will be the singing of our young children."

Mrs. Godwin directed the placement of the wooden buckets among the urns, putting Eleanor in mind of the earthy shepherds mixed in with the choirs of angels. She looked up to find Bram smiling at her, and an unsettling hope rose in her.

After the carols, the children processed out and returned garbed as the holy family and their entourage of angels and shepherds with a real baby in arms. Eleanor sniffed back a tear and looked around to see many handkerchiefs deployed.

It was *beautiful*, and *touching*, and *memorable*, just as she'd hoped. Whatever the future held for her, she'd have another perfect moment to cling to.

From across the aisle, Matthew scowled at her, and not even that could mar her pleasure.

THOUGH IT HAD BEEN years since Bram had been in a church for anything but funerals, the rituals had lodged deep in his soul. Unlike other clerics, Mr. Godwin seemed the real article, a man of God who had the kindness to not bore his congregation to tears with long-winded prayers.

Eleanor was beautiful tonight, a red dress peeping from under her cloak. She looked perfectly content among the restless children, her eyes aglow as much as theirs. While the regiment always managed some holiday merriment in their winter camps, he'd forgotten how magical Christmas could be when reflected in the eyes of children.

The service ended, and Godwin stepped down from the altar into the sea of parishioners. Bram struggled through the crowd to reach Eleanor.

Matthew Gurnwood was making for her also. Oh yes, Bram had felt the good reverend's glare as he'd marched in with flowers for his lady. Bram steeled himself for battle and reached her first.

"Eleanor," he said, and "Oh, Bram," she said at the same time, her voice thick with emotion.

He reached for her hand. "Dear Eleanor, will you—"

"Huxley." With the barest of nods, Gurnwood glared at him before turning back to his sister. "Eleanor, come along with us. The archdeacon and I will escort you to the inn."

A jolly-looking older man had joined their little group. He looked vaguely familiar, but Bram couldn't say where he'd met the fellow.

Galt stepped up with Millie, a sly look making his lips twitch.

Eleanor cleared her throat and made introductions.

Felix Millington greeted old Galt and Millie and then addressed Bram. "And you sir, I know well, though you probably don't remember me. I was a friend of your late father and mother. Dandled you on my knee before you were breeched. We were all proud to see you grow into such a fine young man. It's well met, we are." He bestowed an amused look on the joined hands. "Do I detect an understanding here?"

"*Oh.*" Eleanor tugged but Bram clamped his other hand over hers.

"I was getting to that, sir." He dropped to one knee. "Eleanor, I've never forgotten you."

"Here now, Huxley," Gurnwood exclaimed. "What do you think—"

"I wrote to you and when you didn't reply… I assumed… well, I've never forgotten you. Would you make me the happiest of men? Would you marry me?"

Her mouth dropped open.

"You need my approval," Gurnwood sputtered.

Eyes sparkling, her gaze never leaving Bram's face. "You forget, I'm of age, Matthew."

"I'll vouch for this young man's character, Gurnwood," the archdeacon said. "The only question is, what does your heart say, Miss Gurnwood?"

His whole world was in her dark shiny eyes, his future, his hopes, his dreams.

"I love you, Eleanor."

WE MUST TALK, he had said.

Instead, he was sweeping her away with the suddenness of his proposal and she was being carried away, again.

And yet, and yet… her hand felt right in his. Matthew had whispered pious calumnies against Bram's character, yet everything about Bram felt honorable, and true, and right.

"For pity's sake, Ellie," Galt said, and Millie shushed him.

Eleanor touched his strong jaw and swept her thumb over his cheek. Tenderness flooded her, and desire swept through her again. "I've never forgotten you, either, Bram." She took in a deep breath.

She'd prayed for wisdom. And guidance. And an angel to show her the way.

And courage. She'd be stepping out into the unknown.

"Yes," she said, taking a leap of faith. "Yes, Bram, I will marry you."

Bram shot to his feet. Huzzahs sounded around them, and her feet left the ground as he tossed her up into the air.

"Kiss her," someone said.

And he did.

EPILOGUE

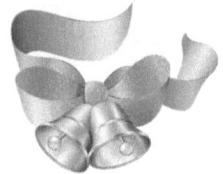

*O*ne week later

Three clergymen had officiated their wedding that day, the archdeacon himself fetching the license from the bishop in Chichester and insisting on having part of the honor along with a smiling Mr. Godwin and a very subdued Matthew.

Perhaps, under Mr. Millington's influence, her brother would shed some of his pretentiousness.

What with the New Year's Eve celebration and the day's nuptials, the assembly room behind the Royal George Inn had never looked more festive. Nor had Eleanor ever seen such conviviality: farmers, gentry, and the Brockton Manor crowd more or less mingled—less in the case of Lady Felicity and of course, her own brother, Matthew.

After the fine luncheon, Bram accepted congratulations and good wishes, never very far away from her. The weather had turned foul, and the quartet the viscount hired sent word that they had to beg off. But an intrepid farmer pulled out a violin, and so there would be dancing.

She hadn't danced with Bram since that long-ago party.

"A waltz," he called.

"I've never waltzed," she whispered.

"It is," he said, waggling his eyebrows, "the next best thing to making love."

She went up on her toes and set her lips to his ears and said, "Why not skip the next best? The bridal suite is ready."

His eyes lit, his lips turned up in a slow smile, and his hand flattened against her back. "Follow my lead, Lady Huxley."

He tucked her close, his touch radiating heat that unfurled within her. The dance floor cleared for the newlyweds, the bow scraped across taut strings, and Bram swept her closer still, his lips hovering, tantalizing and close, as they circled and twirled, and one couple, and then another, and another stepped onto the floor.

Dizzy with the motion, his masculine scent, and sheer desire, she barely noticed when they passed through the doorway and stood in the lamplit passage that led to the inn's reception room. A grinning Alexander Grant closed the door behind them, leaving them alone in the dim light.

Bram pulled her against him, pressed his lips to hers, and then she was floating as he swept her up.

"On to the best thing?" she asked, laughing.

He growled an answer into her ear and took the stairs two at a time, freeing a hand to open and close the bedchamber door, and finally setting her on her feet.

His strong arms came around her, and he raised her chin with one finger, a look of wonder in his eyes.

She took in a breath. "Well?"

The spell broken, he chuckled. "The best thing for tonight. And every night." His thumb swept her lower lip. "But the very best, Eleanor, is knowing I'll have a lifetime with you."

THE END

ABOUT ALINA K. FIELD

Award-winning and USA Today bestselling author Alina K. Field earned a Bachelor of Arts Degree in English and German literature but prefers the much happier world of romance fiction. She makes her home in Southern California, and between wrangling a terrier, a chihuahua, and two feisty grandkids, she's hard at work on her next historical adventure.

You may recognize some of the characters in this story from the earlier stand-alone romance novellas, *Rosalyn's Ring*, *Courted by the Earl*, and *The Marquess and the Midwife* as well as *A Leap Into Love*, where Eleanor Gurnwood made her first appearance.

You can find more books by Alina K. Field and meet more of her characters at https:/AlinaKField.com/Regency-Romance/.

SOCIAL MEDIA FOR ALINA K. FIELD

You can learn more about Alina K. Field at these social media links:

Facebook: https://www.facebook.com/alinakfield
Twitter: https://twitter.com/AlinaKField
BookBub: https://www.bookbub.com/authors/alina-k-field
Instagram: https://www.instagram.com/alinak.field/
Goodreads: https://www.goodreads.com/author/show/7173518.
Alina_K_Field
Pinterest: https://www.pinterest.com/alinakf/
Newsletter signup: https://landing.mailerlite.com/webforms/land
ing/z6q6e3

AN ANGEL'S PROMISE

BY RUE ALLYN

A MACKAI FAMILY HOLIDAY SHORT STORY

Artis MacKai might be only a little girl, but she is not going to let a blizzard, wolves, or a deadly enemy stop her from rescuing the stolen mare and foal who are the hope of her family. It will take the spirits of her parents, a determined boy, and her desperate brother to save her.

CHAPTER 1

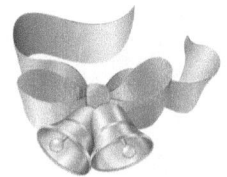

*J*anuary 1286, Northwest Scotland

Eight-year-old Artis MacKai huddled into her brother's great cloak and clung to the back of his huge black destrier. She was not certain which was worse: the biting wind and icy snow that blinded her or the anger Raeb would unleash on her for riding his cherished *Ionraic Bleigeard* through a blizzard and straight onto the lands of their enemies, clan Marr. Presently, the storm was the only enemy she faced. But she'd rather encounter a dozen lazy Marr guards than endure her brother's wrath.

That worry and the destrier's heat kept her from freezing in place. She'd crept away from Dungarob Keep and its stables before dawn. Not that she could see much through the blizzard, even then. The changing light told her dark had fallen long ago. But the *Bleigared* pushed on with little urging. Perhaps he, too, knew that, should their mission succeed, more than two lives would be saved. Fail, and she would die along with the destrier and much, much more. Worry about Raeb's anger was pointless, if she and the *Bleigared* did not survive. The cold that numbed her gloved fingers told her that they must find *Aingealach Spealp*, Angel's Spirit and her foal of three months soon, or death was a certainty. She urged the noble stallion to greater speed, and despite dangerous footing, his devoted heart responded, parting drifts like the hand of God parted the seas for Moses.

A wolf howl ripped down the lashing wind and sent shivers along Artis' spine. She had not thought she could be colder. A flurry of yips and growls mixed with the trumpeting neighs of an angry horse. *Bleigared* raced from the trees and plunged down a hill with a rock fall at one side.

As they neared the clearing at the bottom, Artis could see a blur of dark shapes circle and leap, seeming to attack the snow. Wolves. She had no weapon save the long knife she'd taken from the armory just before borrowing *Bleigared*. She should turn her mount and run. A scream of pain followed the angry trumpeting. A MacKai would never run. That other horse was in trouble; it had to be *Aingealach Spealp*. Artis added her own howls to the fray and prayed *Bleigared* would be able to fight off the pack with hooves and teeth as he did knights in battle.

The collision of stallion and wolves was horrifying and should have knocked Artis from her perch. Two of the beasts fell beneath *Bleigared's* flailing hooves. Another sailed through the air, sent aloft by the other horse. The destrier had a wolf by the neck, shook it, reared up, and tossed it into the snow beyond sight. Artis could now see two large wolves attacking a horse the color of sea foam. *Aingealach Spealp*!

Out of the swirling white, a giant, storm gray wolf leapt for the destrier. The great horse reared. Artis lost her seat, flying in the opposite direction as *Bleigared* twisted to attack the wolf. She lost her breath when she hit the ground, and all she could do was pray that the horses would win the day.

"Nay, my sweet Artis is too young to perish." The words strangled from Baron Bothan MacKai's throat. His words, like his fear, would not matter for he could do naught to stop the events unfolding below him.

"Do something, Bothan. We cannot let our daughter perish." To living ears, Lady Ailith's scream was an unearthly howl.

"Beloved, we are spirits. What can we possibly do? I cannot form a fist, let alone hold a blade if I had one." Her husband wailed sorrow and frustration.

These past months, since their murders, helpless to aid or comfort those they loved, the couple had watched their children suffer and struggle. Whatever cause imprisoned the two of them on earth, it forced on them the parents' greatest torment—the inability to aid their suffering children.

Fury at the circumstances blew from Ailith's mouth like the gale swirling about them and the fight below. "We have our love for Artis and all our children. That will never die and is the strongest of weapons. Because you love them as I do, be assured your love will do the same." The strength of that love tossed Bothan to where *Bleigared* fought the monster wolf. What force allowed Artis's father to grab hold of the black's mane, he would never know. But grab he did, pulling himself close and clasping the steed about the neck. The action must have hurt the horse as much as it astonished Bothan MacKai, for the stallion fled faster than the airborne wolf spun.

As horse and husband vanished into the storm, Lady Ailith MacKai's love-borne fury bashed the wolf against an ice-covered boulder. The beast's ribs cracked loud as ice over a winter sea, and it slid to the bottom of the stone, where the blizzard rapidly interred it.

A COLD MORE CHILL THAN the devil's heart blew past Artis, and at last her lungs filled. Beyond her the wolf faltered in mid leap. *Bleigared* pivoted and dashed into the blizzard as if pursued by a banshee.

Before her eyes, the wolf, still in mid-air, spun and shook. It uttered a horrible gurgling howl before flying, as if thrown, against a large boulder where it slipped down the icy surface to the snow then it lay still. The carcass disappeared beneath snow that swirled and tumbled faster than Artis could see.

Still dazed from her fall, she knew what she'd seen was not possible, but she also knew beyond certainty that everything she'd seen had happened, exactly as she'd seen it. No one but she would ever know the truth of what had happened here. She was so very cold and so very tired. This is what Mama had warned all her children would happen if they strayed beyond Dungarob Keep in such weather.

"Yes, it will mo leanabh eolach, but I'll not let you die if I can prevent it."

Ailith breathed the words, praying her daughter would feel her mother's love if not actually hear the words.

The words crooned in Artis' head, and warmth covered her body. Above her the snow slowed and dropped like milkweed seed to one side or the other.

"Mama?" No one but mama called her 'my knowing child.' No one but mama truly understood that Artis' gift was not a sight but a knowing. The who, what, when, and where of the things, Artis knew mattered little. What was important was that, when she knew a thing, the thing was always true.

"Yes, dearling. I'm here. I'll keep you warm for as long as my love can last."

"*Aingealach Spealp,* Mama. She's out there with her foal. The wolves were attacking her. I knew . . ." Exhaustion silenced Artis.

"I know mo leanabh eolach. Save your breath, as I can hear your thoughts. However, I have not the means to move you."

"But the wolf?"

"Aye, God's love gave power to my rage at the wolf. But I've no rage for you, and thus no strength to move you. However, I can call my Angel's Spirit. If she can come, she will."

To Artis, it was as if a song had come to soothe the beast of the angry storm. The lulling tune inspired a craving for closeness, impossible even for Artis in her weakened state to resist. She struggled to rise. That miraculous warmth that warded off the snow and wind pressed her back. Then hot breath blew from *Aingealach Spealp's* muzzle. Artis turned her head and smiled at the horse. But the mare stumbled to a halt beside her, folded her legs and sank down into the snow a short distance away. Blood oozing from gashes in the horse's side bore testament to the damage done by wolves and the great effort the horse of the angelic spirit had made to come to Artis. In the small space between mare and girl, a black foal settled. Warmth from both mothers sheltered the children. Familiar lullabies reached Artis' ears, and for a while she, the foal, and the mare languished in the warmth and safety of her mother's love.

"Why did you brave this storm, daughter?"

The question wove between the words of the song.
"I had to help you keep your promise."

"Aye, to fail in a promise is to live a lie."

"If your spirit leaves the earth with a lie, you cannot live in heaven with God."

"I should never have promised you could have the foal."

"Please don't say so, Mama. You made the promise out of love, and you did not know Laird Marr would have you and papa murdered. Together, love will help us keep your word."
Ailith chuckled.

"I suppose this is something you know."

"Yes, Mama."

"Very well then. We will wait for help to come.
Rest now."

The tune Ailith sang kept worry away from her daughter, but that worry was very real. Ailith did not know how long she could protect her child. Much as she wished to hold Artis, the last thing Ailith wanted was for her *leanabh eolach*, her knowing child, to perish before she had a chance to really live, to learn the wonders of the world and the glory of a beloved's heart. *Hurry, my love. Hurry, Bothan. I am fading, and without help Artis has too little time.*

CHAPTER 2

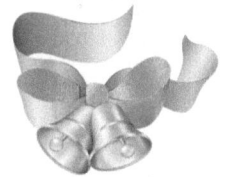

*B*aron Bothan MacKai clung to the stallion's neck. He had to
believe he could do so only because of the love he bore his
children. He had always been proud of the steeds bred from MacKai
stock. Knights came from all over Christendom to persuade the head
of clan MacKai they deserved the privilege of purchasing a MacKai
destrier for themselves or a MacKai palfrey for their ladies.

The destrier Bothan rode plowed through drifts and skidded along
icy streambeds. One of the best MacKai steeds ever bred, the horse
had been given to Raeb, Bothan's son, when that young man had left
to foster with an English family, distant relatives through marriage.
Months had passed before Raeb, now Baron MacKai, could make his
way home and take up management of the estate. Bothan knew his
son planned to try to steal back the horses that were his birthright. He
knew Marr as well. Raeb would fail. At fifteen, he was tall and strong
and showed great promise, but he was too young—in Bothan's
opinion—too inexperienced, to defeat a madman like Laird Marr.

Raeb was also too young to shoulder the burdens murder had
thrust upon him. Those burdens included seven sisters. Bothan had
always thought of his daughters as his jewels. Raeb was his blade, built
for war and leadership. But the girls had been the shining light of

Bothan's life. He wept for all of his children and swore, if vengeance from the grave were possible, Laird Marr would suffer eight times the hell Bothan suffered now.

Strong and true-hearted, *Ionraic Bleigeard* could only do so much. The horse had long ago dropped from a run to a lope then a jogging trot and now walked, head bent against the blizzard. Bothan could see nothing but the white of the storm against the black of night. All he could do was to urge the steed onward. Was it prayer or desperation that, after an eternity in the snow, Baron MacKai imagined he could see light streaming from an arrow slit in the wall of his ancestral home?

The *Bleigeard* was stumbling.

> "Don't give up. Your stable is nigh. You'll have oats and hay and warmth. Loving hands to curry and sooth you. Just keep going."

Even to Bothan's ears, the words blended with the moaning wind. How could a horse understand that?

But the destrier plodded on. When he stopped, Bothan could not understand why until he thought he heard voices mingled with the wind.

"Check the postern gate. That huge beastie could not have gotten far."

> "It is sorry, I am, Ionraic Bleigeard to have to hurt you more, but this is the only way I know to gain the attention of the living."

With that, Bothan let out a scream that made the wind itself freeze in its tracks. The blowing snow parted to reveal the huge gates of Dungarob Keep.

"Holy Mary, mother of God. What was that?" swore a fear-laden living voice.

The *Bleigeard*, none too happy at having his half-frozen ears blasted, reared up and pawed at the huge gates before him.

"Call the guard. Get the Baron. We're under attack."

Bothan wailed.

"Noooo. Let us in."

Weary though he was, the *Bleigeard* continued to batter the gate.

MOMENTS EARLIER, inside the keep, Raeb MacKai's sister Sorcha limped to a halt in front of him. "Artis is missing."

"What do you mean she's missing!" Raeb stared at the accounting book before him. He'd added the columns three times and arrived at a different calculation each time. He hated numbers—especially when they never said anything except there was not enough money.

"I mean, she's gone. Your sisters and I have searched the entire keep, and she is nowhere to be found. I have the clansmen searching the grounds now."

Raeb silently grumbled an oath. "Artis will never miss her favorite feast day, and Epiphany is tomorrow. She's probably found some hidey hole where she can make her gifts in secret."

"Had I not already searched the keep, I might agree with you. But she's not here, and there's more bad news."

What could be worse than learning that his youngest sister vanished and his clan was completely destitute? "And what is that?"

"When the stables were searched it was discovered that someone has stolen several small bags of oats and your prized destrier, *Ionraic Bleigeard.*

"What?" He roared and leapt to his feet. The destrier was the only horse he and his family owned. Every other horse still in the stable belonged to one of the loyal guardsmen.

"Raeb," Sorcha MacKai said. "I think you understood me perfectly. Your precious beast is missing as is our sister. Though I'm not certain which concerns you most."

"I'm sorry, Sorcha. Of course, it worries me that Artis is missing.

But she goes missing so often, and always turns up. *Ionraic Bleigeard*, on the other hand, should always be where I last left him and that was the warmest part of the stable."

Sorcha clasped her hands together. "I understand, you've too much to worry you, and now this. But believe me, brother. Artis is not in the keep. I'm worried about her. She's grown more and more silent every day since our parents were murdered. The closer we get to Epiphany the more silent she becomes. 'Tis because of mother's promised gift; I am certain."

He stared at Sorcha's serene expression and the hands folded gently at her waist. He believed she was frantic, but in the last six months she'd taught herself to bury every emotion so deep only the brother closest to her in birth could see beneath the outward calm. She amazed him. Where did she get the strength to portray peace when disasters struck at every turn? Especially given what she'd suffered. He shoved a hand through his hair.

Guilt still haunted Raeb. He'd been too far away to aid Sorcha and his parents when Laird Marr had turned on them. Though he'd left on his father's orders; he'd enjoyed himself too much in England to even think of traveling back to Dungarob for a visit. And look what had happened. He cursed England and himself.

"It is not your fault, Brother. No one could know Marr would be so crazed when my betrothal with his heir was ended."

"Perhaps. It was a madness most evil that caused him to murder our parents and force your horse off a cliff. But I should have been here. Do you know, the day it happened, I was dancing with my foster sister at a fair."

"And if you think our parents would want you to never have had that happiness, you are more than a fool, Raeb. We must live now, not in a past that cannot be changed no matter what our regrets."

She had more than a few regrets of her own, he knew. "You are right. I suppose Artis said nothing to anyone of where she was going?"

"I asked and no, she said naught to anyone in the keep."

"Aye, even at eight years old, the child is smart enough to know she'd be stopped before she could take two steps into that foul storm." Weariness sounded in every word.

Sorcha gripped his hand. "The only way she could get out of the keep is if no one knew she'd left. With this storm, she could have departed by the main gate, and no one would have seen her."

Was it possible? He hadn't thought of anyone leaving the keep in such a blizzard. Even a horse thief would seek shelter, but not if the thief was a sister on a mission. And with Artis every cause was always a mission.

"I may know where to look for her, but I'll have to borrow a horse to find her."

Sorcha's eyebrows rose. "Borrow Dougal's. Our captain's steed is near as swift as the *Bleigeard*."

"I'll speak with him on my way to the stable." Raeb took a look at his sister's face, noting the frown line between her brows. "Is there aught else I should know?"

Sorcha pressed her lips together as if choosing her words. "'Tis not just the storm that worries me."

"That blizzard is more than enough for concern. What else?"

"That monstrous destrier of yours will kill her. She's too small to be able to get a saddle on him."

Raeb shook his head. "No. You know Artis's way with animals. The *Bleigeard* will do her bidding, and she'll nae have to say a word to him. Now that I think on it, you did not say any of the saddles were taken. A horse thief surely would have needed one to control my favorite mount even in good weather. The *Bleigeard* is not an easy horse at the best of times."

"So, Artis rode your great beast bare backed to go and help a creature in need, but how do you know where to look? How would she know where to find the mare and foal? I realize she has a gift, but…."

"You said it yourself. Epiphany. She's been pleading with me since that awful day in May to steal back the MacKai horses. She told me she knows Mother's soul will not get to heaven if her promise is not kept. Our sister's gone to find *Aingealach Spealp* and bring her home, so mare and foal will be safe here before Epiphany. Our mother's promise will be kept."

At that pronouncement, Sorcha paled, and she shook visibly. "She's gone to Strathnaver? They'll kill her."

"Aye, if they know she attempts to steal back one of our horses, they would. Perhaps this blizzard is a blessing after all, for you and I both know the old laird is too lazy and selfish to even send a servant to care for one animal let alone an entire herd in this kind of weather."

By the time he finished speaking, Sorcha had restored her rigid control. "Then hurry. Borrow the best horse you can find and hurry."

In that same instant, a guard arrived with the news that the keep was under attack at the great east gate.

When the source of the supposed attack was discovered, Raeb donned his second-warmest cloak and rushed to the stables. At the sight of his destrier he breathed a tiny sigh of relief. Yet his worry increased tenfold. His treasured *Ionraic Bleigeard* had returned on his own, but where was Raeb's even more treasured youngest sister?

A draft of air whispered past his head.

> "Borrow Dougal's steed. It's near as good a horse as the Bleigeard."

Raeb turned a circle looking for the speaker, but found no one. "Dougal," he said to his oldest friend. "I must borrow your horse. Organize the men who have their own mounts and follow me as quickly as you can. And send a message to Sorcha that my sisters are to prepare a hot meal and warming cures for all who brave the storm. I pray we find Artis in time." More explanations than that could wait.

"Let me help you get saddled," his friend said as they set off at a run.

CHAPTER 3

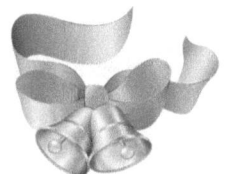

*W*armed by her mother's love, Artis had managed to pull the foal into her lap and crawl closer to the mare. They huddled together and waited. In her mind she could hear her mother singing.

> Oh, hush thee my dove, oh hush thee my
> rowan...

Strong and clear, the voice, the song restored the hope Artis had when she set out on her journey to see her mother's promise kept. The storm, the wolves, the weariness had battered that hope, and now Mama renewed its strength. All would be well.

Then *Aingealach Spealp*'s breathing started to labor, coming both harsher and weaker as the night lingered. The foal struggled from Artis' lap to nudge at its mother, knowing something was wrong when the mare gave no response beyond a soft whinny.

The harshness left *Aingealach Spealp*'s breath, reforming into a quiet wheeze scarce audible above the groaning wind.

"No, Mama, please. Tell God to save *Aingealach Spealp*. Her child needs her. You and I know how very much a child needs its mother."

"God knows of our need and your worry, daughter. I must use what strength I have to keep you safe until help can come."

Tears formed in Artis' eyes. "She's not supposed to die. If she dies, the foal will die, and you will not be able to keep your promise. I know God won't let this horrible thing happen. I know it."

Silence reigned for a time.

"I may know a way we can keep her alive for a time, my knowing child. But you will have to sing the lullaby."

"Why can you not sing, Mama?"

"I will be busy, sweet girl. I will use some of my love to live for Aingealach Spealp."

And Artis knew. "You have not enough love left to keep us warm, live for the mare, and sing."

"That is right. So, sing now."

"*Oh, hush thee my dove, oh hush thee my rowan...*" Artis began.

The mare's breathing steadied, and she nuzzled her foal.

The cold crept in very little by very little, as the snow ceased falling.

"*Oh, hush thee my lapwing, my little brown bird.*" Artis sang louder, though she did not feel like it. The foal, the mare, she, even her mother, all needed courage and comfort. Artis knew she could do this, though her heart hurt at the truth of the sacrifice her mother was making.

"Why are you singing?"

"Who is that?" Artis paused her song but started up immediately when a chill breeze crossed her cheek. "*Oh, fold thy wing and seek thy nest now,*"

"I'm Naff." A slim figure not much taller than Artis herself stepped from the trees on the Marr side of the clearing and showed itself to be a scrawny lad.

"You can't be." Artis spoke between lines of song. "Rubbish cannot walk and talk. *Oh, shine the berry on the bright tree.*"

"It's what they call me. So, I must be."

"*The bird is home from the mountain and valley.* If it's a Marr who calls you that you should not listen."

"Why not?"

"Because they are too stupid to take proper care of their animals, and cannot know what is a proper name. *Oh, hush thee my lapwing, my little brown bird.*" Artis repeated the short song.

"The Marrs are not stupid. Just cruel," remarked the lad as he came closer.

"Cruelty is stupid." Artis was certain. "*Oh, fold thy wing and seek thy nest now...*"

The boy shrugged. "Why are you here, and why do you sing?"

"I'm here for the same reason you are." The moment he'd appeared Artis had known why he'd come. "*Oh, shine the berry on the bright tree.*"

"To find the mare and foal?"

Artis nodded and kept singing. "*The bird is home from the mountain and valley!*"

"How could you know they would be here? Where to find them? Who are you?"

Artis smiled and patted the snow-covered ground beside her. "Come sit with me," she spoke between snatches of song. "It's warmer here. I will tell you everything. Then you will choose a new name for yourself, and we will name the foal together."

"Do you have any food? I'm fearful hungry." The boy frowned in doubt. "I'm not sure I can think of a new name."

"I'll help you. As for food," she shook her head. "I am sorry, I have none. But sit. It is warmer. *Oh, hush thee my dove, oh hush thee my rowan.*"

Finally, he sat. "It is warmer. A bit."

"*Oh, hush thee my lapwing, my little brown bird.*"

"You should call yourself Fionnlagh. For I know you to be a

warrior, and you have come to me through the dark white of snow this night. Now, sing with me, and it will be warmer still."

"*Oh, fold thy wing and seek thy nest now,*" they warbled together.

He didn't sing well, but he tried. "Fionnlagh," he tried the name. "Aye I fight a lot, so I must be a warrior. But I've no other name to go with it."

"When you need one, it will come to you." Artis turned her head to smile at him. For a moment, warm became hot. "I'm Artis MacKai. I have the knowing. That's how I am here and how I know you will find your name."

"*Oh, shine the berry on the bright tree.*"

"May I see the foal? The Earl calls the mare Justice. He always laughs when he says it."

"Hmph. Much he knows about it. The mare belonged to my mother, and her foal was promised to me. Her name is *Aingealach Spealp.*"

"Angel Spirit," whispered Fionnlagh. "That is a much better name than Justice."

"Mama promised the foal to me."

"Then the foal's name should be Angel's Promise." Fionnlagh gave a firm nod.

Artis beamed at him. "That is a perfect name. Angel's Promise he shall be."

The heat fled. Cold wrapped foal and children in a frigid grip.

"Oh no, we forgot to sing. Quick Fionnlagh, sing."

"*The bird is home from the mountain and valley.*" Their young voices rose, but the wind howled just as loud.

"Mama, I'm sorry, please stay."

"It is I who am sorry my knowing child, my sweet girl. I thought my love was strong enough to keep you safe, warm until your father could come with help. Know that we will stay as long as we can, if you are to join us."

148

"He's not far, Mama. I would like to come with you, but I do not know if I can."

"*Oh, hush thee my lapwing, my little brown bird.*" Her mother's spirit joined the chorus. The cold lessened a small bit. However, the mare's breathing ceased, and her body went still.

"*Oh, fold thy wing and seek thy nest now.*"

Short moments before Bothan returned, the foal lifted its head with a snort, looking toward its mother. Then it let out a high-pitched squeal.

"*Oh, shine the berry on the bright tree.*"

Together Artis and the lad stroked the foal as they sang. Soft tones, soft strokes, and warm love. But Artis knew that both her mother and the mare were beyond reach.

"*The bird is home from the mountain and valley!*"

The last words faded, and their voices fell silent.

The foal emitted one long squeal.

Tears froze on Artis' face. For once in her short life, she did not know if the echoing voice she heard in her head was true or only what she wanted to hear.

The wind picked up. Girl, lad and foal huddled together, their life's heat seeping away with each breath.

BOTHAN CLASPED his wife's spirit close to his own. They were both fading. He'd had his doubts, but his wife had always believed love was infinite and all powerful.

He watched helpless as the blizzard resumed and covered his daughter, the boy who'd come from who knew where, the foal and the mare's body. Soon, too soon, boy, girl and foal would be dead as well. Could he and Ailith last long enough to greet their daughter as she left the world? Would he go with her to heaven? Artis was an innocent, despite what she called her 'knowing.' He, however, had done many a thing that could bar him from paradise.

"Did you get to Raeb?"

"I did, but the storm is fierce, I do not know if even he and his men can save Artis."

"It is in God's hands now."

They fell silent for a time.

Beside him his wife moaned.

"Are you in pain my love?" Bothan asked. "I feel it too. A pulling, like a great tide that refuses to allow any foothold."

"We must hold, nonetheless, husband. The children, the foal, they are not yet dead."

"Then we shall stay. Let the devil himself come; we'll not yield until Raeb can get to Artis."

RAEB HAD JUST DESCENDED a hill bordered by a rock fall when he heard a high-pitched horse's squeal. The sound was weak, but he was certain he heard it. He kneed his borrowed steed in the direction of the noise. The snow was deeper here, up against that fall of rocks on the windy side of a clearing.

The squeal came again. Longer, weaker. Was he getting close?

It was his mount that had the good sense to stop.

"You are too well trained a beast to halt for no reason." Keeping a firm hand on the reins, Raeb dismounted and nearly stepped on a body. He bent, brushing snow from the slim form. "Artis?" Panic overtook him, and he shook the body to wake whoever it was. "Artis!"

"No," said a boy's voice. Snow flew from his tossing head, and he patted the ground on his far side. "She's over here."

All Raeb could see was a hump of snow. He brushed and dug, and at long last found a small hand. He rescued her body from its snowy tomb, cradled her in his arms and wept. "Artis."

Hot tears fell on her face and refused to freeze. Beside him he heard the boy, off key, singing, "*Oh hush thee my dove, oh hush thee my rowan.*"

Tears streaming, he stared at the lad who'd placed a hand on Artis' head. Was the boy mad? Had he murdered, Artis, not the cold?

"Sing with me," the boy said. "She'll hear you and wake up."

"How?"

"She told me before she went to sleep. She said you would come, but she had to sleep so she could keep the foal alive until you got here. It was my job to stay awake and be in your way so you would find us. I'm sorry I didn't stay awake as long as I should. But we'd better start singing before she goes to sleep forever."

The lad croaked out another line. "*Oh, hush thee my lapwing, my little brown bird.*"

Raeb knew the tune well. It had been one of his mother's favorites, and she'd sung it to each of her children from the day they were born. He added his rusty baritone. He hadn't sung, had not wanted the joy he knew song would bring, in many long months.

Their voices lifted, and Raeb looked up to see the men who'd followed him into the blizzard to find Artis. All of them in the saddle staring, and all singing at the tops of their lungs.

Unable to compete with the loving chorus, the wind fell silent.

Raeb could swear he heard the two greatly missed voices of his parents crooning the lullaby.

Artis opened her eyes, smiling at her brother. "I knew you would come."

"Why, sister? You nearly killed yourself, and me with you."

"I had to help Mama keep her promise

Raeb could only stare. "But the promise was a foal. Where?"

"Here." Artis lifted the cloth of the cloak that covered her to reveal the foal warm and alive. "This is Angel's Promise."

He gathered his sister, who would not release the foal, and with Dougal's help, mounted his borrowed horse, carrying two precious lives before him.

"Dougal, take that boy up behind you. I've yet to learn how, but he played some part in saving my sister's life."

Dougal took the boy up, and the cavalcade of searchers turned for home.

"Yes, I know, Raeb. You want me to explain everything." Artis said.

"That I do, but after you are home and I am certain of your well-being."

Later, much later, Raeb knew he would laugh with relief and sing the carols and holy songs of the season in gratitude for his sister's life and her certainty of his parents' fate. Even later, probably years later, he believed he and his clan would face and somehow overcome severe difficulties. But now, today, as pale winter sunlight broke through the cloud cover. He knew joy.

The End

A NOTE TO READERS

This story really does end with the gift of Raeb's renewed joy and the lives saved. But you deserve to know that Bothan and Ailith met their heavenly reward with the knowledge that Artis, the boy, and the foal all lived. Eventually Artis and Fionnlagh will get a longer story leading to an HEA for each of them. However, I've many other tales to pen before I can write that story. While you wait, I suggest you take a look at *Knight Defender*—Raeb MacKai's story—or *Knight Protector*—Sorcha MacKai's story. Receive a FREE download of *The Taming of Iver MacTavish* a Clan MacKai secret bride novella by subscribing to Rue's News here. Thank you very much for reading. Please send your thoughts on the story to me personally via email to Rue@RueAllyn.com

ABOUT RUE ALLYN

Award winning author, Rue Allyn learned story telling at her grandfather's knee and has been weaving her own tales ever since. She and her husband of more than four decades (try living with the same person for more than forty years—that's a true adventure) have retired and moved south. When not writing, enjoying the nearby beach or working jigsaw puzzles, Rue travels the world and surfs the internet in search of background material and inspiration for her next heart melting romance. She loves to hear from readers, and you may contact her at Rue@RueAllyn.com. She can't wait to hear from you.

Learn more about Rue at:

Website: https://RueAllyn.com

To get *Knight Defender* follow this link--https://books2read.com/u/4EQ6de

She would never wed a Scot. He would prefer death to marriage with an English woman. So why do these two natural enemies each pretend to agree to marry?

She wants a life dedicated to the support of a nunnery not a loveless political marriage to an overbearing enemy. A growing passion for the man spoils all her plans. A weak simpering English woman is not his idea of the ideal wife. But when she turns out to be more than a match for him, he cannot help but fall in love. Even when they discover love, can these two enemies create peace or will the hatred between countries separate them forever?

Discover whether political loyalties or love wins this passionate battle. Purchase your copy of *Knight Defender*, book three in Rue Allyn's Knight Chronicles, now.

SOCIAL MEDIA FOR RUE ALLYN

You can learn more about Rue Allyn on these social media links:

Website: https://RueAllyn.com
Facebook: https://www.facebook.com/RueAllynAuthor
Twitter: https://twitter.com/RueAllyn

ROOM AT THE INN

BY CAROLINE WARFIELD

A fatherless child requires a village to care for it, provided they have room in their hearts. When a cold-hearted baroness makes it impossible for the tenants of Little Hocking to care for one little boy, the Honorable Declan Alworth steps up to make room in his heart and his home for the little treasure. How can the vicar's niece, Maera Willis, resist either one of them?

Written to order for Denise Austin with gratitude for her interest in my work.

Author's Note

I occasionally offer the right to specify elements for a made-to-order story that would be the exclusive property of the winner for two months as the grand prize in a contest. This effort is the result of one such contest. She asked for a sleigh and a secret baby, and so this story began.

CHAPTER 1

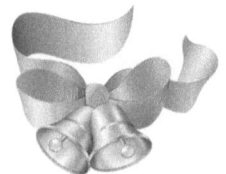

"*H*is lordship is late this month."
Maera Willis kissed the top of little Samuel's head.
"How can he stay away from this little angel?" She hugged the boy
close.

Jenna Mullins smiled over the laundry she folded. "He does dote
on the boy, but the weather…"

The woman had a point. The December ice storm had been brutal
and the snow that came after made the roads and even walking
treacherous. Maera knew walking up from the village had been foolish, but the draw of the baby compelled her. She longed for one of her
own, and couldn't resist the opportunity to hold him.

Samuel gave a little burp and smiled up at Maera. *How can a father
farm out a treasure as adorable as Samuel?* she wondered. *If he kept him at
his side, as a father ought, ice and snow wouldn't matter. If he truly loved the
little one, he would have him in his home.*

Another insight came to her, one even grimmer. *Unless, of course, he
has a wife who doesn't know about her husband's sins.* Anger for Samuel
and for the wife followed the thought.

"What of his mother?" she asked, letting curiosity get the better
of her.

"You wouldn't know, would you—you being newly come to Little Hocking," Jenna said, lifting the basket of nappies up onto a shelf. "Isabelle Grimm were a foolish girl, make no mistake, taking up with some man. No harm in speaking of it now, I expect."

Jenna wiped her hands on her apron and sat across from Maera, giving little Samuel a fond pat and a sad smile. "His mother's dead these six months, poor duck. Childbirth fever. His lordship found this little one crying in the cottage and brought him here to us. Cold and wet he was, but none the worse for wear. Arranged a funeral for her, his lordship did. Generous man."

Same man? The one paying for her son no doubt. A niggle of guilt reminded Maera she ought not jump to conclusions, but what was she to think with this poor tyke alone in the world. Outrage filled Maera. *Jenna thinks him generous? He could hardly do less for the woman who bore his son.*

"Davie! Mind the soup pot," Jenna shouted. She rose and pulled her youngest son away from the hearth. "You boys take your rough-housing outside, snow or no snow," she ordered. With five children of their own, Jenna and Jonah Mullins managed a busy house. Thomas, her oldest boy, helped his father with the stock in the barn. Peg, a year older than Thomas, tended Martha, just a toddler, quietly in the corner, sewing clothing for a straw doll.

"Samuel must add to your burdens, Jenna," Maera said.

"All babies are a bit of bother, but he's a good one. And his lord-ship's coin is a help, what with the baron raising rents," Jenna replied, picking up her mending. "I appreciate your attention, Miss Willis, but you best get yourself home. It threatens snow again. I won't have the vicar cross with us."

Maera's Uncle David served Little Hocking, a poor living in a remote part of Westmoreland. When his letter came in the wake of Aunt Martha's death, Maera happily responded. He needed a house-keeper and a teacher for the dame school. She needed an excuse to leave her brother's house.

"I fear you are right, Mrs. Mullins," Maera said, laying Samuel in his crib. "Give my regards to Jonah. I hope we'll see you at services on Sunday."

"God and the weather willing, Miss Willis. God and the weather willing," Jenna said wearily. "Thank you kindly for the visit and the apple compote."

Maera, wrapped in her thick cloak and bundled in scarves, trudged down the lane in front of the Mullins's farm, head down into the wind. She didn't see the sleigh that flew around the bend until almost too late. When she did, it startled her so badly she slipped backward into the ditch, landing awkwardly with her feet up one side and her head at the bottom.

Momentarily stunned, Maera couldn't move.

She scraped the snow from her face and peered up to see a pair of angry eyes, so brown as to be almost black, glaring over the edge at her.

"Are you an imbecile, woman? You could have been killed."

Heat so strong it ought to have melted the ice filled her. "Me? You almost mowed me down. I'll have your apology," she shouted back.

Oddly, the eyes warmed and the man standing above her, arms akimbo, began to laugh. "You sound feisty enough. You can't be too badly hurt."

Staring past her skirts where they had begun to bunch toward her knees, and her boots, toes pointed at the heavens, her fury gave way to humiliation. "If you were a gentleman, you would look the other way and help a lady up."

Her statement added to his hilarity. "Which do you want me to do, my lady—look away or assist you?" he gasped between laughs.

DECLAN—THE Honorable Declan Alworth—bit his lip and reminded himself he was indeed a gentleman. He had to remind himself twice. He had no business laughing. Relief that he hadn't killed the reckless chit made him silly —it was his only excuse—and he couldn't think

165

how he would extricate her from her predicament without making it worse.

He studied the situation carefully from the heels of her well-made half boots resting against the top of the ditch, past the shapely ankles in warm woolen stockings, down to the skirt bunched up at the girl's knees, to her awkward position at the bottom of the ditch—

Goodness! If a glare could kill, I would be dead.

"Well, are you going to quit ogling my ankles and help me out?" she demanded.

"Be patient, I'm studying the situation. There has to be a way…" *If she were a barrel of nails, I could build a ramp and roll her up. If she were a pallet of lumber, I could bring in a winch—*

She rocked to one side in an effort to sit and fell back with a thud. *Thank God she didn't break her neck or hit her head on a rock*, he thought. *Stop thinking like an engineer and get her out of there.*

"What do you suppose is under all that snow?" he called down.

"Me!" she responded through clenched teeth.

At least she has wit. "I mean next to you. Rocks?"

"I don't feel any."

"Well, we'll know in a moment." He jumped in beside her, feet first. Fortunately, he did not hit rocks or turn his ankle. Unfortunately, his good boots sank into two inches of oozing mud, and his resulting language further called his claim to gentleman status into question.

Lifting the girl proved difficult. He tried pulling her by her hands, but the mud she had fallen in held her fast, and every time he pulled it threatened to suck her back. Every time she did her skirts skittered a bit further up her legs.

Her very shapely legs. Declan began to rethink his assumption that the victim was a young girl.

When he reached down, pulled her shoulders so he could get an arm around her waist, and lifted her into his arms, he knew his assumptions were a great distance from correct and thanked the angels for it. He discovered the womanly curves that had been hidden under woolens and snow. He had not held such a delectable armful in a long while, and he rather liked the sensation of a woman in his arms.

"Well, do you plan to just stand here?" she demanded.

A very opinionated woman in my arms! That felt good as well. He liked a woman with backbone. "I'm trying to figure out how I will climb that steep slope while carrying you. He judged the distance and the angle. He couldn't account for the slide of the mud, but he judged three firm strides upward would do it.

"If you're not going to get on with it, put me down. I'll—"

Yes, three strides. Being correct pleased him. It always did.

Jenna's boys met them at the top of the road, mouths agape.

"Good lads! Alert your Mam and open the door for me." They ran to do as bid, and he savored the feel of her as he strode toward the Mullins cottage.

"Where are you going? Put me down! I can walk. I—"

"Are you always this managing?"

"I beg your pardon?"

"It's a clear enough question. Do you generally give orders to your rescuers? Based on your carelessness, I assume you've had many."

"I never—"

"You've never had a rescuer? How impressive. Kindly knock on the door."

"I beg your pardon? Oh." The woman looked over her shoulder and realized he had carried her to the cottage door. She raised a hand to oblige, but it opened before she could, revealing Jenna Mullins with Samuel on one hip, and her younger boys in her skirts.

"Miss Willis! Davie and Jake said you fell arse over applecart."

"Correct. This lady has taken a fall. My fault I fear." He set her gently on her feet, cupping one elbow to steady her. He sent the boys out to see to his horses.

"Miss Willis, is it? Are you related to the vicar in Little Hocking?" She gaped at him, and he didn't wait for a response. "You seem steady enough," he went on. "Have you pain anywhere?" He yanked off his muddy gloves, tossed them on the floor, and reached up to run his fingers through her hair, checking her head for lumps and bumps. The silky curls distracted him, and he may have gone on longer than necessary.

That awoke her from her stupor. "Kindly remove your hands, sir!" she demanded. "I am quite well. I am indeed the vicar's niece, and I will return to the vicarage forthwith."

She stamped her foot for emphasis. *She seems well enough. Stubborn though.*

"What do you think, Jenna. She's had a bad tumble. Should we trust her on the roads?"

"You look well enough, Miss Willis, but you can't be too careful about falls."

"Nonsense. I broke my fall and didn't hit my head. It was just, er, awkward. I'll just take my leave; I've imposed on you enough."

"True enough. We've gotten enough mud and melting snow on Jenna's floor. It might be best if we both leave." He looked down at the Willis woman. "I saw no carriage. How do you propose to return to the vicarage?"

"I will walk, of course."

"That you will not. I cannot allow it," he said. No gentleman would let her walk in this weather. Not when he had a perfectly good sleigh.

"Unless you plan to hold me prisoner, I will do as I please, your lordship."

She made the title sound like an insult. *Maybe it would be, if it were accurate.* "No," he said.

"No?" she demanded.

"No lordship," he corrected. "I am the mere second son of a baron, so it is Mr. Alworth. That is supposed to make me 'honorable.' Jenna forgets. Or Mr. Declan if you will." He raised an eyebrow to ask her which she preferred.

She ignored him, choosing instead to lift her firm little chin and sweep from the cottage, the impact of her exit somewhat dampened by the squish of her wet boots and her muddy, rumpled clothing. The sway of her hips, however, appeared no less enticing in spite of the mud.

He sighed deeply at the slammed door. "I'm sorry Jenna, but I'm afraid I can't stay to help you with the mess," he said picking up his ruined gloves. "And I will miss my time with Samuel. I'm staying through Twelfth Night at the baron's request, however, and I'll be able to come over as much as I like. Tell Jonah we're finally going to look at the drainage problems." He reached inside his greatcoat and pulled out the purse he brought for Samuel's care. "For this month," he said.

He didn't wait for Jenna's thanks. He did what a gentleman would do. He chased after Reverend Willis's stubborn niece.

CHAPTER 2

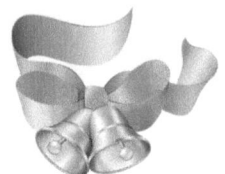

"The family would be grateful, Declan, if you would refrain from making a spectacle of yourself in the village."

Irene's voice grated on Declan's nerves more than usual. He'd had a difficult afternoon, and he wasn't in the mood for his sister-in-law's imperious dictates or contemptuous tone. He had promised Rod he would stay a month to see to the drainage in the lower fields, but he had no idea how he could bear his brother's wife that long.

Irene glared the length of the dinner table. *She's just warming up. Any moment now—*

"It is bad enough you humiliate us with your insistence on dabbling in trade. You could at least refrain from lowering behavior here where our neighbors might see or hear."

And there it is. It always comes back to my business, as if building bridges were one of the deadly sins. He clenched his teeth against his usual defense of honest work, but couldn't resist one retort. "I should think you would be pleased that I don't require an allowance from the estate. I know Roderick is."

Irene looked as if she had bit into something vile. *She hates it that I don't rely on an allowance from the estate. If I did, she'd have leverage to make me dance to her tune, like she does Rod.* He pitied his older brother.

170

Roderick might be Baron Rockledge, but Irene controlled the purse—and her husband.

"But trade, Declan! They titter behind their fans at the assemblies. As if that weren't enough, word of your bastard has reached the Marchioness of Oglethorpe."

Declan's eyes flew wide. *They think Samuel is mine?* He glanced at his brother who seemed to be fascinated with the blancmange and jam in front of him, eyes resolutely down. *I suppose it was inevitable. Let them think it.*

"Oh yes, Declan. Don't look shocked," Irene went on, becoming more agitated. "Do you think I don't know you visit the Mullins farm to pay for his care? Lucy Maguire delighted in telling me that piece of information. The entire county enjoyed the salacious gossip after your last visit. I can hardly show my face for shame. When the squire's daughters came for tea, they attempted to pry details from me. All I could do was lament our family scapegrace. The entire county knows, Declan. You've not made any effort to hide it."

Declan stabbed into his pudding, and tossed it into his mouth. It tasted like sawdust. He glared at his brother, who refused to look his way.

Irene ignored them, wrapped up as she was in the sound of her own voice. "And now you attempt to ruin the vicar's niece in broad daylight in front of the entire village."

That got Declan's attention. "I beg your pardon, Irene. How could I ruin the lady? I drove her home in the sleigh. She was attempting to walk home along the icy road, and I feared for her safety."

"You were seen!" Irene shook with indignation. "A farmer saw you force her—force her—into your vehicle, and her covered with mud. Were you rolling on the ground? Have you no shame?"

The stubborn woman required a bit of convincing. It was hardly coercion! "That's enough, Irene. Berate me all you choose, but Miss Willis is an innocent. Draw in your claws and leave the woman alone."

"I suppose I'll be forced to dine with them," Irene huffed, baffling Declan by her turn of mind.

"Why is that, my dove," Roderick asked, puzzled enough to join the conversation at last.

"To deflect any scandal, we must put on a brave face. We will have to attend services on Sunday. Declan will behave like a gentleman for a change, while you and I greet the vicar civilly. We will invite him to bring his niece to dinner, thereby showing we have nothing to hide. That should silence the gossips."

"Or set them off," Declan retorted. "They'll have it I'm courting the woman. I won't put her in that position. What will happen when I leave?"

Irene flicked a signal to the butler and rose. "As to that, I suggest you take your bastard with you. Miss Willis will have to brazen it out. Unless, of course, she is the mother of the creature. Then you can continue your illicit affair in Glasgow. I am decided on it. You must remove the little by-blow." She turned her penetrating gaze on her husband who visibly cringed. "Roderick, I insist you force Declan to do just that. I will leave you to your port."

She sailed out the door, which closed behind her silently on perfectly oiled hinges.

Roderick gave a shuddering sigh. "Really, Declan, must you set Irene off over dinner? It quite ruins my appetite."

"Me? She lies in wait to bait me so she can have reason to lament my sad lack of respect for my status in life. She hasn't forgiven me for evading her attempt to marry me to the Marquis of Oglethorpe's youngest."

"The chit came with a hefty dowry. You could have given up that foolish start of yours and lived like a gentleman."

"My business isn't a 'foolish start.' I build things, Rod; things that will last. I would go mad sitting on a piece of land watching peasants till it for me while their families go hungry. At least my business pays workers a decent wage, and gives me a sense of worth." Sometimes Declan wondered how he and his brother came from the same family. From the look on his face, so did Roderick. "About the baby—" he began.

"I don't suppose you would oblige Irene and remove the infant from the area," his brother murmured.

An angry retort came to Declan's lips—several of them in fact—but most would be pointless. "His name is Samuel," he insisted. *Our father's name.* He stared into the rich ruby liquid in his glass and went on, "I would take him, if I had a house and a way to care for him, but I have neither at the moment."

When his brother didn't respond to his dig about the boy's name or argue about moving him, sorrow sat like a rock in Declan's belly. "Still, it might be better all around," he said, "if that is what you prefer. I could oversee his care more easily." He met his brother's eyes. "And I would have no reason to come back here again," he added softly.

MAERA WIGGLED to find comfort on seat cushions lumpy with age. She rode in a lumbering old sleigh—borrowed for the occasion from Mr. Macaulay, the village physician—and sighed. Her uncle handled the ribbons, leaving Maera to her irritation.

"Really, Maera, you act as though I'm carting you to your doom. We're responding to a dinner invitation, not a writ of execution," Reverend Willis said.

"That woman looked at me as if I might soil her hem," Maera complained.

"The Baroness Rockledge has a haughty edge, I'll grant you," her uncle answered.

"An edge? It is a wonder the entire shire doesn't bleed when they encounter her sharp tongue." She took a breath. "The Baron seemed harmless enough. Why do you suppose they invited us?"

"She told us—due to your unfortunate accident. They wish to make amends. Mr. Alworth appeared genuinely regretful."

"The arrogant miscreant probably regrets that he has to endure dinner with me."

Her uncle chuckled. "You two do seem to strike sparks off each other. I found him to be a perfect gentleman when he brought you home, and quite charming on Sunday."

Maera puffed out her cheeks. "I might find him more 'charming' if he didn't leave that darling boy in the care of strangers. Samuel is precious; he shouldn't have to suffer for his father's misdeeds."

"Really, Maera, I thought you were too wise to believe all the gossip you hear. Jonah Mullins tells me his lordship fusses over the boy and never fails to pay for his keep." He raised a hand to stop any retort. "Enough— One other thing I want you to remember. The church in Little Hocking is a poor one. We rely on the baron and baroness's good will. I need you to charm the woman."

It might be easier to charm a snake, Maera thought, but Uncle David meant well. His work mattered to him and to the people of Little Hocking.

"I will be on my best behavior," she said just as the sleigh pulled up to Rockledge Manor. A man skipped down the steps to open the door. A familiar voice and equally familiar laughing brown eyes greeted her. Mr. Declan Alworth held out his hand. "May I help you down?"

To refuse would be churlish, and Maera had demonstrated enough of that sort of behavior in their first encounter. "Certainly, Mr. Alworth. I thank you," she said as sweetly as she could, causing the fascinating lines at the corner of his eyes to deepen in amusement. *He knows a bouncer when he hears one*, she thought.

He led her to a perfunctory greeting by Lady Rockledge and bored inclination of the head from the baron. *A person could freeze to death in their company*. The Honorable Declan appeared a model of openness and warmth by comparison, wretch though he might be.

Conversation in the drawing room proved as brief as it was awkward. When weather proved all too brief a topic, Reverend Willis asked after the baron's two sons, both away at school. Neither parent seemed particularly interested.

Maera breathed a sigh of relief when they were called to dinner. The baroness took her place at the head of a table too long for five people, so long she had to raise her voice to speak—or, as Maera thought, *make pronouncements*. It could hardly be called conversation.

The baron sat at the other end; Uncle David next to him. That left Maera marooned in the center across from Declan Alworth.

As a footman served the soup course, the baroness announced, "You will find the dinner more refined than you are used to, I fear. Our chef has superior skills and an excellent reputation."

Maera found the soup over spiced and unpleasant.

"Not as good as Jenna's rabbit stew," Mr. Alworth murmured, eyes alight.

Maera bit her lips to keep from laughing. The baroness didn't notice; she continued her lengthy discourse on her chef's *bona fides*, from the duchess who praised his béchamel sauce to the countess from whom she coaxed him away. She seemed eager to particularly point out those ladies jealous of her success.

The subject lasted well past the meat course, leaving Maera free to concentrate on her plate, avoid Alworth's dancing eyes, and wonder what her father and the baron found to say to one another.

When the footman cleared the cheese course, she was relieved and grateful to have only two savory dishes to choose from. She had feared the miraculous chef might have produced a dozen, but then the guest, a mere vicar, hardly demanded his best efforts.

A pointed announcement that, "Young ladies today do not know how to dress," an outright insult to Maera who wore her second-best gown, a simple rose muslin with lace at the neckline, launched Lady Rockledge into a long catalog of the young women of the county, critiquing each one's poor taste and fashion *faux pas*.

The diatribe drew a pained and—to Maera's surprise—sympathetic glance from Mr. Alworth, but the baroness droned on.

Maera absently accepted an iced cake from the footman, her mind absorbed in trying to picture the gentleman across from her with the tiny baby she had held just that morning. Jenna claimed he came often, and Maera had begun to believe it. She was so lost in thought that a demand from the baroness left her in the uneasy position of not knowing the original question.

"You will, of course, say yes," the woman demanded.

One did not say no to a baroness, particularly this one, but Maera had no idea what she was being asked to do. The intense expression on Mr. Alworth's face gave her no clue. Her uncle and the baron waited expectantly for her answer. She could admit she had not been listening, but the consequence of that could be unpleasant.

"Yes, of course," she said, hoping it had to do with parish charities.

"Of course," the baroness echoed, diving into her cake, for once blessedly silent.

Declan Alworth peered at her curiously, his eyebrows raised. "I will pick you up at the vicarage at one tomorrow," he said. She blinked. He narrowed his eyes. "For our outing," he said. "To the castle ruins."

Her heart dropped to her feet. "Of course," she mumbled. "Our outing."

CHAPTER 3

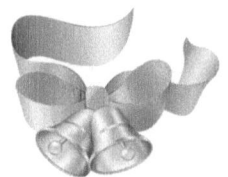

*D*eclan half expected the lady to beg off. It had been obvious Miss Willis wasn't listening when Irene instigated a ride out with him. She'd been trapped, but when he arrived promptly at one, she didn't even keep him waiting, as any of Irene's fine friends would have.

A plump little maid answered his knock at the vicarage, but Miss Willis herself emerged from the parlor immediately with her cloak over one arm and a fur muff in the other. She wore a mauve gown chosen for warmth that still managed to bring out the color in her cheeks. He wasn't sure if she flattered the gown or the other way around. Either way the result was pleasing indeed. He found her appearance striking, out of the common way, and utterly attractive.

He bowed and helped her with her cloak. When he led her outside to his waiting vehicle, she cast the thing a skeptical glance. "Another sleigh?" she asked.

"My brother's second best, unfortunately. Irene needed the good one to pay calls," he said with a grimace. The shabby sleigh was more farm vehicle than proper conveyance. He handed her up. "I considered bringing my curricle," he went on as he jumped up beside her. "But the roads…"

"Is that one safe?" she asked warily.

"It is fast," he replied.

"That isn't what I asked. You may remember I've already had a sample of your driving."

"Why, Miss Willis, I do believe you are teasing me," he said as his team trotted out of the village. "Shall we see what this old thing can do?"

She glared at him. "Even I know the road is pitted from our erratic weather in addition to the snow, and I don't believe for one moment you would risk those lovely horses," she said indicating the pair of bays.

"You have me there, ma'am. They are mine, not the baron's, and they were a bit of a luxury. I prefer to keep them in good health. They got me here from Glasgow in good time, and I need them to take me back in three weeks."

That subject exhausted, they rode silently as they tooled along at a moderate pace.

"What did she say to you?" he asked giving voice to one of the things that had worried him the night before when Irene and Miss Willis left the men to their port. "My sister-in-law, I mean."

"That's plain speaking!" she responded.

"Yes. I prefer it. It is one of the things I like about you." *Ah, a smile at last. Plain speaking it is!*

"Since you asked, and prefer bluntness—she told me you needed only a good woman to cure you of your wayward ways. I fear she hinted I might be the one."

The face he made must have been ugly, judging by the way she winced. "What did she say made up my wicked ways?" he asked.

Miss Willis stared at her lap. "She didn't."

He refused to mention Irene's beliefs and attitude toward Samuel. He let out his breath. "I am sorry. My sister-in-law has no guard on her tongue. Plain speaking is one thing; manipulation is another, and I fear she forced you into this outing. I regret that she put you in such a position. She hopes to see me wed because she believes I will stop disgracing the family by dabbling—her word not mine—in trade. I am an engineer, Miss Willis. I hope that doesn't offend your delicate sensibilities."

"You work for your living? How marvelous!"

He grinned. "Why, Miss Willis, I am shocked. Surely, you don't believe a gentleman should dirty his hands in actual labor—and I assure you I do. I don't hide behind my desk."

"Why ever not? Too many ancient houses are headed by men unwilling to work and desperate for funds."

"Forced to marry money or starve?"

"Is that what happened to your brother?"

"You are as shrewd as you are beautiful," he said bringing a delightfully rosy blush to her cheeks.

"She controls the finances, I suspect," she said.

"Yes, and she controls my brother as a result. It irritates her no end that I earn my own living and owe nothing to the estate so she cannot control me as well. She's doomed to disappointment. Fool that she is, she doesn't see that a wife will want keeping and the work will become even more necessary."

"I'm impressed Mr. Alworth. And you pay for your son's keep as well."

"Samuel?" he choked. The truth stalled on the tip of his tongue.

"Of course, whom did you think—" she gaped at him for a moment and then sank back against the seat, obviously embarrassed. "He isn't your son."

Shrewd indeed. "He is in every way that matters." Declan actually hadn't thought of it before, but once said, it felt right. Rod would never claim the boy, not while his harpy of a wife stood over him. The lad deserved a father who cared.

"But you are not his sire," she mused. "Who is?"

"There are limits to plain speaking," he replied, leaving her to her own conclusions when he changed the subject. If the shire didn't know Roderick fathered the boy, it wasn't Declan's place to unleash the gossip. It wouldn't be fair to Samuel. "Have you been to the castle ruins before? Your Uncle David seemed to indicate you had not at dinner last night."

"He is correct. Aside from throwing us together, why did Lady Rockledge suggest the ruins?"

"To impress you with my consequence, of course, by showing you our ancient roots in this county. Our family built the old stone heap sometime lost in the mist of ages past. I always suspected she was sorry the castle fell down. She would have liked to hold court over a castle rather than a mere manor house."

They turned onto a narrow lane leading uphill. "Come, Miss Willis, prepare to be impressed—if not by the collapsed glory of my ancient pedigree, then perhaps by the brilliant explanations of a structural engineer."

CHAPTER 4

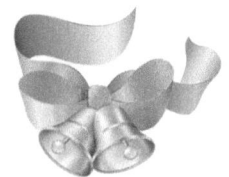

*M*aera smiled from the window when the baron's sleigh came to an easy stop in front of the vicarage. Second-best it might be, but perfect for today's purposes.

The Honorable Declan—that is, Mr. Alworth—walked around and smoothed a hand down the neck of first one horse and then the other, speaking to each in turn. When two village boys ran up to see the horses, he gave each a penny to hold his reins.

Goodness! The man is as kind to his beasts as he is to everyone he meets. Ever since their ride out he had become "the honorable Declan" in her mind because she suspected it described him exactly. He had rescued and paid for the care of a baby not his own. He refused to reveal the boy's actual sire, although Maera had her suspicions, and he treated everyone regardless of age or station with respect. He also behaved as a perfect gentleman toward Maera. *Honorable indeed.*

She hurried to the door, not waiting for him to knock. He grinned broadly when the door flew open. "I do like a lady who doesn't keep a gentleman waiting," he said, studying Maera from the tips of her serviceable half boots to the scarf she wound around her chin on top of her cloak until she felt her cheeks heat and she feared her face had gone a blotchy red. He winged an arm. "Shall we away then, since you are so anxious for my company."

He helped her into the sleigh, climbed up, and pulled a carriage robe over her. She waited until he took the reins to deflate his overblown self-worth. "I'm actually anxious for another gentleman's company," she said pertly.

"You wound me!" he retorted, giving the team their head with no sign of any actual distress. "You find younger gentlemen perhaps more to your liking?"

"Indeed."

Some of the gentlemen in question, Jenna Mullins's sons, waited for them in the farmyard.

"Da says we're to help you fetch greens for the church," Thomas, their oldest, called before the sleigh came to a stop. All three boys appeared delighted with the prospect.

"You are indeed," Maera told them. "But I need a cuddle from little Samuel first." She began to step down on her own, but the boys' sister Peg, who came out the door bundling up her cloak, overheard and dampened that idea.

"Samuel is sleeping, Miss Willis. Good thing, too," she said casting a victorious glance at Thomas and climbing into the back of the sleigh, "because Mam says I can come fetch greenery too." The boys scrambled into the bed of the sleigh behind her.

Declan's eyes twinkled. "Well, that's that, then. Shall we go, Miss Willis?"

She sank back into her seat with a sigh. "Lead on, sir."

Many hands might have made short work of gathering greens, if not delayed by flying snowballs, excuses to run up and roll down the hillside around the castle grounds, and much hilarity in the process.

With the sleigh almost full of branches, Maera followed Peg slowly up the hillside, delighted by a stand of holly they found. They clipped sprigs full of berries steadily until a well-aimed snowball hit Maera between the shoulders. Peg gasped and Maera turned slowly to see the honorable Declan attempting to look innocent while three boys peeked from behind trees giggling. She leaned over and whispered in Peg's ear.

Maera settled her best school mistress face on, pressed her hands together primly, and stepped slowly but deliberately toward Declan, with Peg following behind, hidden in Maera's skirts. The three boys slipped out of hiding, wide-eyed and watchful, as she came within five feet. With a savage whoop Peg leapt out from behind Maera, hit her brother Thomas square in the chest with one snowball, and just clipped Jake's ear with another. Maera, meanwhile, darted between the trees scooping up snow, Peg on her heels, and the battle was on.

"Not fair four against two," Peg shouted.

The ladies watched while the boys—Maera viewed Declan as an overgrown boy in this case—conferred. Waving Mr. Alworth's white handkerchief, Jake plodded toward them having been the loser of their consultation.

"Mr. Alworth said a man must do the honorable thing," Jake moaned.

"Come on, Jake, let's take them down," Maera shouted, turning the boy's face from downcast to gleefully fierce. She watched Declan kneel to show Davie how to make the best snowball and her heart turned over when he ruffled the boy's hair and lifted him to throw it over the bush where Peg and Jake hid. The man winked at her and then threw one of his own, right at her shoulder.

"Foolish man, I have armaments at the ready," she called pelting him with three in a row,

It wasn't long before all six of them, convulsed in laughter, exhausted, and covered in snow, agreed to call truce. "Until we can resume another day," Declan said, with a smile Maera thought he intended just for her.

The boys helped pick up holly branches and load them in the sleigh. Declan ordered them to sit on the sides, their feet among the greens, but Peg objected.

"What about mistletoe? Won't there be a kissing bough?" she asked hopefully.

"Not at the church! My uncle would find that inappropriate," Maera sighed.

"Do you need one at the manor?" the girl asked Declan hopefully.

"I fear the baroness disapproves of bringing the forest into the house," he said, shaking his head in disbelief, likely, Maera thought, for the benefit of the children.

Peg looked so downcast Maera wondered what village boy she hoped to catch under a kissing bough. *Thirteen is a difficult age.*

"Tell me, Thomas, does your mother object to mistletoe?" Declan asked.

The boy scowled with distaste. "No. Fact she had Da bring some last year and the two kissed the lot of us under it."

"Luckily, I know the best tree," Declan said.

Moments later he lifted Jake, who climbed up like a monkey and dropped a large cutting of mistletoe down to them, before climbing back down and jumping into Declan's waiting arms.

"Well done, lad!" Declan said, scooping up the sprig and eyeing Peg with a teasing glint. "Shall we test it out?" Thomas and Jake backed away and broke into a run toward the sleigh, gagging dramatically. Davie stood wide-eyed and watched.

Peg stared up at him, stars in her eyes. "No, Mr. Alworth. I'm but a lass. Best test it on Miss Willis."

"Declan…" Maera began when he made a predatory move in her direction. She took one step back only to come against the tree trunk. He came forward until his face was within inches, raised the sprig of mistletoe over her head, and studied her face carefully.

He means to kiss me. Maera couldn't think clearly in that precise moment, but she rather thought she wanted him to. She stood frozen in place. Suddenly he winked mischievously and darted in to kiss her cheek.

"It works well. Your mother will be pleased," he said casually, handing the mistletoe to Peg.

Behind his back Maera let out the breath she had been holding and steadied herself.

"Don't encourage him, Peg," she rasped. "Some men are horrid teases." And this tease would likely haunt her nights.

DECLAN SAT across from Jonah Mullins in the cozy kitchen, let the fire's warmth seep into his bones, and sipped Jenna's hot chocolate, while the hum of excited children recounting The Great Snow War to their mother filled the air.

He listened to Jonah with half an ear. His eyes, his mind, and a growing piece of his heart occupied themselves entirely with the woman who sat in the corner cuddling baby Samuel. Maera's serenity and joy filled his soul. The kiss had teetered on disaster. When he leaned in to peck her check he meant only to tease, but desire over-whelmed him and froze him in place. He thanked whatever angels guarded fools that he came to his senses before he embarrassed the woman in front of the children.

"Has he not spoken to ye?" Jonah's conversation deserved all of Declan's attention, and he pulled his mind from the soft curve of an arm around a little one to the man across from him.

"My brother has spoken to me of little except the drainage in the lower fields, the one area where I am of some use."

"We're going to dam the burn, then?"

"Not dam it; divert it, and set up a drainage pond. That will keep that strip of land you hold beyond it from flooding, and give several tenants more arable land as well. I'm proposing a bridge to enable you to bring in the crops with less trouble too. Come out with me when I check my calculations, and see if I've missed anything."

"He'll raise the rents."

Again. The word hung in the air. Mullins farmed the same bit of Alworth land his father and grandfather had. His father and Declan's dealt fairly with one another, and the Mullins family prospered. Since Rod assumed the title five years ago, relations had not been the same.

"Probably. Let's hope higher yields make up the difference." There was nothing Declan could do about it in any case except try to improve the land when asked. Maera nodded over Samuel's head, and he realized with a start she had been following the conversation. Her approval gratified him.

"It's that sorry we are you're gone to Glasgow, Mr. Declan. You are sorely missed," Jonah said.

"Will all your boys want to farm, Jonah? Or will you send one to apprentice with me in time?"

"Me, Da!!" Jake interrupted. "I want to be a builder." At nine he was yet a bit young but it wouldn't be long. Declan wondered if Jonah could spare him.

"Someone has been appropriating all my snuggle time," Declan said rising to his feet. He reached for Samuel, and she gave him over without objection. The boy had grown in the past month.

Declan rubbed his nose in Samuel's hair and then bumped nose to nose. The baby reached up and grabbed the scarf tied loosely around Declan's neck. "Oh no, you don't," the man said, repeating his words in a silly voice until he drew a smile and a giggle from the boy.

Maera pretended upset. "Fickle. The lad is fickle."

"He loves his father best," Declan said, drawing a gasp from Jenna. He looked at her sharply, realizing what he said and opened his mouth to speak, but shut it.

"Or at least the man who is as good as," Maera put in, smoothing the moment. Jenna smiled and went back to her cooking, the moment gone. "As much as I'd like to linger, we best get the rest of the greenery and holly to the church before dark," Maera went on.

Peg came up to take the baby, "Afore you go, Miss Willis, may I ask something? It's about the pageant," she said shyly.

Christmas Eve was two days away, and Peg had the central role in the pageant this year; Mother Mary herself. Maera couldn't imagine what the girl wanted. "Of course, dear. What is it?"

"I've been thinking. We practiced and practiced with that little rag doll, and here's this perfect baby. Why can't Samuel be the Christ child?"

Jonah chuckled and Jenna, Maera, and Declan gaped. "Would it work? What do you think, Jenna?"

"If you mean his behavior, I'd say if he's dry and fed, yes, it would work. He's an easy baby. But Mr. Declan, we've not had the boy to church yet." Jenna watched him warily.

What will the congregation think of a parentless child? The thought hung in the air.

Maera spoke first "Why not? I should think my uncle and the congregants would love a real baby." She looked from one to the other. "In any case, he'll be the most innocent person in church."

Wise as she is beautiful, Declan thought. "That settles it. Samuel, you are going to star in the Christmas pageant." He kissed the boy and handed him to Peg.

CHAPTER 5

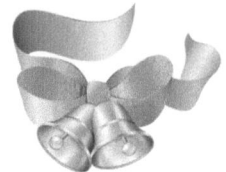

*T*he next two days flew by. Between decorating the church, tidying the vicarage, helping with baking, and rehearsing the pageant with the children, Maera should have had no time to think about Declan Alworth. Except he insisted on carrying in branches, climbing ladders, and hanging greens around the ceiling of the little stone church, an exercise that required removal of his coat to reveal muscular shoulders when he stretched up to hang garlands. Except he decided to bring the Mullins children to practice. Except he stayed and let baby Samuel nap in his arms. That sight and his smile sent her to bed each night considering mistletoe and what might have been if Peg hadn't been close by.

It is a wonder my thoughts aren't entirely scrambled. The day arrived, however, without disaster, and Maera walked over dressed in her warm mauve wool, the one that made the oh so honorable Declan's eyes light up. She came along the side of the church but stopped around the corner when she heard his voice.

"It matters to the tenants, Irene. My brother's presence matters, and therefore so does yours," Declan said. "I wish your boys had come home for the season."

Maera couldn't make out the baroness's irritable sounding retort, but the woman's voice rose when they reached the door of the church. "Really, Declan! Pine branches? Rather pagan isn't it? How does the vicar permit it? Oughtn't frivolity be saved for Twelfth night?"

Not frivolity—joy! Maera bit her lip to keep from speaking. She paused a moment and then came around in time to see the children marching over from the bakery where they had gathered in the assembly room above it. Her heart lifted at the sight of crooked angel wings, shabby shepherds, and kings in paper crowns. She pulled them all into the vestibule with a finger to her lips, allowing room for smiling latecomers to scurry by.

At a signal from Uncle David, Martin Carpenter, the baker's elderly father, raised his fiddle, and a hush came over the church.

To the sound of his playing, the children processed down the aisle and took their places at the front. Thomas—solemn, as Joseph—led Peg by the hand. He carried a bundle slung over one shoulder, meant to look like luggage. Maera breathed a prayer that the little angel inside it would stay quiet in the short distance from vestibule to altar.

She let out her breath when they arrived without incident and he set his "bundle" behind the cradle, hopefully uncovering the baby's face as she told him to. The congregation, too busy chuckling over Mickey Fuller's enthusiastic. "NO! There's no room in the inn," didn't notice. But when Thomas responded, "But my wife is expecting a baby..." Samuel let out a squawk. Peg leaned over to pick him up and Uncle David leapt in with "And she brought forth..."

Peg stepped back and knocked the cradle over, the snickers turned to laughs, and the girl began to weep. Thomas, ever the gentleman, righted the cradle, took Samuel and laid him in it. "And we'll put him in a manger," he said. "The cows are happy to oblige."

By that time, Maera had slipped down the side and urged her angels to sing, which they did with good heart, almost loud enough to be heard over a crying baby. Maera gestured to Peg to pick him up. The girl obliged, sitting gracefully down on the altar step as they had planned and cuddling Samuel on her shoulder until he popped his fingers in his mouth and stopped crying, allowing the kings to make their hasty entrance and the entire cast to make their bows to raucous applause.

The children trailed out and Jenna Mullins herded them back to the assembly room while Uncle David kept caroling and sermon brief.

Maera stood by her uncle on the steps greeting the joyful congregation that exited with congratulations and happy stories about pageants past. "Always some excitement," Mr. Carpenter told her. "It's what they expect. Little ones are a joy."

Maera's smile froze at the sight she saw over Mr. Carpenter's shoulder. The baroness glared at her and swept up to the vicar. "I assume you were not aware that the creature foisted on you for this farce of a pageant is base born. My brother-in-law's mischief is a disgrace." She didn't wait for an answer. She pulled in her skirt, and flounced toward the baronial sleigh—the good one, Maera noticed.

Staring after the departing sleigh, Maera realized the baron didn't wait for Declan either.

"I'm sorry for the disturbance, Reverend Willis." His deep voice reverberated through her as he spoke behind her. She turned to see her uncle shaking his hand, sympathy in his expression.

"We've had worse, Mr. Alworth. Children are always unpredictable. This bunch carried on admirably."

"I believe he meant the baroness, Uncle," Maera said.

Uncle David's eyes twinkled. He knew full well what Declan meant. "Well, she is one for denying folk room at the inn. I'll give you that."

Declan relaxed at the vicar's words and offered her his arm. "Shall we congratulate the angels and their crew? The Carpenters promise biscuits and cider," he said, by way of invitation.

Soon the sound of fiddles and laughter drove ugly thoughts away as Maera watched children dart about, old friends share greetings, and Declan Alworth smile at the festivities with Samuel nestled on his shoulder. Most folks seemed to view little Samuel with compassion as the blessing he was. It took an aristocrat—and a petty, mean one at that—to fuss about a baby's bloodlines in church.

A FEW DAYS LATER, with Boxing Day gone, trouble struck and Declan's mood sank.

"I'm that sorry, Mr. Alworth, but the baron gave me no choice." Jonah Mullins's distress as he described the baron's threat to put him out if his family continued to care for Samuel added to Declan's growing anger.

Declan swallowed the string of curses that leapt to his lips. The outrageous threat—Irene's no doubt—eradicated what little respect that remained in Declan's heart for his brother. Only care for Jonah Mullins gave him strength to hold on to his self-control.

They had come out to examine their flood prone areas, stream flow, and Declan's proposed site for a drainage pond when Jonah pulled him aside. Three other men, Roderick's tenants every one, stood in embarrassed silence some feet away pretending not to listen.

Every word will be repeated in the pub tonight and passed on to wives and sisters before bed.

"He said little Samuel offended the baroness's 'delicate sensibilities' on Christmas Eve, and he has to go. She won't have him in a tenant cottage. Didn't he tell you the same?"

"No, he did not." *The coward.* "Tell me again how much time he gave you?"

"Twelfth Night," Jonah said morosely. "He said the boy must go or —" the farmer bit his lip. "He said he'd raise the rents so high my family would be out on the road."

"Eight days. About a week," Declan murmured. "Not even enough time for me to get to Glasgow, make arrangements, and come back." He glanced over at the embarrassed faces under the tree. "No one else in Little Hocking will dare take him."

Jonah shook his head sadly. "No, Sir. I expect not. We've enjoyed the boy, me and Jenna. We'd happily keep him, but I can't afford double rents or worse—eviction. I have my children to think about."

Declan clapped a hand on Jonah's shoulder. "It isn't your fault—it's the baroness. Thank you for telling me right away."

"Can't you talk to your brother? Change his mind?"

"My brother and I speak of little besides drainage," Declan answered and the truth of it sank like a stone to his belly.

"I wish—"

Declan gave Jonah a sharp glance, guessing what he meant. Since Roderick's lady had provided him with two sons, there was no hope of Declan inheriting and improving the lot of the barony's tenants. The boys always seemed decent enough to their uncle, but the way they were alternately spoiled, abused and neglected, the tenants might not be any better off when the eldest's time came.

"This wouldn't have happened in your Da's day, Mr. Declan," Jonah went on.

"No, it would not have. He was a man of kindness and compassion." *What in God's name happened to my brother?*

Declan shook with the force of an indrawn breath. "My brother and I are overdue for a talk. You're right about that." He turned on his heel and walked to his horse grazing in the meadow.

"Mr. Declan," one of the men called, "Aren't we going to see about the drainage?"

He turned the horse's head toward the manor. "My brother will have to see to his own fields," he shouted back, regret for the fate of Roderick's tenants choking him.

CHAPTER 6

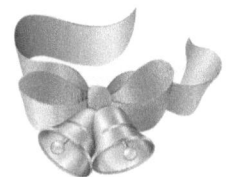

$\mathcal{M}$aera knew she ought to go but, distressed as she was over Jenna's news, she couldn't make herself rise. She stared at the sleeping baby.

"But surely another family can be found," she said again.

"Not in Little Hocking. They'll run whoever tries it out o' their homes. Her ladyship wants the little angel where she can't see him, and that's no lie," Jenna told her. "Poor mite. Not his fault."

The baroness thinks he's her husband's by-blow, Maera realized. She could see in Jenna's face that she knew it too. *The woman feigns outrage to deflect attention. She ought to aim her anger where it belongs—at the baron.*

"Then we'll have to take him at the vicarage," Maera said decisively.

"And have your uncle lose his position?" a deep voice bellowed.

The women spun around to see Declan in the doorway, removing his hat. Jake took it and his scarf too.

He strode toward the women with a thunderous expression, softened only slightly by the sight of the sleeping baby. He turned a chair around backward and straddled it.

"You must have figured out by now, that my sister-in-law has determined to banish Samuel from the neighborhood. I won't have you putting the reverend's position in jeopardy."

"Your brother can't be as unreasonable as that! Can't you talk to him?" Maera pleaded.

"Since I just left him nursing a black eye and my sister-in-law in hysterics, I'm not even sure I'm welcome back tonight."

"What did you do?"

"I reminded him of his responsibilities."

Maera darted a glance at Samuel.

"Yes," Declan said. "Samuel as well. I believe the reply was, 'don't try to blame your carelessness on me.' He's a damned poor liar." He peered up at their hostess. "Sorry, Jenna," he mumbled.

"Don't you go apologizing to me, Mr. Declan. You've done your best for the boy. Is it the orphan asylum?"

"Good God, no! I'm taking him to Glasgow. It is for the best. If he stayed here, Irene would poison his life. Her venom would do him more harm than my brother's neglect."

"But can you manage it, Mr. Alworth?" Maera demanded.

"Given time, very well. I planned to take him as soon as I had a house, and... someone—a nursemaid and a nursery. I haven't had time."

A wife. He needs a wife. Maera thought. *No nursemaid will work in a bachelor establishment.*

He must have seen her dubious expression. He ran a hand through his hair, mussing it. "I'll manage. I'll have to, won't I? I came here to ask Jenna to make him ready to travel. Pack his belongings and—" He waved a hand in the air. "Things."

"You can't possibly mean to—" Maera began.

"Can you have him ready tomorrow first light, Jenna? And perhaps take time to write notes for me about feeding and such?"

"Alone? How are you even going to travel alone with a little one? Are you going to stop every hour to change him? Feed him? You can't —" Maera's agitation grew with every word.

Declan studied her solemnly. "Come with me," he said.

His words knocked her back on her heels. She gaped like a fish.

Jenna glanced from one to the other. "You ought to take a woman, Mr. Declan, that's no lie, someone to care for the boy, but no respectable unmarried woman will travel alone with a man."

"I'll have to hire a less respectable one. Someone at a coaching inn looking for a few coins."

Maera gasped.

Jenna shook her head. "I know you're a good man, but folks will talk. You'll make the lad's situation worse, you will." She turned her gaze pointedly on Maera. "The man needs a wife, and I'm not afraid to say it."

Silence lay thick in the cottage until Jenna rose and shooed her children out the door. "We'll just go see to the stock. In the barn," she said, shutting the door on Maera and the honorable Declan.

Maera felt herself go hot and then cold. She suspected her face had become a mass of red blotches. "Jenna can't mean you ought to snatch a wife up off the village street, anyone who comes along."

"Not just anyone, no," he murmured. "She has a point though. I thought of asking Peg to come as nursemaid, but Jonah would have my head."

"You asked me to come," she reminded him.

"I spoke without thinking. If you leave with me, Irene will have it about that you are Samuel's mother and my—" He broke off, but Maera understood his intent.

"She'll say I'm your mistress."

"You won't be able to come back, and your uncle will suffer for it."

Maera stared at her lap unseeing while she ran all the choices through her mind over and over finding no way out. She looked up at Declan who seemed as troubled as she.

"Jenna is right. I need a wife. You could marry me," he said. He rushed on, gesturing with one hand, before she could reply. "I know it isn't the proposal a woman dreams of, but we get on well, don't we? I would make a faithful husband and—and we'd have Samuel." His hand moved toward Maera as if to touch her cheek, and then fluttered to his lap.

Maera glanced at the baby who stirred in his sleep, and couldn't hold back a smile. *Samuel. Yes*. The idea that she could be his mother warmed her heart.

Declan went on, trying to cajole her now. "I confess I don't have a house—I just never got around to getting one—but I will. It won't be a manor house; just enough for a family, children."

Children. Plural. Everything marriage entailed came crashing in.

Her distress must have communicated itself to her face—because Declan leaned closer. "I'm sorry this is all so fast. Come to Glasgow with me. We won't rush this marriage business, at least after the vows are said. You can stay in my apartment above the shop while I look for a house and then we'll see."

Does he think it's the house that matters? Maera opened her mouth to tell him what he could do with his ridiculous proposal, but the words would not come. Samuel needed her. How could she say no. *Dear God I've only known this man for three weeks. How can I say yes?*

Declan ran his hand through his hair, the now familiar gesture making him even more attractive, which didn't help her state of mind. She lay awake nights thinking of his kiss as it was. She had to be rational about this.

"I've upset you," he said, "And I'm sorry. It was a ridiculous impulse. I have to take Samuel away from here before more people get hurt. I'll be taking him in the morning. If you think of any solution to my problem before then, I'll be grateful. If not, the lad and I will manage on the road. We'll figure it out, he and I." He touched the little one's foot under the blanket with a gesture that melted Maera's heart to a puddle.

When he looked at her under thick lashes, she suspected he knew exactly how attractive he was. "You haven't told me no outright. Will you at least sleep on it? I leave in the morning. If you don't come, I'll have my answer."

Maera nodded. "I'll think of little else," she said. "How can that woman be so cruel to an innocent child and her husband's tenants? Has she no heart?"

"None that I've noticed," he sighed. He rose to go. "I have to gather my belongings. I want to finish my drawings for the drainage project. Jonah can handle it if the baron allows it."

Even in distress he still thinks of others... He's a good man, gloriously attractive and... Maera shook her head to clear it. "You said you wouldn't be welcome back. Where will you sleep?"

"My brother's stables," he said with an attempt to grin. "Simon, the head groom won't give me away, and he'll help me sort my curricle and team. I'll break in after dark and fetch my belongings."

"You're leaving your childhood home," she said with sudden insight.

"No. Not anymore. It hasn't been since my father died and Rod married Irene. I prefer to stay away."

He left her there next to the baby, as confused as ever. *Sleep on it, he said. How does he think I will manage sleep at all?*

THE LAD OWNS LITTLE ENOUGH, Declan thought, as he tied the bundle of blankets and baby gowns next to his trunk on the boot of his curricle. *I'll fix that as soon as we settle in.* He placed the parcel of nappies and a jug of milk mixed with gruel under the seat up front. A wooden box Jonah nailed together lay on the floor next to the driver' side and the wooden rattle he'd given the boy lay on the seat. He made a quick prayer of gratitude that at least the weather had turned and the roads improved.

Jenna stood in the shelter of the farmhouse, with little Samuel in her arms, bundled against the cold, worry in every line of her face. Declan flashed her a smile he intended as reassuring and checked the bridles and harness, though he needn't have. Old Simon knew his job.

He leaned his head against the neck of one of the horses, patting its side and garnering strength from the unruffled animal. Maera hadn't come. Any doubts he had about how badly he wanted her evaporated when the sun rose and she did not appear. He doubted he would return to Little Hocking, and he likely would never see her again. The hole in his heart throbbed. *I didn't even say a proper good-bye.*

Leaving the shire proved more difficult than he had claimed the day before. He grieved the loss of the brother of his childhood, but would not miss the man his brother had become. Other folk would be harder to forget. *And Maera...*

"Thank goodness! I was afraid we were too late." The one voice he knew he would miss flew like an arrow across the farmyard.

She stood at the edge of the lane clutching a portmanteau, anxiety marring her expression, and time stilled.

She came and the portmanteau means— "You're coming with me!"

Her smile wobbled but her answer was firm. "Yes. Samuel and I are coming."

The paralysis that had frozen him in place at the sound of her voice lifted and he reached her in a few strides. "Let me take that from you," he said, sucking in a breath when he realized Reverend Willis stood behind, her frowning deeply.

"This is bad business," the vicar said.

"I know I'm only a younger son, but I can support her, believe me. My business prospers. I will take good care of her."

The old man waved his words away. "I know you have the finances, and I had hoped the two of you might make a match, but not like this, not this rushed affair." He gestured toward Samuel with his head. "Bad business treating an innocent baby this way, driving him— and you—out of your home, and in winter too."

Declan took one of Maera's hands. "We'll make a new home. A good one," he said fiercely.

Reverend Willis stood a little straighter. "See that you do—by special license if you can, or banns if you must, but as soon as possible once you reach Glasgow," he said, his voice harsh.

"No need," Maera said softly, shocking both men. She glanced from one to the other. "It's Scotland, isn't it? We don't need a license. What did you think I meant?"

The vicar looked as relieved as Declan felt. *She plans to go through with it. She's going to marry me.*

Maera shook her head and thrust the portmanteau into his arms. The assured, determined woman had reemerged. "You best get that stowed so we can be on our way if we don't want to wander the road north with a baby any later than we have to."

Declan stood rooted to the spot holding her bag while she accepted Jenna's hug along with the swaddled baby. She frowned at his curricle, a vehicle better suited to racing than family transportation, he realized. "I hope that thing makes up in speed what it lacks in comfort," she said. Her raised eyebrow sent him scurrying to help her up and tie on the bag, while she tucked the little one into the box under woolen shawls.

"You didn't bring much. Even Samuel has more," he muttered, pulling the rope tight.

"Uncle David will send the rest; he has your direction."

He watched the sky as they drove out the lane and onto the main road. "Early yet. We should be in Scotland by nightfall, the Good Lord willing."

CHAPTER 7

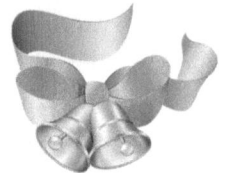

"We can't go on much longer; I fear for him in the cold," Maera told the man at her left shoulder. Little Samuel lay nestled against her breast inside her cloak, his woolen shawls over both of them, but still she shivered. Her feet felt like blocks of ice. It had gone full dark, and fear added to her distress. Visions of nighttime road hazards—from brigands to unseen obstacles—taunted her.

"I know this stretch of road. There is an inn coming up soon," Declan replied.

"We should have stopped at the last inn," she mumbled.

"Still England," he replied.

"Why does that matter?"

"When we stop and I declare you to be my wife, I want it to be true —or as near as— lest you have repercussions."

"So that's it? We'll stand in front of some innkeeper and declare ourselves married?" He didn't immediately reply, and another thought struck Maera. "For it to be real don't we have to... complete it?" Even in the frigid wind her face heated.

"Not in some traveler's inn. We'll see a minister when we get to Glasgow and do the thing properly, and we'll 'complete it' as you put it in a warm bed in our own home. But for tonight, for the benefit of the inn folk, we'll declare it, yes."

Long excruciating minutes later—probably less than half an hour in actuality—they pulled into a coaching inn. Declan tossed the reins to a hostler, lifted her, still holding the baby, and carried her into the common room, sat her by the fire and demanded hot cider "for my wife."

He knelt next to the chair and took one hand, rubbing warmth into it. "I have to see to the team. I won't be long. They carried us over thirty miles today, and need their rest as well, if they're to take us the rest of the way."

The innkeeper's wife bustled over, a mug of mulled cider in hand, to coo over the baby. She pulled a wide stool over so Maera could lay him down and free her hands. "Welcome to Gretna," the woman said. Lowering her voice to a whisper, she asked, "Be you wed actually? Willing?"

She assumes—but they must see eloping couples often. Maera couldn't formulate an answer. Willing? Yes. Wed? Perhaps not yet. She nodded silently sipping the welcome warmth.

"You best get papers witnessing it for the little one's sake," the lady advised. "I kin tell you the best place."

Maera found her wits. "We plan a church ceremony in Glasgow," she responded.

The innkeeper's wife sighed deeply, patting Samuel's foot. "After the fact is better than naught. Do y'trust the man?"

"With my life." Maera didn't even hesitate. Declan would keep his word.

A stable hand brought Samuel's bundle of necessities just as the boy began to wake, fussy and irritable. The inn found milk, and they showed her to a room with a warm fire, heavy quilts and reasonably clean sheets. She quickly changed him, adding the wet ones to the oilcloth bag Jenna had thoughtfully included, lay his shawls near the fire to dry, sat on the edge of the bed, and began to help him take the milk.

Declan came up after what seemed an eternity, carrying the

makeshift cradle from his curricle, and Maera's heart lifted at the sight of him. The innkeeper followed with a tray of hot stew, warm bread, and cider. He put it on the table and bowed out.

"Is he well?" Declan asked.

"As can be. Warm, dry, and fed. We're managing," she responded.

Declan put the cradle down between the bed and the fire where it would be warmest and she would hear him. He fell to his knees next to the bed.

"I'm so sorry," he murmured.

"Whatever for?"

"Putting you and Samuel through this."

"I think blame lies with the baroness," she replied.

"I could have stopped sooner. My pride—"

"Your *care* made decisions difficult. We're here and no harm done."

"We can slow down now, and take the rest in easy stages," he told her.

"Now that I'm your 'wife?'" she asked.

"We'll make it formal, I promise, but yes. There's no going back, Maera."

"No," she sighed. *As if I'd want to.* She reached out and brushed his hair back. "You look exhausted."

"You as well. I'll go back down and sleep in the taproom," he said.

That made her laugh. "Won't that undermine your declaration of marriage?"

He grinned up at her. "Perhaps. But I promised you we would not consummate this marriage on the road and I meant it." His eyes, black and intense, drew an answering warmth in Maera. "Lying with you—being here—I'll struggle to keep my word."

She wanted to tell him not to be so noble, but common sense told her he was right. Rumpled, dirty, exhausted in a lumpy bed near a fussy baby—all of it doused any romantic feeling. Her respect for the man grew.

"Stay with me," she said impulsively. "Sleep on top of the covers if you want. We're both too tired to get up to anything anyway."

He started to shake his head no, but conceded she had a point.

They went to bed fully clothed after Samuel went back to sleep and they had devoured the hot meal. Declan arranged the quilts for maximum privacy in a narrow bed.

Maera curled to her side on one edge next to the cradle, Declan's back to hers, and wondered how she would endure his closeness without touching him.

"How long?" she whispered in the dark.

"Long?"

"I should say how many days—to Glasgow that is?"

"In easy stages, four..."

It seemed an eternity but she knew they couldn't maintain the pace, not traveling with a baby. "Let's do easy stages," she replied, but she heard his breathing even out and thought perhaps he slept.

A baby's cry and a shaft of sunlight woke her after what felt like mere moments. Maera flopped over onto her back to find herself staring up into dark eyes and a warm smile. Declan leaned over her on one elbow and brushed back her hair with his other hand. "I like you by me," he said, his voice husky.

I like it too...

Before she could say the words, his mouth met hers and she lost herself in his kiss, reaching up to put her hands around his neck and tug at the hair curling in the back.

She gasped for breath when Samuel's cries became frantic and Declan pulled away. "I'd call that a promise," he said hoarsely before rolling over and standing. "Can you manage Samuel? I'll see to ordering breakfast."

DECLAN'S easy stages stretched into noon of a fifth day. His relief at the sight of his business premises almost equaled his concern about the impression it made on the travel-weary woman at his side. "I warned you it was my workshop," he said.

Maera's smile could have been stronger, but she didn't complain.

God bless the woman, she never complains. He'd slept in the stables at coaching inns the last four nights, unable to stand the temptation of having her close, and she didn't try to argue with him. The babe had become increasingly fretful with erratic feedings, bad weather, and strange beds. Now that he had them home, he promised himself he would make it better.

He helped her down and led her through the door to what had been his entire world a month ago, but which appeared little enough with Maera at his side. On the other side of the door was a counter with open workspace behind it. The door to his office lay to the right and beyond it, the stairs to his apartment, his tiny entirely inadequate apartment.

"Declan!" his foreman called. "Well met. You didn't warn us you were com—" The man's voice fell off when he spied Maera. The other four men laboring behind him stopped to gape as well. As if seeing them for the first time, he wondered what Maera made of the dirty, smelly crew of builders. There would be more. Men came in and out between this place and the work site.

"Soon-to-be-Mrs. Alworth, may I present my foreman, Frank Price." Still gaping, Frank touched his forelock and dipped his head. "And behind him Charlie, Arnold, Hamish, and Ian." They did the same.

Finding his voice, Frank said, "Welcome," swallowed deeply, and said more forcefully. "Congratulations!" He came forward to shake Declan's hand. "Is this the wee one you had in foster?" he asked peering down at Samuel. Blessedly Declan saw not one sign of judgment or even speculation in the man's eyes.

"It is, and this miraculous woman has agreed to help me improve the lad's circumstances. Let me see them upstairs, and then I need your help. Ian, be a good lad and see that some hot water is brought up, would you now?

He led Maera toward the stairs where she surprised him. She reached the third step and stopped, forcing Declan to stop with her. She turned to look down at the men who had followed her every move with astonished stares.

"It is good to meet you, gentlemen," she said. "I can see why Declan is proud of you. Thank you for your congratulations." Their wonder fed his pride in this marvel who would be his wife.

She gazed around his sitting room. The tiny kitchen in its alcove, just visible through a pair of curtains, always seemed adequate to him, but now… "it isn't much, I know."

"It's clean and warm. We'll be comfortable here. We can take our time about the house." She smiled up at him. "There is room for Samuel here."

He sagged with relief. "The bedroom is through there," he said pointing to a door, and I've a copper tub hanging on the wall if you want to, ah, bathe." The word seemed to stick in his throat. "Ian's fetching water."

"I'll need to do laundry soon too. Samuel went through all his clothes and nappies."

Nappies. One more thing to worry about. He ran his hand through his hair absently nodding. *Where does a man buy a woman a dress to be married in? And a ring?*

"I'm going to find a minister who will marry us quickly. Will tomorrow be too soon?" he asked.

She frowned. "Would he do it today, do you think? We promised Uncle David as soon as may be possible."

His heart galloped in his chest, and her glance toward the bedroom door didn't help. "I can ask," he rasped. "You make yourself comfortable."

He left her then, his mind wandering in circles about rings, flowers, and how fast he could hire a laundress.

CHAPTER 8

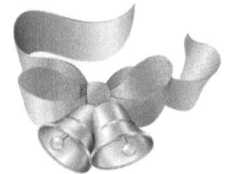

*H*ot water proved a blessing. Declan's workers carried their bags up as well, and two hours later Maera felt more human. She had bathed, washed her hair, sponged her rose muslin dress, and shook out the wrinkles. The workroom below had gone silent. She wondered if they'd all gone off to the worksite he mentioned.

She wandered about the rooms, unpacking and tidying. Where the workshop appeared neat and bustling, his rooms looked sadly neglected and lonely. She'd soon fix that.

Clean rags in Declan's tidy little kitchen proved excellent nappies, and Maera found one clean gown for Samuel, a pretty thing Jenna had embroidered blue flowers on, one she suspected had already dressed more than one Mullins child. Once he was fed and clean, she wished Declan would see him before he needed to be changed again, as babies do. She tied his bonnet under his chin.

As if conjured by the wish, she heard Declan bang through the door and take the stairs two at a time to burst into the room. Her heart soared at the sight of him, and Maera wondered if she would ever grow used to it.

"It's set. I hope you're ready. The minister wishes to do it now," he told her.

She felt like he devoured her with his eyes, sending a jolt of pleasure through her.

"What did he say?" The words were thick in her throat.

Declan feigned an irritable face and put on his best Scots brogue. "'Tis better to marry than to burn in Hell. Best do it quick, Sassenach…"

They laughed together at that, and she knew it for the blessing it was. Their life would have laughter.

"What are you carrying?"

"I almost forgot. Nappies," he said putting them down on the table.

She laughed again. "Not precisely a young girl's dream of a wedding gift, is it Samuel?" she said rubbing the baby's nose with hers.

"Perhaps this is better," he said handing her another package, taking the baby so she could open it.

She gasped at what it held. "Declan, this feels like silk!"

"I hope so. That's what I bought."

She held it in front of her. The blue, green, and mauve exactly complemented her dress. "It is beautiful," she breathed.

"I thought you ought to have something beautiful for your wedding," he said sheepishly. She threw her arms around him, baby and all, and kissed him fiercely. "Did I do well?" he whispered against her mouth.

"Oh yes," she whispered back, and she kissed him again, only to have him pull away.

"I need to change my clothes. You and Samuel will show me up." The bedroom door vibrated with the force of closure.

He emerged in a fine black jacket, the white of his cravat and shirt gleaming above an embroidered waistcoat. Only his boots spoiled the picture of the perfect upper-class gentleman.

"I haven't had much use for fancy shoes or dancing slippers lately," he said by way of apology.

"You are a vision of perfection to me, Mr. Alworth," she said.

"And you are a vision of all that is beautiful to me, soon-to-be-

Mrs. Alworth," he replied. They grinned at each other like fools. She pulled her shawl around her shoulders and picked up her cloak. He tucked the baby in one arm and gave his other to the bride.

She stepped down into the workshop to see that Declan's men had returned wearing clean shirts and wicked grins. A plump little woman introduced to her as "Mrs. Frank" clapped her hands in delight.

They all trooped after her to the kirk where the dour old minister heard their vows and unbent to bless her with a twinkle in his eye. He made sure they signed two copies of the marriage lines, one to send to her Uncle David in Little Hocking.

When they walked back home, Maera was astonished to discover the counter in the workroom covered in a linen tablecloth with a vase of flowers at either end. A cake had place of honor in the middle, watched over by three Price children under orders from Mrs. Frank who seemed to be the mother hen of all these men. Someone managed to find a bit of brandy and soon a jolly party ensued.

Samuel was handed from person to person and the boy proved to be as friendly as he was bright. He sagged at last in his new father's arms, sound asleep.

"There now," Mrs. Frank announced to one and all, "We've worn out the wee boy, and I suspect our bride is dead on her feet as well. Get you gone now."

The men all began to leave, shouting their final congratulations. The cheerful little woman reached up and took Samuel from Declan. "Frank and I will take this little treasure home for a night or two. Don't you worry Mrs. Alworth. We can take care of him."

Declan reached behind the door and handed Frank the package of baby things. Before Maera could object, the Prices were gone and they were alone.

"You conspired in that!" Maera said leaning into Declan's shoulder.

"She offered," he said, kissing the top of her head.

She turned in his arms until they were face to face, their breaths mingling. "Are we well and truly married now?" she asked.

"We will be very soon," he replied, "But there's something I forgot today."

Her head jerked up. "What can you have forgotten?"

"To tell you something important."

She opened her mouth to say something else and he silenced her with a finger. "Before we do this, you need to know that I love you." Her eyes flew open, but he continued without letting her speak. "I think I loved you since I peered down in that ditch and you demanded to be rescued. I'd have taken the time to court you properly if I hadn't been forced to leave."

"Is that all?" she demanded.

He nodded, unable to speak.

"Good. Because I love you too. I think I've loved you since the first time I saw you holding Samuel." Their matching grins surfaced again. *This is going to be a happy home.* "And if you don't mind," she said, "could we go up and get on with being married?"

He kissed her first, as deeply and possessively as he'd wanted to for weeks, scooped her into his arms, and started up the steps. "I don't mind, Mrs. Alworth. I don't mind one bit," he murmured, nibbling her ear.

THE END

ABOUT CAROLINE WARFIELD

Caroline Warfield has been many things. Now in at least her third act, she works in an office surrounded by windows where she lets her characters lead her to adventures in England and the far-flung corners of the British Empire. She nudges them to explore the riskiest territory of all, the human heart. Love, after all, is worth the risk.

Find more books by Caroline Warfield here: https://www.caro linewarfield.com/bookshelf/

While this little story stands on its own, most of Caroline's novels or novellas inhabit one of two shared universes. Her *Dangerous Series* (set in the Regency era) and her *Children of Empire* series (set in the Victorian era, and many of her novellas share characters. *Duke in All But Name*, (released December 2022) introduces the *Entitled Gentlemen* series, which shares the world and characters of *The Ashmead Heirs* series. The two worlds may yet collide.

SOCIAL MEDIA FOR CAROLINE WARFIELD

You can learn more about Caroline Warfield at these social media links:

Website: http://www.carolinewarfield.com/
Goodreads: http://bit.ly/1C5blTm
Facebook: https://www.facebook.com/groups/WarfieldFellowTravelers
Twitter: https://twitter.com/CaroWarfield
Email: warfieldcaro@gmail.com
Newsletter: http://www.carolinewarfield.com/newsletter/
BookBub: https://www.bookbub.com/authors/caroline-warfield
You Tube: https://www.youtube.com/channel/UCycyfKdNnZlueqo8MlgWyWQ

ZARA'S LOCKET

BY JUDE KNIGHT

A run-in with the adult son of the household leads to dismissal for governess Zahrah ibnit Yousef, or Zara MacLaren as the household knows her. Turned out on a Christmas Eve, her circumstances go from bad to worse when she is robbed and then arrested.

Goldsmith and jeweler Simon Marshall recognizes the locket a young aristocrat tries to sell, and it leads him on a hunt for Zara, the friend of his childhood. He finds her. He finds trouble, too, and joins her in her incarceration.

They need a Christmas miracle. It will take a pair of charitable gaolers, a little Christmas cheer, and the timely intervention of family to bring this story to a happy ending.

This story is dedicated to Zara Heflin, who won it as a prize. She gave me three ingredients, and I wrote this story to include them: a spirited heroine who is loyal to those she loves and adores animals and books, the friends-to-lovers' trope, and a locket.

CHAPTER 1

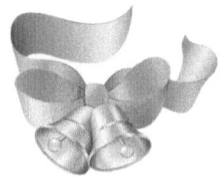

*S*omeone had wrecked the small windowless room the Strickland household provided for the comfort of their governesses.

At first, Zahrah was inclined to blame her charges. The three children currently consigned to her care were hell-spawn—encouraged in their defiant disobedience by parents who chose to believe them angels, and to ignore any evidence to the contrary.

However, even their most strenuous efforts to chase her away had resulted in nothing worse than frogs in her shoes, mud puddles in her bed, and a bucket of slops balanced on a door. And their behavior had improved since she began telling them stories at bedtime on any day in which they had all three attended their lessons and displayed the manners they had formerly trotted out only with their parents and their older brothers and sisters.

At the moment, with Christmas approaching, she had an extra carrot to offer them. The Strickland family did not decorate for Christmas, but Zahrah had asked and received permission to decorate the nursery and schoolroom. The children were looking forward to it, and so was Zahrah. It would make up for not being with those she loved for the festival.

Zahrah sorted her way through the mess. Her mirror broken. Ink thrown onto a watercolor she had tacked to the wall. Her clothes not just tossed around, but ripped apart. Worse still, pages torn from her few personal books and other pages defaced with splotches of ink.

This was not the children. They lacked the strength for such destruction. And they didn't, she was certain, hide this degree of spite.

It could have been a servant, she supposed. They were stand-offish and unpleasant, but none hated her, or had cause to.

The wooden box her brother had made and given her for her last birthday lay in pieces, its contents gone, or hidden in the clutter, perhaps. The bits and pieces were mostly worthless to someone else. Cheap pieces of jeweler suitable for a governess, most of them with happy memories of the person who gave them to her, or the occasion on which she bought them. The latest letter from her mother, set aside for a rereading. A button that she had not yet had time to sew on a cuff.

And her locket. That was the one item she hated to lose. Her father had commissioned it for her sixteenth birthday, and she had worn it daily ever since. She had only taken it off because the catch had been broken in the scuffle with Gerard Strickland.

The oldest Strickland son had been brooding for the past two weeks, ever since his ambush on her had resulted in a threat to his person, backed up by the knife she always carried. Yes, and he had been muttering threats when none of the other Stricklands were around to hear.

She had taken no notice. What could he do, after all?

Well. Now she knew.

She looked at the piles she was forming—a large one of rubbish and smaller ones of items for repair. The few bits and pieces her intruder had left undamaged, she put on her dresser ready for packing. The loss of her locket was the last straw.

She had negotiated a truce with the children. She had ignored the hostility of the servants, the rudeness of the family. She had also ignored Gerard's suggestive comments and evaded his wandering hands, until he lay in wait for her one evening and she had to use her knife to threaten that part of his anatomy that seemed to do most of his thinking.

"I will release you if you promise to leave me be," she had told him. He had tearfully demanded her promise that she would not tell his father. She already knew there was no point in complaining to the nasty cockroach's mother. Lady Strickland would take her eldest son's part if he were caught assassinating the King. Lord Strickland was more reasonable. However, she had agreed. "If you keep your word, I will keep mine," she said.

Which meant she was now released to do what she should have done in the first place.

But downstairs Marsh, the snooty butler, informed her that Lord and Lady Strickland and the young sirs and ladies were out for the evening. Ah yes. A Christmas Ball at the manor of the Earl of Brent and his lady. The two elder daughters of the household had been talking about it for weeks.

No point in staying up, then. Here in the country, people often stayed out until first light, when the roads were safer for the horses.

Zahrah asked the butler to find Mrs. Giltawny, the housekeeper. "I want both of you to meet me at my room," she said. "Someone has destroyed my things, and I wish for witnesses to see the damage that has been done."

Marsh sniffed. "I daresay the children would be glad to see the back of another governess," he said, his tone suggesting that, in Zahrah's case, he agreed with them.

"I was with the children all day," Zahrah told him. "I went directly from their bedsides to find my room in chaos. I have an idea who is responsible, and will share that with you shortly. Now fetch Mrs. Giltawny, please."

He sniffed again at her tone of command, but did as he was told.

His supercilious mien dropped away into a void of shock when he and Mrs. Giltawny arrived.

"I started tidying so I could see what could be salvaged," Zahrah explained. "This pile is beyond repair." She lifted the closest item, the remains of a pair of stays, slashed with something sharp until it was barely recognizable. Marsh blushed as he averted his eyes.

"It was never one of the maids," Mrs. Giltawny insisted, and Marsh chimed in. "Nor any of the men."

Zahrah agreed. "None of the servants, I agree. And not the children, either. I strongly suspect that the person who did this was seeking revenge because I rejected his advances."

Mrs. Giltawny immediately leapt to the same conclusion as Zahrah. "Mr. Gerard."

"Surely, Mrs. Giltawny, a gentleman like Mr.—" Marsh began, but Mrs. Giltawny spoke over him. "Now then, Mr. Marsh, you know as well as I do, I have to send out the maids in pairs when the young master is at home, and when the mistress dismissed the last governess, she was in the family way. She said it was Mr. Gerard, and all the mistress had to say was she must have asked for it, but I don't believe it, not ever so, for he never waits to be asked, and that's a fact."

A fact Zahrah would have appreciated knowing. Though—to be fair—she had seen Mr. Gerard as a threat from the first time he'd leered at her and asked her to read him a bedtime story.

"If you would, Mrs. Giltawny, I would like my trunk fetched so I can pack," she told the housekeeper.

Mrs. Giltawny gave her the first friendly smile Zahrah had seen since she entered the house. "I don't blame you, dearie. Have somewhere to go, do you, and a bit laid by?"

That was the rub. She could, of course, return home. And if she told her father why she had not seen out her first quarter, he might never allow her to take another position. He had argued against her taking the first one, five years ago. He had pointed out, quite accurately, that she had no economic need to work.

She had retorted that her need was emotional. As daughter of a duke's governess and the man the ton saw as his steward, she did not fit into the world of nobles and gentry. As Zahrah ibnit Yousef ibn Ahmed—Zahrah daughter of Yousef son of Ahmed—she had no place among the servants. Her father was vizier and best friend to the Duke of Winshire and her mother, Patience, was the lady to whom the widowed duke had entrusted the rearing of his younger children.

Her younger brother Jamir was making his own way in the world. She demanded the right to do likewise. So, she anglicized her name to Zara, took on her mother's surname, and accepted her first position.

Zara MacLaren had been a governess for the past five years. Her first post had ended when her students left her; their father had been posted to Portugal. The next two had been temporary contracts. This was the fourth. Retreating to the family home in Shropshire after only two months with the Stricklands felt like a defeat.

However, that was merely pride speaking. She would not stay where she was not valued; where she was attacked and her things pillaged. She would pack and be ready to leave as soon as she had given her notice to her employer and told him exactly why. Or, at least, as soon as she had wrested her locket from his appalling son.

CHAPTER 2

*T*he young man arrived ten minutes before closing. Simon Marshall pegged him as a gentleman by his arrogant bearing and his clothing—on the flashy side of tasteful, but clearly expensive. He was a seller, Simon decided, rather than a buyer. Whereas someone interested in the jewelry Simon made would look around at the tasteful displays in their glass cases, a person with items they hoped to sell checked first that no-one who might know them was lurking anywhere in the shop.

Simon's heartfelt sigh at the interruption to his evening was entirely internal. He could hear his mentor's voice as clearly as if the old jeweler had stood at his shoulder. "Today's seller will become a buyer on the turn of a card. Be respectful, but don't be taken in, Simon. Most of what they want to sell is trumpery, and some of it is stolen."

Sure enough, the young man—Simon guessed in his early twenties—took a quick turn around the shop, glancing across the displays with no interest, and came to a restless stop in front of the counter and Simon.

"Good evening," he said, with a smile that was meant to be charming but didn't reach his eyes.

Simon inclined his head politely. "Sir," he replied.

The man frowned and cast another glance around the empty shop. He lowered his voice. "I was told you buy jewelry."

"Sometimes," Simon admitted. "If it is of adequate quality and demonstrably not stolen."

The flinch was minute, and Simon would have missed it if he had not been looking. "Nothing of the sort. No, indeed." The man's eyes drifted to one side, staring over Simon's shoulder as if to seek inspiration. "It's my mother," he decided, and the small tension lines around his eyes relaxed as he decided on his story. "Gambling debts, I'm afraid. I promised to sell a few of her trinkets. On the quiet, you understand. Wouldn't want the pater to come down heavy on the old dear."

The smile with which he finished was a touch anxious.

Simon could tell an outright lie when he heard one. However, before he could formulate the words to turn the man away, his visitor pulled a handful of chains and beads from his pocket, dumping them on the counter and going back to fish for more.

"Take a look. Tell me what you think. How much you will give me?"

Simon's rejection froze on his tongue as his eyes were drawn to one item. There could not be two such lockets in all of England. It was a standard two-part round locket cast in gold; two hinged sides fastening together to enclose the contents. The central decoration within the jeweled frame of each circle set it apart. Where one might expect flowers or swirls or other such decorative motives, the marks etched into the gold were—or so he had been told—phrases in Arabic. On the upper side, a quote from a Persian poet "Everything you want, you already are." On the rear—he turned it over—the owner's name. Zahrah ibnit Yousef ibn Ahmed.

He traced his finger over the name, remembering a golden summer in Oxfordshire, the summer after he finished school, before the breach with his uncle. The Duke of Winshire owned a nearby estate, and was making an extended visit with his retinue. The cottage where Simon had lived with his nurse since he was a baby was close by. The unwanted

225

bastard of an earl's unwed sister, he lived more than a mile from his uncle's house but less than five minutes' walk from that of the duke.

Only ten minutes from the village, too, where he had for years spent every minute he could steal away with the local metalsmith, learning to make fine goblets and delicate jewelry.

Simon had first met Zara at the lake that marked the boundary between the two properties. She had been fifteen, two years his junior and hovering between school room and drawing room. Her dark hair and bronzed skin set her apart from the pale English beauties of her age, as did her ambiguous social position—neither gentry nor servant in a world that ranked everyone and treated them accordingly.

One misfit to another, he and Zara had become friends. She had introduced him to her brother, her mother, and the two youngest sons of the Duke of Winshire, whom Mrs. MacLaren had raised with her own children. The lessons he had learned in that family's charmed circle of welcome had given him the courage to strike out on his own path.

He had fallen more than half in love with the beautiful maiden who made it all possible, though he knew better than to risk his new friendships by showing it in any way.

The gold locket had been her sixteenth birthday present from her father, and was the first commission Simon had been trusted to undertake on his own. He knew every detail of it as well as he knew his own name.

How did this noxious dandy get Zara MacLaren's locket?

"A pretty piece, is it not?" The man was shifting uneasily from one foot to another, every now and again shooting another look over his shoulder to check that the shop was still empty.

Simon came out from behind the counter, turned the door sign to 'closed' and locked the door. "There. Now we shall not be disturbed." He smiled as he prowled towards the man who had Zara's locket.

Alarm flared in the eyes fixed on Simon's, but the fool gulped down his own disquiet to demand, "How much will you give me?"

Simon smiled, hiding his disquiet and his anger behind an affable facade. "It all depends. Let us discuss it over a drink." He rounded the counter and reached beneath it for a bottle of brandy and two glasses. He kept it for indecisive buyers, who relaxed over a drink and found it easier to make up their minds.

The idea certainly appealed to this would-be seller, who nodded eagerly before questioning Simon's response. "What do you mean, it depends? Do you want this stuff or not?"

Simon led the way to the small sitting area, and the man followed him, or rather the bottle he held up as a lure. Simon poured two fingers-width into a glass, and the man watched the golden liquid as if it promised life itself.

Simon managed to make his voice deceptively mild, though his emotions were anything but. "How did you come by the items, Mr. er... I don't think you mentioned your name?" He put his hand on the glass closest to the man, and left it there, as if he had forgotten to lift the glass and pass it over.

"Strick— er. Yes. That's it. George Strick."

He hadn't taken his eyes off the glass, and Simon pushed it over.

Simon pretended to take a sip from his own glass, and explained, "I have to ask, you see. If anyone brings in items to sell, I need to ascertain their provenance. I'm sure you understand."

Strick, or whatever his name really was, tossed back his brandy and held out the glass for more, even as his eyes shifted so they did not meet Simon's. "I told you. They're my mother's."

Simon nodded, as if accepting the patent lie. "It is just that there have been a number of jewelry thefts near here, and the constabulary are watching the jewelers. We have to account for every item that passes over our counters." His own lie, he flattered himself, was delivered with far more confidence, the key to believability.

Strick paled, and cast a panicked glance at the door.

Simon pulled a rueful grimace and filled the man's glass. "The fools have stirred up a wasps' nest, that's for certain. Stealing from people with powerful connections. I hear the Bow Street Runners have sent a couple of their best men down. Any thief with any sense won't be stealing within one hundred miles of here. And if they have taken anything, they won't be trying to sell it."

Strick proved his title to idiot of the year by standing. "I'll just be going, then. Since you don't want to buy."

Simon filled the man's glass again. "Don't be in a hurry," he coaxed. "There are always ways, you know. After all, a man needs money to live, and I daresay your need is greater than," he raised one eyebrow and said, with a twist of his lips, "your mother's."

Strick settled back into his seat and gulped down his third brandy in ten minutes. "You have that right," he complained. "The way I see it, the silly bitch owed me, coming on to me like that then stopping me from taking what she promised. She pulled a knife on me! Can you believe that? A bloody servant!"

Simon sternly suppressed the urge to punch the rest of the information out of the piece of obnoxious pond scum. In a straight fight, he would win. But unless he killed the man, act two of this play would be Strick complaining to the law, and Strick was a member of the gentry while Simon was a merchant.

His unsupported word would not be believed, and Strick's would. It was as simple as that.

He continued to ply the man with alcohol and teased the story out of him a bit at a time, right down to his real name and the address at which Miss MacLaren served as governess to the younger children of the parents who had raised this turd.

Six glasses in, Simon helped Strick—Strickland, rather—out the door, and across the road to the inn where Strickland had taken a room. "Don't you worry about a thing," he assured Strickland, for perhaps the third or fourth time. "I'll look after the items for you, and pay you what you deserve as soon as it is safe to do so."

"You're a good man for a commoner, Marshall," Strickland said, attempting to slap Simon on the back, but slipping off balance.

Simon resisted the urge to let him fall flat on his face, and instead gave him a shove that propelled him across the inn doorstep and halfway into the common room, where he fell into a chair and sat slumped, a silly smile on his face.

"Mr. Strickland might need some help up to his room," Simon told the innkeeper. The man had become something of a friend over the four years that they'd worked on opposite sides of the street. "Is there any chance you could find a way to keep him here for a couple of days? And do you have a horse I can hire? He has stolen from a lady of my acquaintance, and I need to check that he has not left her in dire circumstances."

"You should call the constables," the innkeeper advised.

Simon shook his head. "He is the son of a lord."

The innkeeper grimaced and expressed his opinion in a foul oath. He narrowed his eyes at Simon. "But you're not letting it go, are you?" he asked. "Whatever you're planning, you're grinning about it."

"I think you will enjoy the joke," Simon agreed. "The defenseless governess he chose to assault had a knife she knew how to use. She threatened his ability to father children and he backed off, but stole from her in revenge. What he doesn't seem to know is that she has powerful connections, and I'll get a letter away to them before I leave Birmingham."

He laughed as Strickland slumped further in the chair and began to snore. "Strickland might as well enjoy the next couple of days sleeping off the brandy I poured into him. You and I might be cautious about assaulting the son of a minor lord. But the lady is the goddaughter of a duke, and grew up with two of his sons. If they give him the beating he deserves, the weight of our unfair system will be on their side." Actually, Simon was not certain that 'goddaughter' was the right description. But the duke certainly stood in place of an uncle to her.

Simon itched to deliver the miserable scum sucker to the duke and see justice administered. But the more urgent need was to reach the Strickland manor. He had to return Miss MacLaren's locket, and satisfy the burning compulsion to see she had not been harmed by the actions of this immoral sprig of the nobility.

His imagination was feeding him a lurid carousel of scenes. Zara cast penniless from the house. Zara handed over to the law for accusing the son of the house of theft. Zara alone and friendless.

The innkeeper looked Strickland up and down. "If he attempts anything with one of my girls, I'll finish what your lady friend started," he warned. "Come on. I'll make sure you have the horse you need."

While the horse was being saddled, Simon hurried back through his shop, catching up the discarded jewelry as he passed the counter on the way to the back room and the stairs to his room, where he threw a change of clothes into a bag.

From what the villain said, the ride to the Strickland manor took around six hours, but that was in daylight and the sun had already set. Travelling at night would be slower and more dangerous. A wise man would wait until morning.

Simon changed into riding breeches and boots and hastily wrote a note to Miss MacLaren's father, and a second to the Duke of Winshire. He grabbed a warm coat, muffler and gloves. He'd have need of them before morning. Within ten minutes of leaving Strickland to the questionable mercies of the innkeeper, he was clattering back down the stairs to send his letters on their way and take the horse to rescue the lady.

CHAPTER 3

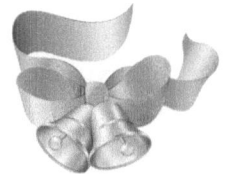

*Z*ahrah trudged down the muddy road towards Market Bosworth, where—or so she had been told—she could catch a coach to Birmingham and then a further one in the direction of home. One for Shrewsbury would be ideal. Her money would not stretch indefinitely. She'd retrieved the pouch she'd taped under her bed and added to it one month's worth of pay, reluctantly disbursed by Lord Strickland.

The limit on her funds was the reason she was walking. She had no idea how many nights' accommodation she would require on the road, and the trip from Shrewsbury to her father's manor would mean either hiring a conveyance or paying for a room and waiting for someone to fetch her.

The morning had started with an unpleasant interview with her employers, during which Lady Strickland had loudly protested her son's innocence (and therefore Zahrah's guilt) and then succumbed to hysterics.

Lord Strickland had hustled Zahrah off the premises, refusing to allow her to say her goodbyes to the children. He paid her half what she was owed, grumbling all the while that he truly owed her nothing, for she had provoked his son and then lied to get the poor boy into trouble.

If Gerard Strickland was a boy at twenty-five years of age, his father and mother were much to blame. Zahrah kept that thought to herself along with her recognition that both parents believed their son's culpability and wanted to get rid of her before she could spread the news. At least Lord Strickland's sense of urgency led him to order a groom to drive her into the village in the gig the housekeeper used for shopping.

She'd arrived to find that the biweekly coach to Birmingham had left at dawn. Rather than wait three days for the next, she had paid the inn to store her trunk until sent for and set off for the market town.

It had seemed a sensible decision at the time, with the skies clearing after the overnight rain. Not so much now, an hour and a half later and less than halfway there. The clouds had gathered again, and she could smell the rain in the air.

She had refused two offers of rides from passing carters. One had leered at her, and openly suggested she sat upon the wherewithal to pay for a ride. The other seemed innocuous enough, but appearances can be deceptive, and besides, the cart behind him was piled high with smelly manure, malodorous fragments of which adhered to his person.

Better drenched than assaulted again, she thought, as her hand crept almost without her volition through the slit in the side seam of her skirt to touch the handle of the knife strapped to her thigh.

But the driver simply touched his fingers to his droopy hat and continued on his way.

She plodded on as the skies darkened and the satchel that had felt so light when she tucked a few essentials into it at the inn dragged more and more heavily on her shoulder. *What a way to spend Christmas Eve!*

She lost herself remembering Christmases at Wind's Gate, the principal residence of the Duke of Winshire. Her father was Muslim, her mother Christian, but both enjoyed the festivities for the sheer fun of them.

In her mind's eye, she could see them and her brother Jamir in the ballroom, part of a laughing crowd making swags and wreathes from greenery collected that morning. They would have taken up residence in the rooms reserved for them in the great sprawling castle a day or two before Christmas Eve to be part of the festivities.

Perhaps they were thinking of Zara, imagining her making decorations in the schoolroom with her charges.

Instead, she was shivering in the cold wind on this interminable road. Then the rain started.

It was the kind of rain to run through. Soft, but persistent, she could have dashed from a carriage to a door and caught nothing more than a few drops to be shaken off the heavy wool of her hood and cloak. Instead, as the minutes passed, she could feel it seeping through the fabric, making first her hair and shoulders wet, and then, by increments, her arms, her back, her chest.

As thunder rolled overhead, with flashes of lightning briefly illuminating the path, she did not dare take shelter under any of the trees that occasionally dotted the landscape. By the time she saw a tumbledown cottage in one of those brief bursts of light, she was wet to the skin all over.

Even so, she approached with care. Worse things might happen to a woman alone than being soaked in a storm.

She circled the cottage, clambering over bushes and around small trees. No smoke. No light. No noise. The two small windows were too grimy to peer through. The door hung slightly ajar so she could look through into a deserted interior.

She had to lift the door to open it enough for her to slip inside. It scraped on the ground, but moved sufficiently to give her access. Inside was a single room, with a fireplace at one end and a number of objects that, as her eyes became accustomed to the gloom, she identified as fragments of wood that must once have been furniture.

They could now be firewood, she decided. She put her satchel on a peg next to the door. Using touch as much as sight, she selected some pieces that would fit in the fireplace without being further broken. A bird's nest found on the mantelpiece would suffice for kindling. From her satchel she retrieved her flint and steel. It had been wrapped in oilcloth with the book she had packed to keep her company on the coach. No chance of reading in this light!

Still, she soon had her fire going, and for a miracle, the chimney still worked. She had feared she would need to share her temporary accommodation with the smoke. With the fire to supplement what little light trickled through the dirty windows she could now shut the door to exclude the cold breeze.

Most of it, at least. Threads of icy air seeped around the edges where the door failed to fit.

Now to get dry. Zahrah managed to prop some of the larger bits of wreckage into racks to hang her clothes near the fire. Now she was no longer walking, removing the damp fabric from her cold clammy skin had become imperative. And her spare gown was nearly as wet as the one she was wearing.

Fortunately, the spare chemise was more or less dry, and so she donned that and hovered near enough to the fire to warm one side at a time until the heat from the fire finally managed to overcome the damp chill of the room.

After a while, she replaced the book in the oilskin bag and sat on it, leaning against the wall. Lightly dressed as she was, it wasn't warm enough to sleep. Probably just as well, since who knew what kind of vermin might have invaded the place. As long as she was moving, they were probably more frightened of her then she was of them. But she would hate to wake up and find a rat or a spider investigating the human who had encroached on their territory.

If only she had enough light to read by. Instead, she found herself revisiting the encounter with the Stricklands, and with their son before that. It was futile. She could not have done anything differently, apart from resigning as soon as Gerard Strickland showed his true colors. She had been so certain she had put him in his place.

Her mother would say, "Now, Zahrah, you can do nothing to change the past. Consider it only to learn from it. What could you do differently next time?"

Would there be a next time? Her father would be reluctant to let her take another post, especially if he learnt the details of how and why she left this one. Zahrah was not even sure she wanted another post. Her experience so far had done much to explain why most governesses she had met had taken up the role out of necessity rather than desire.

Zahrah enjoyed teaching, and her first position had been all she hoped for. Her students were two lively intelligent girls with beautiful manners, who were a delight in the schoolroom. She shared responsibility for them with a team of nursemaids, who took care of them from teatime until after breakfast the next day. And she enjoyed a position of honor in the household, with the servants deferring to her as a lady, affection from her students, and both gratitude and respect from the parents.

The second and third positions had been temporary. In each case, she had been appointed to fill in for another governess—one who was ill and another who had been given leave to attend a family funeral. In both cases, she had been pleased to leave.

The children in the first temporary post had been sullen and resentful. She had been fully responsible for their care day and night, except on her half-day out. She could not say what the parents were like, since neither she nor the children were called into their presence at any time during her stay. Both the housekeeper and the butler warned that the children must, at all times, stay out of the public rooms of the house and their parents' rooms. They were to be neither seen nor heard. That was only the start of a long list of rules about where they could go and what they could do. No wonder the poor things were unhappy.

Zahrah invented several games that could take them on adventures without leaving the nursery, and by the time their regular governess was well enough to take up the role again, they cried to see her go.

The second family had the opposite problem. Zahrah's charge was the heir and only child of elderly parents. They doted on him. They insisted on seeing him as frail, though to Zahrah's observation he was sturdy enough and would have been all the better for some exercise in the open air. They refused to allow him to be thwarted in any way, and employed a governess to teach him because they felt a tutor would be less sympathetic to his many crotchets and caprices.

He sulked for most of her fortnight with him, resentful that his beloved Miss James had left him, even to attend the funeral of her brother. Zahrah finally discovered his passion for painting, and the last two days were relatively pleasant.

Then came the Stricklands. Once again, she had managed to negotiate a truce with her pupils, but the servants were the worst she had dealt with so far, the parents pompous and unfeeling, and the obnoxious Gerard downright dangerous.

Though she had been promised a nursery maid, the woman was usually off doing some other tasks for the housekeeper, so that Zara was once again in sole charge of three lively children from the moment they woke until they went to sleep at night.

She had little to do with the other older children of the family—the vile Gerard and two sisters. They never visited the schoolroom to see their younger siblings, and had only unpleasant remarks to make to them should they encounter them on the stairs.

If she took another post, she would be interviewing her employers with much more care than she'd used to date!

By the time the rain stopped, she had nearly run out of small pieces of wood to feed to the fire, and her clothes were closer to damp than to sopping wet. By the position of the gleam behind the clouds that denoted the sun, she had about two hours before it was too dark to continue on her journey. She donned her damp dress and cloak, packed everything else into her satchel, knocked the dying embers into separate corners of the hearth, and exited the cottage, pulling the door as far shut as she could.

Before long her boots, which had begun to dry, were soaked through again, as it was impossible to avoid all the puddles. She continued on, encouraging herself with thoughts of a night in a comfortable inn: a warm bed, a hot meal, and perhaps even a bath.

Tired as she was and lost in her own thoughts, she did not hear the man until he was nearly upon her, leaping suddenly out of the ditch to grab at her arm. She whirled away at the last moment, but not soon enough to prevent him from ripping her satchel from her shoulder. He came after her, a knife in his hand, his gap-toothed grin indicating he expected a swift victory.

Zahrah backed away, buying herself time to unfasten and drop her cloak and draw her own knife.

He checked for a moment at the sight of her weapon. "What you plan to do with that sticker, silly wench?"

Zahrah took a fighter's crouch, narrowing her eyes. The awkward way he held the knife spoke of incompetence. She was reasonably certain she could beat him in a fair fight. On the other hand, he was heavier than her, and more desperate. She could not afford to get close enough for his weight to give him the advantage.

She let a small smile play around her lips, as she swayed from foot to foot, weaving the knife in a pattern designed to draw his eye. "Come here, and you will find out."

His grin faded and he rocked back on his heels, his voice still defiant. "I'll come 'ere all right, and give ye a poke, and that I will."

Zahrah laughed. "The last man who tried that felt my blade on his balls. Come here, and you'll never poke anyone again."

He took another step back, so Zahrah tried a step towards him. "Drop my satchel, and I might let you go in one piece." The success of her bluff was mixed. He took off at a run, but he snatched her cloak up and carried it and her satchel off with him.

It was, she supposed, a small price to pay for not being assaulted, but it was a nuisance nonetheless. She chased him a few steps for the appearance of things, but he scuttled away through the hedge faster than she could have imagined, and she stood on the road listening to the retreating sound of him crashing through the undergrowth.

She regretted losing the book, she regretted more the pouch containing most of her money. Thank goodness she had put a couple of coins under the lining of each boot. Hopefully, it would be enough for accommodation tonight and a seat—even an outside seat—on a coach to Shrewsbury.

One thing was certain, she concluded as she continued walking, it was time to set her pride aside and use some of her slender resources to send a letter to her father.

CHAPTER 4

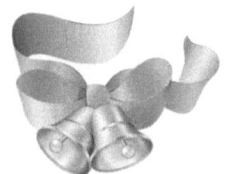

*T*hanks to rain and rutted roads, and a cast shoe in the early hours of the morning, Simon finally arrived at the Strickland manor just before noon. Perhaps he should have stopped at the inn to tidy himself, but he was driven by an impelling conviction that Zara was in danger, and he must reach her before it was too late.

He handed his horse to the stable boy who came running to meet him, took off his outer coat, and dusted his hat before walking round to the front door. It was answered by a butler who took the dignity of his position across the line into pomposity.

"Please let Miss McLaren know that Mr. Simon Marshall is calling."

The butler put his already elevated nose higher. "Miss McLaren is no longer employed in this household." He allowed himself a smirk. "She was let go this morning."

Simon shoved his foot across the doorstep and his shoulder to the door, preventing the man from shutting the door in his face. "Then present my name to Lord Strickland. Tell him I have information about his son."

The butler glared. "You will have to wait outside." Again, he tried to press the door shut.

"I will not." Simon pushed the door wider, and stepped over the threshold. "Give my message to Lord Strickland. I will wait here."

The butler sniffed, but quite rightly doubted his ability to physically remove Simon. Instead, he ascended the stairs at the back of the hall.

Simon waited, looking around and listening to noises from upstairs. It sounded as if two or more children were having a contest to see whose temper tantrum could be the loudest. Among the screams and unidentifiable shouts, he clearly discerned Zara's name. "I want Miss McLaren. I want Christmas. Bring back Miss McLaren."

Evidently, the butler had told the truth about her having left. It appeared, too, that she was not totally unappreciated in this house.

It must have been a good ten minutes before the butler returned to escort him up to the next floor. The sounds of chaos from the schoolroom were a floor or two higher, and continued unabated, muffled a little when the butler ushered him into the drawing room and closed the door behind him.

"I am Lord Strickland," said the florid man whose garishly embroidered waistcoat strained at the buttons. "What is this about my son?" He did not introduce Simon to the lady beside him, a gaunt female overdressed for a day at home in silk and ruffles.

Simon got straight to the point. "Yesterday afternoon, Mr. Gerard Strickland attempted to sell me a number of baubles and several valuable jewelry items that he admitted he stole from Miss MacLaren who was, until this morning, employed in your household. I wish to find Miss MacLaren. Can you tell me where she has gone?"

Lady Strickland sniffed. "You are mistaken. I gave my son some items to sell for me."

"Indeed? Then perhaps you can explain why I recognized one of those items as belonging to Miss MacLaren, and your son confessed to the theft?"

"Lies!" the woman shrieked. "Lord Strickland, have him arrested for his lies."

Simon turned to address her. "I can call the constables, if you wish.

They will be very interested to discover how your son obtained a locket belonging to the goddaughter of the Duke of Winshire."

Lord and Lady Strickland exchanged alarmed glances, and it was the lord who answered. "Rubbish. The goddaughter of a duke would not be working as a governess."

Simon shrugged. "She is following in her mother's footsteps, I imagine. Lady Patience was a governess before she married the duke's closest friend, and became foster mother to the duke's younger children." It was a slight exaggeration, but good enough.

"It is my jewelry, I tell you. My locket," Lady Strickland insisted. "You cannot prove otherwise. And the MacLaren woman has gone. We dismissed her this morning for impertinent lies. You have no business here. Lord Strickland, have the man thrown out."

Simon continued as if she hadn't spoken, addressing Lord Strickland. "The locket is a unique piece, made for the lady's sixteenth birthday. It has her name on the back and a quote from a poem on the front."

"You see!" Lady Strickland crowed. "It isn't the same locket. This one just had some chicken scratching on it. Not any words."

"Her name and a quote written in Arabic," Simon explained, and added. "Her father wrote the words for me to copy. I knew it again immediately. Can you tell me where Miss MacLaren has gone?"

"As my wife said, she left this morning." Lord Strickland's nostrils were flared and his voice tight, but he retained some decorum, which was more than could be said for his wife, who had burst into noisy tears and was drumming her heels on the floor. Clearly, the acorns upstairs had not fallen far from the oak.

"Can you tell me where she went?" Simon asked, maintaining his own decorum with an effort, when what he wanted to do was throw punches and bang heads.

"One of the grooms took her to the inn. I believe she intended to catch a coach. and that is all I can tell you." Lord Strickland had pulled the bell rope while he was speaking. To the butler when he entered, he said, "Show this man out, and don't allow him inside again."

The butler went to take Simon's arm, but desisted at a warning glare. "One more thing, Lord Strickland. If your son returns home, tell him to leave again for his own good. I suggest he gets as far away as he can. Australia might be far enough. The lady he attempted to debauch is, as I mentioned, the goddaughter of the Duke of Winshire. The duke has six sons and four daughters, all skilled with weapons, and all of them regard Miss MacLaren as a sister. Her own brother is one of the finest swordsmen I know and an expert marksman. When I tell them that your son attacked the lady and then stole from her, England will not be large enough for him to escape them."

Lady Strickland gave a louder wail and her tears redoubled.

Simon continued. "If I were you, I would hope His Grace or one of his children catches your son first. For Miss MacLaren's father and brother will also be hunting him. Yousef ibn Ahmed is the duke's dearest friend and was his vizier and a general in his army when the duke was a king in the East. And his son Jamir ibn Yousef is a fine young warrior, who loves his sister very much. I have no idea what they might do to your son if they reach him first."

At that, he turned on his heel and walked out the door. The butler made no attempt to accompany him, instead scurrying downstairs, probably to share the scandal to which he had just been made party.

CHAPTER 5

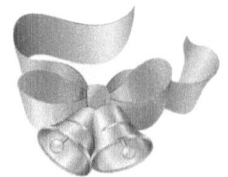

The village lockup was at least dry, and the constable's wife brought Zahrah a couple of warm blankets as well as a pot of tea and two large slices of fresh bread with cheese. "For while you are in my husband's custody, you are his responsibility, and I won't have you starving to death or shivering your way into an ague," she insisted.

For all her brisk manner and her practical reasoning, her eyes were kind, and she thawed still further when Zahrah thanked her. "Someone taught you nice manners, even if you are an Egyptian and a thief."

"My father was born in Egypt, but my mother is as English as you are, Mrs. Barker," Zahrah said. "And I am no thief. The money was my own, my pay from the position I left this morning, and all that I have left after I was accosted by an actual thief."

She had told the constable that when he arrested her. She had limped into the village, her gown torn, her hair a bedraggled mess, and attempted to use a silver crown to pay for a room at the inn. The innkeeper refused to believe she had come by it honestly, and the righteous citizens present in the taproom dragged her to the Barkers' house and insisted that the constable lock her up.

"As to that," Mrs. Barker replied, "you can tell the magistrate all about it, but not until after Christmas, for he has gone to visit his daughter and her children in Birmingham, bless the dear sprouts. Meanwhile, I will make sure you have a share of our meals, and you will have a warm bed out of the rain. If you would like, we can decorate in here for Christmas! Now don't you worry, dearie. Sir William —that's the magistrate—he'll sort it all out when he returns."

She bustled off, closing and locking the door between the lockup and the Barkers' family quarters. The lockup was divided into three spaces. Bars formed two cells for prisoners, and the rest of the room held a table, a chair, a bookshelf, and a fireplace.

The constable was not, at the moment, in the room. He had locked Zahrah into one of the cells, chivvied the jeering onlookers out through the outside door, and disappeared through the inner one.

He had not returned, but Mrs. Barker had lit the fire when she came with her tea tray, blankets, and good advice. The woman was clearly in favor of looking on the bright side, and she was not wrong. Zahrah was grateful for food and shelter.

Grateful, too, that if English justice proved to be unreasonable, at least she would not be hanged out of hand. She would undoubtedly have time to get a message to her family, if she could find a way to pay the postage. Perhaps she could sell her boots? Perhaps Mrs. Barker would help her?

She regretted the loss of her book, though with the storm outside making the sky dark, reading was probably not an option. Not without a good lamp, and she lacked even a candle.

As DUSK DREW NEAR, the rain turned to sleet. Simon's oiled coat still kept most of it out, but the wind drove it up under his hat to melt on his neck and drip down beneath his collar, and his moleskin trousers were damp against the flanks of the horse, the moist portions growing ever larger.

He kept on, promising himself respite when he found Miss MacLaren comfortably ensconced in some inn's private parlor, perhaps warming her toes by the fire as she read a book—her favorite activity on cold dismal days.

Once. Long ago. For all he knew, the adult woman was very different to the girl who had been his friend. It was the Zara of yesteryear, though, who drew him on, and he could not rest until he saw her safe.

At the inn near the Strickland's manor, they had told him she had paid for her trunk to be kept until sent for, and set off to walk to the market town. "There's a coach there every day, see?" The innkeeper explained. "Not like here. Twice a week, it is, and last time were yesterday ago, see? She didn't want to wait. She could walk it, she said, and off she went."

"In this weather?" *You let a lady set off alone on a strange road in a storm? What kind of a villain are you?* Those were the words thundering in his head, but he kept them behind his teeth. Still, the innkeeper must have sensed them, or perhaps his own conscience was playing the same refrain, for he protested, "It has only just come on to rain, see? And there's traffic that would give her a lift, like, if she had a mind. In fact, Barnstable, the smith, went to town this morning. He might have picked her up along the way. You can ask him when he gets back."

Simon wasn't prepared to wait, but he elicited a detail description of Barnstable the smith and his cart before setting off along the road. He kept a sharp eye out as he went, but saw no sign of anyone who might be the lady he sought. Would he recognize her? She had been sixteen last time they met, and that was nine years ago. But her lovely dark brown eyes with their heavy brows and long lashes were emblazoned on his memory. They would not have changed, surely?

He stopped the smith just a few miles out of the market town. The man had seen Miss MacLaren that morning, and had offered her a ride, but she had insisted on walking. "I haven't seen her on my way back, though, so if you didn't find her, I guess she found a ride with someone else."

He told Simon how to find the inn where the coach for Shrewsbury stopped. The London coach was owned by a different line, and stopped at another inn. Simon got directions to that one, too, for good measure.

But when he questioned the servants at first one inn and then the other, no one fitting Miss MacLaren's description had sought food, accommodation, or a coach ticket.

He left a short note for Zara with each innkeeper, and with each of the landladies the innkeepers sent him to—the women who offered rooms by the night. Drawing a blank at these, he hired another horse and set off for the only village on the road he had already traversed. In the opinion of those he had spoken to, the lady he sought might well have taken shelter from the rain at the small inn there.

The village in question was about a third of the way back to the Stricklands'. It would be a little over an hour's walk—or an hour and a half in the conditions, which were turning ever more dismal. On a fresh horse, Simon made good time. Nonetheless, he and the horse were relieved when a turn of the road suddenly disclosed the village before him just as the storm-darkened sky was losing the last of the light from the setting sun.

The inn was easy to find, the only large building, apart from the church, in the huddle of little cottages. Simon rode through large gates into a stable yard large enough for a coach and six, but currently deserted in the driving sleet. He dismounted and led the horse under a lean-to roof in front of the stables. "Ho within," he shouted.

A groom scurried out to take his horse, and pointed to a door on the other side of the stable yard which let directly into the inn. "Reckon maister'll find ye a bed," he said.

Simon would ask after Zara first, but he'd be going no further tonight. Not in the dark of the storm at night on a road he didn't know. If Zara had not taken shelter here, he was at a loss for what to do next.

The door let into a taproom resplendent in ivy, tree boughs, and mistletoe. Simon stood for a moment just inside, looking around. As he took off his dripping coat, his hat and his gloves, he concluded that most of the villagers must be home snug in their cottages, that the half-dozen men playing a raucous game of darts were well into their cups, and that the burly fellow leaning on the other side of the bar was his best source of information.

This man greeted him as he approached the bar. "Room for the night, nineteen shillings. Includes stabling for your horse, a hot dinner, and breakfast in the morning."

"Excellent," Simon said. "And right at this moment, I would appreciate a pint of your ale."

The barman called through a door in the back wall, telling someone named Betty to turn down the sheets in the green room and bring through a plate of her stew. The darts players all turned to watch, as if Simon was the entertainment of the evening and they were waiting for him to begin a song or a dance.

As the innkeeper turned to pouring the ale, Simon broached the topic of his search, raising his voice a little so that all of the occupants of the taproom would hear.

"I am looking for a lady. I arrived to visit her at the Strickland manor near the village of Wesney, and discovered that she had set out for Market Bosworth, where she intended to catch a coach. I have asked along the road, and in Market Bosworth. She does not appear to have arrived. She has not taken shelter here, by any chance? Miss MacLaren? A well-spoken lady, in a green cloak, I believe. She was working as governess for Lord and Lady Strickland, and she is making her way to Shrewsbury to join family for Christmas."

There was silence in the taproom, all eyes on him. Then one of the dart players spoke. "Friend of yours, is she?"

"We have known one another since we were children," Simon explained. "I am concerned that she may have met with some trouble."

"Egyptian lady." That was another of the dart players, the comment a statement, not a question.

Simon frowned. Zara's father was, in fact, from Egypt, but he did not think that was the kind of Egyptian this villager meant. The term —or its derivative gypsy—was commonly used to mean the Romanichal, that wandering race whose members were outsiders wherever they went, and therefore favorite scapegoats when things went missing.

Still, that the man mentioned Egyptians in relation to Miss MacLaren gave him hope she had reached this village.

Cautiously, he answered the statement with the question, "What makes you say that?"

While they had been talking, the dart players had all come up to the bar, and all of a sudden, the bartender said, "He's the one, all right. Take him to the constable, lads."

Without further ado, one man latched onto each of Simon's arms, one scooped up his coat, hat, gloves and saddlebag, and he was marched back out into the freezing night and along the road to a cottage just outside of the village, where they thumped on the door.

"Here, what's this?" asked the man who opened the door.

The person who had described Miss MacLaren as Egyptian appointed himself spokesman. "See here, Mr. Barker. This is the man that his lordship told t'innkeeper about. The Egyptian's accomplice. He was asking after her over at the inn. Didn't know we were already onto her. Thieving whore."

"Miss MacLaren is a lady," Simon said sharply. "Keep a civil tongue in your head." He addressed Barker directly. "Do you have a magistrate in this village? If so, I would like to have a word with him. I believe I can clear up these misconceptions."

His captors jeered, and the spokesman said, "Listen to the pretty words, and him a thief like the woman."

Barker confirmed Simon's suspicion that Strickland had prepared this reception committee when he said, "Mr. Simon Marshall, is it not? I regret that you will not be able to see Sir William Blaney, our magistrate, tonight. He is spending Christmas with family. If you would step this way, you can reassure yourself that Miss MacLaren is safe and well, and I'm sure we can clear this all up in the morning."

"Here," said the spokesman. "What are you up to, Mr. Barker? You've got to arrest this man. We captured him, and we get the reward."

Barker sighed. "Bill Miller, your brain is pickled in gin. Leave thinking to those that are good at it and get along home. Come inside, Mr. Marshall, and the rest of you get along."

He led Simon inside, and shut the door on the faces of the darts players.

"Am I correct in thinking that Lord Strickland arrived here before me, and set the villagers against me and the lady?" Simon asked.

The constable ushered him along a small hall. He did not answer directly. "Sir William is an honest man, Mr. Marshall, and a clever one. His goal is to find the truth. If Lord Strickland has lied, he will find out and see that justice is served."

He opened a door at the end of the hall. The room on the other side had an open space with a table and two cells, barred but with wide open doors.

Simon stepped forward with a glad cry. "Zara!" There she was in one of the cells, dressed in an ill-fitting gown and looking weary, but whole and uninjured.

She was seated at a small table and being served dinner. It smelt wonderful.

CHAPTER 6

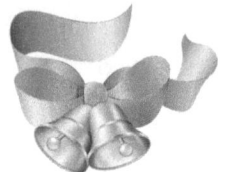

"*A*nother for dinner, Mother," Mr. Barker told his wife. Zahrah looked up just as the man with the constable said her name. It was not someone she knew. At least—surely the hazel eyes were familiar? "Simon?" It must be seven years since she last met him.

"You remember me!" He sounded surprised. And delighted.

"Of course, I do. Mrs. Barker, Simon is the goldsmith who made the locket I told you about." She had poured out all her woes to Mrs. Barker while they decorated the gaol for Christmas. Although she had not told Mrs. Barker how much she had admired Simon when she was a girl of sixteen. Ever since, she had measured every man she met against him. No one had ever come close to the standard. "We have not met in more than seven years! Simon, how do you come to be here?"

Simon felt inside his pocket and pulled out a leather pouch. "I've been looking for you since this morning, ever since I called at the Stricklands' manor to return these, and found you had been dismissed."

"I resigned," Zahrah insisted, then cooed with delight as he poured the trinkets and baubles she'd thought gone forever into his hand.

"How did you get those?" A silly question, for surely, he must have received them from the son of her former employer or someone who knew that nasty rotter.

Simon was not done. He put the trinkets back into the bag and felt inside his coat, coming back out with her locket. "I have a jeweler's shop in Birmingham. A man came in yesterday evening and attempted to sell me these things. Of course, I recognized the locket straight away." He put it in her hand. "So, I offered him a brandy, and kept pouring more until he told me everything."

"Gerard Strickland," Zahrah stated, without looking up from the open locket. "Look, Mrs. Barker. My parents." Strickland had been too stupid even to remove the miniatures.

Simon nodded. "Strickland. I took him back to his inn, left him to the landlord, and set out to see if you needed my help. And here I am." He turned to the constable.

"Mr. Barker, is it? Mr. Barker, Miss MacLaren is innocent, and so am I. I can explain what has happened."

Mr. Barker gave a small bow. "Thank you, sir. I would appreciate your explanation. I have already made a record of what Miss MacLaren has to say. I should explain, however, that I must insist on you and Miss MacLaren being our guests until Sir William, the magistrate, returns and makes a ruling."

"But we've done nothing wrong!" Simon protested.

"Mrs. Barker explained to me," Zahrah said. "There'll be no travelling until the weather clears, and we'll not be given a room at the inn; not after Lord Strickland has put a price on our heads."

"He has got those drunken hotheads nicely worked up," grumbled Mr. Barker, "and what Sir William will say about it when he gets back, I do not know." He shook his head, and appealed to Simon. "An information has been laid, Mr. Marshall. I might think it is a pack of nonsense, but that is not for me to say. I need to keep you in custody until I can tell a magistrate what I have been told by various sources and what my own investigations lead me to believe. But what my dear wife says is also true. I want to keep you safe, so I cannot let you go. As long as the weather prevents you from leaving, the innkeeper and

251

his idiots will take the law into their own hands if they think I have let it out of mine."

It was clear that Simon didn't like it. "Will you release us when the weather clears?" he asked.

"Well, Mr. Marshall, Sir William will certainly be back on the first day fit to travel."

Mrs. Barker chuckled. "A few days of his grandchildren is quite enough for him, poor man."

Simon was inclined to be indignant. "So, you insist on keeping us until Sir William hears our case? Even though you recognize it as a farrago of lies?"

Zahrah felt it was time to play peacemaker. "Simon, will you not agree that we cannot travel during this storm?"

Simon's nod was reluctant.

"And Mrs. Barker is a marvelous cook." She indicated her half-eaten dinner. "We shall enjoy Christmas with the Barkers and let the future look after itself. After all, even if Sir William proves not to be the honest man that Mr. Barker believes, Mrs. Barker has agreed to post letters to the Duke of Winshire and my family as soon as the weather allows the mail to get through."

Mrs. Barker clucked in annoyance, picking up the plate of food. "And here you have let your dinner get cold while we've been talking. Why don't the two of you come through to the kitchen and we'll all have our dinner together."

"Do I need to remind you, Mother," said Mr. Barker, "that Miss MacLaren and Mr. Marshall have been arrested, and are my prisoners?"

"They will be just as much in your custody in the kitchen, Mr. Barker," his wife pointed out. "And it is not as if you believe them to be guilty."

Mr. Barker muttered about his personal beliefs being nothing to do with the point, but he made no further objection.

ONCE HE'D HAD time to think about it, Simon could see the sense in staying where they were, at least until Sir William returned and could hear their case. As Zara pointed out, once the magistrate could travel, so could the mail. Simon was as certain as Zara that her father and the duke would come to their aid as soon as they heard of the need. Whether Sir William deserved Mr. Barker's faith in him or not, the duke would see to it that Zara was protected.

Over dinner, Mrs. Barker was trying to persuade her husband to put his prisoners up in their guest bedrooms. "After everything Miss MacLaren has been through today, and wet as she was when she arrived, that nasty cell is far too cold. We shall have her coming down with an ague!"

"Would it help if I offered my parole?" Simon asked. "Miss MacLaren, too, if she agrees."

Barker regarded him thoughtfully, and Zara gave her enthusiastic endorsement of the idea. "I accept your parole," Barker said. "You don't leave this building without my consent, mind."

"That's fair," Simon agreed. In this weather, he was more than pleased to be safe and warm. "Miss MacLaren, what did happen to you today?"

By the time they had eaten their way through Mrs. Barker's roast mutton and vegetables, followed by a deep-dish apple pie served with custard, Zara and Simon had both shared their adventures since the day before yesterday, and they had learned a little more about their hosts.

Barker's primary role was schoolmaster. It was not a full-time position in this rural environment, where children provided important labor to their families. Sir William insisted that all of his tenants and laborers with children older than six and younger than twelve sent them to Barker for nine hours schooling a week.

So, Barker worked three hours in the morning on Mondays, Wednesdays and Fridays, except at peak sowing and harvest times. Being village constable as well, thanks to the house that came with the job and a small stipend, helped Mr. Barker make ends meet.

Mrs. Barker took in a little sewing and occasionally worked at Sir

William's manor when one of the senior female staff members took leave or when Sir William entertained.

By the time they had helped Mrs. Barker to make up the beds in the guest rooms, Zara could no longer control her yawns, and Simon was also feeling the effects of a sleepless night and a day of riding.

He refused a bedtime drink, and carried up his own hot jug of water for a wash before he got into the clean sheets.

His last waking thought was more of an image—Zara, laughing from across the kitchen table. With a smile at the memory, he slipped into a deep and dreamless sleep.

CHAPTER 7

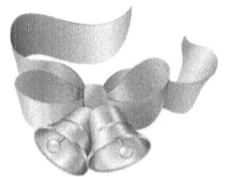

"*I* expected a much more active Christmas," Zara said to Simon, as they washed the dishes.

She was wearing another gown of Mrs. Barker's, her own having been laundered and hung up in the box room under the eaves to dry. Like the one she wore last night, it was a little too tight and rather short, displaying more of her charms than was comfortable. A base-born jeweler had no business lusting after a duke's goddaughter.

Simon washed another plate and stacked it for Zara to dry. They had sent the Barkers off to the Christmas services, promising to clean up after breakfast. "What would you be doing now if you were still at the Stricklands?" he asked.

"I would be at church with the children, if it was not raining too hard to take the carriage out. If so? Acting out the nativity, or roasting chestnuts over the fire, or singing carols. I had promised them a holiday from lessons on Christmas Day, and one needs many different ideas for entertainment when the weather is poor. This is much more peaceful, but I am sorry for the children."

"They were upset," Simon told her, and shared what he'd overheard of the yelling from the direction of the Strickland schoolroom.

"Poor children. They are obnoxious little devils, but I feel sorry for them. Their parents seem to have no interest in them at all, and their older brother and sisters notice them only to scold, criticize or tease them."

"How on earth do you teach creatures like that?" Simon wondered, making a start on scrubbing one of the pots that Mrs. Barton had set to soak before she left.

Zara laughed. "I find that bribery works even better than threats." She shot him a sideways glance. "For example, I found they loved stories. So, I would tell them a bedtime story if they managed to attend all meals, stay attentive in class, and refrain from major infringements of the rules. Active goodness, rather than simply avoiding trouble, might win them dessert, or a run outside, or a lesson they particularly liked—Judith was fond of drawing, for example, and could be convinced to keep her clothes neat all day and refrain from attempts to strangle her brother in return for a lesson in perspective or shading."

Simon tipped the dirty water from the pot and examined it to see if it needed any more scouring. "I think you must be a very good teacher, Miss MacLaren." He had another scrub at a recalcitrant bit of cooked-on matter.

Zara shrugged even as she blushed. "My mother was a very good teacher. When I am in doubt, I just think, what would Mother do?" She took the clean pot from him and began to dry it. "What of you, Mr. Marshall? What would you be doing on this Christmas Day if you had not come after me?"

"Work on one of my commissions, perhaps?" Simon mused. "I do not open the shop on Christmas Day. I am usually open late on Christmas Eve, and I do a half day on the Feast of St Stephen."

"You do not spend time with family or friends?" Zara asked.

Simon shook his head. "My friends are busy about their own affairs, and I have no family—or none that care to claim me. You do not need to feel sad for me, Miss MacLaren. I have a craft I love and that brings me a good living. I have much more than many. Shall I put the kettle back on the hob and make us a cup of tea?"

"You do that, and I will cut us a slice each of Mrs. Barker's fruit cake," Zara offered.

She returned to the topic when they were sitting in the Barker's parlor, each with a cup of tea and cake on a plate. "Please tell me if I intrude, but is your uncle no longer..."

Oddly enough, though he'd never spoken about his family to any of his friends, it seemed natural to tell Zara the truth. After all, when she had known him, he had been an acknowledged member of his uncle's family—even if tucked away on the corner of the estate, with the exact relationship never spoken.

As it happened, her locket had been the catalyst for the breach. The Duke of Winshire had been so impressed he had praised Simon's craftsmanship and artistry to the earl. It was the first the earl knew of Simon's work with the metalsmith. Simon was summoned to the main house, to his uncle's study. "Now that you have left school, boy, you will need a profession. If you wish to join the army, I will buy you a commission. Likewise, the navy, I suppose. Otherwise, I have a friend whose steward is looking to take an assistant. It would be a good opportunity for you. And if you do well, you can return here and take over when my steward retires."

Simon, glowing from the success of the locket, replied, "It is good of you, uncle. However, I have already decided on a profession. I intend to be a goldsmith. Perhaps, you might be willing to help me gain an apprenticeship?"

He did not expect the fury that broke over him. Simon would do what he was told. He might be baseborn, but he was still a member of the family, and his choice of profession reflected on his uncle and cousins. "The idea of you preferring *a trade*," this word redolent with disgust, "to an honorable profession!"

Simon told Zara some of this, though not the connection with her locket. "After that, I left. The metalsmith gave me a recommendation to a friend of his in Birmingham. My uncle refused to sign the articles of apprenticeship, but I took legal advice. I was nineteen, and even I didn't know my exact relationship to him, or who my parents were. Since the earl was not legally my guardian, he could not stop me from signing on my own behalf. When I completed the apprenticeship, my master took me into partnership, and I inherited his workshop a year ago."

His uncle had written one final letter, repudiating the relationship in terms that gave Simon a clue to his origins. "I always wondered who ruined my sister. Given your low tastes, I can only assume that the villain was from the lower orders."

Zara was indignant on Simon's behalf. "You're better off without him," she proclaimed. "Yours is an honorable profession, and even when we were young, you were very good at it. Men like that are part of the reason I became a governess. They think they are so much better than everyone else, and that gives them the right to trample on people's feelings."

That led to the story of the miserable time she had had as part of the fashionable world, and her decision to leave it all behind and, as she said, do something useful. "After all, it was very clear that I was not going to find a husband in London's ballrooms." She sighed. "Nor anywhere else, it seemed. Those who might have interested me were too afraid of my father and the duke to show even the politest interest."

Is she hinting she would find a man like me acceptable? He thought not. Surely, such a hint would come with a sideways glance or some indication she was conscious of him as a man.

Nonetheless, perhaps there was hope.

Is hope the word I mean? Precisely what am I hoping for? The answer was there, in his mind, as if it had been growing since yesterday evening when he saw her in that cell, totally composed and cheerful despite the circumstances. Or perhaps the dream he had refused to consider seven years ago had merely been dormant, waiting for the chance to bloom.

Zara doing dishes with him in the comfortable little apartment above his shop. Zara pouring him tea and sitting with him in his parlor. Zara in his bed. Her warmth and her bright curiosity would be an asset there as in all parts of his life. Zara as the mother of the children he had never thought to have.

She was frowning slightly. "Is anything wrong, Mr. Marshall?"

"You called me Simon once," he blurted.

She nodded, smiling. "Simon, then. And you must call me Zara. I suppose the rules of propriety might be suspended, at least as far as names go, while we are guests of the Barkers."

He would accept that. And perhaps, before their time with the Barkers came to an end, he could win the right to call her by her first name for the remainder of his life. Yes, and other, more intimate names, too.

The Barkers arrived back from church as he thought about the word he most wanted to call her, letting it resonate through his mind. Wife. He had a matter of days to court her, before the magistrate arrived to set them free (he could consider no other outcome). Before he had to return to Birmingham and she to her family.

He had to make them count.

ZAHRAH WAS ENJOYING her first family Christmas in years, for Mr. and Mrs. Barker had taken their two unexpected guests to their hearts, calling them by their given names and involving them in both the chores and the entertainment.

Simon spent part of Christmas afternoon outside chopping wood and doing other chores under Mr. Barker's supervision. Mr. Barker had found him a pair of working boots and a heavy coat. Mrs. Barker wiped away a tear. "They were my Robert's," she explained. The Barker's only son had died at Waterloo, eight years ago. "Such a waste," Mrs. Barker said. "All those young men, from all those different countries, and in the end, the French have a king again and very little has changed."

Mrs. Barker would not let the melancholy moment last. She led Zahrah through to the parlor, where two modest but pretty gowns were spread out over the sofa. "These belonged to my Maudie. She left them in a trunk in the box room when she married, a long time ago. They wouldn't fit her now."

Maudie, it transpired, had married a clerical man. She, her vicar, and their six children lived in far-off Devon. Mrs. Barker lived in hope that one day she and Mr. Barker would save enough money for a visit. "Maudie would like us to move there, but what would Mr. Barker do for a living? And our other daughter, Clara, lives with her family in Yorkshire. She has only the two children, and visits us most years, when the harvest is in and before lambing starts."

From which Zahrah gathered that Clara had married a farmer.

Mrs. Barker and Zahrah worked together to sew the alterations to fit the dresses to Zahrah's shape, taking in a few seams and adding hem ruffles cut from another garment. "It is so nice to have young people in the house for Christmas again," Mrs. Barker said. "We shall have such fun. What do you say to helping me with the dinner? And perhaps after dinner, we can sing Christmas carols."

They made an early start on the singing, Zahrah and Mrs. Barker, caroling their favorites as they prepared duck with sage and onions, half a dozen different dishes from vegetables that had been dried or otherwise preserved for the winter, and a pork hock basted with cranberries and roasted at the side of the fire. Then there were the sweet dishes. The star was the Christmas pudding in its cloth, made weeks ago but now simmering on the back of the stove to heat. Zahrah helped Mrs. Barker make a pie with minced meat, dried fruit and fragrant spices. Whole baked apples went into a pot with hot coals heaped on it, and in another pot, a water bath held a bowl where custard flavored with brandy was slowly setting.

"We have locked all the animals away in the barn," Mr. Barker reported when he led Simon into the kitchen an hour or more after they'd gone outdoors. "It has started to snow. We'll be snowed in by morning—no travelling for several days."

Zahrah found she didn't care, and Simon didn't seem bothered either.

"You will not lack for firewood for every room, Mother," Mr.

Barker added. "Young Simon here has chopped and stacked a great mountain of wood within easy reach of the kitchen door."

"And dear Zara has worked hard on dinner, Mr. Barker." Mrs. Barker beamed. "I am so happy to have the two of you here with us, Zara and Simon."

They spent the afternoon while the dinner cooked reading in the parlor, which contained a copious bookshelf. Both of the bedchambers upstairs also boasted bookshelves stuffed with well-thumbed volumes. Biographies. Adventure. History. Botany. Even novels. Zahrah buried herself in the first volume of Jane Austen's Sense and Sensibility, while Simon discovered Waverley, by Sir Walter Scott.

The dinner was a great success. Zahrah was enormously proud to have had a share in its creation. Afterwards, as promised, they sang carols. Simon proved to have a lovely tenor. Mr. Barker declared that he could not sing to save his life, but he accompanied them on a mouth organ.

They finished their evening quietly, listening as Mr. Barker read from the first chapters of the Gospel according to Luke. After that, it was time for bed. Zahrah and Simon said goodnight to Mr. and Mrs. Barker at the foot of the stairs, as the older couple's bedchamber was on the main floor.

Upstairs was under the eaves, with the box room and two little bed chambers. Zahrah paused with her hand on her door handle, reluctant to see the evening end.

Simon was looking up. She followed his gaze with her eyes. A bunch of mistletoe hung from the ceiling. *That wasn't there earlier today. Was it?*

Simon looked a question at her. With the sense that she was about to take a leap into the dark, Zahrah stepped up to him and looped her arms around his neck. *Now what?* She had experience of men attempting to steal a kiss, but none of freely giving and receiving one.

Simon bent his head, going slowly, and softly laid his lips upon hers. She felt the tingle run through her body. She pressed closer, and he deepened the kiss, covering her lips with his own, one hand firmly on her back.

Zahrah's thoughts scattered. She lost track of her surroundings and everything else except the sensation of Simon's lips, his tongue sliding across hers, his firm hand anchoring her to his body, his other hand gently caressing one breast.

When he broke the kiss, she stared at him, dazed. He looked no less befuddled.

She leaned towards him again and he pressed a light kiss to the corner of her mouth. "I hope this means you are open to my courtship," he murmured. "Or do I need to apologize?"

"Don't you dare apologize," she scolded. She was recovering a few of her wits. "Courtship, Simon?"

Anxiety flickered in his eyes. "If I do not presume. If you could imagine marrying a tradesman of little fortune and murky birth."

"Very easily." If the tradesman in question was Simon. "Yes."

His anxiety melted into the beginnings of a smile. "You can imagine?"

"Yes, you may court me. But first, kiss me again."

CHAPTER 8

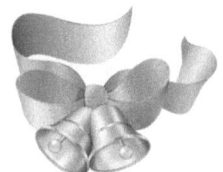

The snow continued all the next day. Simon started the morning by escorting Zara down to breakfast, stopping on the landing to make further use of the mistletoe. After breakfast, he dug a path to the little barn, and Mr. Barker milked the cow while Simon put out feed for the cow, the two pigs, and the poultry.

He spent the rest of the morning sitting next to Zara on the window seat in the parlor, a blanket around the two of them against the cold beating in from outside, talking about everything under the sun.

They both admired the prison reform campaign of Elizabeth Fry, and both wanted to see slavery abolished throughout the British Empire. Neither of them much liked Queen Caroline but they agreed she had been treated unfairly. Both cautiously supported political reform, though not with the violence that had been seen in other countries. They both enjoyed music. Zara played the piano. Simon had no such skill but hoped to hear Zara play one day soon.

After lunch, Mrs. Barker declared she could do with a little afternoon sleep, and Mr. Barker would like one, too. He looked surprised at the suggestion, but said nothing after a nudge with his wife's elbow.

"Is Mrs. Barker matchmaking?" Simon asked.

"Helping our courtship along," Zara suggested. Simon had no objection to that.

The afternoon followed the pattern of the morning, but with the addition of some rather adventurous kissing.

Simon would have liked to explore even further, but he was a gentleman, after all, and Zara was not yet his wife, or even his betrothed. "Is it too early to ask you to marry me?" he asked, and was surprised when she pointed out they had only known one another as adults for two days. "It seems like much longer," he said.

They grew closer with each day that the storm lasted. When the day dawned clear on the twenty-ninth of December, they were almost sorry. Except that, by then, they were both looking forward to a future together. Not that Simon had actually proposed. Not yet. But they both knew the question was coming, and what the answer would be.

The outside world intruded almost immediately, with the villagers calling to see how Mr. and Mrs. Barker had weathered the storm. If they were surprised to find Zara and Simon being treated as honored guests, most of them accepted that Mr. Barker knew best. The innkeeper grumbled, but subsided after Mr. Barker demanded to know whether he was more interested in justice or in the reward Lord Strickland had offered.

Apart from the mail, which struggled into the village that morning, and left with letters for Zara's family, no other travelers managed the journey for another two days. Thawing snow made the road a boggy mess by day and froze into a treacherous ice sheet at night.

Zara and Simon, with Mr. Barker's blessing, walked around the village, visited with friends of the Barkers, admired a baby that had been born during the storm, and spent two hours touring the church with the vicar, and listening to his stories of parishioners down through the ages.

Simon had never found anyone who was easier to talk to than Zara. He even told Zara about the heavily-veiled stranger who called into his shop late one afternoon not long after he had taken down the former owner's name and replaced it with his own.

"She was a countess; Lady Burnham. I had never heard of her, and my face must have shown that, for she put up her veil and burst into tears." His own eyes treacherously watered as he remembered the scene. "Zara, she was my mother."

He was silent for a minute, remembering her tears and his own indignant shock, which melted as he heard the rest of her story. "After I was born, my uncle arranged for her to marry a Scottish earl, to reinstate her in Society. They had managed to keep her condition a secret, but they had to tell her suitor, of course."

"Could she not have taken you with her?" Zara asked. "No. I suppose not, if no one knew you existed."

"Her husband didn't want me—which, I suppose, is understandable. And what you say is true, I suppose. How would they have explained a new-born boy a couple of weeks after the wedding? My uncle agreed he would keep me, but her husband demanded that she promised not to try to contact me or see me. My uncle used to send her a report on my wellbeing once a year, until I left home when I was nineteen. Then she lost track of me, until she saw the advertisement for my shop in a London newspaper. She came to Birmingham expressly to see me."

The visit had healed some wounds and opened new ones. He now wrote to her at the same address his uncle used to use. One letter a year, just reporting on his wellbeing. "I'll have something exciting to tell her when I write my Lady Day letter this April," he told Zara, and looked around to make sure they were unobserved before he kissed her on the nose.

"I have brothers and sisters I have never met," he said. That was sad, too, when he thought about it. He suggested that they visit the bakers and buy some of his sugar buns. "One each to eat on the way home, and four to have with our supper with the Barkers," he proposed.

Halfway through the day, on the last day of the year, the world ended their idyll. First came Lord Strickland, storming into the house shouting for Mr. Barker, and abusing him for releasing his prisoners.

"I'll take them into my own custody, since you have failed in your duty," he pronounced.

Mr. Barker politely noted that he did not work for Lord Strickland, but despite his calm approach, the situation rapidly devolved into a stand-off, as Strickland called on his servants to subdue the constable and seize the miscreants, and Simon stepped up beside Mr. Barker ready to fight.

But suddenly the servants were surrounded by villagers, who hustled them none too gently off the Barkers' premises. Zara had run out of the back door and gone for help as soon as Lord Strickland burst in the front door.

Strickland removed himself to the inn, swearing he would have the pair of them before nightfall.

Next to arrive was Sir William. He had not even managed to arrive home. Strickland saw his carriage as it passed through the village, and insisted on pouring his own version of the tale into the magistrate's ear.

Sir William came straight to the cottage, politely acknowledged Mr. Barker's introduction of Simon and Zara (despite Strickland's splutters), and asked them all to wait elsewhere while Mr. Barker gave his report in the parlor.

He emerged to say that he intended to go home to his manor and change, but would hear the case at the manor in one hour.

After he and Strickland had left, Zara grabbed Simon by the hand and led him up the stairs to their landing. "Quick," she said. "It is time for your proposal."

"Are you sure?" Simon asked. "I've been ready for days, but if you want more time, I don't think we need to rush. I'm sure Sir William will believe us. Did you see how he squelched Lord Strickland every time the man tried to speak?" He chuckled at the memory.

"We do need to rush," Zara insisted. "Sir William came from the West. How long do you think the journey will have taken my father and brother after they got my letter?"

Simon had not thought of that. "Good point." He had been planning his proposal for days, but he couldn't remember what he meant to say. He knew he was going to go down on one knee, so he did that. Then he thought he had better tell her how he felt. "Zahrah ibnit Yousef ibn Ahmed. Zara MacLaren. I love you."

There. He had got that out. He looked up at her, still waiting expectantly. *He had forgotten the question.* "Will you marry me?" Not as poetic or as elegant as he had planned. But she was smiling.

At that moment, a thunderous knock on the door was followed by Mr. Barker's voice. "No need to... Oh. You must be—"

"Yes!" Zara exclaimed. "Yes, Simon, I will marry you."

FATHER, walking into the house a pace before the Duke of Winshire and two paces ahead of Jamir, looked up the stairs to see Simon on his knee and Zahrah hastily exclaiming her acceptance before anyone could interrupt.

Simon, she was pleased to note, withstood the full weight of Father's glower without an outward sign. He stood, offered her his hand, and escorted her down the stairs and into her father's arms.

"You will tell me more later about this suitor, Zahrah. But first, how are you? Have you been hurt? Insulted? What do you need from me?"

Behind him, Simon was greeting Uncle James, the duke, and two of his sons, as well as her brother. From what she could hear, they all remembered him from that summer so long ago, and the duke had received his letter, sent before he left Birmingham.

"Perhaps we should go through to the parlor and tell your family the whole story," Mr. Barker suggested. "The magistrate will hear your case in one hour's time."

The Duke of Winshire, his foreign retainers, and his unusual horses had been the subject of many a cartoon in the newspapers. Perhaps that was why Lord Strickland was nowhere to be found when it was time for the hearing, and Sir William sent a couple of footmen to fetch him.

After Sir William had listened to the case against Zahrah and Simon, and dismissed it, Lord Andrew Winderfield, one of the duke's sons, and several of his retainers rode to Strickland's manor to find the family gone. According to the disgruntled servants, who had all been dismissed without notice, they had left in haste not an hour before the duke's son arrived.

He had not paid for his meal at the inn, either. Nor had the innkeeper received the reward he was promised. Simon's opinion was that it served the innkeeper right.

CHAPTER 9

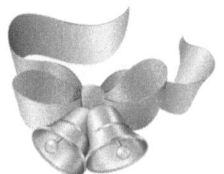

*Z*ahrah hesitated at the door of the little church in Wingatt, the village at the mouth of the pass that the fortress of Wind's Gate had been built to protect.

Now that her wedding was finally here, she wanted to savor the moment. She had been betrothed for four and a half interminable months, surviving on frequent, sometimes daily, letters and three brief meetings with her beloved.

Twice, he had closed up his shop for three days and come to her. Birmingham to Wingatt was a full day's travel each way, so each visit had been frustratingly brief.

Brief, too, had been her stay in Birmingham for the assizes last month, when Gerard Strickland had appeared to answer for several crimes, not only those against Zahrah. He had been arrested trying to board a ship for the colonies, and his father was to stand trial in the House of Lords for a web of debt and lies uncovered by the duke's investigator.

Zahrah spared a prayer for the children, who had apparently been taken in by relatives. She could not be angry with any of them. Even Gerard, though she was happy he was no longer free to hurt other women. Still, if it had not been for his attempt to sell her locket, she and Simon might never have found one another again. Tears rose in her eyes at the thought.

Her father patted her hand on his arm. "If you are having second thoughts, my beloved one, say the word and we shall go home. Forget the infidel. I'll buy you a kitten."

She punched him with her other hand. "Waladi! You promised to behave."

His eyes twinkled. "And now you are smiling, my daughter. Shall we go and put your groom out of his misery? He is a good man."

Yes. It was time. Her smile grew as she thought of him waiting anxiously by the altar.

They passed through the doors, and there he was. Her beloved. Her unexpected Christmas present. Her Simon.

SIMON COULD NOT QUITE BELIEVE she was here, and this was really going to happen. Yousef Effendi, her father, had informed Simon when they first sat down to discuss the betrothal that he had wanted a Muslim, and preferably a nobleman, for his daughter.

Zara was neither impressed nor bothered. She pointed out that the only noblemen she knew were not Muslim, and all the Muslims she knew were married.

"One of them might be persuaded to take you as a second wife," Yousef replied. "Or a third, perhaps, since you are so old."

"He is joking, Simon," Zara assured him, while Simon was still choking on his indignation.

"In my society, it is considered bad manners to punch your father-in-law," Yousef intoned, his visage still stern and serious.

Simon caught a slight crinkle at the corner of his eyes, and a twitch of the lips. "I shall take that under advisement, sir," he replied.

After that, they went ahead with the plans for the wedding.

Even so, for months, Simon had waited for someone to put a stop to the wedding and now she was outside, in the foyer. That was what her brother had said when he came up the aisle escorting her mother five minutes ago.

Simon turned to look at the door again. That's when he saw the couple in the back row. The lady was hidden from view by a bonnet with veil, but he knew her escort. His uncle had come to his wedding, which surely meant the lady with him was Simon's mother?

He forgot all about that when the door opened. Zara was here. His bride, allowing her fearsome father to place her hand in Simon's.

The wedding was simple; the minister not long-winded, thank all the powers. Simon spoke his vows loudly enough to ring through the church, his eyes on Zara's the whole time. Then she spoke hers, and in no time at all the minister was presenting them to the congregation as Mr. and Mrs. Marshall.

The couple from the back stood to leave, but the lady paused in the doorway and lifted her veil. With her eyes on Simon's, she blew him a kiss, and he smiled back at her and nodded. "Your mother?" Zara asked? She did not wait for an answer, but waved, and the lady slipped out of the door after Simon's uncle.

Somehow, though it had never occurred to him it would matter, the little interaction between the woman who bore him, and the woman he had come to love put an extra gloss on the already wonderful day.

Suddenly filled with more joy than he could express, Simon Marshall bent and kissed his bride.

The End

ABOUT JUDE KNIGHT

Jude Knight always wanted to be a novelist, but life got in the way for decades and she nearly lost the dream. She wrote a thousand beginnings, but it took a huge life event to shove her into writing an ending. That was in 2014. Eight novels and counting later, plus short stories and novellas galore, she's living her dream: writing historical fiction with a large helping of romance, more than a dash of suspense, and a sprinkling of humor.

Learn more about Jude at:

Website and blog: http://judeknightauthor.com/

The characters in this story belong to Jude Knight's Regency world, a fictional place in which any of Jude's characters might wander into any of her stories. In particular, the Duke of Winshire is hero of his own series, The Return of the Mountain King, where you will meet his friend and vizier Yousef, and Winshire's sons, daughters, nieces, and other relatives. Also, his long-lost love, Eleanor and her son the Marquess of Aldridge, who are more inclined than any of Jude's other characters to go series hopping.

SOCIAL MEDIA FOR JUDE KNIGHT

You can learn more about Jude Knight at these social media links:

Website and blog: http://judeknightauthor.com/
Subscribe to newsletter: http://judeknightauthor.com/newsletter/
Bookshop: https://judeknight.selz.com/
Facebook: https://www.facebook.com/JudeKnightAuthor/
Twitter: https://twitter.com/JudeKnightBooks
Pinterest: https://nz.pinterest.com/jknight1033/
BookBub: https://www.bookbub.com/profile/jude-knight
Books + Main Bites: https://bookandmainbites.com/
JudeKnightAuthor
Goodreads: https://www.goodreads.com/author/show/8603586.
Jude_Knight
LinkedIn: https://linkedin.com/in/jude-knight-465557166/

THREE SHIPS

BY ELIZABETH ELLEN CARTER

Laura Winter lives on a tidal island that is home to a lighthouse. On a late November day, a violent storm brings not only the handsome Lieutenant Michael Renten but also a clutch of pirates bent on wreaking mischief.

CHAPTER 1

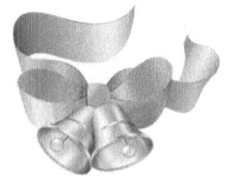

I saw three ships come sailing in
On Christmas Day in the morning.

"Goin' to be a bad storm, Miss Laura. I can feel it in me bones, I can."

Mr. Fletcher pointed a thumb at the barometer hung on his wall. Even without reference to the brass and rosewood instrument that was the man's pride and joy, Laura Winter knew him to be correct.

There were other signs—the shift in the on-shore breeze and the way the clouds banked on the horizon.

"Indeed, it will be," she agreed, handing over a list. "Which is why I want to get more provisions; in case we're cut off from the mainland for more than a day or two."

"Not good just afore Christmas," the grocer observed, taking her list.

The middle-aged shop keeper, his starched white apron stretched over an expansive belly, scanned the piece of paper.

"Dickie!" he called in a booming voice, "Come out here and fetch these items for Miss Laura."

Richard Wells poked his head out from the back storeroom. Dickie to everyone at Ashton-On-Sea, and rarely seen dressed in other than his customary faded overalls, smiled at Laura and took the list from his boss.

"Be sure to pack it up nice and good, mind," Mr. Fletcher admonished before turning back to his customer. "You'll be wanting Mrs. Parker's home-made apricot preserves as well, I dare say?"

"Yes, please."

"Three?" the grocer asked hopefully.

Sly old fox! Laura smiled to herself.

She shook her head.

"Just one will be fine, Dickie."

From behind Mr. Fletcher, Dickie offered an approving grin.

"Be ready for you in an hour, Miss Laura," he answered before setting to work to fill her order.

Laura thanked the men and left the shop, the little brass bell on the door tinkling as it closed.

She paused to look out towards her home.

The view half a mile out to St Joseph's Rock was one she never tired of—the pile of sea-darkened rocks at its base, the solid large mound of rock topped with grass from which the lighthouse rose, gleaming white, its mullion windows sparkling in the mid-morning sunlight. It was home, and she considered it with not a little pride.

According to local legend, St Joseph's Rock was the place where Joseph of Arimathea landed in England, accompanied by Jesus as a young man.

Laura doubted the story herself, but ever since the verse by that poet William Blake was published a few years ago, visitors aplenty had come to their corner of the Devon coast during each summer season.

Thus, the legend grew and was embellished by the entrepreneurial townsfolk who supplemented their fishing income by making souvenirs.

Though bright, the late November day carried a chill and Laura turned her face up to the sun to feel its warmth on her cheeks. She balanced the wicker basket on her arm and brushed a strand of red-gold hair from her face.

The clock on the nearby church tower chimed the tenth hour but her musings were interrupted by Reverend Harman. He had been a boxer before taking holy orders and, although older now and a little softer around the middle, he still carried a fighter's physique.

The cleric fell in step with her as she walked down the main street of Ashton-On-Sea, its rows of Tudor-era buildings huddled together against the sometimes-harsh weather as they had done for three hundred years.

"How's your father, Miss Laura?" he enquired. "I paid a visit with him earlier this week and he assured me his foot was well on the mend. Choir practice hasn't been the same without him."

"Stubborn as always!" she exclaimed with equal measures of affection and exasperation. "I finally managed to persuade him to let me check the light twice a day, but he still insists on climbing those stairs to wind the clockwork. Only Mother could persuade him to take care of himself."

Reverend Harman offered a sympathetic smile in memory of Laura's mother who died five years ago, when Laura was only fifteen.

"Well, you only just have to ask if there is anything you need," he reminded her. "So don't be stubborn like your father if you want help."

The mild admonishment of his words was softened with a smile.

"Yoo-hoo, Reverend!"

They turned at the call.

Across the street Mrs. Merriwether waved. She was a large woman with an equally substantial bosom and reminded Laura of a beautifully beribboned figure eight.

Next to her, Miss Jones, the school mistress, thin and reed-like, remained at her shoulder. Her no-nonsense expression quailed many a schoolboy into obedience yet beneath that hawk-like expression lay a character with an equally sharp sense of humor.

"Oh, Reverend," called Mrs. Merriwether, "we need to talk to you about some last-minute preparations for the Christmas fete."

"Hello, Laura!" she continued. "Thank you for the beautiful quilts, I'm sure they'll fetch a great price for this year's charity."

Laura accepted the thanks and excused herself. Living on a tidal island had its advantages and one of them was the ability to graciously take leave from drawn-out conversations by pointing to the change of tide.

Indeed, St Joseph's Rock was quite accessible via the causeway at low tide but completely cut-off during high tide and the storm surges that regularly battered the exposed coast.

And in truth, out to sea clouds were gathering as dark as bruises, edging the horizon as a sharp gust of breeze cut up the promontory. Even at this distance, Laura could see the flag by the lighthouse snap to attention.

By the time the church bells chimed one o'clock, she had returned to Fletcher's Fine Emporium to find Dickie loading the last of her order onto the small horse-drawn cart.

"Mr. Fletcher asked, what with your dad laid up with a bung foot and you there on St Joseph's on your own like...well, if you need a man about, he said I should go with you."

Try as he might, Dickie could not hide the hint of a frown on his brow and Laura recognized its cause immediately.

"That's very sweet of you," she said, causing Dickie to blush, "but I know Kitty has been waiting for you to take her to the dance this Friday and she would be most disappointed if you didn't go."

The young man's face lit up.

"You're a real friend, Miss Laura. Anything you need, don't be afraid to ask, now. It would be my pleasure."

It was not until she was crossing the causeway in the cart that she allowed herself a gentle laugh at Dickie's delight in not being pried away from his sweetheart. The thought caused her to reflect.

It was only in the past year she'd pondered the notion of having a beau of her own and her mind idly considered those eligible as she negotiated the path home.

Not that there were many eligible. The fight against Napoleon's armies had occupied and taken many a young man. Those who remained were more like brothers to her. Laura couldn't see herself accepting a proposal from anyone of them, even if they should offer.

The muted clip-clop on the cobble-paved causeway cut through her thoughts. The tide was rising faster than it usually did and the horse sloshed hoof deep along the path said to have been laid by the last of the Saxon rulers.

No, she decided, the man for her must be dashing but kind; intelligent but with a sense of humour; brave and handsome.

Where on earth would she meet such a paragon in a small seaside town? One would simply have to fall into her lap.

CHAPTER 1

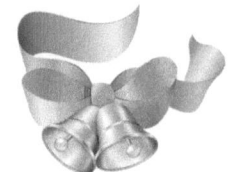

*B*y the time the horse and cart had negotiated the tight, steep turns up the path to the top of St Joseph's Rock; small waves were breaking over the causeway. Laura looked at the sky ahead, a crisp formation of arcus cloud approached like the advancing tide, heading for the coast.

"Papa, I'm home," she called, her arms filled with the first of two small crates. There was no answer, but that didn't alarm her. His badly-sprained foot wouldn't stop him hauling himself up the one hundred and eight steps to the top of the tower to use his telescope and check his barometer, to take notes on the storm to come.

Laura set the load on the kitchen table of their cottage and called from the bottom of the stairwell that led up to the light.

"Papa?"

"You're back, dear girl!" a voice echoed down the void. "Just one more measurement, and I'll be right down to give you a hand."

Laura grinned and shook her head.

By the time he had managed to get downstairs, she would have brought in all of their provisions and unharnessed Acorn the horse. Not that she minded. Laura took an interest in her father's weather recordings—those measures of the scale and scope of the weather influenced the livelihood of everyone in the district.

And indeed, she was correct. By the time her father joined her, Laura had begun the heavy weather routine her father had taught her as a child —persuade Milly the goat into her pen, chase the chickens back into their coop inside the stone-walled courtyard, and then take a walk around the perimeter of the lighthouse and its cottage to close the storm shutters.

The sound of a timber door slamming against the stone wall alerted her to her father's arrival downstairs.

She hurried around the lee of the building to find him outside and struggling to manage his crutches and the heavy cloak across his left arm.

Peter Winter, despite ruddy and weathered features that were testament to a life dedicated to the sea, was still a handsome man in his early fifties. He shared his daughter's bright green eyes and ready smile.

"I don't know who is supposed to be looking after whom here," he said, offering her the cloak.

Laura accepted it and was grateful for its warmth.

Walking side-by-side, they abandoned the protection of the light-house walls to venture closer to the southern end of St Joseph's Rock. Spray reached them even at that height as waves whipped up by the coming storm crashed and broke apart on the massive black boulders below.

Laura was about to make a comment when she found her father staring straight out to sea. She folded her arm into her father's and looked out to sea also. The storm clouds edged closer and heavy rain fell like a black curtain across the grey sea about a mile away from the shore.

"There's a boat out there," she said.

"Aye," he muttered more to himself than her, "but there were two a couple of hours ago."

"Together?" she asked, but her voice was carried away unheard in the rising wind.

Laura's father turned and hobbled back towards the lighthouse, moving swiftly on his crutches. Laura glanced back at the sea. Silhouetted by a flash of lightning, a ketch battled the increasing swell.

She followed swiftly toward the lighthouse, noticing the sharp splinters of afternoon sunlight still falling inland, a reminder of the changeable weather on the Devon coast. No sooner had the door slammed behind her than her father called.

"You'll have to give me a hand, love," he called down from the top of the stairs which he had ascended backwards on hand and seat with his bandaged foot straight out in front.

His crutches were propped at the bottom of the stairs and the edge to his voice spurred her on. Her father rarely asked for help.

The clatter of her footsteps on the iron treads competed with a roll of thunder. Laura reached the light tower just a few steps behind her father and helped him to stand so he could half-hop, half-limp about the room.

As she lit the wicks for the lamp, she could hear the clank-clank sound of the clockwork mechanism being wound. She closed the lens and, with a clunk as her father engaged the mechanism, the large lantern started to rotate, sending a shaft of light through the panes of glass that could be seen miles out to sea.

"Do you think it was one of our boats?" she asked, breathless from the burst of activity.

The fishing fleet at Ashton-On-Sea was one of the main livelihoods in the town but she knew a vessel lost on the rocks of St Joseph's would mean more than economic loss.

"I don't know," her father admitted. "I thought I counted all the fleet in about an hour ago. I hope whoever it is so fool hardy to have been caught up in the storm makes it to port before the worst hits."

As the lantern lens swept around again, she could see the firm set of his jaw and tight, worried lines around his eyes.

"This is going to be a big one," he said. "I can't ever recall the barometer dropping so quickly."

The wind died down as though the storm was holding its breath for a moment. It was an eerie sort of calm. Lightning heralded what was to come.

One-one thousand, two-one thousand, three-one thousand, four...

Crack!

The thunder snapped and popped, the sound echoing noisily in the center of the lighthouse tower.

Then the rains came, hard driving torrential rain that beat against the shutters, demanding entrance.

The returned wind howled and rose.

"You go below, love," said her father, "I'll be right behind you."

Downstairs, Laura lit a lamp and set it on the kitchen table before tending to the fire in the hearth in preparation for making dinner.

Thunder rumbled overhead once more and Admiral and Whisky the cats, one black and the other brown, scampered in to sit by the warmth of the fire and to eye any tidbits that might drop to the floor at mealtime.

The frequent Atlantic storms had ceased to frighten Laura many years ago. The stone walls and storm shutters protected them from the elements, though the shutters were rattled on their hinges by wind looking for ingress.

Nonetheless, Laura had a little ritual that gave her confidence in the face of the most ferocious tempests. It was silly really, but she felt better for doing it. As she began to chop the vegetables for the evening meal, she looked around the kitchen.

On one of the two blue-painted Welsh dressers were bottles of neatly labelled antiseptics, and crisp new bandages wound and stacked in tidy rows along with other medical miscellany. They stood like little soldiers at attention, waiting to be called to duty.

She surveyed them at a glance then looked over to the rear door. By it, a key hung on a brass loop. It opened the storage shed at the far end of the courtyard, where ropes, pulleys and nets were kept in good order to help rescue the crew of foundering vessels. Stores of powder were held there too—blue light for flares, black powder for the signal cannon—and all were assiduously checked every month.

Laura heard the clatter of her father taking up his crutches in the stairwell just as lightning once more flashed overhead. The accompanying crack of thunder was deafening.

Despite his name, Admiral wasn't very brave; neither was his sister. Both cats beat a hasty retreat under one of the dressers.

Laura and her father were as prepared as they possibly could be. Hopefully it would be enough should the boat they had seen be driven on the rocks.

SOMETIME IN THE early hours of the morning, the storm abated.

Despite being hampered by his injury, Laura's father was already up and outside in the still gusting winds, opening the storm shutters. Little by little, a pale rosy light filled the parlor and the kitchen.

Red sky in the morning, sailor's warning.

He had hung the kettle over the kitchen fire too and it was beginning to boil as Laura entered the room. She quickly prepared a steaming hot mug of tea and took it out to her father. He exchanged one of his crutches for it and gamely held the mug in one hand as he limped over to check the storage shed.

Laura released the chickens, which spilled out pell-mell from their roost to peck at the wind-whipped grass, little bothered by the two cats that playfully stalked them, and went to milk Milly. Afterwards, the goat gamboled out on to the grass, bleating her appreciation.

Laura took the milk inside and emerged again with a small telescope.

"I'm going to check the cliff edges," she called to her father, waving the spyglass. He was now at the stable door and raised a hand in acknowledgement.

She started with her favorite view, one which looked back to Ashton-On-Sea, but this morning the view was not good.

Several vessels had broken their moorings and were bobbing unmanned in the roiling sea inside Ashton Quay. Some dinghies were now little more than matchwood, first washed ashore then pushed further onto The Strand by waves that breached the sea wall by several feet even as she watched.

Not surprisingly, the causeway was completely submerged and would likely be so for several days. Spumes of white flecks shot many feet up in the air, filling the atmosphere with salty brine.

St Joseph's Rock was now an isolated island, only a quarter of a mile in area. A small grove of stunted trees, tenaciously gripping the Rock, formed a natural wind break on the western side. Laura edged around them to peer thirty feet down to where, in fine weather, a small sandy beach would be.

Something caught her eye. As a wave receded, the shape resolved itself.

It was not piece of flotsam but the body of a man, face down on a large boulder.

CHAPTER 2

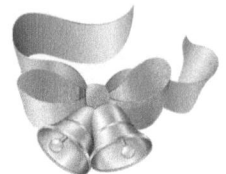

*L*aura's father watched her shoulder the long coil of rope.

"I'm not happy, dear girl. I should be the one going down there, not you."

She gave a pointed look at his injured foot. The way down to the beach was not sheer but it was no gentle slope either and the footing would be treacherous. "Well, needs must," she replied firmly. "I'll be back quickly."

His response was a grimace. He secured the trailing end of the coiled rope to Acorn's saddle.

"Watch your step, Laura," he admonished.

Trailing the rope out as she went, Laura picked her way with care down the side of the hill where the low-growing grass was slick. She grew up here and knew the cliffs well enough to treat them with respect. The saltiness from exploding waves filled her nostrils. She could even taste it on the back of her throat.

The beach filled and emptied as the waves churned in.

She scrambled over one rock, then around another to reach the man. The hem of her skirt darkened in the splashing water.

Still a few feet away, she called out.

"Sailor! Sailor, ahoy!"

The man remained still.

Laura looked back up the thirty feet to where her father peered back, concerned. He called to her but his words were ripped away by the wind.

Her only choice was to approach the man.

The sailor's shirt was torn and shredded, the sodden fabric dark and clinging to the contours of his back. His black hair whipped in the wind like the damp grass around the chickens.

She touched his cheek. His skin was cold.

It might already be too late!

Laura drew a deep breath and grasped his shoulders.

"Come on sailor, time to wake up," she said hopefully, shaking him.

The man obliged her with a groan; Laura matched it with a sigh of relief.

"Help is here," she said.

The man raised himself to his elbows and looked blearily at her. It was hard to determine his age. He seemed much younger than her father but older than Dickie Wells.

"Where are you hurt? Your back? Your legs?"

The man sat up gingerly, shaking his head at each question.

"We're going to haul you out," she said.

The man looked her up and down and flashed her a quick smile, his pale blue eyes twinkling with sudden merriment.

"My guardian angel..." he rasped, interrupted by a hacking cough. "Where is the rest of your heavenly choir?"

"It's just me and my father," she said, pointing up the cliff. Laura shucked off the remaining coils of rope and looped the end under his arms, tying it around his chest to create a harness.

Despite his ordeal, the man seemed well enough, and fit too—his shoulders broad and muscles firm around his arms.

He tried to rise to his feet but stumbled. Laura caught his wrist to support him and he hissed in pain.

She glanced down and saw his wrist had been rubbed red raw. The man shook off her hand, ignoring her scrutiny and whistled sharply towards her father on the cliff.

The mysterious stranger limped across the rocks to a grassy area as Laura's father drove Acorn to take up the slack and then, with a jolt, the rope tautened and he began to climb the steep hill, supported by the rope.

Guardian angel... Laura shook her head. With the speed he was making his way up the cliff, the sailor was the one who seemed to have wings. However, it also appeared he had sense enough to realize how weakened he was. He had not refused the assistance of the rope (which, Laura reflected, might as easily be being used now to haul his lifeless body up the slope) and he stumbled repeatedly, the rope all that prevented him from tumbling back down.

By the time she regained the top, the sailor was on his haunches, recovering his breath as her father untied the rope around his chest.

The man stood, wincing in pain. He was tall, a good inch taller than Laura's father who remained watchful and wary of the man.

An hour or so later, they had learned his name but not much more.

Michael Renten sat hunched on a chair before the kitchen fire, his hands around a mug of tea. His loaned clothes did not fit well but at least they were clean and dry.

"I couldn't get down to the base of the rock but from what I saw up top there don't seem to be any more survivors," Laura's father said after a long period of silence.

"And you're not likely to either, sir."

"I thought that might be the case, Mr. Renten."

Laura's father folded his arms and rested against the frame of the door that led to the lighthouse tower. Even on crutches, he was still an imposing figure.

"So would you mind telling us the full story?"

Laura frowned. "We've rescued people from the rocks before, father, and we've never demanded an explanation from them."

Admiral jumped up on the arm of the chair and nudged Laura's shoulder with his head. She stroked him absently.

Her father nodded at their guest.

"This man's wrists were bound together. He could be an escaped convict."

The young man spat out a bitter laugh, looking at his wounded wrists.

"An elegant deduction from the evidence but completely the wrong conclusion."

"Then explain yourself."

"I am a lieutenant in His Majesty's Waterguard. I was instructed to work in league with a group of blockade runners from Cornwall to identify their ringleader. They made a rendezvous with another vessel yesterday."

With a sigh, the man put down his cup and rubbed his wrists.

"One of the men from the other boat recognized me; a blackguard with whom I once served in His Majesty's Navy," he continued. "The men might have gutted me then and there, but their leader decided to bind my hands and toss me overboard just as the storm was bearing down."

Laura looked to her father and said nothing. The story seemed plausible.

Renten sighed. "I don't expect you to believe me, but if you sent someone to contact the Customs House at Plymouth…"

"We're completely cut off until the swell has died down," she said before her father silenced her with a cautioning glance.

The young man turned to Laura as if noticing her for the first time. "Indeed, miss?" he responded.

He was a handsome man to be sure. His hair had dried to a rich dark brown and, not bound with a ribbon, it fell to his shoulder.

He gave her a quick smile before turning back to her father.

"Do you have signal flags?" he asked.

THE SIGNAL of fourteen flags was too long for the flagpole so Laura's father suspended a line from an upper window in the light house to the pole. It read *Authenticate Agent MR*

As Lieutenant Renten caught up on sleep in a storeroom hastily turned into quarters, Laura set an extra place at the table for their guest.

"Do you believe his story?" she asked her father. He took his time in answering. "I suppose we'll find out in a few days," he answered in a noncommittal tone.

"I wonder what happened to the other two ships."

"Probably long gone, miss. If they were wise, they would have headed out to sea."

Laura jumped at the unexpected voice.

Rested, washed and shaved, the lieutenant looked more handsome than ever. She couldn't help but picture him in his dress uniform, sharply pressed navy-blue jacket with white collars and cuffs and bright brass buttons…

Stop it! She rebuked herself and quickly looked away, pretending to find the corned beef cooking in the pot to be particularly fascinating —yet not before she caught a glimpse of amusement in his expression.

The fine late autumn day was drawing to a close and Laura's father hoisted himself up on to his crutches ready to wind the clockwork.

"Can I assist you with the light, sir?" asked Renten.

The lighthouse keeper hesitated.

"A small service to help repay your hospitality," the lieutenant pressed.

The older man accepted, and the two ascended the stairs to the light.

THE MANTEL CLOCK in the parlor chimed seven and there was no sign of her father or the lieutenant.

"Where could they have gone?" she asked the cats. Whisky merely blinked at her but Admiral looked sharply toward the door and made an odd little growl.

"Stop it," she said, reprovingly, but she too wondered whether she had heard anything amiss. Admiral gave her a disinterested glance back.

A stiff evening breeze picked up. That would explain it. Admiral stared intently at the door.

"No, you are not going outside."

Laura cast her eye about and saw the scraggy ends of the meat that she had set aside.

"Here." She held a piece up for him to see and it met with his approval.

Now that the cats are fed, what about the men?

Laura opened the connecting door to the tower and laughter met her ears as the two men descended.

"I thought I was going to have to send a search party for you two!" she said as they entered the kitchen, but her exasperation was quelled by the pleasure her father was clearly having in the lieutenant's company.

"My fault entirely, dear lady."

Renten bowed formally so she curtsied in response.

"Well, my dear lieutenant, you can make amends by helping me bring the plates to the table."

As they sat down to eat at the kitchen table, Laura heard Milly bleat once outside then stop.

No, it was nothing, she thought. Just the wind.

CHAPTER 3

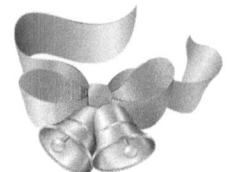

*T*he evening went splendidly. The lieutenant was convivial company and demonstrated through his actions as well as his words that his claim of rank was not unfounded.

Indeed, he had impressed Laura's father to the extent that he brought out a bottle of port after dinner. The two men stood by the fire with a glass each and Laura sat opposite with some needlework—anything to stop her restless fidgeting.

She watched Lieutenant Renten beneath her lashes.

It would have been lovely to have met him under other circumstances, Laura thought. A tea dance perhaps, where he would be in his dress uniform and she would be in a pink—no, a green, sprigged dress.

He would approach her, bow and say—

"Are you feeling all right, love?"

Laura started.

"I'm sorry, father. I was wool-gathering."

A blush crept up her cheeks and she pointedly kept her face away from their visitor. There was a silence which threatened to be awkward before Renten spoke.

"May I ask what happened to your foot, Mr. Winter?"

"Too much Whisky."

"Oh…" said the lieutenant, unsure how otherwise to respond.

Laura held a smile in check at his expression.

Then, as if on cue, a furry, orange-brown streak sped across the room, narrowly missing the man.

"Meet Whisky," said Laura. "Around her, no one is steady on their feet."

And they all joined in the laughter.

As the evening wore on, Laura's father excused himself to check on the light once more before retiring, politely refusing the lieutenant's offer to do it for him. To Laura's surprise, Renten then offered to assist with cleaning the kitchen.

They chatted over the chores, and she found out the lieutenant was from Dorset where his family still lived. He had a sister who was to have her coming-out next summer and a widowed mother whom he was supporting.

Laura listened and waited for mention of a wife. The fact there was none made her unaccountably glad.

She told him about the offer to train under Miss Jones to become a school mistress in town and start as a teacher the following September, and of her interest in keeping meteorological records like her father.

Suddenly, as quick as a flash, Whisky raced across the kitchen again, under a chair, around a table leg, through Renton's legs and skidded on the slate floor to come to a halt right by the back door.

A strange note came from her throat, a chattering sound, not quite the same as her hunting sound.

"Whisky! What are you doing, you daft cat?" Laura called. "Shoo! Get away from the door, go sleep in front of the fire like your brother."

Over the wind outside, Laura could hear shuffling noises but dismissed them as nothing more than Milly and Acorn in their stalls.

The cat, its gaze fixed on the door, reversed a few paces, back arched and a ridge of fur rising up at the tail.

Laura reached for a broom propped in the corner when Renten grabbed it. Their hands barely touched but the warmth of his lingered as she allowed him to take it.

"I'm going outside to check."

Laura shook her head. "Really, there's no need, there's always odd sounds when the wind pushes on shore like this..."

He put a finger to his lips to silence her and unlatched the door, slipping around it and closing it behind him with nary a sound.

Laura continued tidying up and kicked herself.

He was being polite and you had to embarrass him and yourself.

Humph! 'Going outside to check'! How many times had her father used a similar excuse of 'going for a short stroll' to conveniently answer the call of nature?

Countless, countless times.

Laura Ann Rose Winter, you are a goose of the first order!

Yet that didn't explain why he took the broom...

Oh well. Least said, soonest mended, she thought.

The best thing would be to put Lieutenant Renten out of her mind. After all, the crossing to Ashton-On-Sea would soon be passable and him gone, chasing ne'er-do-wells, pirates and smugglers on behalf of the Crown.

Still, when she had thought of a man falling into her lap, she never considered he might be washed up on shore!

The thought made her giggle out loud and Admiral raised a sleepy head from his place at the fire to look at her.

Laura placed her hand over her mouth at the sound of boots at the kitchen door. It wouldn't do for him to see her like that.

The sound of the boots grew louder.

What on earth was he doing? Dancing a jig?

A figure burst through the door. She noticed a sharp blade glinting in the lamp light before realizing the man was not Renten.

He grinned evilly and held the knife forward. Laura screamed.

Admiral leapt to his feet, fur standing on end making him near double in size. He ran straight in front of the advancing man, tripping him and bringing him to his knees. His weapon clattered loose onto the floor

He swung a fist at Admiral and the cat yowled at the blow, then doubled back and with a one-two strike of his claws, drew blood from the back of the intruder's hand.

Laura picked up a small skillet and brought it down with a dull clang on the man's head. He gasped and slipped unconscious to the floor.

Another man burst through the doorway. Laura brandished her skillet and screamed again.

"It's me!" said Renten, raising his hands in a placating gesture. "I don't have time to explain. Lock all the doors and windows now. I'll deal with this one."

Startled by his sudden appearance, with thick dark hair wildly disheveled by the wind and the alertness and command with which he carried himself, Laura hurried to comply.

"What's going on?" Laura's father yelled from the stairwell door; his face flushed with the exertion of rapidly descending the light house.

"The brigands are on the island," Renten called, while he bound the still-unconscious invader hand and foot with strips of wash cloth.

From another part of the house there was the sound of breaking glass.

"Papa!" Laura called.

Renten arrived to her aid.

She stood to one side of her bedroom window armed with a fire poker, jabbing at the arm of the man trying to feel his way to the latch that would open the sash.

That wasn't working so she struck a forceful downward blow and the arm withdrew accompanied by a yowl of pain, along with a trail of blood.

Immediately another face appeared in the window. A bearded face, angry and scowling, that looked briefly into the room directly at the lieutenant then ducked away.

"Renten! Come out here, you scurvy dog! I thought your death was too good to be true. You've got more lives than a cat."

Laura turned to see Renten draw himself taller. It was clear he knew the man.

"I'm surprised the storm didn't put you in Davy Jones' locker," the lieutenant retorted.

"Not before I see you in hell with me!"

"Manners, Blackwell! There's a lady present!"

There was a momentary pause before the bearded face again loomed in the window, this time glancing left and right. Laura brandished her poker once more as the man's gaze fell upon her.

"Beggin' your pardon miss," the scoundrel known as Blackwell said rather formally. "Now if you wouldn't mind persuading your houseguest to leave with us, then we will be all on our way peaceable like.

"You see, I have a dozen good strong men here who are capable of taking apart your cottage stone-by-stone."

Laura turned to look at Renten.

Then she saw her father appear at his shoulder and raise his musket.

CHAPTER 4

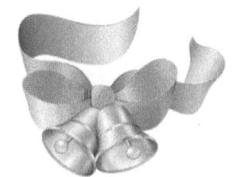

"*I*'ll decide who is a guest in my home and who is not."

Laura's father cocked the weapon to add emphasis. The click was crisp, unmistakable over the sound of the wind.

The face in the window disappeared into the blackness outside.

"Well, it wouldn't do to be too hasty now, would it?" ventured Blackwell in a conciliating voice, a little distance away. "I'll tell you what I'll do. My men will keep guard while you all get a very nice night's sleep."

"I'll tell you what we'll do," Laura's father continued. "One of your men has already made himself at home here, so we'll keep him as our guest overnight."

"Which one, Renten?"

"Smithy," the lieutenant answered.

There was a grunt, then the sound of murmured voices as though a consensus was being sought.

"All right, keep the zounderkite for the night," agreed Blackwell. "We'll parley in the morning. First light."

Over the sound of the wind, the sound of tramping feet could be heard leaving the courtyard.

Renten swiftly opened the windows and pulled the storm shutters closed over the now broken windows. He turned back to his hosts and folded his arms. His expression was grim.

"Mr. Winter, Miss Winter—you have my apologies," he said. "Should you wish to toss me out, I wouldn't blame you."

"Don't be daft, young man," Laura's father scoffed. "So, what are we going to do to sort these blighters out?"

Laura watched Renten consider her and her father for several long seconds, and she realized she was still gripping the poker. Her father held the musket across his chest.

Then a broad smile spread over his face. Laura felt her spirits lighten immediately.

"Well," said the lieutenant, "with Smithy safely tucked away, there are twelve of them and three of us. I think the odds are in our favor."

He turned to Laura. "Miss Winter... Laura," he continued, "I suggest you get some sleep. It's going to be a long night."

Laura was prepared to argue when her father stepped in.

"The clockwork will need to be wound twice more before morning, dear girl, and I'll need to show the lieutenant the caves."

Renten looked intrigued. "Caves? Are they easy to find?"

Laura's father shook his head slowly and grinned. "They're not, and no one knows the Rock better than me."

"It looks like I'm outnumbered, but you–" she said to Renten, poking his chest with a finger, "you make sure my father doesn't lead you into trouble."

He gifted her with a wink.

"I'm good at following orders... more or less."

As THE BEAM of light swept around, Laura could see a schooner at anchor off the island. A small bonfire burned on the headland, highlighting four small tents. Earlier, she saw figures walking about, but Blackwell was apparently being as good as his word.

As the night wore on and Laura wound the clockwork mechanism for the last time before dawn, the fire on the headland had burned down to glowing red coals.

She must have slept after that, with Whisky and Admiral curled up beside her, because she wasn't awakened by the pre-dawn light but by an insistent knock on the door below.

"Miss Laura!" She recognized the lieutenant's voice. "Quick as you can. Join us downstairs."

Had she missed something? She straightened herself quickly and swiftly descended the spiral staircase. Her father was in the kitchen; the smell of cured ham and eggs along with the earthy pungent aroma of freshly fried mushrooms filled the room.

He handed his daughter a full plate—a man-sized serving. She was about to protest when he pivoted across on his good leg to grasp the back of a chair at the table where Renten sat tucking into his food.

He sat down, taking several mouthfuls of food before he noticed his daughter standing there looking at him askance.

"Eat up, dear girl, we have a lot of work to do."

Laura slowly sank into her chair and put a forkful of food into her mouth. Her father looked ten years younger. She hadn't seen that spark in his eyes since her mother passed away.

"What do you two have planned?" she asked, suspicion dripping from each word.

Renten put a finger up to ask for silence as he shoveled the last of his breakfast into his mouth and washed it down with a swig of tea.

"Your father showed me through the caves."

Ah, thought Laura, that explains the mushrooms for breakfast.

"All I need is some blue powder, black powder and a little time."

Renten's and her father's enthusiasm was infectious and Laura found herself catching it too.

"What do you need me to do?"

A FOURTH HAD JOINED them after breakfast, albeit reluctantly. Smithy was seated miserably at the table, his bound hands and feet covered by a large cloak, his dirty pale hair plastered with a mixture of coal dust and fat to darken it.

At a distance he would pass for the lieutenant. A musket aimed at his head by Laura's father ensured his ongoing compliance.

Laura waited at the back door until she heard the cellar door close. Renten was on his way through the narrow and dark labyrinth of caves and fissures that would open out to the sea.

Her father remained out of sight and nodded.

She emerged into the morning sun and the courtyard seemed deserted, although she was certain someone would be watching, hence the ruse with Smithy.

Adjusting the empty basket on her arm, Laura turned to see a man emerge from the shadows.

He had an overnight growth of whiskers only, so he was not Blackwell.

"'Owdie miss," he greeted with a laconic drawl as he made his way towards her.

"Good morning," she said crisply.

"'Ow's our friend inside then?"

"Look for yourself."

The man did and saw a black-haired figure sitting with his back to the window.

"Excuse me," said Laura, sweeping past him. "I have eggs to collect."

Laura opened the door to the coop and the chickens rushed out, following their long-practiced routine of milling in the courtyard before rushing out the gate and onto the grass.

Inside the coop, Laura reached into the laying box to collect the eggs, mindful of the man watching her. Then she felt her bottom being pinched.

Laura stood, banged her head on a roost and let out a yelp of surprise.

There followed immediately another high-pitched scream but it didn't come from her. Wild flapping filled the air and Laura stood back as the man tried frantically to protect his face from the wild pecking and scratching of the coop's very angry rooster, King.

He stumbled backwards out into the courtyard and ran blindly in a small circle with the rooster attached to his head. "Help! Help!" he cried, but when he dislodged the fowl after several frenzied seconds it was too late to stop himself crashing headlong into the courtyard wall.

The man slumped to the ground and King shook himself down and strutted outside to join the hens.

Laura slipped out of the coop and bolted the door behind her, regarding the unconscious man with satisfaction. One down, eleven to go. She calmly released Milly from her pen and Acorn from his stall before returning to the house.

"Father?" she called, bolting the door.

"In here, my girl."

She found him in the parlor where it appeared Smithy was now being made 'comfortable' in front of the bay window. Then the figure slumped forward.

"What happened to him?"

Laura's father hauled the figure back up but it was not Smithy. The cloak was now wrapped about her father's bolster pillow with collar turned up and a broad-brimmed hat covering the 'head'. It seemed that her father had fashioned a mannequin.

"I couldn't leave Smithy to help you so I tossed him back in the cupboard," he said by way of explanation. "Then I saw you and King had sorted the other one out so I threw this together."

Laura nodded at the mannequin. "That's not going to fool Blackwell for long."

"It doesn't have to—just for long enough."

"Well, you're going to get your chance," said Laura, pointing out of the window. "Here comes Blackwell now."

They watched the menacing figure approach the front door with purpose.

Then a series of crackles and pops disturbed the morning air as a bright white flare burst in the sky to their left, and sea birds screeched and flew away from the noise.

Laura and her father rushed outside.

Beneath the flare burst, at a distance, Renten stood with his back to the cliff on the shore side of the Rock. At his feet sat a small iron cauldron and a candle stub in a glass lantern.

"There he is, grab him!" yelled Blackwell to two of his men. The pair sprinted across the grass with Blackwell following.

Laura's father put a restraining hand on her arm, bringing her to a stop just outside the door.

"There's nothing we can do from here."

"But—"

"Just wait."

The two men had now pulled out their swords and yelled damnable threats as they closed in.

"Why doesn't the lieutenant do something?" Laura whispered tautly.

"Just wait," her father insisted.

Blackwell too had stopped running as he watched his two men close the gap. They were now only ten yards away when Renten picked up the lantern, pulled out the candle and dropped it in the cauldron.

The blackguards closed in—five yards, two yards—then the powder in the cauldron ignited. Renten disappeared in a flash of light and billowing smoke.

The two men ran into the miasma and, a moment later, their cries of distress were heard as they ran right off the edge of the cliff.

Laura gripped her father's hand at the sound and the sight.

When the white-blue smoke cleared, the cliff edge was deserted, save for the cauldron.

CHAPTER 5

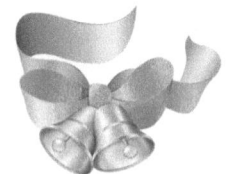

*L*aura cried out but her father held her firm. She looked at him and he kept his head down too in case Blackwell, standing aghast only a hundred feet away, turned and saw him grinning.

"Calm yourself, dear girl," her father reassured her as Blackwell now ran over to the cliff edge, "not everything is as it appears. Trust me—the lieutenant is perfectly safe."

More of Blackwell's men joined him on the cliff edge and he ordered them to descend in search of their companions.

Laura cocked her head. "What have you and he been up to?"

"No time to talk now. Get up the tower, my girl, and hoist a new message. We need help from the shore."

Laura nodded, already mentally counting out the signal flags she would need.

"What are you going to be doing?" she asked.

"I'll secure the cottage then join you in the lighthouse. Our friend Mister Blackwell will not be happy shortly."

Satisfied with the arrangements, Laura retrieved the flag box and climbed halfway up the stairs to the small window. She pulled the previous signal in like so much laundry, then set the new message.

She completed the climb to the top and looked out. Even without a spyglass, Laura could see stirring on the shore already. She chanced a look over in the other direction. A flushed and angry Blackwell stood halfway between the cliff-edge and the lighthouse, looking up at the signal flags and her. Laura offered a cheeky wave.

His face turned a furious puce shade before he turned and erupted into a tremendous bellow to his men on the edge of the cliff now hauling their injured compatriots up off the rocks below.

Milly the goat wandered into view, her ears erect at Blackwell's roar. Laura watched the animal's head drop as it ran as fast as her four little legs could take her—right at Blackwell's rear.

The man was cannoned onto his face and Milly bleated her satisfaction before trotting off.

Laura doubled over in laughter but then stopped abruptly as a door slammed downstairs and there came the sound of drawers being opened and closed violently. Her heart pounded. The villains were inside and ransacking her home!

Then came her father's voice: "Laura! Where's my telescope?"

Her heart resumed its normal rhythm.

"I have it up here with me," she called down.

She heard him close and bolt the connecting door to the tower and start making his way, seat first, up the stairs.

"Head up to the light and tell me what you see," he called ahead.

From her vantage point, she could see Blackwell had regathered what remained of his dignity and his men. The leader gesticulated wildly with his cutlass. She then trained the telescope across to Ashton-On-Sea.

The townsfolk, attracted by the flare, were now reacting to the flags. She saw Mr. Fletcher and Dickie, the Reverend Harman and a few other townsmen casting off in the roiling and choppy waves that still separated St Joseph's Rock from the shore.

Laura relayed the information to her father.

"And what of Renten?" his disembodied voice demanded. "Check the schooner!"

"The schooner? How on earth did he get there?"

She edged around the lantern to look south though the telescope. Renten was just bringing a dinghy alongside the schooner.

Her father spoke from the doorway as he struggled to his feet.

"Where the lieutenant dropped off the edge of the cliff is a small ledge and fissure. You know the Rock is full of them. That one leads across to the ocean side but is narrow and hazardous. The lieutenant's mission was to draw Blackwell's men shore side then slip through to their vessel."

Laura put the glass back to her eye and could see the lieutenant's dark hair ruffle in the breeze and his shirt stretched taut across his back as he hefted a small barrel on to his shoulder.

"What in heaven's name is he doing?"

Renten nimbly climbed up a rope ladder and tossed the barrel on the deck before scrambling up over the deck rail himself.

"He has a surprise planned for our visitors," said her father, limping to her side.

Laura passed the telescope to him. To her surprise, he didn't spare a moment looking at Renten, but instead set the focus on the brigands on the ground.

They too had noticed the two small boats from Ashton-On-Sea making their way to Saint Joseph's Rock. Blackwell's men had gathered around him.

Without the advantage of the telescope, Laura could only guess at what they were saying. They did not look at all pleased.

"We need more time," her father muttered, handing her the telescope once again.

"More time for what?" she asked to an empty room. Her father was already making his way downstairs.

She followed after him.

"Father!"

He was hobbling precariously down the stairs for speed, putting the least weight possible on his injured foot.

"We need a further distraction. The signal cannon should do it," he called back to her.

Laura followed him into the kitchen where he opened the pantry door. From behind a sack of potatoes, he pulled out a small barrel similar to the one she had seen the lieutenant carrying.

"Gunpowder! Mother would be cross at you bringing a whole barrel into the house!"

He ignored her scolding, instead telling her to fetch along a couple of the small cannon balls he had hidden among the onions.

Outside, on the eastern side of the lighthouse, the small cannon stood pointing out to sea.

Her father prepared the cannon, priming it with gunpowder and lighting the fuse as Laura nervously waited for them to be discovered by one of Blackwell's men.

As good fortune would have it, they remained out of sight behind the cottage, arguing volubly with their leader.

"Right-o Laura, get back inside—"

Bang!

The little cannon fired, the report disproportionately loud to its small size, and it immediately attracted attention.

In fact, before they could go more than a few paces, ten men with cutlasses drawn stood between them and the safety of the cottage.

Blackwell stepped forward.

"You," he thundered, his arm shaking with fury as he pointed to them. "You two have become too meddlesome."

"Big Arms! No Nose! Take them inside and tie them up." The two men who stepped forward clearly deserved their nicknames. They pinned the Winters' arms behind their backs and began marching them towards the cottage, Laura's father moaning in pain at being forced to put weight on his injured ankle.

Behind them, Blackwell roared at his men.

"The rest of you find that fool Smithy and look for Tinder while you're at it. He's not been seen since first light. He can't have gone far on this flyspeck."

Close to the cottage, the lighthouse keeper stumbled.

"Father!" Laura cried out in alarm. "You big brute, let go of me. My father is hurt!"

After a few strong tugs, No Nose decided to let her go. She rushed to her father and wrapped her arms around him.

"Just a few moments more," he muttered. "A few moments more..."

"Hey! What you be mutterin' 'bout?" Big Arms asked.

Laura helped her father back to his feet and he took a hesitant step towards the cottage. Then a smile split his face as a flash of light, brighter than the sun, was reflected in the cottage windows.

Laura turned rapidly to see the strange phenomenon and a fraction later the sound caught up.

BOOM!

CHAPTER 6

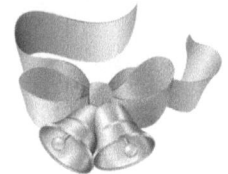

One of the schooner's large spars shot a hundred feet straight up in the air, and Laura watched agog as the large lump of timber began falling down again.

"Thunderation!" said Big Arms, and he and No Nose took off in the direction of the blast, though it was clear they could do little of use about it.

Then Laura's father tugged her towards shelter as debris began raining down on the Rock.

Acorn galloped as fast as Laura had ever seen him, quickly followed by Milly and the chickens, all of which all huddled in the courtyard vocalizing their distress, the sound echoing around the stone enclosure.

Admiral and Whisky peered out from behind a curtain, their tawny eyes wide and round.

Blackwell and his men stood at the southerly point where their clipper was now nothing more than flotsam.

"Quick as you can, love, back inside," Laura's father urged. "If Blackwell was angry before, he's going to be furious now."

"What are you going to do?"

"I'm going to meet our friends from Ashton."

Laura shook off her father's hand and ran back to where No Nose and Big Arms had dropped their weapons as they fled. She picked up both blades and returned with them.

"*We're* going to meet our friends from Ashton," she corrected him. "No one is going to drive me out of my home."

She thought her father may be angry at her disobedience. Instead, he grinned and urged her to run ahead of him.

"That's my girl," he muttered with pride.

By the time they had reached the path that rose from the submerged causeway, Reverend Harman, Fletcher and Dickie had been joined by a group of twenty other men—fishermen and farmhands, smithies and merchants—all of them angry.

"Where are the scurvy-dog scoundrels!" demanded one.

"We'll drive them back into the sea!" added another.

Reverend Harman called for calm and Laura's father briefly told the story of the past three nights.

The crowd grumbled.

"Eh Dickie, you bring enough rope to secure these blackguards?" asked Fletcher of his assistant.

The young man pushed his way forward with a bundle of rope across his shoulder.

"I did, sir!" he said, bustling to the fore.

The grocer leaned in. "Now that would be the old stock, not the new that came in the other day?" he muttered.

"Oh, yes, Mr. Fletcher, the old stuff just like you said."

"Good lad," replied the older man, then, noticing the reproachful looks from the others, he straightened his back and rubbed his belly. "It's still good rope, well proven…"

"Then round them up, men," Reverend Harman instructed, rolling up his sleeves, apparently ready to put his boxing skills to the test if need be. "These villains can cool their heels in one of the empty ware-houses until the Waterguard arrives in the morning."

With the exception of the Reverend, Laura noted, everyone was armed—cutlasses, pistols, hoes and clubs—and they marched with purpose towards the southern point where Blackwell and his men remained, disconsolate at their loss.

At the sound of the approaching posse, Blackwell turned. A menacing grin spread slowly across his face. He drew his cutlass and stepped forward.

"We may have lost our ship, but we're not going to surrender meekly to a group of lily-livered townsfolk, are we men?" he called.

"Yes, we are!" they replied.

Blackwell turned back glacially.

"Men?"

They looked at one another, and Big Arms, who appeared to have been appointed spokesman of those who remained fit for battle, stepped forward, rubbing the back of his head ruefully.

"Actually, Mr. Blackwell, the men 'ave all agreed we're going to give up smuggling."

Murmured agreement rippled through the gang.

"I mean, it's one thing to bring in contraband from the Frenchies, but tying up that customs man and throwing him overboard in a storm was criminal."

"You *are* criminals!" Blackwell insisted.

"Aye, but we're not murderers."

One by one the men dropped their weapons and raised their arms above their heads—all except Blackwell who was quickly disarmed and restrained by two of the blacksmith's men.

"Sir, miss," said Big Arms, addressing Laura and her father. "I'm very sorry to have 'arrassed you. You won't have any trouble from us again, I'll promise ye that."

Laura's father nodded his acknowledgement but Laura had lost interest in the proceedings.

She wandered to the edge of the cliff. The sea was beginning to calm, already returning to the rhythm of the days and the seasons which were long familiar to her.

It tugged at her, filling her with a strange longing.

The sun had moved past its zenith and golden tipped waves shimmered on the horizon. Amid the debris from the schooner, the small boat from the vessel was bobbing near the rocks, unattended.

The lieutenant!

She hadn't seen him since the explosion. Was he safe? Had he fallen overboard? Had he made it off the schooner at all?

His absence jolted her into action.

At the northern end of the Rock, the prisoners were already being ferried across to the mainland in groups.

Now there was only a handful of men waiting for transport. Her father was speaking to the Reverend.

"Father, have you seen Lieutenant Renten?" she interrupted.

"There he is," he said, pointing to one of the boats making its way back to Ashton-On-Sea with the prisoners. Laura's heart skipped a beat as she identified him from his dark hair.

As though he was aware of being observed, he turned and appeared to be looking straight at her.

No, surely that couldn't be; he was four hundred yards away, and yet he raised his hand and gave a salute. She raised her hand in return and his salute turned into a wave.

Despite the chill in the air, warmth bloomed through her.

WHAT REMAINED of the year raced through like the squalls that sweep in from the Atlantic.

The excitement caused by the arrival of the brigands ebbed after Blackwell and his men were taken away. Life returned to normal.

The fleet went out to catch fish between the winter storms and the Ashton-On-Sea Christmas fête was judged to be the best yet.

With his foot fully healed, Laura's father had taken his place in the choir, much to the delight of Miss Jones who also invited Laura to teach the youngest children at her school after New Year instead of the next school year.

Yet despite the festivities and parties, Laura felt something amiss.

Lieutenant Michael Renten.

How odd that someone she had only known for a short time and under the most extraordinary circumstances should occupy so many of her thoughts.

She had been among the townsfolk gathered on the quay to farewell the dashing young officer but in the press of the crowd it would be a mistake to believe that, as he stood looking back on the gangplank, he was looking for her.

And surely it was a silly romantic notion born from reading too many novels that it seemed to her their eyes met for that briefest moment before he was urged on to the clipper by the bosun.

Laura never spoke these thoughts aloud.

Only her private diary knew her secrets—a record of one moment in time when she had a brush with adventure and romance—a precious memory to treasure.

Perhaps that would be enough.

CHAPTER 7

Christmas Day
        St Joseph's Church at Ashton-on-Sea was beautifully lit
that morning. A myriad of candles burned in every candelabra,
casting a merry yellow light on the colorful hand-sewn silk pennants
that hung from the walls.

Laura wore her warmest wool dress in a deep red. It was a festive
color which matched her mood. On her coat was a lovely gold-enam-
eled brooch, a gift from her father.

Reverend Harman delivered the sermon from the Book of Isaiah:

For unto us a Child is born,
Unto us a Son is given;
And the government will be upon His shoulder.
And His name will be called
Wonderful, Counsellor, Mighty God

The choir took up the theme with excerpts from Handel's Messiah,
which they had been rehearsing since September.

Laura listened proudly to her father's rich tenor. He looked
wonderful in his choir robes of scarlet red and white.

As the recital continued, Laura felt a small rush of cold air from
the doorway as latecomers joined them.

Not very surprising, she thought, not glancing back but enraptured by the candle-lit choir. Summer might bring the sun worshippers looking to take a rest cure by the sea, but Christmas brought the pilgrims looking to capture a moment of spiritual connection, no matter how tenuously arrived at.

The choir did not disappoint with its recital, nor Reverend Harman when he stepped forward and read Blake's poem, the one adopted for St Joseph's Rock.

And did those feet in ancient time
Walk upon England's mountains green?
And was the holy Lamb of God
On England's pleasant pastures seen?

As the congregation stood together to sing Hark! The Herald Angels Sing, Laura could not help but think of Blackwell's brigands during the opening verse and she wished them reconciled.

And, outside after the service, she looked across to the lighthouse, its tall whitewashed tower gleaming in the winter sun. The tides favored them today. It would be hours before they needed to consider a homeward journey.

Laura spotted a familiar face and rushed towards him.

"Dickie! Congratulations, I'm so glad you proposed." Laura hugged Dickie, then Kitty, a pretty little blonde girl, the daughter of the local tailor who was receiving good wishes from everyone in the parish.

Even Mr. Fletcher, who was normally so gruff with his assistant, stood beaming with avuncular pride.

"Tell me, Laura," said Kitty, "who is your father talking to?"

"I'm not sure," she admitted. The man must have been among their latecomers but he had his back to her.

He was dressed in the uniform of a naval commander—crisp white breeches topped by a rich navy-blue coat trimmed with gold braiding and buttons on the sleeves. A single gold epaulette sat on the left shoulder.

Then, for the first time, she noticed the other smartly-dressed naval officers among the congregation. She looked for a lieutenant's uniform and found it. Its wearer was talking to the reverend's wife.

Laura turned away.

It wasn't him.

"Laura!"

Disappointment dampened her cheer, but she forced a smile and turned to her father's call.

"There is someone who is very keen to renew his acquaintances with you."

The commander turned and she found herself face to face with the man who filled her dreams and the pages of her diary.

"Miss Winter, a great pleasure to see you again."

His warm and ready smile faltered for a moment before Laura realized she hadn't returned his greeting but was simply staring at him open-mouthed.

She recovered herself.

"The pleasure is mine, *Commander*."

To her surprise, he blushed and his smile turned shy.

"My commission is only a week old. I'm still not used to hearing it," he admitted. "With your father's permission, would you care to take a walk, Miss Winter?"

To Laura's mind, her father gave his permission with too much enthusiasm, even excusing himself before she could accept the offer herself.

Renten offered his arm. She took it and they strolled toward the Strand.

The quayside no longer bore evidence of the storm but was now home to three new ships she didn't recognize—a fine single-masted cutter, an elegant sloop and a smaller boat better suited for navigating the shallow inlets along the coast.

"We arrived just as the service was beginning. I came straight to the church," he said.

He told her that, after Blackwell's capture, due in no short measure to her and her father, he was promoted.

"I asked to take a brand-new posting, right here," he said.

"How long has my father known?"

"A week, possibly two. I wrote to ask permission to court you when I learned of my promotion. Why?"

He paused and grinned as the answer came to him.

"He never told you, did he?"

"He did not! The sneak."

"Disappointed?"

"Never," she said sincerely.

Laura stepped closer.

She could feel his warmth and she placed both hands in his and squeezed them gently.

He raised her hand to his lips and kissed it.

"In fact," she said, "It is a Christmas wish come true."

Then let us all rejoice again,
On Christmas Day, on Christmas Day;
Then let us all rejoice again,
On Christmas Day in the morning.

The End

ABOUT ELIZABETH ELLEN CARTER

Elizabeth Ellen Carter is a USA Today bestselling author and award-winning historical romance writer who pens richly detailed historical romantic adventures. A former newspaper journalist, Carter ran an award-winning PR agency for 12 years. She lives in Australia with her husband and two cats.

Learn more about Elizabeth Ellen at:

Website: https://www.eecarter.com

The fast-paced humor of Three Ships is in contrast to Elizabeth's usual style, but has in common with her other stories a love of thrills and suspense. Her latest novel is Deceiving the Duke, which sees impoverished Scottish Lady Ruby McAllister seeking to make a dying duke honor a promise to her late father. Posing as a night nurse to get closer, she finds herself attracted to Seth Musgrave, the duke's estranged son. He also has good reason to dislike his meanspirited father, but what if he learns the woman he's falling in love with is deceiving the Duke?

SOCIAL MEDIA FOR ELIZABETH ELLEN CARTER

You can learn more about Elizabeth Ellen Carter at these social media links:

Website: http://eecarter.com
Facebook: https://www.facebook.com/ElizabethEllenCarter
Pinterest: https://www.pinterest.com/eecarterauthor/
Instagram: https://www.instagram.com/elizabeth_ellen_carter/
BookBub: https://www.bookbub.com/authors/elizabeth-ellen-carter
YouTube: https://www.youtube.com/c/ElizabethEllenCarter

THE BEAU OF CHRISTMAS PAST

BY CERISE DELAND

Years ago, Alyssa and Gabe were caught enjoying a Christmas kiss, which broke Alyssa's betrothal to another man, and caused the pair to be exiled, far from their families and one another. Home for Christmas, will they find the past something to be overcome? Or fulfilled?

CHAPTER 1

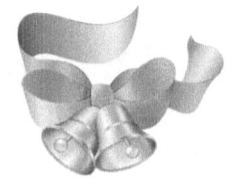

 *ecember 16, 1818*
         London

"But Gabe, you must come!" His oldest friend grinned at him. "Third time is a charm!"

Gabriel Shaw did not put any stock in superstitions. He had the successes of hard work to his credit and little in this world had come to him by serendipity. So, when his cousin, the ninth earl of Darby, died in September and the family solicitor sailed to him in Venice to announce that Gabe was the tenth earl, he laughed first, drank excessively second, and wrote to his assistant in the City of London third.

Life did not come at him in threes. Usually only in ones. One directive by his grandfather, the eighth earl, to improve the old family import business alone. One bequest by his dying father of one hundred pounds sterling to save the business that had been decimated by the wars of the little Frenchman. Followed two months later by one order from his uncle, the newly minted ninth earl, to leave England and never show his face there again.

Frowning at his friend, whom he'd loved since they were at Eton, Gabe shook his head at the man's invitation to attend his and his wife's Christmas festivities. He chose his words carefully, despite their camaraderie since age six. Barrington's Christmas ball five years ago had seen Gabe in his first pickle with a charming girl. Barr's ball the following year had been the second with the same irresistible lady. It had also been the very event he had attended that precipitated Gabe's quick banishment from good society. "I have not danced in years."

Lord Barrington, the sixth earl of his family, lifted his brandy and wiggled his long pale brows in jest. It was ten in the morning at their London club, but Barr was toasting Gabe's change of fortune. "I do not expect you to waltz, old man."

"I gather Dora is short on single men for the holiday?" he teased. Gabe liked Barr's wife. Always had. A second cousin of his own on his mother's side, Dora possessed a gaiety that was not only natural but enduring.

"We need you. Besides, you must go north to inspect your estate sometime. Sooner would be best, and you know it. Come. We will make your days pleasant. You will not be drawn down by old memories."

Gabe savored another taste of his brandy. The best memories he had of Barrington Priory were two Christmases long ago. The first, five years ago, found him in a broom closet with a giggling girl. The second, one year later, found him in a butler's pantry with that same lovely creature. It was also the event when both of them were discovered by her fiancé that had inspired his uncle to exile him. "Ironic, isn't it, how life can play tricks on you?"

"In your case, Gabe, yes. You've had more than most. But your luck is turning. Come to Yorkshire for Christmas. Dora wants you. I do. So do the boys."

"And does Dora's best friend attend?" He locked his gaze on Barr's, fearing his answer and wanting it in the affirmative all at the same time.

"She does."

She was the very reason he should not go. Exile to all the marvels of Cadiz and Casablanca, Florence, Venice and Athens had not dashed her from his memory.

"She has been with us for four months now," Barrington said.

"After her father and her brother Malcolm died in July, she lived in a small tiny cottage in Bradford on one of their unentailed properties. Dora invited her with us because we need help with the boys."

Both of the lady's relatives had been severely injured in the same carriage accident. Upon reading the news in the *London Times*, Gabe ordered his man of business in the City to get all the details from the family solicitor.

"Malcolm lingered longer than his father," Barrington said and drained his glass. "But he could not overcome the pain of his injuries."

Gabe had never gained anything without observance of logic. "She is in mourning still, Barr. She won't agree to celebrate with you." *Or me. Definitely not with me. I was the cause of so much of her suffering.*

"Dora insists on it. Says she needs a happy Christmas. As do you."

"Oh, Barr. Please. I am the new earl of Darby, tenth of my less than noble lineage. Rich beyond my expectations or my station. In trade, for God's sake. What right have I of happiness?"

"Every right. You'll make a damn sight better earl than ever the last three of your family. Trade, be damned, or in your case, applauded. You've earned your right to claim the land, the houses, and title. Justice that you have it all, I say, it is. But you will have your hands full. If rumor is true, your predecessors were thieves of the profits for gaming hells and actresses. Now no arguments. Write them at Darby Park to open the doors and windows to a new day in your house. Then come to Christmas at Barrington Priory." His friend winked at him. "Third Christmas is the charm!"

CHAPTER 2

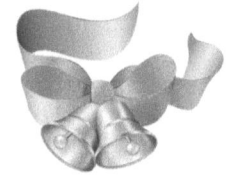

Wednesday, December 22, 1818
Ripon, Yorkshire

"Reginald! Come back here this minute!" Alyssa darted after her eight-year-old charge. "You've left your scarf!"

"Auntie Al!" cried Thomas, Reggie's six-year-old brother. "He took my skates!"

"Grab his, Thomas. We'll catch up and get yours. Not to worry." She snatched up her own skates, caught his little hand and urged him along the nursery wing toward the stairs. "If we want to have a good long time at the pond, we've got to hurry while the sun is out." *Besides, your mother is in a tear to get there soon.*

"Alyssa!" Her friend Dora called up to her from the second floor. "I've got Reggie in hand. Let's go!"

"We're coming, Dora!" She scooped up Thomas in her arms and took the hall at a clip. "Your mother wants us to get there quickly and have a good turn round the pond before the sun goes down."

Why that should be today of all days was a mystery to Alyssa. The four of them had gone skating every day for the past four, and Dora hated to ice skate.

"Mama said she'd give us extra pudding tonight for going to the pond again!"

"Indeed, she did. Aren't you thrilled?"

Thomas mashed up his charming mouth in a pout. "Pudding, yes. But skating. No. It's cold, Auntie Al."

True. "Mama wants you to have a bit of fresh air. Good for you."

"I want to stay here and ride my horse."

Alyssa took the stairs like a woman on fire. "I understand." *I'd prefer to stay home where it's warm and let you ride your horse, too.*

"Ah, here you are!" Dora greeted her at the second landing and tugged on her gloves. "Let's hurry."

I am!

"What," Alyssa asked as the four of them left the front steps and rushed along the snow-covered pebbled drive toward the carriage, "is your new fascination with skating?"

"I like it." Her lovely pal pushed up the collar of her scarlet Spanish mantle and grinned at Alyssa with excitement akin to a schoolgirl.

The two boys jostled each other to climb into the seats, Reggie elbowing his brother in a torment older brothers reserve only for their younger siblings.

"Since when?" She had a suspicion Dora had a new project up her sleeve. Dora never did anything with frantic energy unless she had a master plan. Skating the past four days was her newest *magnum opus.*

"I always have. Just this year the ice is so perfect."

Alyssa suppressed a shiver, settled into the squabs and huddled inside her fox-trimmed pelisse. "Perfect for Highlanders. Not for those of us with the coast and salt in our veins."

"Bah!" Dora settled into the squabs next to Alyssa, then knocked the roof for the coachman to drive on. "You know you like the fresh air."

"Riding," she grumbled. "Not skating."

"Don't be a noodle. You used to like skating."

"I did." She remembered the day, the hour and the circumstances when she no longer enjoyed gliding on the ice. She also remembered the man who saved her. "Until I broke my leg."

"You were ten." Dora rolled her big blue eyes at her. "You healed! Look at you now. You walk. You run. You dance."

"I skate only because I want to keep up with Reggie and Thomas."

"And me."

Alyssa inhaled. "And you."

"I think I may have found a new governess," Dora said at last, shoving her hands in her coat pockets.

"Here in Ripon?" Alyssa was surprised, because Dora was very particular about the instruction and care of her two boys. Since dismissing her last governess five months ago, she had interviewed two applicants from a service in York and received a pile of recommendations from an advertisement she'd taken in a London newspaper. The very reason Alyssa remained at Barrington Priory with Dora and her husband Barr was at their special request to help care for Reggie and Thomas. Alyssa welcomed the company. Living alone in her little cottage in Bradford was not what she had planned for herself. But circumstance had intervened, and she was, at twenty-three, the spinster she'd never imagined she'd be.

"She lives in Canterbury."

"Good heavens, Dora. She'd come all this way just for an interview?"

"She needs a position. So, yes. She would."

"And if you don't like her? You'll send her back?"

"I told her I would pay for her fare."

"Good of you." Dora was nothing if not fair. "Does she come soon?"

"Tomorrow."

"My goodness! The day of your ball and mere days before Christmas. Has she no family?"

"None. That's one reason I thought it fit to bring her on. Give her a happy holiday."

"I hope you like her. It would be sad to turn her out afterward."

"I've few doubts. Besides, I want you to meet her, too. Before you go home. You are so instinctive with people. If you like her, I know she will be a proper fit."

The reminder that she had decided to go home after the new year made Alyssa shiver a bit more. She liked her visits with her cousin and her little family. It gave her a glimpse of home and husband and children, all which she might have had... if she had found a better man than those three whom she had rejected.

"Ohhh! Look, Alyssa!" They had rounded a copse of tall snow-capped firs to gaze upon the shimmering ice of the local pond. Reggie and Thomas clamored to get out. The boys spied their two closest friends, two little girls who glided over the ice, sending up to the crisp air the chirps and calls of children at play. "The Darby girls. Company!"

Alyssa was used to seeing the girls here, and she welcomed their presence. Reggie and Thomas were well-occupied with them about. The girls, orphaned daughters of the late Lord Darby, lived far down the road in their manor house near town. They usually came by their coach, that stood apart today by the copse. They also usually came accompanied by their governess, a Miss Perkins of pursed lips and narrowed lids. But today the girls glided around the pond, calling to each other, and waving to Reggie and Thomas, escorted by a dark imposing man.

Alyssa blinked at the vision. He was...

A tall, elegant form in inky black great coat and fine top hat. He stood to one side of the pond, his gloved hands clasped together at his waist, as he waited silent and serene while the Barrington carriage rolled to a stop before him.

He was more man than she remembered. Why would he not be? It had been four years since last she saw him. In a butler's wine cellar. The light of one candle highlighting the ebony waves of his hair and the lush sweep of his lips. The air humid and intoxicating, full of the angel's share of whisky and wine, and the devil's appeal of his woodsy cologne. The night dangerous with its promise of a marriage proposal for her, but not from him. No. From him, a kiss that buoyed her heart with longing she might escape the dreaded fiancé and instead claim him as her beloved. He of other kisses in a broom closet the previous year. He of other Christmas balls when they were young. He of her hopes. He of her vain desire for him because he was a second son of a second son and no match for her father's intention to get her at least an earl. He of all her dashed hopes. He of the flashing grey eyes that focused on her now.

He did not move. He did not smile. He did not even seem to breathe.

At once, Alyssa understood what was happening here. "He is why we've come to skate today."

Dora grinned and shivered, triumphant. "Of course, he is. He wondered if you'd remember him. You do. I told him, and so did Barr, that you had never forgotten him."

"How good of you," she managed to say, though her heartbeat was too rapid to stop her from clasping her hands together too tightly to indicate nonchalance. "You arranged this."

"We did. He did. Home from his travels, he is. For good, too, now that he is the new earl. Aren't you delighted?"

WHAT WAS HE DOING HERE? Ha! Acting like a love-sick boy, yes! To his shock. Where was the man who could have a Tuscan contessa as his paramour for the summer or enjoy the invitation of an acclaimed Parisienne ballerina without regret?

Yet he could not take his eyes from the vision who beamed at him.

He had no rights to try to redeem himself in her eyes. He had hurt her. Worse. He'd destroyed her. Yet here she was, smiling at him as if it were five years ago, or four even, and nothing disastrous had befallen her. She climbed down from the carriage, her lovely face alight with welcome.

This ripe creature coming straight toward him was overjoyed to see him. Her cousin was chatting on about *how wonderful this,* and *how superb that,* as he gazed like a besotted child at the woman he'd always fancied and fought for words that might not sound trite.

Today, she wore a blue green woven wool that replicated the

uniqueness of her eyes. Her face was a perfect oval, and her cheeks were plump above hollows that gave her a sophistication she'd not yet claimed at eighteen. Her hair, still that irrepressible cloud of burnished blonde, escaped her blue silk bonnet. The rest of her was more rounded and, dare he say, more delectable than he had ever predicted she might become. Her breasts alone inspired in him a hard response that would make skating damned impossible.

"You've come to Darby Park for Christmas," she said as she left her hand lingering in his. He noted she did not call the Park *home*. Smart girl. She knew better. But went on with, "Oh, you do look well. I see your little cousins are enjoying your company, a boon for them, I am sure. Plus, Dora and Barr are thrilled you've come north. Dora has told me so just now."

"You did not know before seeing me that I'd arrived, did you?"

She shook her head. "Though I expected you'd come eventually to your domain, today I evidently was meant to be surprised." She cleared her throat and feigned a rueful look at Dora. "The ruse succeeded, and I am surprised. But very pleased to see you, my lord."

"I will turn and march right away, Alyssa, if you continue to *my lord* me."

"Then you will be Gabe to me. As ever you were."

He lifted her gloved hand and kissed the back. "As ever I wish to remain."

A *frisson* swept through her. What was that about? Had she heard intonations in his words that implied all the sentiments he had never voiced? He was so full of regrets, so eager to make amends to her for all that had gone wrong for her after their last rendezvous in the wine cellar, that he was not surprised. He probably wore a sign on his great coat that listed his many sins against her.

"Shall we skate?" she asked with both brows in a gleeful arc he remembered so well. She was still the imp with whom he had spent years of his youth learning how to dance and letting her crush every one of his toes.

He rubbed his hands together. "Nothing better, Al, my girl!"

She threw back her head to laugh at his use of her old diminutive name and took a look at the new blades that he'd slung over his shoulder. "Come along then. To the bench! Tie them on!"

Impetuous. He'd always been so with her and no one else. It's what had gotten her in trouble and him driven away. Spur of the moment choices were not his usual mode. Prudent actions were his forte.

When he left home four years ago, he had only three wishes. He wanted to lift the family company from bankruptcy to singular superiority. He wanted to show those who thought him less than he was that he would acquire the name and fame of a man of the world. He thought he would forget the young woman who'd taken his arm and run with him into the shadows of closets and cellars for the raptures of decadent kisses. He had easily achieved the first two. Never the last.

Now, by the grace of all that he had accomplished in this life, he was here to improve his fortunes further. At the urging of his friend Barr, he'd returned to the Park and persuaded the few remaining staff up to snuff. He'd acquainted himself with his cousin's daughters, poor sweet chicks who needed mothering and fathering to keep them in tow. Before he'd left London to come north, he'd even armed himself with fine winter tailoring and ordered this new pair of skates. Which he now had to don.

All the others, children and Dora and one of his grooms included, had taken to the ice. Alyssa and he warmed the wooden bench.

Getting his skates securely tied was a trial. He was all thumbs, his mind on how she smelled of roses and fresh soap. "I think the shoemaker made the wrong size for me."

"Let me help," said the woman who could not seem to stop smiling at him as she went to one knee in the snow before him. Her position had him sucking in his breath. She appeared to be his, his alone, and bent over in such a way that his physical delight in her jumped to uncomfortable new heights.

"You're binding them too tightly," he complained with a laugh. "My blood will stop flowing." *In truth, all of it's already gone to one particular part of my anatomy.*

"They have to be tight, Gabe. We must hurry. The sun will be down soon," Alyssa said, as she yanked at the leather straps and wrapped them around his trouser legs. "There you are. Stand up now."

He winced, grateful for the fall of his coat over evidence he wished to do other things than skate. But he stood and, dubious of his ability to hold his balance, he sailed off with her right at his side.

"You do well, sir. One would think you've been practicing."

"I've had other things to do that kept me from this."

"Business." Her blue-green eyes flashed as they took the pond in a slow circle. "I've heard. You've done well. Worked hard. So, there's been no time for fun?"

"Very little." He did not wish to discuss what he had done for enjoyment. He'd pensioned off his contessa months ago, and the liaison with the Parisienne had been nothing more than a week's brief interlude.

Their silence stretched out. That was his fault. If he wanted more communication, he would have to encourage it by sharing more than he had.

"I worked hard at building the company. We had agents stationed in port cities, of course. But many were so old, or so discouraged by Napoleon's customs men, they did nothing. I had to pension off most of them and replace them. Luckily, many who were qualified and who wished the positions were our original agents' sons and daughters."

She skated closer to him, her gaze on his full of surprise. "You hired women?"

"Of course, I did. Why not? Women can strike a deal sooner and often with better profit than men."

"I would agree! I hope to do the same."

"Oh?" *How?* "You want to come work for me?" He could dream of that.

"I would if I could, Gabe. But I know nothing of trading goods." She lifted her shoulders and skated on; her lips pursed in contemplation. "I will use what I do know to build my own business."

"What would that be?"

"A book shop. I will open one this summer. By then, I will have acquired stock enough to open."

"A shop! That's superb. Where?"

"Ripon. I must find a space I can afford to rent and repair to my needs. Just to start and then, as I earn enough, I will buy the space and live above."

If she were to run a shop in nearby Ripon, he could see her and visit whenever he came to Darby Park. That filled him with joy... and a need for her company he hadn't acknowledged in a very long time. Four years, in fact.

"Why do you wait to act on this idea to open the shop?"

"Money, of course. What else does anyone wait on, eh?" Her cheeks pinked in embarrassment. "I will have saved enough by then to live for a month or two. By then I will also have bought enough books to stock my shelves. People love to read. It's healthy for them to sit quietly and enjoy communion with another person's ideas and experiences."

"You are buying books with savings?" That was a conclusion and intrusive to ask, but he was horrified she was reduced to scrimping her own means to fund her worthwhile project.

"Yes, of course."

"Why?" He halted in the middle of the pond and caught her hand to make her stop and face him. His question was forbidden. No one inquired about the finances of another. Yet he would learn this about her.

"It is the only way."

"Your father left you no means?"

She rolled a shoulder, squinted at the horizon, then faced him. Her lips were drawn flat, her eyes dazed. "My father left me two thousand pounds."

That was all? The man had offered her fiancé a dowry of ten thousand and two acres of land on the edge of the town of Ripon. "Why not grant you the ten he would have given to whatever his name was?"

"Talbot. Lord Talbot. Eight thousand went to him."

Bastard. "As recompense for his so-called 'pain and suffering', I would guess?"

She nodded her head once, then broke away.

He pushed off and caught her around the waist. "Tell me the rest."

"No," she bit off, gazing straight ahead.

He slowed in time with her measured glide, but with his hand to hers, urged her more nearly against his side. He felt her heat, her supple body in flow to their syncopated dance over the ice, and his desire flared like fire to hold her against him face-to-face, breast to his chest, hip to hip, her luscious thigh to his own.

One glance at her face and his heart wrenched. Tears glistened on her lashes.

"What happened after you broke it off with Talbot?" Barr had written that, after their discovery in the wine cellar, her father had demanded she retire to his smallest estate in Cornwall. She had remained there until weeks before her father died last year.

She came to a stop on the edge of the pond. "I lived at one of Papa's holdings outside Truro in Cornwall. A good life it was, quiet and peaceful. Few knew me or of my reputation. Papa had told me when he banished me that he did not wish to hear from me. I did not communicate with him, even when he wrote he was ill and dying. I could not forgive him for his treatment of me. But on his death bed, he wrote once more and begged me to come to him. I did go and saw him before he took his last breath. He asked for my forgiveness for what he'd done. I gave it. Who does not on such an appeal? Yes, well. He said he had made reparation for his harsh treatment of me. He gave no details. But the next morning, a bare hour after he had passed, my cousin, Papa's successor, the newest Lord Margrove, invited me to the reading of the will." She inhaled and shook her head, her blue-green eyes hard as stone. "But there was nothing in Papa's last testament that could be construed as reparations for me from him. I was granted only the two thousand he had told me was left after compensating my former fiancé, Lord Talbot."

"Sweetheart," Gabe whispered and pressed her close to his heart, one hand to her nape. Dora would not ridicule him or Alyssa for this. One of his young cousins, however, stopped skating to nudge her sister and point to them. He would talk with her later. "Men can be so cruel."

"To women," she said, pulling away to stare into his eyes with a solid determination. "And to other men as well. You had the same done to you."

"We were each cast out."

"For kissing each other," she said in a melodic whisper on the wind. Her lashes fluttered and she beamed at him. "I never regretted it. Not once."

"I owe you—"

She slanted two fingers across his mouth. "No, Gabe. You owe me nothing. Your kisses showed me that I could never have married Talbot." She squeezed his arm. "Now enough of the past. I see Dora waving at us. She and the boys are ready to go home. I would guess you are coming to dinner tonight, too. Are you?"

"I have been invited, yes."

She tipped her head and grinned at him. "Well, for goodness' sake, come along then! You must tell me tales of Venice and Rome and all the lovely old places a lady only reads about in books."

"Only if you come ride with me in my coach up to the Priory."

"An offer I cannot refuse," she said and hugged his arm as they called to the girls to join them. The youngsters giggled and elbowed each other, knowing they joined a man and woman interested in each other.

As the four of them took the short drive up to the Barringtons' house, Gabe marveled at the surprises that could be positive and change one's life. So rare, so welcome. Like the surprise of sitting and watching the love of his life across from him, happy to see him, forgiving of all that had passed between them.

What, he reminded himself, he needed foremost was to stick to a healthy dose of reality. To wit, the lady before him might have kissed him years ago. She had lost her fiancé and reputation because of it, too. But she was older and wiser now and her kisses, he was quite certain, were not on offer.

For if his kisses had once shown her she should not have married Talbot, that did not mean they had ever proven she should have married him.

CHAPTER 3

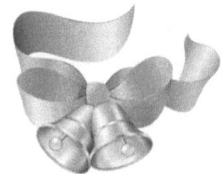

"What was your assessment of the condition of the house, Gabriel?" Barr asked him as the footman served the dessert.

Alyssa noted this was the first such question to Gabe about his new situation.

They sat at the candlelit table. Sconces on the walls flickered with the glow of more candles throwing mellow tones across the faces of the four dining. Gabe's wards, Rosalind and Marie, were dining with the boys up in the nursery. The four adults could enjoy their frank conversation without hindrance.

"The manor house is in poor condition. The roof needs new shingles. A leak has ruined the servants' back bedrooms on the fourth floor. The floors have not been scrubbed or waxed in years, I'd say. And the window dressings are in tatters. If the house were not so close to town and to the tenants' cottages, I'd shutter it up or let the wild boars have at it. My cousin, God rest him, gave no thought to the place."

The sound of children laughing came through the floorboards.

Gabe frowned. "Nor did he fill his two children with the care they have needed since their mother died."

"They've come here," said Dora, "to play with Reg and Thomas."

Gabe cast her a loving look. "For that, I am grateful. They need to feel wanted."

"Everyone does," Alyssa added on impulse. "Losing one's mother leaves an open wound in one's heart."

"I cannot be their mother," Gabe said, twirling his wine glass, then taking stock of Dora, Barr and her. "But I can provide a comfortable home and a fond uncle's guidance now that I am here."

Dora nodded. "I know you will do more than that, Gabriel."

Barr shook his head. "You must call on us if we can provide any help. I understand four of your tenants have left for York. Two of them were handy with carpentry and stonework. We have two such men with those skills here and I would happily send them to you."

"The same," added Dora, "for your house staff. My housekeeper told me last week that your scullery maid has left and so too your upstairs maid."

Gabe cleared his throat. "My butler tells me they departed because they did not wish to serve me."

Alyssa recoiled at the news, angry for his loss. "Better that they go."

He stared at her with those bright grey eyes. "Agreed. I have enough work to do to straighten out the house and improve the estate's crop production without having to play sycophant to those who believe me capable of seducing innocent women."

"Many," Dora said, "have forgotten." She didn't elaborate, but the looks that were exchanged round the table told the tale. A few did remember the scandal that had resulted in Gabe being sent away and Alyssa's broken engagement and banishment.

"I have no need to curry anyone's favor," Gabe said, a sting to his tone that would warn anyone away. "I've too much work to do. Tenants, animals, land—all need to be nourished. Like all else I own, I will give them my fullest attention."

Alyssa knew the challenges he faced were enormous and would make a less determined man pale. Yet Gabe would prevail because he had the dedication to urgency and excellence.

"Have you any thought," asked Barr, "how to juggle that with the management of Shaw Imports?"

"I did not set foot on the ship for home before I had secured the company's future. I left my man of business in charge in Leghorn with orders to tighten the reins on all our offices along the Mediterranean. When he believes he may leave it to operate efficiently at a distance, he comes north to London, then to me."

"You sound as though you've thought of everything," Barr said.

"I do hope you have it in mind to enjoy yourself here." Dora lifted her glass in a toast to Gabe. "We've invited half the shire for tomorrow night's ball. I'm sure you will remember many of them."

Alyssa bit her lip. *Perhaps he does not wish to.*

"I will do my best, Dora." He lifted his wine glass and sipped, more gracious about this topic than Alyssa. "Four years is a long time. I had no time to gauge anyone's reactions to my uncle's decision. I left the next morning for London and beyond."

"You are not angry," Alyssa said with shock and delight.

He settled his gaze on her with a serenity she applauded. "A useless emotion now that circumstances have changed my life entirely."

Alyssa admired his resilience. His expression in the glow of candlelight afforded her a renewed appreciation of his striking black hair and sun-kissed complexion. The turn about the ice had added a healthy red to his cheeks. As for his lips…

Well. She took a deep breath and forced her gaze to her plate.

His lips had always been a special point of her desire. They were generous. In a complementary line to his wide jaw, his lips were firm. But when he spoke, they formed perfect words given forth in a heartfelt baritone. And when he smiled, they went wide with glee. When he kissed, his lips turned kind. And demanding.

Ravenous.

That was the word that set her breasts to tingle.

Ravenous.

That was the thrill she relived over the past four years every time she closed her eyes and…

"Alyssa?" Dora called to her. "I say! Are you ill?"

343

Her eyes snapped open. "Not at all. Don't mind me. A moment's memory of a past Christmas. I am so excited for tomorrow night's ball. And happy to be here." She threw a smile at Dora and Barr. A glance at Gabe told her he considered her with narrowed circumspection and a heat that told of old desire. *Well, yes.* The man knew her too well.

"I'LL WALK you down to the foyer, shall I?" Alyssa had to have a few minutes alone with him. The evening conversation had been more than friendly, convivial really, but she required more specifics about his immediate plans. Tomorrow night would give her nothing in that regard, either. One look at the newest Earl of Darby in a formal cut of black attire, and the local maidens would drool to be presented and happily hand him their dance cards. Alyssa would stand no chance of a few minutes of frank conversation.

The four stood in the family parlor. Dora had indicated she would roust the children from their play and get the girls to come down.

Barr, too, was ready to retire. "A late night tomorrow."

"I look forward to it," Gabe said to his friends and bid them good night. To Alyssa, he offered his arm.

They took the stairs, the old butler waiting patiently for them at the door.

Gabe allowed the man to assist him with his greatcoat and thanked him for his service. "I will speak with Miss Waring," he said, and the man bowed himself away.

"You'll save a place for me on your dance card tomorrow night, I do hope?" He gave her the lift of that wicked dark brow and put his hands to her upper arms.

"All my dances will be open. Pick any one you'd like."

"I'll take them all, Al."

He was too charming. She tipped her head and grinned at him. "To the shock of the neighbors."

"To hell with them," he bit off and lifted her chin. "I come tomorrow night only to dance with you."

"You will disappoint every young thing for miles around."

"I wish to gain only your favor." He brushed his thumbs across the arch of her cheeks. "Will you dance with me?"

So full of the enchantment of him, tears welled in her eyes. "If I do, we'll create another scandal."

"Third time's a charm, Barr told me last week."

She sniffed back tears and swallowed loudly.

He gathered her against him, his lips in her hair.

She clung to him shamelessly. "I never thought to see you again."

"Nor I you, my darling."

His endearment brought out a sob, and she clutched him closer. Her cheek against his warm hard chest, she ventured, "Do you stay in Darby Park for long?"

He was suddenly speaking against the lobe of her ear. "As long as it takes to right all past wrongs."

At his words, she wanted to rub herself against him like a cat. Instead, she fought to be wise. "The crop failures have been devastating. Bountiful yields could take years."

"I give it months here, then south to London. I commit to coming back and forth. I'll not see my business fail because I devoted myself exclusively to this. But I wonder," he said as he lifted her chin, "how long you remain here."

"After Christmas I return home." She should leave soon to save herself heartache at losing him once more.

"Might I persuade you to stay longer?"

She must not. To stand near him, to admire him, to want him so was more dangerous than ever it had been. He was older, more virile, worldly, and she was more smitten by him than she'd thought possible. To even gaze upon him this close was to melt into the euphoria of wanting him. Still, she could be foolish enough to ask, "How would you do that?"

"I'd kiss you in the middle of a grand foyer against all our precedents." He grinned, his mouth brushing across hers in soft waves of pleasure. "How successful would that be?"

"Very. No one is left to part us."

"Or send us away."

The patter of little feet upon the marble had her lowering her forehead to his chest. The next sound was Dora clearing her throat as she descended the stairs.

"Tomorrow night," he whispered and stepped backward.

In another moment, he and his wards vanished into the blustery winter night.

CHAPTER 4

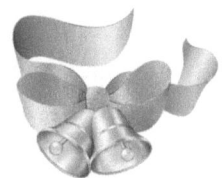

She climbed the stairs and went to her bedroom, deriding herself for her naiveté. She let Dora's maid help her out of her dinner gown and dismissed her. Like a sleepwalker, she went into her dressing room and picked at the bodice of the ball gown she'd wear tomorrow night.

Four years old, the dress was still pretty. Of French gauze over a pink silk slip, the gown fit her only because she'd sewn gussets into the side seams to accommodate her larger bosom. Given her meagre circumstances, enlarging the dress had been the only option for her if she wished to attend Dora and Barr's ball. Before Gabe's arrival, she hadn't minded that she would be so attired. But now, she would not attract him. Others would. Could.

She was foolish to want him. Silly to think that now, when he'd made his fortune and the earldom had also come to him, he could want her. His affectionate nature was an offering he'd always given her. His embraces, his delicious kisses he had always conferred upon her in sequestered spaces. Never in open regard. She understood why. The restrictions he lived with had painted him into the margins of his family's and his social class's order. Years ago, he had no titles or earnings—and by all, was considered to have no prospects. He was a spare's spare. One of the forgotten men of a family whose nobility should have granted him more than the honor of bearing their presumably respectable name. He had been unfairly and damnably discounted.

While she, too, was held in as little regard. A female of no consequence. Without desires of her own or ambitions to improve her station, save to be anything more than some man's wife, mate, in charge of his house, his servants and hopefully his children. She had a dowry then. At ten thousand pounds, it was a goodly sum that mere whispers of its size set bachelors aquiver with expectations of financial liquidity. A few even condescended to speak of acquiring her for her comeliness or even her intelligence. Talbot, the one man whose proposal had met with praise by her father, had proudly offered her his dead mother's dower house. "To live in, year-round," he had notified her the day her father approved his offer. "My mistress prefers the manor house."

That woman was now spending Alyssa's eight thousand. For many years, she cursed the woman's very name. Alyssa had given up her anger the day her father died. She decided that no longer would she allow resentment of Talbot and his doxy to destroy the serenity of her days.

Tomorrow she would welcome Dora's choice of governess for Reggie and Thomas. Tomorrow night she would enjoy the musical ensemble Dora and Barr had hired to play at the ball. She would dance. Once with Barr. She always did at their parties. Perhaps once with Gabe.

Then the day after Christmas she would go home to her comfortable cottage four miles away and prepare for the new year. In it, she promised herself to open her bookstore and look into offering her books in a lending library. Perhaps teach in the village church school to earn extra money.

Her life was rich. She had promised herself that. And she would make it so.

December 23, 1818

Darby Priory

The next afternoon, as Rosalind and Mary rose from the dining room table, so did Gabe. The girls were agog to be invited to the Priory to celebrate the Barringtons' annual Christmas ball with their friends, Reginald and Thomas. Because the dancing would continue to the wee hours, the girls would spend the night. As would Gabe, too.

He had prepared in London for this Christmas after Barr's invitation. Though at that point, he had not met his two charges since they'd been toddlers, he wished to give them gifts to mark the occasion of their new relationship. Their mother had died three years ago. Their father, his cousin, had not been a generous man and Gabe feared what the girls might have learned from him about the nature of men and family affection. Whatever caliber his cousin's displays of affection had been toward his daughters, Gabe knew the problems his own sire's indifference to him had generated. He wished not to emulate the man.

As the girls' legal guardian, he would be responsible for them until their marriages or their twenty-fifth birthdays. He wanted to endear himself to them and mark a new life for them and himself. He'd brought to England with him for each of them a fine porcelain doll from his own supplier, an expert craftsman in Naples.

For the adults, he had other gifts he'd claimed from his storage factory near the East India Docks. For Dora, three yards of Morone peony red silk from Lucca. Barr was to have the finest cheroots from his tobacconist supplier in Amsterdam. A gift for Alyssa had been more difficult to select. He did not wish to be forward or lacking in etiquette, and so he could not give too personal an item. Not creamed soap from his man in Karlsruhe or scent from his perfumer in Grasse. Not an item too impersonal such as the royal purple skeins of wool from a mill in Edinburgh. Nor the much-too-suggestive four-foot-length of ivory Chantilly lace from his friend north of Paris.

On a whim to wrap up all of them and give everything to her, he found himself sitting in what had become his favorite chair in the old walnut-paneled library. Drumming his fingers on the arm of the leather chair, he sipped a good Armagnac from his friend in Bordeaux and pondered what to give the woman he loved for Christmas. Here amid the items that infused his lonely childhood with those who had become his erstwhile champions, kings and rogues, knights and mythical heroes who fought against fierce odds, he had valued courage. He had learned to savor the sport of a strong challenge and to demand of himself the subtle art of the shrewd victory.

At once he was on his feet. Here from this shelf, he picked Julius Caesar. There and there and there were multiple copies of Aristophanes' plays. And where…? Where was the one that would make her laugh and cry and throw her arms around him? At least one copy of the poor girl who attracts a prince at his ball had been here. He remembered a very old tattered copy of *Cendrillon* that the girls' mother enjoyed. It had to be here still. The frayed red leather, a collection of…yes! The Frenchman Charles Perrault's perfect little tales.

He'd wrap them all up in swaths of the Pomona green silk from Lyon. To bloody hell with etiquette. He'd give her all! Give her anything. Everything. If only she might give him the one thing he'd never thought to desire. Never before had the right to ask to possess.

Her very self.

CHAPTER 5

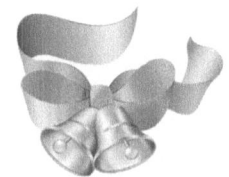

*A*lyssa had not attended Dora's and Barr's Christmas balls for three years after Lord Talbot had decided not to marry her, unwilling to appear in public. Dora had constantly urged her to attend. Insisted even. Only last year had she given in. Tonight, she had a different challenge. Earlier in the evening, she had taken Gabe's hand in a set of country dances, and now she had to stand by and appear unfazed by him dancing with every sweet thing in the shire.

"I've never been to such a ball." The new governess whom Dora had hired today confided in Alyssa. "I do feel out of place."

The young woman had appeared after noon when the family coachman had brought her from the village carriage inn. Dora had interviewed her and hired her, then insisted she attend tonight's gala.

"Please enjoy the evening, Miss Harlan. Lady Barrington means only to welcome you to the house and the neighbors. Everyone here knows Lady Barrington's Christmas parties include all her staff, who come for as long as they wish. Most stay for a few minutes, then return below stairs."

"I have no ambitions to capture a beau here." She cast a covetous glance at Gabe, belying her intentions. "I want only to work for a good and proper family."

Alyssa smiled at her, understanding how Gabe could appeal to her, so well turned out was he in formal black coat and trousers with blinding white stock. "You will have a very happy family to work with here at Lord and Lady Barrington's."

Miss Harlan licked her lips and tore her gaze from Gabe as he ended the latest dance and took his partner to her parents. "I wonder how often Lord Darby visits here."

Alyssa's heart squeezed in want. "Often, I would wager. He is very good friends with your employers."

"Do you visit often?"

Was Miss Harlan gauging Alyssa as her competition?

"Not in the future, no." *I cannot bear the torture of watching him dance with another, let alone watching how other women will pursue him.* "I have plans to open my own shop. That will keep me quite busy."

"How lovely you can find means to do that," Miss Harlan said with envy and a bright twinkle in her pretty blue eyes. "What kind of shop?"

"Books," said Gabe who suddenly appeared at their side and had eyes only for Alyssa. "Isn't that right, Miss Waring?"

"Indeed. A wonderful little place where patrons will find *Gulliver* and *Pamela* and *Childe Harold.*" She had to keep reminding herself of her goals when he stood so close and remained so very far out of her reach.

"A lending library too," he added for the governess's sake. "But that is for the future. For now, Miss Waring, come dance with me."

She considered his hand out before her. A second dance with him would inspire tongues to wag. The daring Miss Waring who'd once been found in a butler's wine cellar kissing the very man who now stood before her. "Of course," she said because she could never refuse the chance to be held in his arms. "A second time they will have to accept."

"Who are 'they,'" he asked with a grin on his face as he led her out, "to deny us the pleasure of each other's company? Unimportant."

She took to the chalked floor like one in a trance. This would be the last time she could stand beside him and bow. The last time he'd put his hand to hers, lead her around the square, and put the flat of his hands to hers as he smiled at her. Never again would she sashay down a column of dancers and meet him, face to face, and admire the breadth of his shoulders and the grace of his form. No more would she call him the fellow she had first loved when she was eighteen and he had caught her hand and hid with her in a broom closet to escape one persistent beau. Nor was he the one who had rescued her from a life of subservience to a self-righteous cad by running with her to the butler's wine cellar and showing her that his kisses were more intoxicating than any other man's could ever be.

As the music died and Gabe took her toward Dora and Miss Harlan, Alyssa could not bear the despair that welled in her chest.

"Excuse me please," she choked out to them. "I feel unwell. Good night to all of you." And she turned away, skirts high, to escape the lure of the man she could never claim for her own.

SHE MADE the second landing of the stairs on her way to the next floor when he caught her by the wrist. "Why do you leave?"

She flinched away from his grasp, yanked her skirts higher and continued her climb. "I'm tired."

"How could you be?" He followed, his long legs eating up the steps two at a time to her one.

"Go back." She stopped for a moment to face him. "I'm coming down with some malady you do not want to catch." Then she raced onward.

"What is it?" He caught her at the top of the stairs and turned her to him, her back to the wall. "Nerves?"

"Don't be silly." She pushed him away and tried to go round him.

He cut her off. "Don't want to watch the *ton* gossip about us together?"

"Absurd." She tried to go the other way round him.

"Exactly my thought." He let her go.

But she'd gone only a step before he circled his arm around her waist and pulled her backward. Then in a thrice, he had some door open, slammed closed, and they were in darkness. With the smell of soap and starch drifting up to her nostrils complemented by the fragrance of his sandalwood and lime cologne, she noted she could not see him. A good thing. *But oh, my.* She could smell him and...

When he cupped her face and put his lips to hers, she could taste him and savor him and swoon in the aromas and textures of his embrace.

"You mustn't kiss me," she objected even as he took her mouth between his chuckles.

"Of course, I must. You are the woman who keeps escaping my grasp." He pecked at her lips. "I won't have it any longer."

"I won't, either," she said as she wrapped her arms around his broad, sleek wool-clad shoulders and kissed him back at her leisure. After all, no one was here to see them or hear them. To badger them or banish them. She could, with impunity, kiss him all she liked, for one last luscious time.

"I want you to marry me," he said with that mellifluous baritone that soothed her soul and lit her heart on fire.

"Oh, Gabe. They'd never allow it." She ran her fingers up through the satin waves of his hair. She'd fantasized about doing that, touching him so, and here in the dark, where no one would ever know, she could enjoy herself.

"*They* have never done anything for me. Nor for you, either. *They* do not matter, my darling. Only you and I. And I ask you to marry me. Soon. Will you?"

"My...shop. I must have it." *Wonderful, Al. The man wants a wife. You want a shop.*

"Have one everywhere."

"What?"

"Have a shop. Have one in Ripon. One in York. London. Rome! Wherever you are, there am I, and there should be your book shop."

In the windowless room, her heart picked up a lively tempo. But she frowned at him. "You are quite mad, you know."

"For you. Yes." He gave a bright laugh. In the close confines of wherever the hell they were, his joy filled the tiny space and jolted her awareness. "I am."

"And you want to marry me?" *Could that be true?*

"I do. I want to be the one who kisses you at every Christmas, every birthday, every harvest dance, for all my days to come. I have always wanted you. For years and years. Since first we found ourselves surrounded by a collection of brooms."

"Hmmm." She liked this conversation. The darkness. And his sentiments.

"And later," he said and nuzzled her neck, his kisses little tickles along her skin, "when we inhaled an angel's share and found ourselves kissing in the butler's cellar. I loved you more then. But I loved you most the next day when you did not marry that foolish man. I loved you every day since then and today, I love you most of all."

He lifted her chin and pushed tendrils of her hair around her ears. His lips nibbled along hers. "I love you, my darling. And I think you love me, too. So, it is only right you marry me and let me love you forever. Don't you think, hmmm?" He took her mouth in a kiss that robbed her of breath and gave her hope. "What do you say?"

"Oh, Gabe. I do love you!"

"That is the woman I adore!" he crowed. "Shall we go tell them?"

"No!"

"No?"

She snuggled up to his warm muscular goodness, and held him tight. "First, I want more kisses."

"Thank God." He gave her one long lingering example.

She tore her lips from his. "But I do have one question."

"What?" He huffed, sounding impatient and miffed.

"Where are we?"

He was silent. Finally, he ventured, "Do you care?"

"Actually, yes, I do. I'd like to tell our children that brooms and wine and...whatever this is, have something wonderful in common."

"I see. Sounds logical. Do you wish me to open the door and find candles?"

She ran her hands up his throat to frame his marvelous jaw and said, "No. Not just yet."

Long minutes later, after he helped her rearrange her bodice and she helped him do some justice to his cravat, they emerged. Gabe found a candle in the hall and lit up the room. Shelves floor to ceiling were filled with milled soaps and bundles of dried lavender, ironed sheets, towels and cotton furniture drapes.

They gazed at each other and chuckled, "The linen closet."

EPILOGUE

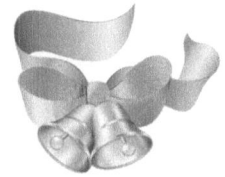

 *ecember 24, 1819*
London

Alyssa stared down at the latest shipment of books from Athens in the crate at her feet. She didn't know whether to laugh or cry or haul them out to the alley and burn them. "How many people in London want to read Plato in the original, Lucy?"

Her assistant winced, crossing her arms and shaking her head at the wooden box that consumed so many square feet of space in the shop's tiny storage room. "Last year, we had four."

"So, we definitely cannot find twenty-six more," Al said and winced at the efforts of her husband to keep her shop filled with the odd, the unique and the definitely unloved tomes of authors of centuries past.

"My lady, I like your husband, I do. The earl is a good-hearted man. But we still have not sold last year's nine copies of *Cicero's Orations,* which the earl recommended to his friends."

"They'd rather read their own illustrious words than a dead Roman's."

The living man of whom they both spoke pushed aside the purple velvet curtain that separated The Twig Bookshop from its storage room and feigned disaster at overhearing their words. "I know my friends consider themselves so clever that all their geese are swans. Good afternoon, my darling." The tenth Earl of Darby kissed his wife on the cheek. "Hello, Lucy."

"Swans!?" Miss Lucy Malvern, who was the Baron Greyhurst's third daughter and a bluestocking who read Greek better than many a Cambridge don, pushed her spectacles up her nose. "My lord, I read your friends' speeches in the *Times* daily, and I submit they cannot even speak the King's good English!"

Al hugged her husband as he swept an arm around her waist. "We are taking your lovely offerings and casting aspersions on them."

"Meaning you cannot sell them." Gabe sighed and shook his head, unfazed by their dismay. "Ah, well! We can hope for a new generation to study hard and do them proud."

Al eyed him. "While we wait years for that to happen, my dear, they clutter up this room. I shall have to offer them up at a reduced price."

"Why not teach a class, offer them up for free?"

Al caught Lucy's eye, and they turned to stare at him.

"*What?*" he said and threw up his hands. "If you can't sell them, give them away!"

Al lifted her chin and nodded. "Why not?"

"Why?" Lucy persisted and shook her head at Gabe. "Your friends won't come."

"They can't be saved, Lucy. Why try? Make the offer to young boys..." Gabe caught Lucy's evil eye on that statement, "and young girls, who want to put a feather in their caps."

"And offer the class for a fee," said Al. "A fine idea."

"And just *who* teaches this class?" Lucy asked with her hands on her hips.

Al and her husband stared back at her.

"I think you are both mad."

The shop bell over the front door ting-a-linged. Lucy huffed and left to serve their customer.

Gabe pressed a lingering kiss to Alyssa's lips. "That's better. I've gone too long without the taste of you."

She pressed the flat of her hand to his greatcoat and chuckled. "The last was only hours ago."

"A man needs his sustenance." He winked at her.

"So does a woman." She confessed to the man whose very breath charmed her. "Did you collect your gift?"

He'd been secretive about a few Christmas presents he'd been collecting while they were in town this month. "I did."

She patted his shoulders and ribs, his arms and drew him near her again. "You have nothing on you, sir. *Where* is it? *What* is it?"

He tortured her like this each Christmas. On the first Christmas of their marriage, they celebrated nearly one complete year of wedded bliss. He'd had the old family parure of diamonds and sapphires reset for her. Six months before she had miscarried their first babe and he wanted to proclaim that she was and would remain the only woman he would ever love. The second Christmas, a month after the birth of their first child, their daughter Rose, he'd imported from southern France cuttings of a new breed of white roses.

Last year, to commemorate the birth of their second girl, Lily, he'd brought from Spain young plants of climbing purple lilies. This year, she'd not become pregnant...and the lack left her fearful she might no longer be capable. She was not yet too old. And her failure to conceive was not because they were less in love. No indeed, they were as joyfully—as scandalously—intimate as they'd been from the day they'd married.

He wiggled his brows. "I have it in the carriage."

"You wouldn't bring it in here to show me?" She arched a wicked brow. They both joked that their two daughters had been conceived in this tiny storage room amid the copious words—usually unsellable—of Caesar, Aristotle and the like.

"I want you to see it. Only you."

His sweet regard brought tears to her eyes. "Oh, my darling husband," she whispered and cupped his jaw. "Before we leave for home, I must give you your Christmas gift."

She'd suspected for weeks now that she might be able to say this to him. To give him the present he always valued above all else she ever purchased for him.

He crushed her close. "I do love you in tiny rooms, my sweetheart. They bring out the minx in you."

"And the mother."

"Yes," he said and kissed her with the fervor that she knew would lead them both straight to a fabulous night in their bed. "Again."

"You knew!" She laughed and threw her head back in glee.

He swept one hand against the side of one breast, then slid it down to her thickening waist and on to squeeze her derriere. "How could I not? I know your body as well as mine."

"What do you have in the carriage? Herbs? Cacti? A jungle?"

"Oh, ye of harsh attitude. Let's get your coat, madam, say *adieu* to your truculent assistant and get in our carriage. Our children await!"

"And so does your surprise gift," she said as she did as he requested, closed the front door and stepped through the snow up into their town coach.

"Ohhh," she breathed as she saw in the seat opposite the marvelous creation that he'd had carved by the master carpenter in the shop two doors down. "He's so lovely. Bright. And his red saddle is so grand. Fit for two girls to ride together. Or perhaps three."

"Three. I told Mister Winslow I wanted the seat big enough that children might share it or grow into it as they did."

She sat, her husband's arm around her shoulders, admiring the handiwork of the carpenter and the thoughtfulness of the darling man she'd married. "You know, I think we should name him."

"Caesar?"

She snickered and tickled her husband's side.

"I thought we'd name him something more in keeping with our love affair."

"Such as?"

"Charm."

She wrinkled her brow at his smiling face. "Because?"

"Third time is a."

THE FOLLOWING CHRISTMAS, when he came to the Twig to fetch her home two days before Christmas, he had in the carriage another rocking horse, a twin to Charm. Well-loved as that horse was, the wooden creature was often argued over and cried upon as well as vigorously—frantically!— rocked.

"What would you name this one?" she teased him as she put her hand over her rounded form, soon to be their fourth child. Perhaps a fourth daughter or a first son. They would learn in April.

"Fourth."

"Ah. As in Sally?"

"Exactly."

On April tenth, Sally was baptized as Sebastian.

THE END

ABOUT CERISE DELAND

Cerise DeLand is the USA TODAY best-selling author of Regency, Victorian and Edwardian historical romances as well as a few contemporary novels. She likes to research abroad, loves to put her characters in real castles and chateaux she has visited and give everyone a happy ending. At home, she cooks a fabulous dinner every night, swims many mornings and coaxes herbs from the stubborn Texas soil upon which she lives.

Visit her at: http://www.cerisedeland.com

RECENT RELEASES

NAUGHTY LADIES SERIES:

Lady, Be Wanton, #1
   Lady, Behave, #2
   Lady, No More, #3
   Lady, You're Mine, #4, Coming Winter 2023

The Lyon's Den novels:
   The Lyon's Share
   The Lyon's Perfect Mate, Coming July 2023

THE BELLES WOULD LIKE YOUR HELP!

Book reviews help readers to find books, and authors to find readers. Please consider writing a review for *Belles & Beaux*, even a couple of sentences telling people what you liked (or didn't like) about the stories. Reviews can be posted on BookBub, Goodreads and on most eRetailers websites. For links to this book on those sites, see the *Belles & Beaux* page on the Belles' website: https://bluestockingbelles.net/belles-joint-projects/belles-beaux/

Malala Fund

The Bluestocking Belles have chosen the Malala Fund as the charity they support, and to which they donate some of their royalties. Periodically, they take on projects intended to directly support this cause, which exemplifies their personal values and intentions: the right of girls and women to do whatever they choose with their lives.

How can you help?

Make a donation to our Team Page at https://www.classy.org/team/89502

OTHER BOOKS BY THE BLUESTOCKING BELLES

Find buy links and story blurbs for all the following books on our website at https://bluestockingbelles.net/belles-joint-projects/

The Bluestocking Belles donate a portion of the proceeds to benefit the Malala Fund.

Desperate Daughters (2022)

Love Against the Odds

The Earl of Seahaven desperately wanted a son and heir but died leaving nine daughters and a fifth wife. Cruelly turned out by the new earl, they live hand-to-mouth in a small cottage.

The young dowager Countess's one regret is that she cannot give Seahaven's dear girls a chance at happiness.

When a cousin offers the use of her townhouse in York during the season, the Countess rallies her stepdaughters.

They will pool their resources so that the youngest marriageable daughters might make successful matches, thereby saving them all.

So start their adventures in York, amid a whirl of balls, lectures, and alfresco picnics. Is it possible each of them might find love by the time the York horse races bring the Season to a close?

Storm & Shelter (2021)

Winner RONE Award for best anthology of 2021

When a storm blows off the North Sea and slams into the village of Fenwick on Sea, the villagers prepare for the inevitable: shipwreck, flood, land slips, and stranded travelers. The Queen's Barque Inn quickly fills with the injured, the devious, and the lonely—lords, ladies, and simple folk; spies, pirates, and smugglers all trapped together. Intrigue crackles through the village, and passion lights up the hotel.

One storm, eight authors, eight heartwarming novellas.

Holiday Escapes (2020)

Holidays, relatives, pressure to marry—sometimes it is all too much. Is it any wonder a woman may need to escape? The heroines in this collection of stories aren't afraid to take matters into their own hands when they've had enough.

These stories are republished here at 20% of the cost of collecting them all from each individual author.

Two bonus short stories round out the collection.

Fire & Frost (2020)

In a winter so cold the Thames freezes over, five couples venture onto the ice in pursuit of love to warm their hearts.

Love unexpected, rekindled, or brand new—even one that's a whack on the side of the head—heats up the frigid winter. After weeks of fog and cold, all five stories converge on the ice at the 1814 Frost Fair when the ladies' campaign to help the wounded and unemployed veterans of the Napoleonic wars culminates in a charity auction that shocks the high sticklers of the ton.

In their 2020 collection, join the Bluestocking Belles and their heroes and heroines as The Ladies' Society For The Care of the Widows and Orphans of Fallen Heroes and the Children of Wounded Veterans pursues justice, charity, and soul-searing romance.

Valentine's From Bath (2019)

The Master of Ceremonies announces a great ball to be held on Valentine's Day in the Upper Assembly Rooms of Bath.

Ladies of the highest rank—and some who wish they were—scheme, prepare, and compete to make best use of the opportunity.

Dukes, earls, tradesmen, and the occasional charlatan are alert to the possibilities as the event draws nigh.

But anything can happen in the magic of music and candlelight as couples dance, flirt, and open themselves to romantic possibilities. Problems and conflict may just fade away at a Valentine's Day Ball.

Follow Your Star Home (2018)

Forged for lovers, the Viking star ring is said to bring lovers together, no matter how far, no matter how hard.

In eight stories, covering more than half the world and a thousand years, our heroes and heroines put the legend to the test. Watch the star work its magic, as prodigals return home in the season of good will, uncertain of their welcome.

Never Too Late (2017)

Eight authors and eight different takes on four dramatic elements selected by our readers—an older heroine, a wise man, a Bible, and a compromising situation that isn't.

Set in a variety of locations around the world over eight centuries, welcome to the romance of the Bluestocking Belles' 2017 Holiday and More Anthology.

It's Never Too Late to find love.

Holly and Hopeful Hearts (2016)

When the Duchess of Haverford sends out invitations to a Yuletide house party and a New Year's Eve ball at her country estate, Hollystone Hall, those who respond know that Her Grace intends to raise money for her favorite cause and promote whatever love-matches she can. Seven assorted heroes and heroines set out with their pocketbooks firmly clutched and hearts in protective custody. Or are they?

Eight assorted heroes and heroines find more than they've bargained for when they set out for Hollystone Hall for a charity ball.

MEET THE BLUESTOCKING BELLES

The Bluestocking Belles (the "BellesInBlue") are seven very different writers united by a love of history and a history of writing about love. From sweet to steamy, from light-hearted fun to dark tortured tales full of angst, from London ballrooms to country cottages to the sultan's seraglio, one or more of us will have a tale to suit your tastes and mood.

Learn more about the Bluestocking Belles at:
Website: www.BluestockingBelles.net/
Newsletter: http://eepurl.com/dAJU_9
Teatime Tattler twice-weekly gossip magazine: https://bluestockingbelles.net/category/teatime-tattler/
Free books: https://bluestockingbelles.net/teatime-tattler-free-books/

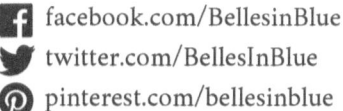

facebook.com/BellesinBlue
twitter.com/BellesInBlue
pinterest.com/bellesinblue
instagram.com/bellesinblue

www.ingramcontent.com/pod-product-compliance
Lightning Source LLC
Chambersburg PA
CBHW060222030726
47499CB00004B/1161